A Cold
White Sun

Books by Vicki Delany

Constable Molly Smith Series
In the Shadow of the Glacier
Valley of the Lost
Winter of Secrets
Negative Image
Among the Departed
A Cold White Sun

Other Novels
Scare the Light Away
Burden of Memory
More Than Sorrow

A Cold White Sun

A Constable Molly Smith Mystery

Vicki Delany

Poisoned Pen Press

Copyright © 2013 by Vicki Delany

First Edition 2013

10 9 8 7 6 5 4 3 2 1

Library of Congress Catalog Card Number: 2012920288

ISBN: 9781464201585   Hardcover
      9781464201608   Trade Paperback

Poisoned Pen Press
6962 E. First Ave., Ste. 103
Scottsdale, AZ 85251
www.poisonedpenpress.com
info@poisonedpenpress.com

Printed in the United States of America

For my mom, with thanks

Acknowledgments

I'd like to thank the many police officers who kindly offered their time to help me create believable cops. In Ontario, Staff Sergeant Kris Patterson, Sergeant Brad Gilbert, Constable Gary Marino, Constable Glenn Relf, and Constable Nicole Lott. In Nelson, B.C. Sergeant Paul Burkart and Sergeant Janet Scott-Pryke.

I owe thanks to Cheryl Freedman for her editor's eye and fun lunches.

I am grateful for the wonderful Canadian mystery community for years of support and encouragement. Robin Harlick, Barbara Fradkin, Mary Jane Maffini, Linda Wiken, Rick Blechta, Anthony Bidulka, Dorothy McIntosh, among many, many others.

And to Barbara Peters, Rob Rosenwald, and the wonderful staff of Poisoned Pen Press for being such a fabulous group to work with.

Chapter One

Cathy Lindsay liked to think she could still be fun, spontaneous, not a slave to routine. She might be a teacher of English to bored (and boring) high school kids, mother of two, wife of one, living in a modern four-bedroom house in a small mountain town, with an SUV and a minivan parked in the two-car garage, the driveway and sidewalk shoveled, the bushes wrapped in burlap. But she could still shake things up if she wanted.

Sure she could.

If she wanted to.

Cathy used to run half marathons. Not anymore. No time with the job, the kids, the responsibilities. She wasn't as fit as she'd once been, so she relied on her regular morning walk to give her energy to face the day.

Energy to do her boring job, to put up with her dull unimaginative co-workers, to teach her lazy students, proud and boastful in their stupidity.

Energy to put up with Gord who was getting lazier and fatter before her eyes. No wonder he was becoming a tub of lard. Look at him at the neighbors' party last week. Vacuuming up the food. She wouldn't have minded how much Gord ate at the party, if he didn't think he could eat like that everyday. She forbade junk food in the house but knew he gorged on bags of chips and cans of pop at the office. He wasn't much of a drinker, though. You had to give Gord that. Even at the party he stuck to two bottles of beer and finished the night with a virgin Caesar.

In only that one thing Gord was like Mark.

Mark.

Who kept himself in shape with hockey and skiing in the winter, soccer in the summer, and jogged and worked out all year round.

Mark. Smart, funny, handsome.

Mark.

Cathy had no illusions that one day she and Mark would fall breathlessly into each other's arms, to satisfy their raging passion for each other. She'd never run away with Mark and they'd never live happily ever after in a rose-covered cottage in the woods. No, she was stuck with boring old Gord. As long as the kids were still kids, still needing a stable home. Gord might be fat, tedious, boring, but he was reliable.

It didn't hurt a girl to have a fantasy now and again, did it? To act on that fantasy even if only a tiny bit. To be teasing, playful, sexy. To play a game; to believe she was attractive enough to catch a man. A man as desirable as Mark.

Cathy usually got out of bed at quarter to six. Today, she allowed herself an extra forty-five luxurious minutes because it was a Saturday and the start of school vacation. Yawning and stretching, she peeked out the window. It had snowed lightly overnight, and the late winter sun cast a cold pale light on the ridge of mountains to the east.

She dressed quickly, enjoying the quiet of the house, so intense it might have been a physical thing. She allowed the silence to wrap itself around her.

Cathy washed up last night's dishes, tidied the kitchen, and laid things out to make a fancy holiday breakfast when she got back. Then she went into the mud room, calling to the dog. She searched for her footwear, tossing boots and shoes and assorted outdoor paraphernalia aside. Finding her boots at last, she sat on the bench to pull them on and tie the laces. Standing, she pushed her arms through her heavy, down-filled coat, and wrapped the pure wool, hand-woven green scarf around her neck.

Spot danced in circles at Cathy's feet, barely able to contain her excitement. Must be nice, Cathy thought, to approach each day as though it would be fresh and fun and exciting.

Pushing aside earmuffs and hats, she found the blue leash on a hook by the door. She snapped it on the dog's collar and felt the strain in her arm as the small animal lunged for the exit.

Laughing, Cathy struggled to pull on her gloves.

At last, prepared for the cold, they set out.

The house she shared with Gord and their children was set on a large property nestled into the side of the mountain. Cathy and Spot waded through snow to the gate and the public trail beyond.

They turned left and walked together along the wide, well-travelled route. Her feet slipped on fresh snow atop compacted ice, but her boots were good ones and she kept her footing.

Soon the path turned into the woods and the row of neat modern bungalows with tidy gardens sleeping the sleep of winter ended, and she could pretend she was in the wilderness.

She bent and unsnapped the leash. A spring uncoiled, the dog charged into the woods.

Cathy laughed and lifted her head to catch snowflakes on her tongue. She held her arms out, delighting in the day. In being alive.

They planned to go skiing this afternoon. It would be fun if Mark was there. She'd suggest, casually, that Gord stay with Jocelyn on the blue runs and Cathy could slip away to race the black diamonds with Mark.

Just a fantasy, a little flirting. What harm could it do?

She smiled as she watched her boot press a fresh print into the pristine snow.

The woods shook with the crack. Birds flew from trees, startled cries filling the cold morning.

Spot immediately lost all thoughts of squirrels and chipmunks. Gathering her courage she hurried back to the woman. To the one she loved.

Cathy lay on the ground, face buried, the snow around her silently soaking up red liquid. Spot recognized that smell: the scent of meat before Gord threw it on the outdoor fire machine or oozing from a squirrel crushed on the road.

Spot crept closer, ears up, nose moving.

She sniffed at the hand. She whined and touched the arm with a paw, but Cathy did not move.

Chapter Two

Constable Molly Smith pulled a couple of containers from the fridge. Cold pizza and leftover birthday cake for breakfast. Yum.

Yesterday had been her mom's birthday. Lucy Smith, known to all as Lucky, was a good cook and a great baker. Molly's dad, Andy, hadn't been. Over all the years of her parents' marriage, Andy insisted on fixing the dinner for his wife's birthday: take-away pizza and supermarket chocolate cake with super-sweet icing.

Andy had died unexpectedly two years ago. Slowly and steadily they were getting over their loss, but there were somethings Molly wanted to remain as they always had. Her mom's birthday tradition among them.

So takeout pizza and store-bought cake it was.

Although she would have preferred if Lucky hadn't invited her friend—Molly shuddered—to join them. Lucky Smith's gentleman friend was none other than the Chief Constable of Trafalgar, Paul Keller. Molly Smith's boss. Her mom and Paul been dating on and off for the past couple of months. Lucky did not want to talk about the relationship, and Molly was more than happy to oblige. The time she'd arrived at her mom's place at six in the morning to find all the lights off and Keller's car parked in the driveway had been traumatic enough.

Molly's own boyfriend, RCMP Constable Adam Tocek, had also come to dinner. Adam's police dog, Norman, and the Smith family mutt, Sylvester, settled themselves in the family room in front of the fireplace with soup bones that had been Adam's hostess gift as logs popped and embers glowed. Sylvester decided Norman's bone looked much better than his. Norman, the far better trained of the two, lifted one eyebrow and gave a single warning growl. Sylvester wisely retreated to the far end of the fireplace.

Lucky reminded them with a laugh of the time the family had been playing cards around the dining room table while Sylvester climbed onto a chair to get to the kitchen table and the remains of the Christmas turkey.

It had been a nice evening. Paul Keller had left, thank heavens, at the same time as Molly and Adam.

Now, she took her Glock out of the gun safe and slipped it into her holster, looking forward to what should be a quiet day. She wiggled the belt onto the most comfortable spot on her hips, and stuffed her uniform shirt in. Trafalgar was a low-crime, generally peaceful town. Nestled deep in the mountains of British Columbia, far from any cities, on the way to nowhere, it was a neohippy paradise, retiree haven, convergence of ley lines, outdoor adventurer's dream, center of the B.C. pot culture. A small town, yet its cops pretty much saw it all.

Today was the first day of March Break. The town would be full because of the holidays and the fast-approaching end of the skiing season. The police could be busy at night with drunken college kids brawling in the bars and drunken families resurrecting long-held grievances, but the days were generally quiet. With today's forecast calling for nothing but light snow and no wind, the roads shouldn't be bad.

As she let herself out of her apartment, the marvelous aroma of baking bread filled the staircase, even though the sun was not yet up. She lived above Alphonse's bakery and loved getting off a tough night shift, arriving home to be wrapped in the warm fragrant air wafting out of the ovens. Alphonse often left a treat waiting for her on the bottom step.

Fat flakes drifted out of a black sky as she walked the short distance to the police station. The lights at the intersection blinked yellow, not a moving vehicle in sight. Street lamps burned, and the police station was brightly lit, but otherwise all was dark. The mountains not yet visible.

She bounded up the steps, ran through the small waiting room, and punched in the code to open the inner door.

Jim Denton was settling himself behind the console, steam rising from the mug of coffee clutched in his hand.

"Morning, Molly," he shouted.

"Morning. Anything much happen overnight?"

He clicked the mouse on his computer. "A lady slipped on the ice in front of her garage and broke her arm. A minor car accident, out-of-towners driving too fast down the steep roads. They would have gone straight over the cliff if not for a conveniently-parked SUV." The screens monitoring the cells in the basement showed no one currently in residence.

"This changeable weather has done a number on the roads and sidewalks," he said, and she grunted in agreement. Temperatures at the lower elevations had played with the freezing point all last week, melting snow during the day and turning it into solid ice overnight.

"You been up to Blue Sky lately?" Denton asked, sipping coffee.

"Ooooh, yeah. And the conditions are *good*." On the mountains it would be good skiing for a couple of weeks yet.

No one else was in and Smith went through some paperwork, munching on cold pizza and cake, until light began creeping through the blinds. She retrieved her hat, pulled on her uniform jacket, and went out back to get a vehicle.

She drove through the quiet streets while the sun rose. The sky was overcast and as light spread across the valley, everything simply turned from black to gray and then the gray progressively lightened. They hadn't had much snow in the night; just enough to freshen everything up and make it look nice again.

She drove down Front Street slowly, peeking in shop windows, looking for something out of place, an open door, a broken window. Most of the stores, including her mother's business, Mid-Kootenay Adventure Vacations, were trimmed with small white lights, an abundance of fake snow and decorations in the windows.

A handful of people were out walking dogs and the snowplow made a sweep down the main street, but otherwise the only activity to be found in the early hours grew in front of hotels where tourists, skis over shoulders, stamping feet and rubbing gloved hands against the cold, waited for the bus to take them to Blue Sky.

Traffic signals had been switched on, lights glinted from behind drawn curtains, signs on shop doors flipped to open, people were walking to work, and Molly Smith was thinking about heading to Big Eddie's to pick up a mug of their special hot chocolate when her radio crackled. Nothing better on a snowy winter's day than a mug of Big Eddie's special hot chocolate.

Unless it was drinking Big Eddie's special hot chocolate heading out of town to Blue Sky with her skis on the roof.

"Five-one?"

"Five-one. Go ahead."

"Hiking trail on the old railroad tracks at the top of Martin Street. Report of a body found."

She checked for oncoming traffic—nothing—and spun the truck into a U-Turn. "They say anything about the condition of the body?"

"Only that it appears to be recently dead. Caller's name is Matt Hornbeck. He'll meet you at the top of Martin Street, walk you in."

"On my way." She punched the console and headed up the mountain under lights and sirens.

Chapter Three

"I'm hungry. When's breakfast?"

"When your mother gets home."

"How much longer's she gonna be?"

"She'll be back soon, honeybunch. It's so nice out, they must be having a great walk."

Gord Lindsay glanced out the window. He'd have to shovel the driveway soon. Again. Cathy loved snow. She loved to ski in it, she loved to walk in it, she loved to play in it, she loved to sit by the window and watch it fall. He, who had to shovel it, hated the stuff.

She was a mountain girl, raised on a backcountry property until she went to university in Victoria and spent a few years teaching in schools around the Island. Then marriage and children and stability. She'd never stopped pining for the mountains and the snow.

He'd always known she stayed in Victoria for him. He liked the ocean.

When she'd been offered a job at Trafalgar District High, he knew it was his turn to make some sacrifices, and so they packed up and moved. He, after all, could work just about anywhere. That had been ten years ago. His Internet development business was thriving, the children were growing strong and healthy, Cathy was, if not happy, at least content.

He was happy.

Most of the time.

But he still hated the damned snow.

He rubbed the top of his daughter's head. Jocelyn was ten, Daddy's girl. That, he knew, wouldn't last much longer. Look at Bradley. The freckle-faced, gap-toothed boy who'd loved nothing more than to kick a soccer ball around the yard with his dad and had wanted to be an air force pilot when he grew up, had morphed into a sullen, swearing, scowling juvenile delinquent.

Bradley had gone out last night, after scarfing down his dinner, despite Cathy's pleas that he stay home, just this once. Play a board game perhaps, do something as a family to celebrate the start of March Break. The door slammed shut behind him, his mindless, unfocused anger at the world reverberating through the house.

Gord had popped his head into the boy's room this morning. Fast asleep beneath a mountain of blankets.

Cathy was an early riser: all that mountain air she'd breathed growing up, Gord assumed. When he woke, her side of the bed had been empty. The kitchen was tidy for a change, dinner dishes washed and put away, coffee-pot full, bacon laid out to thaw, ingredients assembled for pancakes. Cathy liked to celebrate holidays, even a nonoccasion holiday like March Break.

Spot wasn't in the house; Cathy always took her out in the morning. Yes, their dog went by the name of Spot. Jocelyn had been six when they got her, and the girl insisted on naming the mutt for the black dot on her forehead, the only mark in the mass of curly white fur.

Gord glanced at the clock on the stove. Almost ten o'clock. Perhaps Cathy had run into a friend and gone to the friend's house for coffee, lost track of time.

He'd better check. He grabbed the kitchen phone and dialed her cell. The sound of ringing in his ear, and then he heard a traditional ringtone beneath a dish cloth tossed on the counter not more than two feet away. She'd left her phone at home.

"Can I have a muffin while we're waiting?" Jocelyn asked. She looked adorable in her blue flannel pajamas dotted with smiling white polar bears, fuzzy pink slippers, strands of brown hair escaping the pony tail.

"Okay. Then you'd better get dressed if we're going skiing after breakfast."

◇◇◇

The silence was almost total. The gentle whoosh of skis gliding through snow, poles breaking the surface, the sharp puff of his breath. It had snowed in the night and he was breaking fresh trail. The going was tough.

Tough was good.

Tough was what he needed.

His heart pounded a steady rhythm in his chest. Sweat gathered in a pool on his low back and underneath his arms. He'd unzipped his jacket and taken his gloves off about a kilometer back and welcomed the piercing cold.

A line of tracks, paw prints, crossed the path ahead. He slowed to check them out. Might be a large dog, but no human marks accompanied them. A wolf then. A big one too. He'd heard them in the night, calling to each other across the valley. He'd closed his eyes and listened, delighting in the primitive wildness of the sound. He had no fear of wolves. Wild animals didn't frighten him. He'd faced the most dangerous animal of them all.

And he'd survived.

Sometimes he wished he hadn't.

Mark Hamilton dug his poles into the snow and pushed off again. A hill loomed ahead. A steep one. It would be tough going.

Tough was good.

Tough kept the demons at bay. When his muscles ached and sweat ran in rivers down his body and his heart felt like it would burst out of his chest, the demons fell silent. They might still be there, outside his range of vision, hovering in the dark corners of his mind, but at least they were quiet.

A man couldn't ski forever. Nor run nor bike nor lift weights. A man had to slow down; he had to do his job, to live his life. He had to talk to people, smile and be friendly. A man had to sleep sometimes.

Then the demons circled, whispering, calling. Filling his head with pictures of blood and destruction and sounds of terror and pain and the crushing feel of overwhelming loss.

He crested the hill and glided to a stop. Pulling a stainless steel bottle out of his pack, he twisted off the cap, leaned his head back, and glugged water. The drink felt cold on his lips; it dribbled down his chin and into the depths of his two-day growth of beard where it began to freeze.

A raven, black against a stark background of black and white, watched him from the skeletal branches of a dying pine.

Mark Hamilton lifted his bottle in greeting and the bird took flight. He sucked in a deep breath, felt cold air move into his lungs, fresh and invigorating.

In a couple of days he'd have to go back to town. Back to work. What if he didn't go? If he sold the house, he'd make enough of a profit to pay off the mortgage and buy a place out here, free and clear. Maybe he could offer to buy out Jürgen. Not that Jürgen was likely to sell.

A hundred acres of mountain wilderness, a log cabin, a generator, an adequate well. Mark didn't need much else. He could survive, grow vegetables in the summer, can and freeze them to last the winter. Jürgen told him the hunting was good out here, but Mark no longer hunted. He no longer ate meat.

He'd seen blood and brains leaking into the dust, seen creatures, human creatures, struggling to stand with half their head blown off, trying to run without understanding they no longer had legs on which to run.

He'd given up eating meat, and that seemed to appease the demons. Even if only a small bit and for a short while.

He settled into a slow steady pace as he retraced the tracks of his skis. He might want to live out here, in a cabin in the woods. Off the grid. Alone.

But not yet. One day perhaps, one day when it all got too much and it became time to check out. No, he'd head back to town when his vacation ended. Back to the classroom full of slouching teenagers who didn't give a rat's ass about the beauty of mathematics, the gossiping neighbors who tried to fix him up with their divorced daughters, the teachers with their pleasant middle-class lives and sexless husbands.

He didn't like most of the people he dealt with on a day-to-day basis. He found them boring, shallow, self-obsessed. But they, with their chatter and their gossip and their mundane problems, helped to keep the demons at bay.

If he secluded himself in the wilderness it wouldn't be long before his defenses crumbled and he took the coward's way out.

And ended it all.

Through the trees he could see the building. A two-room log cabin in a clearing, close to a small stream, now frozen over. No smoke drifted from the chimney. He'd been gone for four hours, long enough for the fire to go out. Jürgen kept the woodshed well stocked, but Mark would take the axe out later, chop down a couple of dead trees, cut them into suitable size for the stove, stack the logs.

Someday he'd give into the demons.

But not today.

Chapter Four

Molly Smith knew the hiking trail well. She and Adam went there when they needed a walk or to give Norman a run but didn't have enough time to go far. It was located on an old abandoned railway bed, high above the city. Within the town limits, but you felt as if you were in the wilderness. The trail itself was roughly maintained, but nothing else. No restrooms or picnic benches or directional signs. Just a path meandering through thick woods that occasionally opened up to give the best view in Trafalgar. A parking area had been put in at one end of the trail, but people often parked on the streets that ended at the top of the hill.

Trafalgar was built into the side of a mountain; streets got steeper and steeper as they climbed. They also got narrower and narrower as snowplows continually pushed snow up against the edges. More than one vehicle was trapped, surrounded by a mountain of snow where the plow had simply gone around it. The mountain was so steep houses at the top could experience different weather than those at the bottom. Up here, there hadn't been as much melt over the past few days.

A woman waited for Smith at the end of Martin Street. She was young, practically clad in good, but not expensive, winter gear. A shaggy brown dog of indeterminate breed, what Smith's dad, Andy, would have called a Heinz 57, waited politely at her feet. The dog's muzzle and the tips of his toes were as white as the snow he sat upon. Smith pulled in behind a blue Honda Accord that had seen a lot of miles, switched off her lights, and climbed out of the truck.

"That way. It's that way. Hurry," the woman said.

"Hold on a sec. You called in a body?"

"Yes, a woman. She's not far. Rex found her." The dog gave Smith a rheumy-eyed once-over. Not impressed with what he saw, he turned his head and set about chewing at his nether regions.

Another siren broke the quiet. An ambulance, leaving the hospital. Smith glanced over her shoulder.

"You won't need the ambulance," the woman said.

"Are you sure?"

She took a deep breath. "Oh, yes. My husband's with her. He's waiting for you."

Smith stepped onto the path. "Are you coming?"

"I'd…If you don't mind, I'd rather not. I've seen more than enough. And…" she nodded to the dog. "I don't want to take Rex back. Follow my footsteps. It's not far."

"Tell the paramedics where I've gone." Smith broke onto the trail. The snow on the sides was deep, but the path was well used and firmly packed under the fresh dusting. The footsteps of the woman and dog were easy to follow. Below lay the roofs of houses clinging to the edge of the hill, the steep winding road, the quiet town, the black river meandering between the mountains, the bridge leading to the other side.

Smith broke into a jog, calling out as she ran, and before long a man answered, "Over here."

Evergreens were piled with snow, the branches of the few aspens and cottonwoods stark and bare. She rounded the bend and could see him up ahead, standing in the trail. Something dark lay near his feet, not moving. The rocky face of the mountain rose sharply above them.

The man was young, bearded, dressed for outdoors in the cold. He looked at her, but said nothing more.

On the ground, a black coat, a green scarf. Red snow. A dog barked and Smith glanced around. Small and white, the animal blended into the surroundings. It bared its teeth and lunged, but couldn't reach her. It had been tied to a tree by a blue leash.

Smith took off her winter gloves and pulled thin blue disposable ones out of her pocket before dropping to her haunches. A woman lay face down in the snow, her arms spread out to either side. Smith slipped on the gloves and touched her fingers to the skin beneath the woman's scarf. Still warm, but cooling rapidly. Nothing moved. Blood soaked the back of the coat, not a great deal of it. The snow had been churned up all around her by bloody paw prints.

Smith got to her feet. She stepped backward, trying to keep her boots in the prints she'd already made.

She touched the radio at her shoulder.

"Five-one." She coughed to clear her throat.

"Go ahead, five-one."

"I'm at the trail at the top of Martin Street. I need a detective, and he'll be wanting forensics. Probably the RCMP dog also." She looked at the man, watching her with wide eyes. "Is that your dog, sir?"

"No."

"Better send someone from the humane society too."

She heard a shout, probably the paramedics, and called out to them.

Chapter Five

Eliza Winters wasn't much of a cook. Good food, to her, was what restaurant chefs prepared. She'd been a model since the age of sixteen, and for many years food, when she wasn't dining out, was by necessity not much more than rice crackers and carrot sticks. The minimum required to keep body and soul together. Now that she was well into middle age, no longer modeling, she could eat what she liked. But old habits die hard, and she could not summon up much interest in her kitchen.

John stood at the stove, his attention focused on four slices of bacon sizzling and spitting fat in the cast-iron frying pan. He wielded a spatula like a weapon, as if expecting one of the rashers would attempt an escape.

She smiled. Her husband wasn't much of a cook either, but he did like a hearty breakfast on his days off and had soon come to realize Eliza wasn't going to stand at the stove in a frilly apron the way his mother had when he was a young man living at home.

"Perfection," he said, placing the bacon carefully on a layer of paper towel. He cracked two eggs into the hot fat.

"Perfection indeed," she said, encompassing far more than the plate of bacon.

Toast popped up, and he took his attention away from the eggs long enough to flip a slice onto a side plate and present it to her.

"Thank you," she said. John massaged the muscles in her shoulders. He smelled of wood smoke, and his chin scratched against her cheek when he bent over to kiss her.

"Fire lit?" she asked, wiggling her shoulders into the most favorable position.

"Might even last this time."

She twisted to smile up at him, looking forward to a simple day lazing about the house. Together.

The cursed cell phone fastened to his waistband rang.

He tossed her an apologetic grimace and flipped open the phone. "Winters," he barked, sliding the frying pan off the heat.

Eliza always maintained that John had two personalities. His cop face and his husband face. She could see one morph into the other and didn't need to be told this was a summons he could not ignore.

Those separate faces had only merged twice, the night they met when he as a young patrol officer answered her 911 call, and about two years ago when a man she'd once known had been murdered. John had, momentarily, actually believed Eliza, his wife of twenty-five years, might have killed him.

It had taken a long time for their marriage to recover from her sense of betrayal.

But recover it had. She got up from the table and began putting together a bacon and egg sandwich for him to eat in the car.

◇◇◇

Detective Sergeant John Winters drove down the steep mountain road toward town, munching on the remains of his hastily-assembled breakfast. Fortunately, they hadn't had much snow overnight and the driveway was clear. He and Eliza had come to Trafalgar househunting in spring. They'd fallen in love with the house and garden. The view down to the shimmering river was spectacular and not a neighbor could be seen.

They'd been warned that a lot of snow could fall at the higher elevations. He was from Vancouver, and he'd dismissed talk of fourteen feet of snow as an exaggeration.

It wasn't.

Traffic was light this morning. He made it down his stretch of mountain to the highway meandering along the river, over the bridge, through Trafalgar, and up the hills on the other side in near record time.

A police truck and an ambulance were parked at the top of Martin Street. As Winters climbed out of his car, an RCMP vehicle pulled up behind him. Adam Tocek and his dog, Norman, jumped out. Norman's head was up, his ears pointed, his expression eager. Norman loved going to work.

The men, not so much.

"Body in the woods, Molly says."

"Fresh, by the sound of it."

Another car labored up the hill. "Party time," Alison Townshend, the RCMP forensics officer, greeted the men. "First day of school holidays and I have to leave a note for the kids telling them I've gone out. Do you know what we have, John?"

"Sounds like a shooting. Let's go see." He pulled on his gloves and tightened the scarf around his neck. Fat cheerful flakes fell from a pewter sky.

Norman led the way. Trained to follow the freshest scent, he found Smith's trail immediately. Not that they would have had any trouble without the dog. Boot prints made clear indentations in the fresh snow.

Winters shouted, and Smith answered.

No more than a hundred yards along, the path took a sharp bend. Two paramedics were waiting, their packs resting on the ground. They nodded greetings. Smith stood in the center of the path, next to a man. A small dog tied to a tree nearby set up a chorus of frantic barking as Norman approached, straining to free itself from the restraints of its leash.

A body lay on its back in the snow. A woman. Her arms were tucked against her sides, her face wet with melting snow, her eyes glassy, staring up at nothing. As Winters looked, white flakes fell gently onto her face. She did not lift a hand to brush them away. She wore a winter coat, green scarf, gloves, and boots. The coat was spread open and red liquid soaked her chest. Blood spread around her, like broken Christmas lights scattered on a white carpet. The snow was churned up around the body; small paw marks, trailing blood, led to the nearly hysterical small dog.

The paramedics approached. "I've called it, Sarge. No pulse. H.R. zero."

"Did you move her?"

"She was lying face down. We turned her and opened the coat to check for a heartbeat."

"Thanks." Winters pulled out his cell phone. He called Jim Denton and said he needed officers to seal off the area. He wanted the entire walking trail placed out of bounds.

Denton reminded him they didn't have enough officers, some of those with young families had taken vacation time.

"From the parking lot then, to whatever street is after Martin to the east. We're in the middle of a public path. I can't have curiosity seekers picking through the bush for clues, trying to be helpful. Oh, and call the coroner."

Winters went over to Smith and the man standing beside her. Townshend and Tocek hung back, waiting for orders. The paramedics packed up their equipment.

"This is Sergeant Winters," Smith said. "Sergeant, Matt Hornbeck placed the 911 call. His wife was here, but I said she could take her dog home." Her voice dropped. "Hope that was okay?"

It wasn't okay, but he was scarcely going to say so in front of a civilian. Smith should have known better than to display a degree of uncertainty. Just when he thought the young officer was coming along nicely, she slipped.

"What can you tell me, Mr. Hornbeck?"

"Not much. Janice and I were taking Rex, our dog, for a walk. We hadn't gone far when Rex bolted up the path ahead of us. He wouldn't come when we called, which is unusual. He's an old guy and doesn't like to be out of our sight. We followed. This is what we found." He spread his hands.

"Do you live nearby?"

"Redwood Street. We drive up here to walk Rex most weekends."

"Did you touch the body?"

The man turned green around the edges. He swallowed heavily. "Yes, I did. I wanted to help. At first, I figured she'd fallen. Her dog was going nuts, trying to encourage her to get up, I guess. Don't know why I didn't see the blood at first. I touched her cheek. Cold. So cold." He shuddered. "So still."

More people in uniform began to arrive. Falling snow picked up its pace.

"Do you recognize her?" Winters asked.

"No."

"Ever seen the dog before?"

Hornbeck glanced at it. The poor creature was set to pull down the tree to which it had been tied.

"Can't say. It's not an unusual breed. Lots of people walk their dogs here."

"You said the dog was jumping on the woman. How'd he get tied up?"

"I did that. Hope it was okay?" he echoed Smith. "I thought it should be out of the way."

"Is that your leash?"

"No. She was holding it. I uh...sorry, but I pried it out of her hands. I probably wouldn't have been able to stomach it, but she's wearing gloves. Somehow that didn't seem so bad."

"Did you disturb anything else?"

"No."

"How much time passed between finding the body and calling 911?"

"Probably less than a minute. This close to town, cell phones get a strong signal."

"Thank you, Mr. Hornbeck. We'll need you and your wife to come into the station and make a statement. Give your contact information to Constable Smith. I'll call you when I'm done here."

"Sure."

"Did you hear anything? Anything out of the ordinary?"

"You mean like a gunshot?"

Winters did not reply.

"No. Nothing. Lovely and quiet."

"See anyone else on the trail?"

He shook his head. Ice and snow were trapped in his beard and mustache. "No. We only just started walking. There might be people further toward the parking lot."

"Thanks."

Winters left Smith to take Hornbeck's information.

"Let's have a look, Alison." He pulled latex gloves from his coat pocket.

"Humane society's here." Tocek indicated a small woman peering myopically up the path. Norman waited patiently beneath a tree.

"Thank heavens. Let her take that dog away. Man can't hear himself think over that racket. Before she does, Adam have a look at it. Make sure there isn't a clue tucked into its collar."

"Better keep your gloves on," Townshend said. "She may be small, but I bet she's nasty when frightened."

Winters and Townshend approached the body. They crouched down on either side. He was conscious of Molly Smith peering over his shoulder, of the humane society woman talking softly to the frenzied dog. He could hear officers, city as well as Mounties, arriving. He couldn't see them around the bend, but he could hear onlookers and curiosity seekers also gathering.

Snow fell harder now. A light veneer covered the woman's face, melting in the still warm blood on her clothes.

"Gunshot."

"No doubt about it," Townshend replied.

"Hard to tell how many. One maybe. If two, they're together."

"Fired from a distance, probably. Not close anyway. No powder burns."

"Can you tell what type of weapon?" Smith asked.

"Not yet. There's not an excessive amount of blood. She must have died almost immediately the bullet hit."

The woman stared at them through sightless brown eyes. He checked her body. No other visible wounds.

She was probably in her late thirties, early forties. Her shoulder-length blond hair was expensively cut and streaked. John Winters' wife was a fashion model. In her youth Eliza had been so successful she'd sashayed down the catwalks in Paris and Milan for the likes of Dior and Chanel; her pouting face had been on the cover of *Vogue* several times. On occasion he'd found himself being dragged to boring industry parties and dinners to drink European beer or expensive cocktails and exchange empty conversation with mindless models and superficial designers. He knew, more than most men, the cost and effort that went into being beautiful.

This woman wasn't beautiful, but she was well cared for. In life she would have been attractive. Her skin, turning the color of skim milk with death and cold, was smooth and taut. Her mouth was open in a soundless scream, and he could see perfect white teeth. He gently pulled the glove off her left hand. The nails were short, the pink polish unchipped, the fingers long and smooth. A good-sized diamond ring graced the third finger, along with a plain gold band.

"Recognize her, Molly?"

"I've seen her around. Can't think where."

"It'll come to you." Winters pushed himself to his feet, trying not to grimace as his knee protested. He studied the area. Ahead, the trail carried on for about twenty yards before disappearing around a bend. On his left, through a break in the trees he could see the road, houses and garages, gardens and sheds, and the maze of streets leading down to town. On his right, a patch of thick trees and undergrowth, then the rocky mountain face climbing at about a forty-five degree angle. Behind him, the trail went back to where it began. The woman had been struck in the back. He studied the way she'd fallen.

"Adam."

"Here."

"The bullet must have come from that direction." Winters pointed at the mountain. "I'm interested to know what's on the other side of that line of trees. Molly, you've been there?"

"There's a small clearing. The mountain face levels out a bit, but it's very rocky so not much grows. People stop there for a rest or a picnic in the summer sometimes."

"Adam, check it out. You and Norman see what you can find. You'd better hurry, this snow will start covering tracks soon." He glanced up. Snow spilled from thick gray clouds. "I thought we were supposed to get less than a centimeter today."

"Whatever the forecast says," Townshend replied, "I believe the opposite."

"Molly," Winters ordered, "you're with Adam."

Chapter Six

Molly Smith followed Adam and Norman, man and dog fully intent on the job at hand. Norman's head was down, his ears up, his nose moving, casting about for a scent. Adam held the leash balanced in his right hand, waiting to feel as much as see a signal from the dog. All of the dog handler's attention would be focused on his animal. Another officer always accompanied the pair, watching their backs.

Smith kept her own head up, her eyes moving through the trees surrounding them. A shooter had been here. Highly unlikely he'd hung around, but you never knew. He might be watching the police, the dog, the curiosity-seekers on the road. A shiver ran down her back. *Was he watching her, now?* Her Kevlar vest protected her to some degree, but was a high-powered scope trained on her face?

A gray squirrel broke cover and dashed up the trunk of a scraggly cedar. Smith almost leapt out of her boots.

Get a grip.

They slipped into the line of trees. Second growth forest, the area had been logged many times. Trees were tall but thin and close together, the undergrowth thick.

Hard to get a clean shot on a moving person.

In a few steps they emerged into a small clearing with a foundation of solid rock where only a handful of tough saplings and scraggy bushes grew. The undisturbed snow lay deep, higher than the top of Smith's boots. They waded through drifts, feet breaking the crust, while Norman picked up his pace. Adam let him have his head.

Beneath a single pine, drooping with the weight of snow, the ground had been churned up. From there a line of boot prints, coming and going, led west across the clearing to disappear into the woods.

Smith turned. Through the gap in the trees she could see John Winters examining the body, Alison Townshend crouched beside him. Corporal Ron Gavin, Townshend's partner, had arrived and was photographing the scene. The coroner approached as Smith watched, wrapped in a white scarf. Winters got to his feet to greet him. Falling snow swirled around them.

"Bang," Adam said. "A clear shot."

"You think it came from here?"

"Almost certainly. The shooter didn't worry about covering his tracks." Adam pointed to a bright red splotch lying on the ground near their feet. "He didn't seem to worry about it at all." Falling snow was beginning to cover the shell casing, but it was still highly visible. Tocek touched the radio at his shoulder. "You were right, Sarge. Someone was here. The snow's trampled as if he stood around for a while, and he left a casing behind. His tracks head west, probably back to the path. Want us to follow? Ten-Four." He turned to Smith. "Let's see where Norman takes us."

Norman had the scent now and he set off at a strong loping pace following two sets of boot prints close together, one coming into the clearing, one leaving. Smith glanced at them as she passed, careful to keep her own feet out of the treads. Large boots by the look of it. A man's boots.

Not that that was much of a surprise.

Women could kill, but they rarely used firearms and even more rarely would stand in wait, like a sniper.

Walking was difficult. Occasionally her feet broke through the icy crust beneath the fresh snow and she sank almost to her knees. Norman led them back into the line of trees. Naked branches raked at their faces and arms, hidden twigs and rocks tried to trip their feet, snow fell into their collars. Instead of getting brighter, the day progressively darkened as clouds thickened. Falling snow had turned from light fluffy flakes to small, icy pellets.

They broke through the bush and found themselves back on the trail, west of Martin Street. Along this section, the path meandered behind the last row of houses. Many of the homes had gates in fences, allowing ready access to the trail. A German shepherd, even bigger than Norman, leapt against the fence around his property, snarling and barking. Norman ignored him.

They jogged down the path. The prints continued, not far apart indicating that the man had not been running. After about a quarter of a kilometer, Norman swerved, left the trail, and headed down the street. The boot prints disappeared into tire tracks and other footprints, but the dog kept moving.

A family, wrapped in colorful scarves and mittens, children dressed in puffy snowsuits, were erecting a snowman on their front lawn. The bottom pieces were in place, and the two kids were pushing a snowball downhill. They stopped what they were doing to watch the police jog past. Smith lifted a hand in greeting. Faces peered through windows, and a woman came out onto her front porch to watch.

A church occupied the corner of the second intersection. Smith and Tocek arrived to see the last few cars pulling out of the parking lot. The minister stood on the steps, a red shawl tossed over her cassock.

"Oh, no. I hope…," Adam said as Norman veered into the parking lot. The dog ran across the empty space and came to an abrupt halt. He looked baffled for a moment, and then he began casting around trying to regain the scent in the mass of tire treads and foot prints, crossing back and forth over each other. Falling snow gathered in the depressions.

"Can I help you, Officers?" The minister approached, holding her shawl to her throat. She was in her sixties with a helmet of gray hair and twinkling hazel eyes.

"Ma'am," Adam said. "My dog followed a scent here. A man on foot. I don't suppose, uh, you noticed anyone around."

"I noticed a great many people this morning. Makes a change from the rest of the year. I conducted a funeral service." She gestured to a sleek black limo parked at the bottom of the church steps. "I have to get to the graveside. They'll be waiting for me."

"A couple of quick questions first, please," Smith said. "What time did the service start?"

"Nine-thirty."

Smith checked her watch. Ten forty-five. "What time did you arrive? Were there cars here before you?"

"The youth group had a sleepover in the church basement to celebrate the start of March Break. Their parents were told to pick them up by eight-thirty, to give me time to prepare for the funeral, so yes, cars were coming and going all morning. As for the parking lot…The big room in the basement faces out the back. I'm sorry,"

Norman and Adam walked in circles. The shoulders of both man and dog were slumped.

"Can you tell me what's happened?" the minister asked.

"Forensics officers will be here later," Smith said. "But I think they'll only be interested in the parking area."

◇◇◇

Sylvester bounded through snow drifts, and Lucky Smith smiled. The old dog really did enjoy the snow. He loved to climb on the high mounds piled beside the driveway and stand there, proudly surveying his domain. There had been a warm spell earlier in the month and a lot of the snow had melted, but enough had fallen since to return the woods to a vestige of a winter wonderland.

"Seems to have been an incident in town," the man beside her said. "A killing, looks like."

"Oh, dear. A local? Anyone I know?"

"I don't have any details yet. I'll head over in a while, see what's happening. Not that they need me poking around. No one seems to need me much these days."

She gave him a sharp look, wondering if that were a hint, but his eyes were on the dog running ahead. Paul Keller's wife had left him in the fall; their grown children had moved out long ago. Their house sold quickly, and Paul moved to a new condo complex down by the lake.

He'd wanted to move in with Lucky, to the house she'd shared with Andy, to the property at the edge of the woods beside a meandering branch of the Upper Kootenay River where the Smiths had raised their two children.

It was all too much, too soon, and she'd told him she couldn't see him anymore.

But Trafalgar was a small town. Paul Keller was the Chief Constable, and Lucky Smith was passionately involved in most of the controversies that swept through their community.

They'd run into each other at a fund-raising party for Friends of the Library. They'd held drinks awkwardly, chatted about nothing important while canapés were passed and the town's movers and shakers swirled around them. Lucky had bid on a quilt being auctioned. She didn't need another quilt, but it had been made by a friend of hers and she wanted to push the bidding price up. Paul cheered her on. And then he commiserated with her when she won. She'd expected the bidding to go a good deal higher than it had.

The evening reminded her how much she enjoyed his company, so when he asked if she'd like to go to a movie one night soon, she'd accepted.

They hadn't slept together again. She hadn't invited him to her house for dinner, not wanting the opportunity for intimacy to present itself.

He'd known her birthday was coming up. That didn't surprise her: Lucky Smith was not unknown to the police, no doubt her details were easy to come by. When he'd offered to take her out to celebrate, she'd suggested he come to her house for pizza and cake. Somehow last night, as they'd been saying goodnight, Lucky found herself inviting him to drop by in the morning for coffee and maybe a walk if it was nice.

And here they were.

Walking.

Two good friends, walking the dog in the snowy woods.

She reached out and touched his arm. He turned and faced her. He smiled.

She took his gloved hand in hers and they walked on.

By eleven, Gord Lindsay was getting seriously worried. He'd put the pancake ingredients away and taken out eggs and bread. He fried the bacon and a couple of eggs and made toast for himself and his daughter. Bradley was still asleep. Sometimes the boy'd sleep until sundown.

"Isn't Mom coming skiing?" Jocelyn asked, apparently not minding that her eggs were overcooked and her toast burned black around the edges. "She said last night she wants to try out her new goggles."

He stirred eggs around on his plate. He was on the third pot of coffee and his head was beginning to buzz.

He and Cathy had their problems, no doubt about that. But no worse than any other couple. She'd threatened divorce about a year ago, but they'd gotten over it. He *thought* they'd gotten over it.

What the hell was he thinking? If she were going to leave him, it wouldn't be after putting bacon out to thaw on the counter.

She wouldn't leave without her purse and a suitcase and her phone. In fact, she wouldn't leave at all. If she'd decided to end the marriage, she'd tell him to get out.

Something had to have happened. She liked walking the old railroad trail behind the house. Perhaps she'd fallen and couldn't get help.

He pushed his plate aside and rose to his feet. "I'm going out for a bit, hon. You wait here."

"I don't want to wait here. I want to go skiing. The day's going to be over before we even get there. Do you think Mom went without us, because we were still in bed? She's always saying she's going to leave us behind one day."

"The cars are in the garage. I checked."

"Maybe she went with Mrs. Mannstein."

"That's an idea. Call the Mannsteins will you, honeybunch. Ask if they've seen your mom. And…uh…once you've done that, call some of her other friends, okay? Her phone's on the counter."

He saw a shadow of fear creep into Jocelyn's wide eyes. "You don't know where Mom is, do you, Dad?"

"That's why I'm going looking for her. After you've made the calls, tell Bradley to get the hell out of bed."

Gord dressed quickly in outdoor clothes. He opened the back door and peeked out. Footsteps of Cathy and Spot, rapidly filling with snow, crossed the yard and went through the gate.

An image flashed in his mind. Christmas morning at her parents' when Cathy was pregnant with Bradley. They'd had almost two feet of snow the day before, and the stuff was piled to the first floor windows. Her dad kept the property well ploughed, and banks along the walkways and driveway were almost as tall as a grown man. Cathy had burst out of the house and thrown herself into the new snow. "To boldly go," she cried, "where no one has gone before."

Then she threw a snowball at Gord, to where he stood in the doorway, holding a cup of coffee. The ball hit his shoulder, exploding in a puff of powder, she laughed, and he hadn't known it was possible to love someone so much.

He dropped onto the bench and put his head into his hands. Where had it all gone wrong?

Back then, he'd tried to enjoy the winter with her, in the same way that she'd gone sailing with him. The boat had been sold when they moved to the mountains, and these days he didn't even own a good pair of winter boots.

They didn't do much together any more. Nothing you could call fun at any rate.

Tonight, he'd take Cathy out for dinner. Some place expensive and flashy. Maybe he'd go shopping later, surprise her with a no-occasion present. She liked that jewelry store in town, perhaps they'd have something in her taste on sale.

Gord's hiking shoes were scarcely adequate for the deep snow outside. He pulled on Bradley's boots. They were too large, but they'd have to do.

Gord Lindsay left his house and crossed his back yard. As he opened the gate, he glanced over his shoulder. Jocelyn stood at the window of the family room, her face white, her eyes round, the red phone clutched in her small hand.

Chapter Seven

The light snowfall that had been predicted was turning into a near blizzard. Snow whipped around their faces and piled at their feet. Smith, Tocek, and Norman made their way back up the hill after leaving the church. Yellow police tape had been strung between trees and telephone poles at the top of roads ending at the hiking trail. Most of the gawkers had disappeared as the temperature began to fall as fast as the snow.

"Impossible to follow," Adam Tocek said, breath visible in the cold air, to the group of police assembled to hear what he had to report. "The scent goes into a parking lot and then it disappears. Poof. Almost certainly, the perp simply got into his car and drove away. Probably mixed with people leaving church."

"I asked Reverend Watkins to tell the guy who plows the lot not to come until she hears from us," Smith said.

"I doubt we'll be able to single out any particular tire treads even if we knew what to look for," Tocek said.

"Still…"

"Still," John Winters said. "We have to try."

"A lucky break on his part," Ron Gavin said. "A funeral service on a Saturday morning."

"Lucky? Good timing, more likely. He walks down from the mountain casual as can be…"

"Not bothering to hide his tracks," Smith said.

"Having parked his car in the lot so that his trail would be lost, first among parents picking up their kids and then when the funeral ends and the street's jammed full of people and cars jostling for the exits."

"He knew when the service was."

"That doesn't help us much. A funeral notice would have been placed in the papers. Probably an invitation to kids to come to the sleepover also."

"He walked through a residential area after shooting a woman," Ron Gavin said. "That tells me something."

"What?" Smith asked.

"You didn't come across a gun lying discarded under a tree, so he kept it with him. He planned far enough ahead to be able to conceal his route of exit. I doubt he tossed his weapon casually over his shoulder as he made his way through the church parking lot. Any number of people would have seen him, and probably called it in. The weapon had to be able to be broken down, small enough to fit into a backpack or sports bag."

"You have any ideas on that yet, Ron?" Winters asked.

"We have the shell and the casing found in the clearing. They're on the way to ballistics, but they'll be a couple of days getting back to us. Pretty clearly a 12ga."

"Which means?" Smith asked.

"A 12-gauge pump-action shotgun. Affordable, not difficult to get hold of, legally or illegally. It has a folding stock that would fit into a sports bag."

Townshend and Gavin had erected a small tent over the body to keep it protected from the weather. The coroner had arrived, seconded the paramedic's declaration of death, and headed back home to his family, ready to come out again when it was time to take the body away.

Winters shook his head. He had a bad feeling about this. A shot out of nowhere, a quick escape. Almost a sniper attack. Judging by the signs, the killer hadn't tried to approach the woman after he shot her, so any sexual motivation was unlikely. Couldn't have been a robbery. No one would expect a woman out walking a dog on a snowy morning to have her purse on her or more money in her pocket than would buy a cup of coffee.

Appearances, no one knew better than John Winters, could be deceiving. This woman looked middle-class, respectable. Ordinary.

That didn't mean she was.

Could this have been a hit? A contract killing?

A warning to someone else? Her husband, her father?

If organized crime had any presence in Trafalgar, John Winters would know about it. The sort of criminals he dealt with were by and large small-time. Drug pushers. Marijuana gro-ops. Purse snatching and break-and-enters. Men who left the bars on a Saturday night and took out a lifetime of frustration and disappointment on their families. That type didn't keep a distance. If they intended to kill someone, it would be up close and personal. On the spur of a drunken moment, not meticulously planned.

It was possible that this woman didn't live here. Smith wasn't positive she recognized her.

Had she come to Trafalgar for a visit?

And brought her enemies with her.

"The parking lot makes me think of someone well organized. Thoughtful. A planner," Winters said.

"Which doesn't tie with leaving a cigarette butt and a shell casing behind for us to find. He might have simply been lucky about the funeral."

"True."

Winters and Gavin had examined the spot where Adam, and Norman, believed the killer had stood waiting to take his shot. The snow was trampled, the boot prints clear. As well as the highly visible red shell casing Adam had spotted, they found a used cigarette end covered by a light layer of snow. Townshend was up there now, under a hastily erected tarpaulin, sifting through snow and forest debris, looking to see what else might have been left.

"The cigarette could be from someone else," Smith said. "Could have been someone up here earlier who dropped it."

"Perhaps, but you saw only one set of prints." Winters turned at a call. His boss, Paul Keller, suitably dressed for a walk in the woods in high boots, warm coat, thick gloves.

"This snow's going to be a real problem," Ron Gavin said. "We can't cover the entire trail."

"I heard the weather report at uh…Mrs. Smith's house," Keller said. Winters glanced at Molly and saw color flushing her cheeks. "They're expecting ten to twelve centimeters in the next twenty-four hours, more at higher elevations."

Gavin swore.

"Do we know who this is?" Keller pointed at the tent.

"No ID on her," Winters said. "No cell phone. No license tag on the dog. Not even keys."

"Think that's important?"

"The lack of keys likely means she didn't drive up, but plenty of houses are within walking distance. If she were out for a casual outing, she'd have no reason to bring her purse or driver's license. Molly, you were here first. Did you think the guy who found her might have taken her things?"

"He seemed shook up, as did his wife." Smith's face scrunched up in thought. Flakes settled on the brim of her uniform hat. "He didn't have a pack or anything. Lots of pockets in his coat. No, I don't think so, and no one else approached her. From what I saw, there only seemed to be one set of prints near the body. Which would be his. He said he touched her to see if she was alive. The dog had jumped around a lot and mussed the snow though." She turned to Adam. "Can Norman retrace her steps? Maybe he can lead us to where she started from."

Tocek shook his head. "He can't follow two tracks of two different people. Far too confusing. He'd try to take us back to the spot where we picked up the shooter."

"Molly, any more thoughts on where you might have seen her?" Winters asked.

She shook her head. "Nothing specific enough to say."

"I've told Jim to let me know if anyone calls about a missing person. Speculation can wait. Let's see what else we can find before that snow gets any deeper.

"I'd like whatever help you can get for us, Paul. I need interviews with every house between here and the church. Also, people who attended the funeral service and parents who picked up their kids this morning. Ask if anyone noticed a car parked particularly early or someone walking down the hill carrying a large bag."

"I'll call IHIT," Keller said. "It'll be tough getting extra bodies with the school holidays."

"Don't I know it. Anything they can do will be of help." The RCMP Integrated Homicide Investigative Team helped out with murder investigations in British Columbia. "Adam, we don't need you and Norman anymore. Molly, Dave Evans is guarding the top of Martin Street, keeping the log. Go and replace him."

Mark Hamilton opened a can of beans to serve as an early dinner. He dumped the contents into a saucepan and eyed them. Not very much.

He found a second can, added those to the first, and put the pan onto the stove. When he got back from skiing he'd built up the fire. Red and yellow flames roared within, throwing heat around the kitchen alcove. The kitchen, like the rest of the cabin, was small, plain but comfortable and comforting. Open shelves were neatly lined with cans and glass jars. Pots, frying pans, and drying bunches of herbs hung from hooks in the rafters. The cookstove burned wood, the table was hand-carved, the colorful rag rugs on the floor had been hooked by Jürgen's wife, Helga.

While the beans simmered, Mark sliced a baguette he'd bought at the bakery in Trafalgar to go with some good smelly, runny cheese.

In a couple of minutes the beans were piping hot. He tipped them into a bowl, pulled out a chair at the scarred old pine table and sat down. His mother had taught him never to eat standing up. He'd forgotten a lot of things his mom had taught him, but not that. Funny how some things stuck in a man's head.

Unbidden and unwelcome he remembered meals in Afghanistan. He'd first arrived in that miserable country a few days before Christmas. The staff at the embassy in Kabul had gone all out to mark the occasion. A roast turkey the size of a small child and a decorated, although rather odd of appearance, tree. Everyone trying to be festive in the absence of home and family.

He'd phoned his mom in the morning, and she wept plenty of tears. Not having a wife or children to miss, he'd had a good time at the dinner. Plenty of booze was on hand, enough to make everyone stupid. And that pretty aid worker, the one from some well-meaning, well-funded NGO or another, sneaking into his room when the party ended and everyone staggered off to bed.

He slathered butter onto a heel of the baguette, the best part, and tried to remember her face. Hell, he couldn't even remember her name.

She wanted to keep in touch when he left the city. He didn't want complications, so he'd lied and said he had a fiancée back in Canada.

Just as well. She was a nice girl. She didn't need a trainwreck of an emotional eunuch like Mark Hamilton complicating her life.

He glanced outside. Heavy cloud cover, snow falling hard. It would be full dark soon. Dark out here truly meant dark. No houses so no lamps, no roads so no headlights. Not even the orange glow of a city looming over the horizon to break the night. There wouldn't be moonlight or stars tonight either.

He'd lit a couple of lamps against the encroaching gloom. They threw long shadows into the corners. Flames danced in the stove. He listened to the deep silence.

Mark finished his meal. Better get outside, clear off the car, and shovel the road while a bit of daylight remained.

Chapter Eight

Molly Smith stood in the snow, stamping her feet. She'd told Dave Evans he could go back on patrol. He'd given her his typical supercilious smirk, climbed into the truck, and executed what he no doubt considered to be a spectacular U turn, spraying snow in all directions.

For a while there, she'd felt like part of the detective team. Backing up Adam, following the scent, listening in on the detectives' conversation. Even participating when she dared.

And then she'd been sent to stand at the top of the road beside the yellow tape, record everyone official who came and left in her log book, and tell bystanders nothing to see here, move along, please.

Never mind that the temperature had to have dropped ten degrees since she left her apartment in the early-morning dark.

As she held her gloved hands to her cheeks and grumbled under her breath, she struggled to recall where she'd seen the dead woman. The face wasn't particularly memorable, probably didn't even look much in death as it had in life. Smith saw so many people from one day to the next. Around town, at the police station reporting a minor car accident, waiting in line at Big Eddie's or Alphonse's Bakery, standing in the crowd watching an altercation, walking a dog in the no-dog area downtown.

A man approached from the west. Walking fast and looking as though he were not enjoying the outing. A reluctant exerciser, Smith thought.

"I'm sorry sir, but the trail's closed for the day. You'll have to turn back."

"Closed. Why?"

Because I said so, crossed her mind. Instead she said, "A police investigation."

"I'm looking for someone. My wife. I think...she came this way earlier. She's..." his voice trailed off "...been gone a long time."

He was in his early forties, close to the age of the dead woman. Average height, overweight. Except for the padding of fat on his face, he wasn't bad looking with high cheekbones, a straight nose, wide hazel eyes under thick lashes, brown hair wet with snow. He hadn't shaved today and black stubble lay thick on his face and neck. He looked, quite simply, terrified.

"If you'll wait a moment, sir, I'll ask someone to join us." She touched the buttons on her radio. "Sergeant Winters."

"Go ahead."

She turned slightly, away from the man, not wanting him to overhear her. "There's a guy here, says he's looking for his wife. She came this way. Hasn't come back. Hey! You can't go there."

He paid her no attention, but ran down the trail, feet slipping on the snow and ice in overlarge boots.

"He's gotten past me, coming your way," she told Winters. "Stop. Please, sir. Wait here. Someone's coming."

Should she leave her post? Run after him? And then what? Wrestle him to the ground and snap on handcuffs? She took a step forward. She stopped and looked over her shoulder. No one was approaching who had no reason to be here. Making up her mind, she ran after the man.

Winters rounded the bend. He lifted his hand, and the man slid to a stop. They talked for a moment, and then disappeared down the path.

◇◇◇

This could not be happening.

Gord Lindsay had assumed Cathy'd run into a friend, gone for coffee and not bothered about him and the kids and breakfast. She could be a self-centered bitch sometimes. At the worst, she might have taken a tumble, twisted her ankle maybe. Been driven to the hospital and not able to get to a phone to call home.

When he saw the policewoman and the yellow crime scene tape, the marked and unmarked cars and vans gathered at the top of Martin Street, his heart began hammering in his chest and he was suddenly drenched in cold sweat.

The cop mumbled something he didn't hear and turned away from him. Gord ran.

He knew. He knew Cathy was up ahead.

A man approached. Arms outstretched, hands up, he planted himself in the center of the path. "I'm Sergeant Winters," said a calm voice. "Can I have your name, sir?"

All Gord could see over the man's shoulder were trees and snow and gray clouds. "Lindsay. Gord Lindsay."

"Mr. Lindsay, Constable Smith says you're looking for someone. Your wife. Do you have reason to believe your wife might have come this way?"

The man wasn't smiling, but his eyes were kind. Snowflakes dotted his mustache and his short gray and black hair was damp with melting snow.

"What?"

"Tell me about your wife, sir. Mrs. Lindsay, is she?"

Gord nodded. He forced himself to calm down. If the police were blocking the path, he reasoned, Cathy would not have come this way.

"Mrs. Lindsay, yes. Cathy. Look, I've left my children at home. I don't want them to worry. I have to be getting back. Maybe Cathy saw the trail's closed and went around on the street. She and Spot do that sometimes. Thanks, buddy."

Gord had had a heart attack a year ago. It wasn't a real heart attack, but it had felt like one. His doctor told him to take the bout of heartburn as a warning and start taking better care of himself. He used to be so fit. He'd played soccer in university. Ran fifty kilometers a week, sailed every chance he got. Man couldn't get better exercise than a day out on the ocean in his own boat. First came the responsibilities of the job, then the kids, Cathy wanting to have friends over, to visit friends. Too busy, always too busy. Tomorrow he'd go for a run. Start slow, work back up to fifty clicks a week.

Cathy'd be home by now. It was well past noon; she'd be angry at missing the day on the slopes. She'd blame the delay on Gord.

It was always Gord's fault.

Yes, he'd better be getting home. He turned around. The policewoman was watching him, her cheeks red with cold and her eyes bright with interest.

"Spot?" the man said. "Who's Spot?"

"Our dog. Well, Cathy and Jocelyn's dog. I can't stand the yappy bitch myself. I mean, Spot's the bitch. Not Cathy."

"What breed of dog is Spot?"

"Bichon Frise. Not a purebred. Just a spoiled mutt."

"Why don't you come with me, sir?" Gord noticed the police officers exchange a look. A look that might have been tinged with sadness.

Chapter Nine

Cathy Lindsay had been a teacher. Schools were close-knit places, a community tucked inside the larger community. Winters needed to talk to her co-workers, but most of them were very likely out of town. Spending the school break with distant family, skiing in Whistler, sunning themselves on a Caribbean beach. They might even be at home, ignoring the ringing phone in case it was some parent or student calling with a complaint.

If Cathy Lindsay had not been the intended target of the shooter this investigation would be a nightmare.

But, for now, Winters had to assume someone wanted the woman dead. That she had an enemy. A bad one.

Or her husband had enemies so vengeful they killed his wife to make their point.

Detective Ray Lopez was working on a search warrant to get into the couple's bank records. Enemies usually meant money. Large amounts of money coming into (or going out of) accounts. He'd have to try to get access to the husband's business account as well. That might not be so easy. The man owned an Internet development firm. He had an office and employees in Trafalgar and more employees in Victoria. Winters only knew that because a friend of Lopez's wife had used Lindsay's company to set up a web page to promote her home jewelry business.

Winters had been living in Trafalgar for three years now. He still didn't have his finger in a fraction of the complex web of relatives, friends, acquaintances, and simple gossip that Molly Smith and Ray Lopez did. It could be damn frustrating sometimes.

He needed boots on the ground. He needed officers walking the hiking path, knocking on doors of houses that backed onto the ridge or lined the road to the church. He needed people talking to the Lindsay neighbors, Cathy's co-workers. They were a small police service, one of the few municipal forces remaining in the B.C. Interior, dependent on the RCMP to give them what officers could be spared. Not much, but it would have to be enough.

The autopsy was scheduled for Monday. He scarcely needed a pathologist to tell him the woman had died after being shot in the back with a single hit from a shotgun. But, it had to be done. Not everything important was immediately apparent. The body had to be forced to give up its secrets.

Molly Smith was relieved not to see the Chief Constable's car parked in her mother's driveway. He was coming around altogether too much for her liking.

Not, of course, that Molly thought her mom should spend the rest of her life alone after the death of Molly's dad, Andy. Lucky was nothing if not gregarious. She had the widest circle of friends of anyone in the Mid-Kootenays. She was involved in just about any environmental or political issue Molly could name.

And sometimes ones she couldn't.

It wasn't as if Lucky had to worry about being alone in life.

Sure, she probably enjoyed the attentions of a man. Someone to cook for, someone to dress up for, to go out for a quiet evening with.

To, shudder, have sex with.

But did it have to be the Chief Constable of Trafalgar? Molly Smith's boss.

Paul Keller, overweight, out of shape, who smoked constantly and drank can after can of Coke when he couldn't get his nicotine fix. He was well-groomed, always neatly dressed, but he smelled like he'd just stepped back from the line at a forest fire.

Molly wondered how her mother could stand it.

She'd said something to that effect to Adam one night. While they were lying entwined in front of the fireplace in his house in the woods and Norman snored in his sleep and all his legs moved as if dreaming he were chasing a bank robber.

"You know, Molly," Adam said, his finger drawing circles on her flat stomach. "Lucky doesn't want to think you're having sex either. I'll bet she pretends you and I are just good friends."

"Don't be ridiculous. She taught me all about birth control and sexually-transmitted diseases when I was in grade seven. She knows."

"You think she and the Chief are any different than us?"

"It's just that…they're old."

"They're still human, Molly."

"Not my mom."

He'd laughed and gotten up to throw another log on the fire and that was the end of that painful conversation.

"I heard the news," Lucky said, giving her daughter a kiss on the cheek.

"What news might that be?"

"Would you like a drink? There's some wine left over from last night."

"Thanks, Mom." Smith shrugged off her coat. She hung it on the hook by the door beside her dad's cap. No one had had the strength to throw away Andy's favorite hat.

She'd spent her shift up at the hiking trail, guarding the scene and logging visitors. Whenever anything seemed to be happening—forensic vans coming or leaving, the coroner, more officers—a crowd could gather out of nowhere.

They kept the body where it fell for most of the day as the forensics people did their thing both under the tent and in the clearing. Forensics might be an interesting career direction, Smith thought sometimes. She'd have to put in a good five to ten years as a patrol officer before being considered for the course and the job.

Not a lot of openings for forensic guys around here. Ron Gavin would probably be retiring in the next few years, longer for Alison Townshend. Competition for their positions would be fierce; jobs in the beautiful B.C. Interior were in high demand.

She'd spent a good part of the boring day considering, once again, her future.

To stay in Trafalgar, which she loved. Near her mother, whom she loved. With Adam, whom she also loved, but wasn't convinced she wanted to spend her life with. Trafalgar, where she didn't have much of a chance to make detective or even sergeant, never mind go into forensics.

Or to move to a city, to a larger force, to get big city policing experience.

The body of Cathy Lindsay had been removed shortly before six o'clock, as the sun dipped behind the western mountains. A good sized crowd had shown up for that. They stood respectfully watching the covered stretcher being loaded into the coroner's van. A couple of men had doffed their hats.

"Cathy Lindsay, I hear," Lucky said now, pouring the wine.

"Yeah. Did you know her, Mom?"

"No. She didn't teach at the school when you and Samwise went there. Your father got a quote from her husband to set up the web page for the store a couple of years ago. It was quite expensive so we went with someone else. They have young children, I hear. It's going to be hard on them."

"Hard on everyone."

A small town, a well-known family. Yes, it would be hard.

"Have you arrested anyone?" Lucky asked.

"No, and don't ask any more questions, Mom. I don't know anything, and I couldn't tell you if I did. Is that beef stew I smell?"

"It's okay if you don't want to talk about it, Moonlight. I will find out what's happening in town."

"I have absolutely no doubt about that." Moonlight Legolas Smith was the name on Molly's birth certificate and passport.

What a name for a cop. Her only brother had been christened Samwise. Definitely not a good fit for an oil company lawyer.

Lucky and Andy had been hippies when they met. Passionate idealists when they settled in the Kootenays, opened a wilderness adventure business, started a family.

Lucky wasn't an idealist any more. But she was still mighty passionate.

Sylvester gave Molly's arm a shove with his nose, and she obligingly leaned over to give him a hearty scratch behind his ears.

Chapter Ten

The chimes over the door tinkled, and a woman entered the art gallery in a flurry of snow and stamping feet, coffee cup gripped in mittened hands. "Morning," Margo shouted. "Did you have a nice day off, Eliza?"

"Quiet," Eliza replied. Deadly quiet in fact. John arrived home late the previous night. He'd touched her face with freezing cold hands and kissed her with icy lips before heading upstairs for long hot shower.

He came back, hair damp, face shaven, dressed in jeans and a fleece Eliza's mother had given him last year, a souvenir of Venice, Florida.

"Bad one?" she asked him.

"It'll be in the papers tomorrow. Is there anything for dinner? I didn't have time for lunch."

Eliza didn't mind that John had been called out. That the quiet day together she'd planned had turned into just a quiet day. She'd spent it working on gallery business and managing her portfolio before going for a long walk by herself and then eating a light supper in front of the computer. That was the way it was and the way it had always been. Things might have been different if they'd had children. But they hadn't and thus their careers had remained important to each of them and they'd learned to accommodate the other.

Eliza had recently opened two art galleries, which she'd named The Mountain in Winter. One in the fashionable Kitsilano district of Vancouver, and this one in Trafalgar. The Kitsilano store specialized in serious art selling for serious prices, and she had an experienced gallery manager in charge. The Trafalgar store primarily featured paintings by a variety of local artists. The sort of work Eliza hoped would appeal as gifts to residents and visitors. Snowy mountain scenes, impressionist-style watercolors of the ski hills. Everything soft and pleasing. She displayed jewelry as well, delicate handmade pieces of intricately carved and twisted metal. It had proved to be a good decision, and the stock had sold well over the winter season when the town filled with skiers. Not good enough to turn a profit, mind, but that wasn't her concern. Not yet. Give the business another year or two.

The ski hills would be closing in a couple of weeks, and Eliza would feature more traditional art gallery shows until campers and kayakers arrived in the summer.

She managed this store herself. Retail was a new experience for her, and she found she liked running the gallery. She had one employee, Margo Franklin who had no background in the arts but was looking for something not too onerous to do with her retirement.

"I guess your husband's involved in that murder, eh?" Margo mumbled from the depths of the closet.

Eliza refrained from saying, he's not *involved*, he's the investigating officer. "He was called out yesterday, yes."

"Can you imagine? A murder like that, here in Trafalgar. Steve says it must be a gangbanger thing. They mistook her for some drug dealer who'd done them wrong. Or her husband maybe. It was intended as a warning to him. Maybe they got the wrong person. I met her once, I think. Cathy Lindsay. She teaches… taught…at the high school."

Eliza liked Margo. She was a reliable employee, good with the customers, enthusiastic about the art and jewelry they sold.

Although sometimes the woman's constant chatter was almost enough to send Eliza screaming into the street.

Margo leaned over the counter. Instinctively Eliza leaned closer as well. "They say it was a military-style sniper's rifle.

Very hard to get hold of, for anyone who doesn't have the *right* connections."

Eliza blinked and jerked back. "I wouldn't pay much attention to what *they* say."

Margo winked. "Right. You're in the know. My lips are sealed."

Eliza groaned.

Chimes tinkled and the door swung open, saving her from having to make further conversation. Margo hurried to serve customers.

Eliza intended to spend the morning in the gallery, working on the accounts, planning a substantial one-man show scheduled for late spring. If the store got busy she'd stay, help Margo. Otherwise go home.

They were busy. Not many buyers, browsers mostly, people who didn't ski but had come on vacation with those who did.

Margo sold one of the largest and most expensive paintings. Seven thousand dollars for an intricately detailed oil of Trafalgar's Front Street bathed in moonlight on a snowy night. Margo chatted happily with the buyers, an older female couple from Spokane, and made arrangements for shipping the painting.

As Margo was occupied, Eliza rose to greet a new customer. A man, neat and casually dressed in jeans and a leather jacket. "Good morning. Welcome. If there's anything I can help you with, please let me know."

"I noticed that sketch in the window when I was passing the other day. I didn't come in, but it's been on my mind ever since." He was referring to a charcoal drawing of skis piled on racks outside the lodge at Blue Sky. "The simplicity appeals to me. Do you have anything else by that artist?"

"We do. Over here. His name's Alan Khan and he lives in Crescent Valley."

"A skier, I bet."

"Most likely."

She showed him the display of Khan's drawings. Simplicity was his trademark. With a few quick strokes of pencil, pen, or charcoal he could bring an entire vista to life.

They stood together for a few moments, admiring the work. The couple from Spokane left. Mozart played on the sound system.

"Nice. I'm William, by the way. William Westfield." He held out his hand. He was no taller than she, excessively thin. Sunken cheeks in a pale face, deep shadows outlining sharp bones. His piercing blue eyes, the color of lake ice, were dragged down by folds of skin, but his smile was friendly.

She shook. "Eliza Winters. Welcome."

"I was pleased to see the gallery opening. It's a nice addition to the main street. I'm going to be moving soon, to a much smaller place, and I'd like something simple for the room."

"Let me know if I can help you with anything." Eliza left him to admire the sketches. Turning, she almost collided with Margo. Margo's own lovely blue eyes were wide and her mouth half open. She lifted one hand to her throat.

Sensing her behind him, Westfield halfturned. "Hello."

Margo said nothing. She just stared.

Eliza touched her arm. "Show me the paperwork for that last sale, will you?"

"What?"

"I said, I want to see the paperwork. Did you remember to fill out the customs forms?"

She didn't have to ask. Margo knew her job perfectly well. But the way she was looking at Westfield was obviously making the man highly uncomfortable. He shifted from one foot to another. He glanced back at the art, and then at Margo who continued to stare.

"Margo!" Eliza snapped.

The woman almost shook herself. When she looked at Eliza her eyes were out of focus, swimming with tears. "Sorry. What did you say?"

"I want to review the paperwork."

"Right." She bustled across the floor to the counter.

"I'll give it some thought. Maybe come back later." William Westfield sprinted out of the gallery.

Margo watched him go. A smile lit up her face and a single tear dropped from her right eye.

"Do you know that man?" Eliza asked.

"Oh, yes. I'd recognize him anywhere. He's my son, Jackson."

They gathered around the table in the conference room early Sunday morning, coffee and bagels resting by elbows and notebooks. "Let's review what we found at the scene yesterday," John Winters said.

"Fuck all, if I may be so blunt," Alison Townshend said.

"Remarkably little," Ron Gavin added. "Boot prints in the snow, indicating the shooter stood in place for some time. A shell casing, a cigarette butt. A clear trail leading away and getting lost in a busy parking lot. A dead woman. The remains of two shotgun shells. One that went through the body, one that missed and buried itself in a tree, almost certainly because the first one dropped her. I've sent them to ballistics along with the casing."

"Two shots, but only one casing?" Townshend asked.

"That type of shotgun keeps the last casing in the bore. It can be removed by hand, or is ejected when the next shot's fired."

"What did you learn about the dead woman's history?" Winters turned to Detective Lopez, who'd worked long into the night on the computer. Fortunately Lopez, father of school-aged children, hadn't planned on taking any vacation time. "Catherine Marie Lindsay, nee Podwarsky. Age forty-one. No record of any sort. Not even a speeding ticket. Born and raised in Fernie. Got a B.A. from University of Victoria. Taught high school at a couple of public schools on the Island. Moved to Trafalgar with her family ten years ago. Teaches English at Trafalgar District High. Married, two children, Bradley, sixteeen, and Jocelyn, ten."

"The husband?" Townshend asked.

"Gordon Roger Lindsay, age forty-one. Born Victoria. BSc in Computer Science from UVic. Worked for various computer companies in Victoria before starting his own business, Lindsay Internet Consulting."

"How's the business doing?"

"On the surface it's doing fine. Nothing big time, but steady income, enough to support a middle-class family comfortably. Beneath the surface? Too early to tell."

"Any chance he was the shooter?"

"He says he was home with his children all morning," Winters said. "The son was sleeping but the daughter was up. We haven't spoken to the children yet."

"Has he been in the military?" Townshend asked.

"Good question," Lopez answered. "But the answer's no. And as far as I can see at this early date there are no significant gaps in his life where he might have been out of the country for anything longer than a vacation."

"My gut," Winters said, "tells me it wasn't him. I was there, with him, when he saw her. Shock first, disbelief, then he broke down. But I've been wrong before."

"Are the kids okay?" Townshend asked.

"He phoned his mom in Victoria and Cathy's family in Fernie. They're coming today, and a friend spent the night at the Lindsay house," Lopez said.

No, Winters thought, *the kids were surely not okay.* How could they be?

"What do you think, John?" Lopez asked.

"I think this is about as bad a case as we can get. With the holidays we're going to have trouble locating her co-workers and a lot of her friends. Right now, I'm leaning to mistaken identity."

"You think the shooter was after someone else?"

"Possible. He stood in one place for a while, might have been waiting for the intended target to come in range. Did he make a mistake? Get the wrong person? People all bundled up in their winter gear—it can be hard to distinguish one from another sometimes. I've got officers on the trail this morning, talking to people who go there regularly. Maybe someone who walks that path every morning didn't show up yesterday. Or was later than expected."

"We know the son," Lopez said.

"Go ahead."

"Bradley Lindsay. Low grade troublemaker. He's been caught more than once drinking beer in the street, at least once sharing a joint with his friends. He's been drunk and disorderly in the park late at night and driven home by an officer. Remember that arson at the equipment shed at the golf club last month? I'm pretty sure it was him and his pals. Couldn't prove anything."

"Minor stuff," Townshend said.

"That's the things I know about."

"Mighty big leap from a juvenile d&d to killing Mom."

"Just putting it out there."

"Do any of his friends have the resources or contacts to obtain a weapon of the sort was used?"

"Not that I'm aware of. But who knows what people have hidden in their basements."

"A shot like that one," Gavin said, "wouldn't have been exceptionally difficult, but the shooter had to have some skill with firearms. Two shots. The first a direct hit."

"When do you expect to hear from ballistics?" Winters asked, rubbing his thumb across the face of his watch.

"It'll be a week at least. Ten days maybe. Same with getting DNA off the cigarette butt, if there is any."

"If it was a hit by mistake, it'll be a tough one," Winters said. "What do we do on any investigation? We start with the victim. Does she have enemies? Why would someone, anyone, want her dead? Family usually. A friend sometimes. A lover, a person with a grudge. If it was a mistake, if it had nothing to do with Cathy Lindsay? All our normal line of questioning will be a waste."

"There's one possibility that's worse," Townshend said.

"What's that?"

"Random. No motive. He popped the first person to walk into his sights. Because he could."

◇◇◇

"Excuse me, can I speak to you for a moment?" Molly Smith asked the young couple strolling along the hiking trail above town. They stopped and gave her nervous smiles.

She'd been standing here since six a.m. when it was still dark. Told to talk to anyone who walked by. Find out if they came here regularly, and if they did, get their names and numbers so the detectives could ask them about people who were in the habit of hiking here at this time of day.

So far, there hadn't been many to ask.

Today was Sunday. Not too cold, the air crisp and fresh, new snow underfoot. The trail should be as busy as it ever got.

But this couple was the first to come by in a long time.

Word, obviously, had spread. People were keeping away from the path, in case someone was still out there. With a rifle scope trained on their backs. Gavin and Townshend had pronounced themselves finished, the body had been removed, the tent dismantled. The clearing where Norman led them remained closed off.

Kids had been sneaking through the woods earlier, teenage boys, searching for blood spatter in the snow. Smith had ordered them to get lost.

"It's about that shooting yesterday, right?" the woman tittered. "We heard about it at the hotel. They said it's safe to come up. Is it?"

"You don't live around here?"

"We're from Toronto. Here to ski for a week. Great conditions, fabulous snow. Do you ski, Officer?"

"Oh yeah. If you're looking for…" She snapped herself back to the job at hand. Nothing Molly Smith would rather talk about than skiing. She cleared her throat. "I mean, were you here yesterday?"

"The bus picked us up outside the hotel at eight. We got back after dark. Sorry. This morning we decided to have a bit of a lie-in, room-service breakfast, a hike, and go shopping later."

"Thanks," Smith said. "Hope you enjoy Trafalgar. Oh, and the best view on the mountain is at the top of the run called Blond Ambition."

They thanked her, linked gloved hands, and strolled on. The man said something and the woman laughed. As they rounded the bend, a single woman passed them, warmly dressed with a woolen cap pulled over her forehead and a scarf wrapped around her mouth.

In this weather, you couldn't tell a hiker from a bank robber.

"Excuse me," Smith said, "Can I speak to you for a moment?"

"You can speak to me all you want, Molly." Constable Dawn Solway pushed her hat back.

"Oh, it's you. What are you doing up here? I thought Francesca was visiting. Did you have a fight or something?"

"No, we did not have a fight. But we might well if our plans for this evening get screwed up. I got called in. I'm *undercover.*"

"What?"

"I suppose one could get more onerous duties on a pleasant day. I'm walking the trail. Looking for anything or anyone suspicious."

"Suspicious in what way?"

"Maybe the shooter will come back to admire his handiwork. They do sometimes, you know."

An icy finger ran up Smith's spine. She felt very vulnerable, standing at the crest of the hill, exposed.

Solway laughed. "You should see the look on your face." Her own face turned serious. "Hell of a thing, out for a walk and out of nowhere someone blows you away. I'm not surprised no one much is up here today."

"Did you know the woman? Lindsay?"

"Not her, but I've met her husband. Their son's a right tearaway. Always has been. Regular little prick. Been picked up a few times. Daddy hurries down to the station to settle it. You must have run into him at some time or another, Bradley Lindsay?"

"Oh, yeah. Now I remember. He was drunk in the park one night, singing at the moon or some such juvenile stupidity. I drove him home and got his mom out of bed. She was not pleased. I knew I'd seen her somewhere. You think he…"

"Na. He's a kid with no conscience and no impulse control. He might trip his mom at the top of the stairs and cause her to break her neck, think it's a great joke, but he wouldn't go to the time and effort to take anyone out. I'd better be on my way, try to blend in. I'm going to take a break in a few minutes and go to Eddie's. Want anything?"

"A hot mocha'd be good. Heavy on the whipped cream."

"You got it." Solway pulled her hat back down and sauntered off.

Smith stamped her feet to restore circulation. She held her gloved hands to her face in an attempt to create some warmth. Snow had fallen all through the night but stopped not long ago and the clouds had cleared. The sun, cold and white, shone in a brilliant blue sky, and on the ground snow sparked as if diamonds were scattered across it. The glare was so strong she wore sunglasses.

A dog barked and she smiled to see him coming out of the trees. Norman, Adam Tocek following. He gave her a grin. "Looking for a hot time, babe?"

"Where'd you come from?" She greeted Norman with a scratch behind the ears.

"Some detective you are. We came in from the other direction. Sniffing around, so to speak. Wondering if anyone returned to the clearing overnight, slipped under the tape. The snow's deep, all traces of yesterday gone. To my eyes, that is. Norman can still figure out what went on. Sometimes, I know he's trying to tell me, but I'm too darn stupid to understand." He gave the dog an affectionate slap on his solid rump.

"Did anyone? Come back, I mean."

"Don't think so. Trail's pretty quiet today."

"People are spooked. Naturally. Word travels fast, and I'll bet the story's growing in the telling."

"Terrorists in our midst. Serial killers. Slaughter us all in our beds." He glanced back through the trees. "Still tough, though. Whatever happened. You know Doug O'Malley?"

Smith nodded. O'Malley was a Mountie. An older guy, about to retire.

"He took a creative writing class at the college last year. Cathy Lindsay was the teacher. A killing like this. A local, someone a lot of people knew. They're going to take it personally."

They turned at the sound of a car pulling off to the side of the road. Two young women got out, accompanied by two dogs. The dogs ran in circles, churning fresh snow, peeing on everything in sight.

"Back to work," Smith said.

"Catch you later." Norman and Adam slipped back into the woods. One of the new arrivals leapt forward as if to follow only to be brought up short by his leash.

John Winters leaned back in his chair and rubbed his stiff neck. Ray Lopez had gone to interview one of Cathy's friends. Try and find out if the Lindsays were having trouble in their marriage, if they had money problems, if Cathy mentioned that she'd been worried about anything. Winters had arranged to call on Gord Lindsay at two. He had time to grab a coffee before facing the difficult task of asking a man if he'd killed his wife.

Big Eddie's Coffee Emporium was quiet for midafternoon. A handful of skiers were back early, seated around a long table, gripping mugs, nibbling on warm pastries and muffins. They illustrated runs and jumps with swirling arms and swooshing noises and loud laughter. Wet gloves, scarves, and hats were piled on another table, steaming as they dried.

Jolene came out of the kitchen, carrying a tray of cookies, straight from the oven judging by the smell. John Winters' detective powers were at their height when it came to baking.

Without being asked, Eddie poured a large coffee, black no sugar, and passed it to Winters.

"Thanks. I'll have a hot chocolate too, plenty of whipped cream. And two, no make it four, of those cookies, please."

"Bad business," Eddie grumbled.

The colored beads in Jolene's hair clinked as she shook her head. "Bad *for* business. I overheard a couple discussing whether they should pack up early and go back to Winnipeg."

"Because of the shooting?" Winters asked.

"People are saying there's a killer out there." Eddie pitched his deep voice so as not to carry.

"One person has been killed. Unfortunately. We're investigating and expect to make an arrest shortly. I don't think it's a whole lot safer in Winnipeg."

"People want to be part of the drama," Jolene said. "Even if only to clutch their pearls and throw frightened glances over their shoulders. Makes them feel important."

Eddie snorted as he sprayed a mountain of whipped cream onto an extralarge cup of hot chocolate. Jolene selected four of the plumpest cookies and slipped them into a paper bag. Winters pulled out his wallet.

People would be spooked. Rumors were running amok, panic spreading along with misinformation. The dispatchers reported a steady stream of calls, few, if any, of which were of help. A man was seen getting onto a snowmobile with a machine gun poking out of his bag; a swarthy stranger had approached a woman in the street asking for directions; a dog had howled in the night. Jenny Jones, who lived in seclusion deep in the woods and loved nothing more than to "assist" the police, called twice. Once to report snowshoe tracks through her property, and then to say she'd seen an image of the killing in the sparks from her fireplace and could identify the killer. Denton scratched off the regular kooks and sent an officer around to speak to the others.

Winters passed over his money and accepted change which he dropped into the tip jar.

The door opened, bringing a gust of cold and a scattering of snow as a family stumbled in. Mom and Dad in ski clothes, a pack of laughing children in an arrangement of outlandish headgear. John Winters was pleased to see that not everyone stayed at home-cowering under the blankets.

He drove to the top of Martin Street. A cruiser was parked there, and Molly Smith stood on the path, stamping her feet, rubbing her hands together, looking mighty bored. No other cars were around.

Smith walked over as the GIS van pulled up, happy at the break in the monotony.

"Get in," he said, "I figured you'd be ready for a snack."

"Am I ever." She clambered into the passenger seat, and he passed her the cup of hot chocolate and the cookie bag. He kept the engine on, the heat cranked high.

She closed her eyes and took a long sip. When her head came up, the tip of her nose was covered in cream. She wiped it away and said, "Heaven."

"Many people come by?"

"Next to no one. More of us are up here than civilians. I chased off a bunch of local kids who wanted to see where she'd died. Ghouls."

"Anyone showing any particular interest?" For once popular belief was true. Plenty of killers did return to the scene of the crime. They enjoyed watching the fuss they'd caused.

"No one who came this way. Adam stopped by earlier. Norman wasn't picking up anything fresh." She munched on a cookie, catching crumbs in her palm.

"Not much point in keeping you here any longer. I've an appointment to interview Gord Lindsay in a few minutes. Finish your drink and you can come with me."

She grinned.

Chapter Eleven

"What do you mean, he's your son? He didn't recognize you."

"You don't have children yourself, do you, Eliza?"

"What does that have to do with anything?"

"There's a bond, you see. A bond between a mother and her child. A bond so strong it can never be broken."

Margo stared over Eliza's shoulder, a soft smile on her face, a warmth in her heart. The door chimes were slowing to a halt following William Westfield's departure.

He was gone but the air was full of him. His scent, his aura. The totality of his being.

Her son.

How could she not know him?

"It's been a long time," she said to Eliza. "A very long time. But I knew. He recognized me, I could tell. After all those years, the bond is still there."

"Margo, what are you talking about?"

She didn't expect Eliza to understand. Most people, parents or not, wouldn't understand. Only when the bond between mother and infant had been shattered so sharply, so abruptly, so deliberately, did a mother and child know it existed. Like an amputee feeling pain in a limb no longer attached.

She'd tried to explain that analogy to the therapist her husband Steve had insisted she see. The therapist had been a stuffy woman, all power suit and glasses dangling from a jeweled chain.

Pictures of children and grandchildren prominently displayed on her desk. What could she know about Margo's loss?

Margo had refused to make another appointment, and Steve let it go.

Eliza was studying her, a question on her face. She reached out one hand, and touched Margo on the arm with fingers as light as air.

"I had a baby, you see. When I was just a girl. I...gave him up. I didn't want to, but I had to." Margo felt tears behind her eyes. She always did, when she thought about what had happened. She tried not to show her ever-present pain to Steve. He was a good man, a good husband. He didn't deserve to know how much she pined for what she had lost.

"You think this man, William, is that boy? When did you see him last?" Eliza's voice was kind. Soft. Her lovely face was crinkled in concern. Margo decided to trust her.

"The day he was born. They didn't even let me hold him in my arms. They didn't let me say good-bye. One of the nurses was kind. She took me to the nursery window and pointed him out. In my heart I named him Jackson, after his father."

"Oh." Some of the sympathy melted from Eliza's face. Margo didn't care. She knew. She knew Jackson had been here. In this gallery. She took a deep breath, pulled the essence of him into her body, the very body that had nourished him over all those months of her shame and her misery.

"If you'd like to go home I can manage for the rest of the day."

"No, I'll be fine. It's wonderful, Eliza. So wonderful. You're wondering why I didn't say something to him. I want to take it slowly, tread carefully. He wouldn't recognize me, of course, not on a physical level, but I could tell he sensed something about me. Deep down inside he knew. Oh, Eliza. This is so exciting."

The rest of the day passed in a blur of sheer joy. Margo practically danced around the gallery. She dusted and swept with cheerful abandon, she greeted customers with an enormous smile, she swung her arms and moved her body to the music playing on the sound system. Eliza watched her, clearly thinking that Margo had lost her marbles, but she could hardly complain when Margo sold several pieces of art.

She wouldn't say anything to Steve. Not yet. Steve would remind her, in that patient so-understanding voice that drove her crazy, of the other times when she'd mistakenly thought a man was her son. Of course, those hadn't been the same. She'd simply suspected the man in the hardware store, or that guy who came to work on the roof, had been Jackson. It soon turned out they weren't. They were too young.

This time…this time…she knew.

From the street, the Lindsay home looked like any other. The driveway was freshly shoveled, the snow on the front lawn chewed up by crisscrossing boots, paws, and tracks of rolling snowballs used to create a childish snowman. The snow sculpture occupied pride of place in the center of the yard, with carrot nose, black-button eyes, and a red licorice mouth; a layer of fresh power draped over it like a cloak.

Winters and Smith parked in the street. They met on the sidewalk. Smith shifted the weight of her gun belt, clearly uncomfortable at what they had come to do. A battered Ford pickup sat in the driveway. The garage doors were closed.

He hadn't needed to bring a uniform, but Molly was observant and insightful and it never hurt to have a second opinion on a delicate interview.

They walked together up the neatly shoveled path. The door opened as their feet touched the bottom step. The woman was in her late sixties, face heavily lined, hair stuffed haphazardly into a gray bun. She wore faded jeans, a blue blouse under a fleece pullover that was a souvenir of Turks and Caicos. The blouse had become untucked on her right side. Almost certainly this was Gord Lindsay's mother.

She watched the police climb the steps, her face red and puffy with weeping. She twisted a damp, torn tissue in her hands.

"Mrs. Lindsay?" Winters asked, stomping loose snow off his boots.

"No. I'm Renee Podwarsky."

The mother. Not the mother-in-law. Much worse.

"Mrs. Podwarsky, I'm Sergeant John Winters and this is Constable Smith. We'd like to speak to Gord Lindsay, if he's available."

She stepped wordlessly aside and they entered the house.

Winters could smell something delicious roasting in the oven. Behind a door, a dog barked.

"My husband and Ann, Gord's mother, have taken Jocelyn to a movie. Gord's through here." She led the way into the house without looking to ensure the police followed.

Gord Lindsay sat on a reclining chair in the family room. TV remote in hand, a hockey game playing on the flat-screen TV that occupied most of the opposite wall. A mug of coffee rested on the table beside him.

"Mr. Lindsay."

The man turned his head. His eyes were blank, empty, unfocused. He blinked several times. "Oh. Yes. Sergeant, come in. We had an appointment, right." His finger moved and the TV went black.

"I'll be in the kitchen," Mrs. Podwarsky said. "If you need me." She shut the door softly behind her.

"Please," Lindsay said. "Have a seat." He pushed his recliner upright.

Winters perched on the edge of a comfortable leather chair. Smith leaned against the wall.

A fire burned in a gas fireplace. The room was far too hot but Winters did not take off his jacket. This was not a social call.

"Mr. Lindsay," he began. "My condolences on your loss."

"Thank you." A voice drained of emotion. A stock answer to a stock expression of sentiment.

"I know how difficult this must be for you, but questions have to be asked."

"I understand."

"Did your wife have enemies? Anyone who might want her dead?"

A table beside the TV held a cluster of framed photographs. Formal school portraits of a boy and a girl at various ages; the family dressed as though attending a wedding; a beaming Cathy Lindsay with a baby in her arms, and a young child leaning against her leg. Young, attractive, happy.

Gord Lindsay remained silent for a long time, watching the light of the flames play against the wall. Watching, but not seeing. Winters knew to let the man have all the time he wanted. Wait him out.

Smith shifted her feet, but wisely said nothing.

"Enemies?" Gord said at last. He talked to the police, but kept his eyes on the photographs. "You mean like the parent whose spoiled brat of a kid got a lousy mark and wants to have her fired? Or the student in the creative writing class who got mad when Cathy suggested her crap piece of writing wasn't ready for publication? If so, yes, some people don't...didn't like her. I bet there are people who don't like you, Sergeant. But they don't hide in the woods and shoot you down like a dog."

Smith had her notebook in hand. Out of the corner of his eyes Winters saw her jot down the information. Highly unlikely a disgruntled student or parent had killed the woman. But stranger things had happened.

"Your wife walked that route most days?"

Lindsay glanced at the window. The drapes were open and the sun sparked on the white expanse of a good-sized back yard. A child's swing set covered in snow, a wire fence surrounding the property, a small gate giving access to the walking trail. Forest and mountain filled the sky.

"I keep thinking this is some sort of joke, you know. Like she's going to pop up from behind the couch and yell, "Gotcha." And then roll around on the floor laughing."

"Was Cathy a joker?"

"Not anymore."

When a death had been so sudden, so unexpected, it could take a long time for the reality to set in. Years sometimes. Years in which the grieving parent or spouse would see their loved one in the turn of a head or the swing of a hip. On the street, in the background of a grainy amateur video on YouTube. Convinced, despite everything, that there had been some terrible mistake. That the deceased was only joking. John Winters kept his personal life separate from his job, but this once, as he studied Gord Lindsay's ravaged, shocked face, he imagined Eliza heading out the door one morning. And never coming back. How could a man live with that?

He didn't look at Molly Smith. It had happened to her, he knew. Before she joined the police. Something about her fiancé being knifed in an alley in the Downtown Eastside, dead before she made it to the hospital.

He wondered if she were remembering her own pain. He wondered if she saw the man in her dreams, in the shadow of a stranger rounding a corner.

He repeated his question. "Did Cathy walk on the trail every day?"

"Pretty much. First thing in the morning, winter or summer, rain or snow or shine, before the rest of us were out of bed. She might miss a day if we'd been up late the night before or if she wasn't feeling well, but that didn't happen often. If the weather was bad, she might cut the walk short, but she tried to get out."

"Did she always take the dog?"

"Yes."

"Did your wife have a lover?"

Something approaching a smile touched the edges of the man's mouth. "You're asking if my wife was having an affair."

"Yes, I am. Was she?"

"No."

"You're sure about that?"

"Sure as I can be. She taught at the high school during the day, came home after school, went out Monday nights to teach creating writing to adults at the college. Otherwise, she mostly stayed home. She believed in having dinner together as a family, every night. In the evenings she prepared for her classes, marked essays, that sort of thing."

"Girlfriends?"

"She has…had…a couple of friends, yeah. Went to a movie or a play once a month or so, talked on the phone a lot. Nothing much more than that."

"I'll need the names of these friends."

Lindsay waved his hand in the air.

Winters heard Smith shift her feet. She coughed lightly. He hid a smile. Not long ago she would have barged in with her question or comment. She was learning. He gave her a discreet nod.

"You spend a lot of time in Victoria, sir."

Lindsay looked at her for the first time. "I know you, don't I?"

"Molly Smith. I've been to this house before. Concerning your son, Bradley. I remember talking to your wife. She said you had a business in Victoria and spent a lot of time there."

"Ah, yes. Bradley. Sadly, my son is, as the expression goes, known to the police. I still keep the original office on the Island. With staff. I spend about one week a month in Victoria."

Winters said nothing. If Lindsay was away from home on a regular basis, his wife could be up to just about anything in his absence.

"Did you kill your wife, Mr. Lindsay?" Winters asked.

Lindsay didn't react. No doubt he'd been expecting the question. "No, Sergeant, I did not. We had a good marriage, a solid marriage, and I loved her very much." The muscles in his face twisted, but the tears did not fall.

"Is your son at home?"

He grimaced. "It's daylight, so Bradley's at home. Sleeping probably, or pretending he's leading a counterattack on an invading alien army. If Cathy and I did have our differences, it was over that boy. She thought he was going through a stage, and we have to be patient. I thought, I think, he needs to have his head slapped and his allowance cut off."

"I'd like to speak with him."

Lindsay got to his feet. "I'll see if he's receiving visitors."

The front door opened, and voices poured into the house. A smile lit up Gord Lindsay's face. "My daughter, Jocelyn. Home from the movies with her grandparents."

"While you're getting Bradley, I'd like to speak to Jocelyn."

"Checking my alibi?"

"Checking everything. How old is she?"

"Ten."

"You or one of her grandparents can be in the room while we're talking."

"Count on it." Lindsay opened the door. "Ralph!"

"Saw the cop car out there. Don't know why you're bothering Gord when there's a killer on the loose."

"My father-in-law, Ralph Podwarsky," Lindsay made the introductions.

Podwarsky was a big man, solid and weather-beaten with a permanent tan and folds in the skin of his face as deep as trenches. His gray beard was unkempt, his eyebrows long and bushy. His fingernails were ragged and broken, the hands scratched and scarred. Cold gray eyes studied Winters and did not look away.

"Routine questions," Winters said.

If he hadn't been inside, standing on a soft beige carpet, Winters thought the man would have spat.

A girl came to stand behind her grandfather. He put a rough hand protectively on her thin shoulder.

"Tell Bradley the police want to talk to him, Ralph. Please," Lindsay said.

Podwarsky grunted and walked away. The girl slipped into the room. Keeping her eyes fixed on Molly Smith, she went to her father and wrapped her arms tightly around his waist.

"Good movie?" Lindsay asked.

"Okay." Huge brown eyes in a frightened face.

"You're Jocelyn, right?" Winters asked.

She nodded.

"Why don't we sit down? Constable Smith has a couple of questions for you. Is that okay, Jocelyn?"

Smith kept her surprise to herself. She might be in uniform, her belt jangling with weapons and equipment, heavy boots dirtying the carpet, but her blond hair was tied back in a stubby ponytail, her face soft and pretty, her cheeks pink with the heat from the fireplace. Winters knew nothing about children and hoped Jocelyn would relate better to a young woman than a grumpy old man.

"I know this is really tough on you, Jocelyn," Smith began. Her voice hit a high note, and she coughed once to clear it. Her face flushed. "I'd like to ask you a couple of questions, is that okay?"

"Can my dad stay?"

"Sure."

"Okay."

"Did you see your mom yesterday morning?"

The girl shook her head. Her long brown hair was tied into a neat braid.

"Did you notice what time it was when you got up?"

"No."

"Was it still dark outside?"

The girl shook her head. "The sun was up, and it was snowing. Mom was going to make a special breakfast 'cause it was the first day of March Break and we were going skiing after."

"Was your dad in the house?" Smith didn't look at Gord Lindsay.

Another nod. "I was hungry, but Dad said we had to wait until Mom got home. We waited a long time. Then Dad cooked breakfast."

"Was your dad in the house all morning?"

"After we ate he went out to look for Mom."

"Which is when I ran into you, Officer," Lindsay said.

"Was your brother in the house?" Winters asked.

"I don't know. Bradley sleeps a lot."

"I looked in on him," Lindsay said. "He was in bed, asleep."

"Fuckin' right, I was."

They all turned. A boy sauntered into the room. His brown eyes were pin pricks of hostility, his swagger lazy and arrogant.

He wore track pants slung low on bony hips and a torn black T-shirt advertising a heavy metal band, all grinning skeletons and splotches of what passed for blood. He threw himself into a chair and tossed one leg over the arm. He began chewing at a fingernail.

"Come on, sweetie," Ralph Podwarsky said, "Grandma Renee's got a snack ready."

Jocelyn glanced first at her dad and then at Molly Smith.

"Thank you," Winters said. "You've been very helpful."

Jocelyn dashed out of the room, braid streaming behind.

"Your dad says you were in bed yesterday morning," Winters said to Bradley.

"What my dad says is always right. He's the boss." Bradley looked at the woman in uniform. "Smith, eh? I never forget a pig. Not a female pig anyway."

"Watch your mouth," Lindsay snapped.

"Or what?"

Winters studied Bradley's face. The boy's eyes were red, he wiped at his nose with the back of his hand. He'd been crying, alone in his room, probably muffling his sobs beneath his pillow. But he refused to let the grief or the pain show, couldn't drop the attitude long enough to take comfort from his father or his grandparents. To give comfort in return.

"Where were you yesterday morning?" Winters rephrased the question.

"In bed." Bradley looked at Smith. "Alone, more's the pity."

Winters could have laughed. Molly kept her face impassive as she tried very hard not to wince.

Sixteen years old, and the kid figured he knew it all. "When did you last see your mother?"

"Around eight, I think. The night before. Friday night. She wanted me to play games or something stupid. As if."

Gord Lindsay visibly flinched, and Winters wanted to smash his fist into the kid's sneering face. "What happened at eight?"

"I went out."

"Where?"

"Just out."

"When did you get home?"

"Around two. I went straight to my room. All the lights were off and everyone was asleep. I didn't see…" his voice broke. He sniffed, trying to cover the emotion, "…my mom."

The boy looked out the window for a long time. They heard the dog bark and Ralph Podwarsky's deep voice calling to it. Bradley said, "I woke up when Dad phoned from the police station, telling me he'd be a while and I was to mind Jocelyn."

Winters got to his feet. Smith moved away from the wall.

"Thank you for your time, Mr. Lindsay. Bradley."

The boy grunted.

"I'd like to take your wife's cell phone," Winters said.

Lindsay didn't bother to ask why. "It's in the kitchen where… where Cathy left it."

"You were going to prepare a list of her friends." Winters handed Lindsay his card. "Why don't you send me an email? Addresses and phone numbers if you have them, just names if not. Try and think of anyone at work she might have been close to, or any social groups she belonged to." Two IHIT officers were arriving on the afternoon plane from Vancouver. He'd get them making phone calls and knocking on doors. If they found anyone worth interviewing, Winters or Ray Lopez would pay them a visit.

Winters reminded Ralph and Renee Podwarsky and Ann Lindsay to get in touch if they could think of anything further, and he and Smith left the house. The door closed silently behind them.

They walked down the neatly shoveled sidewalk. Smith let out a long breath once they reached the road. "That was perfectly dreadful. What a nightmare."

"For the family, yes. For us too, I fear. You know the kid, Bradley. Any thoughts?"

"He's a two-bit troublemaker. Runs with a crowd of middle-class kids who think they're tough. They wouldn't recognize tough until it's too late. Nothing more."

"Gord Lindsay?"

"Seems to be grieving. Wouldn't be the first husband to off the wife and then be sorry about it."

"Head back up to the trail, will you? Check no one's been where they shouldn't while you were gone. Then go back to town. No point in guarding the scene any longer."

Gord Lindsay wasn't much of a drinker, but right now he sure could use a stiff one.

The house was stifling. Renee had jacked the furnace up and switched on the fireplace. His mother and mother-in-law constantly popped in and out of the family room asking if they could get him anything. A cheese sandwich he didn't want appeared at his elbow, and he was encouraged to eat up as if he were a ten year old. Renee had found a roast of beef thawing in the fridge, and she and Ann were competing to see who could put together the most elaborate side dishes. They'd already had an argument over the virtues of mashed potatoes verses roast potatoes. He'd end up being forced to choke down both.

He wanted to throw the goddamned roast in the garbage. At the very least there must be someone in town who'd love to—like Bob Cratchet at the conclusion of *A Christmas Carol*—have a feast appear on their doorstep.

Cathy had planned on putting the roast in the oven yesterday after breakfast, switch the timer on, and finish preparing the meal when they got home from skiing. She'd even made a pie for dessert. From scratch.

Something seemed to have taken control of Cathy lately. She wasn't usually so dedicated to creating the perfect family setting. In fact, she'd always had a rather laissez-faire attitude to the household. He'd put her change of behavior down to middle-age. Even to "the change," not that there seemed to be any other signs of approaching menopause. Perhaps she'd realized how fast the kids were growing up; they wouldn't be children forever.

Look at Bradley for god's sake. The cute little boy with a nose covered in freckles and an unruly mop of curls, who wanted to go everywhere, do everything, with his dad, had turned almost overnight into a juvenile delinquent stereotype. Whenever Gord saw Bradley, he shuddered to think what Jocelyn might get up to in a couple more years.

Was Cathy trying to hold back time? Gord hadn't thought much about her behavior. He sure was thinking about it now. He was thinking of little else.

She'd started dressing better too. Nicer clothes to wear to work. Tailored suits and silk blouses rather than the pants and T-shirts she'd long favored. She'd gone for a shopping weekend in Vancouver with her friend Carolyn a couple of months ago. Came home with high-heeled shoes rather than practical pumps and beautiful jewelry he hadn't dared ask the price of.

He'd put it all down to changing tastes, to getting older, to seeing the passage of time written on her children's faces. Written on Gord's face.

Was it possible he'd been wrong?

Was she having an affair?

She wouldn't have gone all out planning a nice dinner for the family to impress a lover. Could that have been to assuage her guilt?

He'd told the cop he and Cathy had a good, solid marriage.

It wasn't a lie. Not really. They went their separate ways. Lived separate lives, mostly. Most of the long-time married people Gord knew lived together in mild contempt. Look at Ralph and Renee. Renee never shut the hell up, and Ralph rolled his eyes when her back was turned and spent his time looking for things to do to get out of the house. Gord's driveway had never been so well shoveled. Tomorrow, Ralph said, he'd organize the mess in the garage.

When did Gord and Cathy last have sex?

He couldn't remember.

Was she looking for something her husband wasn't giving her anymore?

Gord headed for the mud room. He had to get out of here.

If they weren't having sex it was hardly his fault. She'd turned as cold as a block of ice the last few years. They still slept together in the king-sized bed, each facing a different wall, the sheets between them as empty as the Arctic Sea.

He tried, now and again, to get something going. She pushed him away and said not with Bradley in the house, sneaking around, listening at doors.

If Bradley was out, there would be another excuse.

Sure, Gord had put on a few pounds recently. But Cathy wasn't exactly the hot chick he'd met all those years ago. He thought about what she'd looked like back then. The firm breasts, flat stomach, muscular legs and arms, taut skin.

He bent to pull on his shoes, grunting slightly with the effort.

Jocelyn ran into the mud room. She grabbed her coat off the hook.

"I'm going for a walk, honeybunch. You stay here."

"I want to come."

"I need some time alone."

"Please, Daddy," she whined. "Don't leave me."

"I won't be long. I'll be back by dinnertime."

She stuffed her hands into her mittens. She pulled her hat down over her ears. He jerked it off and threw it across the room.

"I said no."

She burst into tears.

"For god's sake, you're not a baby, stop acting like one," he yelled.

"Please, Daddy, please."

"Keep crying like that, and I might never come home."

He wrenched open the door. Turned at a movement. Cathy's mother stood there, Gord's own mother peering over the shorter woman's shoulder. Renee stepped into the mud room. Cold eyes fixed on Gord's face, she gathered Jocelyn into her arms. "Grandpa's downstairs fixing the broken shelf. He'll take you for a walk."

"No. I want to go with my daddy! Mommy, I want Mommy!"

Gord slammed the door behind him. He was in the garage. His SUV and Cathy's van were parked in their places. He slapped the button by the wall to open the garage door. He ran down the driveway, followed by Jocelyn's howls. Ralph, dependable as ever, had coated the path with a thick layer of salt. Gord's heart pounded in his chest. He sucked in cold air and gasped for breath.

He fumbled for his cell phone, deep in his pant's pocket. Shaking, gloved hands pulled it out. It fell onto the ground. He swore heartily, grabbed it, and flipped open the lid. Four unanswered calls and six text messages.

He punched a button and listened as the call went through.

Chapter Twelve

Every Monday, Lucky Smith began her day at the Trafalgar Women's Support Center. As well as being a member of the non-profit's board, she taught new mothers and expectant women the importance of nutrition in childhood and pregnancy.

Several members of her class would be away today, gone on vacation, but enough had said they wanted to come she decided to keep the class open.

Lucky demonstrated how to prepare nutritious homemade baby food, introducing infants to solids, and cooking healthy food young children would eat because they enjoyed it in the small kitchen at the back of the center. Any woman was welcome to join the program, but only the marginalized and the young usually did. Middle-class women with working husbands, jobs, supportive mothers of their own, money to spend on the latest parenting books, didn't need Lucky's advice.

Her students were mostly teenagers and a few sad women who'd slipped through the cracks in life. Some, she suspected, came mainly for the food that she handed out after the cooking classes and shopping trips.

The support center was housed in a crumbling 19th century house that had, a long time ago, been one of the most fashionable residences in town.

This morning, Lucky had to give the front door an extra hard shove to get it to open. The old wood was alternately shrinking and expanding according to the weather. They needed a new door. They needed a lot of things—the cosmetics would have to wait. The large main room was freshly painted in neutral beige, the walls covered with mass-produced art of the type that came ready framed. The table tops were dusted, and sunlight poured through sparkling windows, but it was impossible to disguise the grime-stained carpet, threadbare furniture, thin faded upholstery, ill-fitting doors, chipped crown molding, water marks in the decorative plaster of the ceiling, and the crack in the far wall, getting larger almost before her eyes.

Bev Price, the tiny dynamo who was the inspiration and driving force behind the center, sat at her desk in the corner of the formerly-gracious living room which served as her office. She pushed back her chair and gave Lucky a wave.

"Have a nice weekend?" Lucky asked.

"Nice enough. I'm worried about the roof. We lost more tiles last week in that sudden wind. Something's going to have to be done, and I don't know where we'll find the money. Donations are down sharply with the recession, expenses are up. And then there's the furnace, surviving on a wish and a prayer."

As if summoned, the wheezing old furnace rattled to life.

"We'll think of something," Lucky said. "We always do."

"Someday, I fear we won't. Then what?"

Lucky rested her hand against her friend's thin back. "Let's worry about that when the day comes, okay?"

Bev gave her a weak smile. "Okay."

They said no more. Both of them, Lucky knew, were thinking the same thing. The center did such important work, giving babies a good start in life. What could be more vital? Yet they had to beg for funding, scrounge every cent, debate whether to fix the furnace or eliminate one of their outreach programs. When military jets were fully paid for, and prisons being built at the same time the crime rate was falling, and fat business executives dined in expensive restaurants getting a tax deduction on hundred dollar bottles of wine and thick marbled steaks.

No point in getting angry about it, Lucky reminded herself. Such was the way of the world, and she'd find herself in an early grave if she allowed herself to let all the injustices gnaw at her insides.

In which case she would be of no help to anybody.

The door flew open and two young women burst in, stomping snow from boots, pulling off gloves and scarves. Round bellies strained against coats too small to fasten at the front.

"Sorry we're late," the taller one said. "The bus slid off the road on George Street, and we had to walk the rest of the way."

"You're not late," Lucky said, "I haven't started yet."

She watched them head for the back, sheading snow and outdoor gear as they walked. High school girls, the both of them.

Lucky Smith wasn't here to judge anyone. She'd do the best she could to give their babies a good start in life by trying to ensure they were well fed.

When she arrived in the kitchen, four young women were sitting around the table. The other two were mothers now, babies in arms or snoozing in strollers. Heather's baby was feeding at the breast with gusto. Heather was one of the few married women who came to Lucky's classes. She was only seventeen, and Lucky figured Heather would be better off without the husband, a sneering nineteen year old with baggy pants and a whole lot of attitude. Lucky suspected child abuse lurked in Heather's background. The girl was smart and well-read. Lucky was trying to encourage her to finish high school, get into college. Lucky suspected the arrogant husband didn't want a wife better educated than he.

Poor girl, trading an abusive parent for a husband not much better.

Again, not her place to judge.

"She was my English teacher last year," Marilee, one of the expectant mothers, was saying to Heather as Lucky came in.

"Really, what was she like?"

Marilee shrugged. "All right, I guess. Just a teacher."

"Are you talking about Cathy Lindsay?" Lucky asked.

"Yeah. You heard what happened to her?"

"Yes, I did."

"Weird. Isn't your daughter a cop? Who do they think did it?"

"Moonlight and I don't discuss police business." Not that Lucky didn't constantly try to squeeze information out of her daughter.

"Probably the husband." Heather shifted her infant to the other breast. "It's always the husband." She kept her head down, her face covered by a waterfall of dark hair, and Lucky was unable to see her expression.

"Maybe he found out she was screwing Mr. Hamilton," Marilee said.

"She wasn't!"

"Where have you been, Brenda? Everyone knows she just about drools when he walks by."

"Well, pardon me, I didn't know."

"Who's Mr. Hamilton?" Lucky asked, unable to restrain her curiosity.

"The new math teacher. Mark Hamilton. He started at our school in September. He's dreamy, for an older guy. Super athlete type. Mrs. Lindsay's been all over him. Fluttering her eyelashes and simpering. At her age. It's embarrassing. Ronnie Desmond caught them once."

"Caught them screwing!"

"Well, not quite," Merilee admitted reluctantly. "Ronnie says Mrs. Lindsay was leaning in real close, like for a kiss. Her hand was on his chest, like she was undoing buttons. They jumped out of their skin when they realized Ronnie had come in."

Lucky wondered if she should tell the girls to go to the police with this information. So far it sounded like nothing more than gossip and innuendo. Teenagers loved gossip, especially anything to do with sex.

Heck, everyone loved gossip to do with sex.

"The husband did it because she dissed him by falling for another guy. Guaranteed," Heather said, her voice flat and unemotional. Lucky wondered what on earth had happened to this girl to make her so cynical.

"Liam should be ready to begin trying solid foods soon, Heather," Lucky said, reaching more comfortable ground. "What do you think?"

John Winters learned nothing at the autopsy. He'd expected to learn nothing, but these things had to be done.

Cathy Lindsay was a healthy female who had given birth more than once. Her heart and lungs were in good shape for her age, she was not overweight, the pathologist could see no signs of developing tumors or impending illness.

She'd died from a shotgun slug striking her in the back, penetrating her heart before exiting her body.

"She was dead," Doctor Shirley Lee said, "before she hit the ground."

Winters rubbed his eyes. He'd been to a lot of autopsies over the years. Far more than he ever wanted to. In some ways, the physical ways, it got easier. He didn't want to throw up any more, could study mangled flesh and shattered limbs or disembodied organs without feeling faint. Unless the smell was particularly bad it didn't much bother him. But he never stopped thinking of the dead body in front of him, laid out on the steel table under the harsh white lights, as a *person*. A person with a life they'd led, for good or bad—often both. With stories that would never be told and laughs that would never be shared.

Wasn't he turning into a sentimental old fool? He tried to concentrate on the doctor's voice as she methodically recorded her findings.

Doctor Lee walked him to the morgue doors while her assistant tidied up. They'd release the body tomorrow. No need to hold onto it.

Shirley Lee was an excellent pathologist. She seemed, to John Winters, to have no other personality. She always dressed in an expensive gray or navy blue suit with stern lines and a skirt cut sharply at midknee. The high heels she favored seemed more like weapons as they clattered down the industrial hallway warning everyone to be on their guard, rather than an attempt to appear attractive and feminine. She wore her long black hair in a tight bun scraped back off her face. She didn't crack jokes or engage in friendly small talk. Winters got the feeling that the morgue assistant, Russ, lived in terror of the diminutive doctor with the penetrating black eyes and thin-lipped mouth.

It was unusual, in fact unprecedented, for her to walk with Winters after she'd torn off her surgical gloves and said she'd have her report ready shortly.

"They say," she said, drawing the words out, "she was walking her dog."

"Yup. On the old railroad track above town."

They passed a janitor rubbing her mop across dirty boot prints and snowmelt.

"Someone shot her."

"So it would seem."

"Why?"

They reached the doors to the parking lot. Outside, sun shone on mounds of freshly plowed snow.

"If I knew why, I'd be a lot closer to finding the one who did it." Winters studied Shirley Lee. She never asked *why*. The why of violent death wasn't her job. He'd seen her carve up bodies of small children while showing as much emotion as if she were repairing a toaster. Today, something moved behind her eyes. She swallowed.

"Has it come to that? Here?"

"To what? It's an isolated incident, Doc. We'll get to the bottom of it. I'm guessing mistaken identity until I know more. Doctor Lee? Shirley?"

She shook her head, like a dog coming out of the water. She blinked several times, rapidly. When she looked at him again her eyes were their normal black chips.

"An isolated incident. Quite right. I'll send you my report as soon as it's ready, Sergeant Winters." She halfturned, her white lab coat swirling around her legs. "Oh, have a nice day."

She walked away, head up, heels tapping a furious rhythm. The janitor almost fell over her cleaning bucket in her haste to get out of the pathologist's way.

Chapter Thirteen

On Monday, Molly Smith switched to night shift.

Which meant she had the whole day free to go skiing.

Before she even got out of bed, she called the snowline at Blue Sky—ten centimeters of fresh powder had fallen in the night. She threw off the duvet and rolled out of bed, shivering in her cotton pajamas. It was still dark outside and she wanted to be on the hill the moment it opened at first light. She dressed in layers of warm clothes and clattered downstairs with her equipment. Lights shone from the back of Alphonse's and the air was filling with the mouthwatering warmth of rising yeast and baking bread.

She tossed her boots and poles into the back of her aging Ford Focus and strapped the skis to the roof rack. A thin gray light began to spread across the sky to the east as she pulled into the quiet streets.

Everything else in town was closed, but at Big Eddie's the line snaked out the door accompanied by bright light and lively dance music. People dressed in an assortment of ski clothes, passes hanging from zippers, backpacks bulging with spare gloves and packed lunches, happily chatted about snowfall as the line edged steadily forward. Eddie's staff poured drinks and served food with the coordination of a ballet.

Smith wore a red wool hat pulled down over her eyebrows, and a scarf pulled up to her chin. People who met her only when she was in uniform often didn't recognize her in civilian garb. Head down, she shuffled forward, hoping no one would accost her demanding to know what the police were doing about the shooting.

She needn't have worried. People who voluntarily got out of bed at six on a winter morning didn't care about much other than their day's skiing.

She ordered a large mocha and a breakfast sandwich, took the food to her car and munched and sipped as she drove.

The Blue Sky resort wasn't far out of town, but it lay at a considerably higher elevation. The mounds of snow pushed to the side of the road and the weight of snow on the trees got deeper and higher. The gray haze of early morning began to dissipate and a pale sun appeared in a soft, cloudless blue sky.

Molly Smith was one of the first to arrive and she snagged a prime parking space close to the lodge.

She joined the lift line as soon as it opened for the day.

When she was a young teenager, Smith had dreamt of making the Olympic team. She was nearly good enough. Nearly, but not quite. She gave up competition but still thought skiing was almost the best thing in her life. Adam skied, although not as well as she. He tried the double black diamond nicknamed Hell's Vestibule once, and declared, half way to the bottom where he lay on his back in a tumble of poles and skis, marveling that nothing was broken, never again.

She didn't mind. Skiing, to Molly Smith, was a solitary pursuit. Herself, alone with the mountain and the powder.

The lift arrived and she jumped on.

"Gonna be a great day." Her seat mate was a man, early thirties maybe. Good looking under a winter tan and several days' worth of stubble.

"Sure is," she replied.

"Which run are you heading for?"

"Hell's Vestibule."

He lifted one eyebrow. "Starting out adventurous."

"I like to begin as I intend to continue."

He grinned at her through a mouthful of straight white teeth. "I'm Tony."

"Molly." They touched gloved hands.

"Live around here, Molly?"

"Born and raised. You?"

"I'm from the east, been in B.C. for a couple of years. I'm thinking of moving to Trafalgar for the winters. Whistler's getting mighty crowded. Not to mention expensive."

"Not a lot of jobs here," she said.

"I'm a ski instructor in Whistler in the winter. Kayak tour guide in Tofino in the summer." He grinned. "Part-time waiter when the tourist trade dries up. There should be plenty of jobs like that around here."

"Some."

"What do you do?"

"I work for the city."

"Good job?"

"I like it."

The lift chair approached the top and they readied themselves to jump off.

"Race you to the bottom, Molly?"

"You're on, buddy."

Before taking the first run of the day, Smith liked to stand at the top of the mountain. To feel the silence, the wind in her face, the cold in her bones, the snow beneath her feet.

Today, she launched herself into thin air almost the moment the lift deposited her at the top of the run.

Tony was a good skier.

But she was a better one.

She was waiting for him at the bottom when he arrived in a spray of snow and a well-executed hockey stop.

"Glad I didn't wager my life savings," he said, pulling up his goggles.

She grinned. "Catch you later, maybe." She headed back to the lifts, feeling Tony's eyes on her back.

She was considering going for another run or taking a break for lunch, when she heard her name called. Her friend Christa, waving enthusiastically, heading toward her with two children trailing in her wake.

The women hugged their greetings, and Christa introduced her visiting cousins. The boy, Glenn, was around nine or ten, his sister, Amber, younger. The little girl looked positively edible in her powder blue ski suit, hat with bunny ears, and tiny skis.

"I said I'd watch the kids so their parents could get in some good runs," Christa said. "Want to join us?" Christa's look was so plaintive, Smith laughed and agreed. "If there's a contest for cutest skier, you've won," she said to Amber.

"And if there's a contest for fastest skier, I'm going to win," Glenn boasted.

They headed for the bunny hill. Smith usually stuck to the difficult runs largely to get away from the crowds. Today, the bunny hill was packed with locals on school break and vacationers. It was a cheerful crowd, though. Kids learning to ski, grandparents wanting to have fun but wary of a fall, a pack of middle-aged women who'd probably never been on skis in their lives clinging to each other, shrieking, and loving every minute of it.

They skirted a class in progress and joined the line for the rope tow.

"I'm getting hungry," Christa said later, checking her watch. "How about you? Want to join us?"

"Sure." Smith had found herself enjoying the children's company. Their enthusiasm for the sport, for the day, was infectious.

Inside the lodge, they crossed the wooden floor with an awkward gait, waddling in their ski boots, pulling off gloves and unzipping jackets. The cafeteria was packed, but they were able to snag a table in a sunny spot by a window overlooking the lifts when a family got up to leave.

"Do you mind getting the food, Molly?" Christa asked, handing her a couple of twenties. "The kids' dad gave me money for lunch, so it'll be his treat. I'll guard the table."

"Sure. Glenn can help me carry." Smith took orders. The open room was thick with the spicy scent of curry mixed with sizzling grease, damp wool warming in the hot air, and sweaty bodies.

"Hi there. Have a good morning?" Tony, the guy she'd raced first thing, behind her in line for his own lunch.

She gave him a smile. "I had a great morning. How about you?"

"Good. The snow here's fabulous."

"Champagne powder."

"I was hoping to see you up there again."

She edged down the line to the pick-up window, Glenn in front of her. "I've been on the gentler slopes."

"Two children's burgers, salmon burger. Chicken curry coming up," the cook called.

"That's us!" Glenn yelled.

Tony eyed the quantity of food being placed on Smith's tray. He eyed Glenn, stuffing a stray fry in his mouth. Tony's face fell.

"I've been on the bunny hill with the kids," Smith explained.

"Oh. Your kids."

"My best friend's cousins. This is Glenn."

Tony grinned. "Hi, Glenn." Glenn nodded and carried his tray, taking great care, to the checkout counter.

"Hey, buddy. Is this yours?" the cook shouted.

"Sorry." Tony grabbed the offending plate. "Mind if I join you?"

"I want to spend time with my friend. Sorry."

"Understood."

Smith handed across her money; the clerk gave her change.

"How about we meet up later?" Tony said. "Another run?"

"I'll be with the kids until closing."

"Tomorrow then?"

"That's seven dollars," the cashier said. "You've only given me five."

Red-faced, Tony fumbled in his pockets for more money. He threw a second blue five-dollar bill down and didn't wait for his change.

"Tomorrow?" he repeated.

Was Tony flirting with her? He certainly was. It felt nice. He was a good-looking guy; he obviously found her attractive. He was a good skier. What could it hurt? She thought about Graham, her fiancé, dead for almost five years now. She thought about Adam. She thought about putting in a twelve-hour night shift and how she'd feel following that.

"I won't be here until around one."

He gave her a huge smile. "What a coincidence. So will I. Probably hanging around at the top of Hell's Vestibule."

"Molly, are you coming? I'm starving!" An exasperated Glenn said.

"I'm coming. Don't be so impatient." They carried the laden trays to their table.

Molly Smith knew Tony's eyes were following her.

They were busy at Mid-Kootenay Adventure Vacations all afternoon. The town was full of vacationers eager to enjoy the winter sports, and a good number of them had forgotten important pieces of equipment or were looking for end-of-season sales.

Lucky worked the cash register while Flower and James served customers.

As she chatted with patrons, rang up purchases, and generally kept an eye on the premises, Lucky considered her young mothers' group. She'd once overheard a sixteen-year-old explain why she'd deliberately gotten pregnant: "Someone to love." Lucky thought that was perhaps the saddest thing she'd ever heard. How little love must there have been in that child's life.

Lucky wasn't concerned about Marilee. Her parents were comfortably middle class, supportive of her pregnancy, prepared to help with the baby in order to ensure Marilee could continue her education.

Brenda, not so much. The girl was too thin, haggard almost, her stomach protruding from her skinny body as if the bump had been pasted on. She promised Lucky she wasn't taking drugs... anymore. But the girl had other problems: Lucky'd noticed a line of bruises on Brenda's upper arm when she'd taken off her sweater because the unreliable furnace had suddenly decided to go on overdrive. Lucky tried to speak to her about it, asking her to stay after class. Suspecting what Lucky wanted to discuss, Brenda said she had to be going and almost ran out the door.

Marilee had gotten pregnant when her boyfriend said it wouldn't matter if they didn't use a condom—just this once. Brenda, Lucky suspected, had gotten pregnant accidently on purpose in defiance of her parents, an attempt to prove her independence. Maybe so she'd have someone to love.

A couple came into the store. Middle-aged, affluent. He was on the short side, with a comfortable stomach and a helmet of gray-and-black hair. She was tall and leggy, wearing designer sunglasses and red leather gloves and boots. They glanced around before approaching the counter. Lucky put on her professional smile.

The man pulled his right glove off and extended his hand. "Mrs. Smith, so pleased to meet you at last. I'm Darren Fernhaugh, and this is my wife, Rosalind." The woman checked Lucky out. The long colorful skirt, dangling earrings, navy blue T-shirt under a heavy beige sweater, worn for warmth rather than for fashion, the uncontrolled red hair, getting progressively grayer every day. Not impressed with what she saw, Rosalind gave Lucky a cool nod and a smile that didn't reach her eyes.

"Welcome," Lucky said.

"Wanted to introduce ourselves," Darren said. "I've heard a lot about you and your store. Why don't you go and do some shopping, honey, while Lucky and I get acquainted."

"Sure." Rosalind wandered over to the book rack. Outdoor adventure books mostly, some on the environment, a collection on gardening and mountain living.

"You're new to town?" Lucky asked.

"Fabulous place. Don't know why I haven't been here before. You obviously do a good brisk business. Probably slows down in the off-season, eh?"

"We cater to skiers in the winter, hikers and kayakers in the summer. The shoulder season can be slow, yes."

"Not much in the way of year-round vacation homes."

Lucky's ears picked up.

"Good vacation property not too far away would bring a lot of visitors in. People who eat in restaurants, shop." She wondered if his teeth were false, they must be to be that white.

"You have a great selection." Rosalind placed an armful of books on the counter. "You could use some fiction, though."

"Wolf River Books is only two doors down. We're not in competition."

"Nice to see a prosperous main street," Darren said, pulling out his credit card. "Everyone relying on each other, everyone does well."

Lucky rang up the purchases. It came to over three hundred dollars. The volumes with color photographs could be expensive.

Darren punched in his PIN, still chatting about the value of a solid business community.

They left. Rosalind didn't look back, but Darren gave Lucky a cheerful wave.

Weird.

"So that's the devil incarnate," Flower said, leaning on the counter.

"The what?"

"Fernhaugh."

"That's his name."

"You mean you haven't heard? You of all people?"

"Heard what?"

"Fernhaugh represents a consortium that's bought the Grizzly Resort property. Permission was given to the previous owners to develop the land, so all the new bunch had to do was put up the cash. They start work soon as they can dig."

Lucky's first reaction to the news was shock that she hadn't known about it.

Then dismay at the reopening of that controversy. Previous plans to take a section of pure untouched wilderness and put up a fractional ownership resort died when the company pulled out. But not without first causing a substantial amount of conflict in town. Fernhaugh must be going up and down the street meeting the store owners, subtly reminding them that vacation homes meant business. Lucky wondered if Rosalind would actually read any of those books she'd bought.

Her thoughts were interrupted when the bell over the door tinkled. A man came in. "Afternoon, Lucky."

"Good afternoon." She struggled to remember his name. Regular customer, but he hadn't been around much this season. Ordinary middle-aged guy, quiet but friendly. "What can we do for you today?"

"Just browsing, checking out the sales. Business good?"

"We've had a busy season, yes."

"Glad to hear it."

"Have you been up to Blue Sky much this year? My daughter says the conditions are exceptional." Lucky laughed. "She says that every year." William, that was his name. William Westfield.

His lip twisted in a grimace. "I'm afraid I wasn't able to get much skiing in this year. But I still like to look." He was losing weight, Lucky thought. Not that he had much to lose. His cheekbones were sharp, his attractive blue eyes washed out, and traces of pain written in new lines in his face.

He walked to the back of the shop, where the sale merchandise was stocked. Flower hurried to assist him.

The door opened again. Margo Franklin, who worked at Eliza Winters' art gallery a few doors down and across the street. Margo stood in the entrance, her eyes darting around the store. She made no move to come further inside, simply stood there, staring at the back wall and the rack of last season's skis.

James gave Lucky a questioning look. She moved her chin, indicating he should see what the woman wanted.

"Can I help you?" James said. Handsome in a well-scrubbed outdoor sort of way, he'd turned out to be a good salesperson. He was a keen skier, and Lucky knew, although he'd not said so, he'd be leaving come spring. She'd be sorry to lose him.

Margo blinked, surprised James was addressing her. "Uh. I don't think so. No. Thank you."

William heard her voice and turned. He let go of the skis he was examining and they settled back into the rack with a clatter. He stared across the display of goggles and gloves, boots and poles, books and magazines. Margo flushed and mumbled, "My mistake. Sorry." The bell clattered as she left the store. James shrugged.

"That was odd," Lucky said to no one in particular.

"Do you know that woman?" William asked.

"Not really. She's new to town, her and her husband. Retirees from the city."

"She's damned creepy, is all I can say. Following me, watching me. I want to buy a sketch from the art gallery and I feel I have to phone ahead, make sure she's not working."

Another peal of the bell. Lucky had never before noticed how darned annoying it could be. Perhaps because she didn't usually help staff the store, but stayed in the back doing the accounts and such.

This time Moonlight, Lucky's daughter, came in.

The girl had obviously come straight from Blue Sky. Not only was she still wearing her ski clothes, but she had that windblown look of mussed hair and ruddy cheeks, and the gleam in her eyes, the same color as her father's, that she only got after a good day on the mountain.

"I lost one of my best gloves," she grumbled by way of greeting.

"It'll turn up," Lucky said.

"Probably, but not before tomorrow."

"You're going back tomorrow? Aren't you on nights for the next couple of days."

"I am. But, well I figured I could do a couple of hours in the afternoon." She studied the magazine display beside the counter rather than her mother. Something was up, Lucky knew.

She bit her tongue.

"Where did you see the glove last?"

"I must have dropped it in the parking lot when I was loading the car. I'll get another pair now. Have anything good on sale?"

"For you, every day is a sale and you know it."

James tossed her a pair. "Try these for size."

She pulled them on. Flexed her fingers. "They seem okay. Thanks. See you later, Mom. I have to get home and change, and be at work at six."

"Speaking of work..." Lucky said.

"Yes?"

Lucky glanced around the store. William had slipped away without her noticing, and no other customers had come in.

Flower had dropped into a downward dog yoga pose in the middle of the room while James stood listening to Lucky and Moonlight.

The clock behind the counter gave a ding to announce the hour. Five o'clock.

Flower bolted upright and headed for the back to get her coat in anything but a meditative rush. She had an amazing ability to simply live in the moment. James followed at a more sedate pace.

When they'd gone, and James had flipped the sign on the door from open to closed, Moonlight said, "What's up?"

"I heard something about Cathy Lindsay today from some high school students in my group. I don't know if you're interested in gossip, but it might be important."

"What'd they say?"

"She was, according to the kids, having an affair with a fellow teacher."

"Wow. That might be important, all right."

"It's just gossip. You can't use it, can you?"

"We can't take gossip to court, no, but we can certainly investigate and see if there's anything to it." Moonlight pulled a face. "I mean Sergeant Winters can investigate. Not me. Why don't I call him and you tell him what you heard?"

"If you think he wouldn't mind."

"Of course, he wouldn't mind, Mom. Not if you have a lead. This early in an investigation like this one, he'll be working around the clock."

She dug in her bag for her cell phone and made the call.

Chapter Fourteen

John Winters was indeed interested in what Lucky Smith had to say. The woman was an information gold mine. Was there anything going on in Trafalgar she didn't know about?

They should put her on the payroll. Except that she was as likely to inform the other side as to what the police were doing as vice versa. Lucky was a vocal proponent of the decriminalization of marijuana and a vocal opponent of wilderness development. Exactly the sort of idealistic old hippy he'd never had much time for. Until he got to know her, and discovered he liked her very much.

He stopped thinking of Lucky Smith as a double agent, and considered what she'd told him.

With plenty of caveats and warnings and evasions, she'd eventually spat out the rumor from Trafalgar District High School that said Cathy Lindsay was having an affair with a fellow teacher.

Nothing like an illicit relationship to spark murder.

He'd thanked Lucky and walked with Molly to the street.

"Is that important, you think?" she asked.

"Could be. Might be a waste of time. Won't know until I talk to the gentleman in question. You went to that school, Molly. Did you know him? Mark Hamilton?"

"No. Must be after my time."

"Do you keep in touch with any of your old teachers who're still there?"

"I wouldn't say keep in touch, but I see a couple of them around sometimes. In town, at the school if we get a call."

"School's out for the rest of the week, more's the pity, and we haven't been able to interview most of her colleagues. If you get a chance to talk to any of them, ask about this, will you, Molly. No names, just see if they know anything about Cathy Lindsay that's not on the record."

"Mrs. Grady, my old English teacher, plays in the indoor soccer league. I saw her at the rec center a couple of weeks ago when one of the spectators had a heart attack. I said hi and we talked for a couple of minutes. They play on Monday nights. Don't know if they will tonight, because of the break, but I can drop in."

"You're on the street tonight?"

"Yeah."

"If the opportunity presents itself, find out what you can. Don't let it take you away from your other duties."

"Glad to."

She left him with a cheerful wave, and John Winters made his way back to the police station.

Ray Lopez was in the GIS office, fingers flying across the computer keyboard.

"I've a name of a possible person of interest," Winters said, throwing his coat over the rack in the corner. "See what you can find on one Mark Hamilton. Teacher at Trafalgar District High School."

"Sure. He's in the frame?"

"Just a rumor so far, but more than anything else we have."

"Perhaps not the only thing," Lopez said with a grin that was designed to make Winters ask.

He obliged. "What'd you find?"

"Gord Lindsay, the grieving widower, has a business office in Victoria."

"We know that."

"He spends about one week a month in that city. He told you he stays at various hotels, wherever he can get a deal at the time."

"Right."

"On November 15th last, the Victoria police were called to a break-in at a house not far from downtown. Electronics taken, computers, TV, the lady of the house's jewelry. Probably a professional job, clean and neat. No one has been apprehended for the crime, and the property has not been located. What's of interest to us, however, is the name of the homeowner's friend. A friend who had been staying with her for a few days. Gordon Roger Lindsay."

"Same guy?"

"Showed his driver's license as ID. No suspicion that Mr. Lindsay had anything to do with the burglary, mind. He owned a MacBook Pro that was taken."

"Maybe the woman's a relative. A friend he bunked in with when he couldn't get a hotel."

"Might be. She's a single lady, one Elizabeth Mary Moorehouse. Age forty-two. When questioned by our guys about Mr. Lindsay, her house guest, she said he stayed with her regularly. Whenever he was in Victoria. What made that seem important enough to get into the police report is that Ms. Moorehouse is employed at a hardware store where she's a part-time salesclerk. The jewelry stolen was estimated to be of value in the range of three to five thousand dollars."

"You have a suspicious mind, Ray."

"Sadly, I do. As do our colleagues in VicPD."

"So Gord Lindsay has what is quaintly referred to as a mistress."

"Allegedly."

"If he does have a lady he's seeing when in Victoria, for whom he bought expensive gifts, might his wife have found out? And objected to same?"

Lopez lifted his eyebrows in question.

"Anything in that report as to if Ms. Moorehouse owns the house she's living in?"

"No, but that should be easy enough to check. One other thing, insurance. I didn't even need a warrant to find out about that. One of Madeleine's friends is a teacher, so I just asked.

They contribute to a life insurance policy as part of their benefits package. The insurance is intended to be enough to replace lost income for a couple of years. Nothing extraordinary, but…"

"But it would be a hefty lump sum, particularly for someone who has unexpected expenses."

"Precisely what I was thinking."

"Good work, Ray. I'll follow up on Ms. Moorehouse. In the meantime, Gord might not be the only one playing games out of school."

"So you say."

"Get me what you can on a Trafalgar resident by the name of Mark Hamilton. Address and phone number first."

Chapter Fifteen

When Molly Smith got to the office—ten minutes late because she'd stayed at the store to hear her mother tell John Winters what she'd learned—she ran straight to the computers. She tossed an empty coffee cup into the overflowing trash can and logged on. The computer told her that the gym in the rec center was booked tonight from eight to ten for the indoor women's soccer league.

"You're late," Staff Sergeant Al Peterson, her immediate boss, stood in the doorway, arms crossed over his barrel chest, scowl fierce.

"Sorry, Sarge. I was helping Sergeant Winters with his inquiries into the Lindsay murder."

"Were you promoted to detective while I was on coffee break?"

"I found a witness, you see. I had to wait with her until the Sergeant arrived to get a statement." That was stretching the truth somewhat. Lucky Smith wasn't going to run away without the stern eye of Constable Smith on her.

Peterson wasn't buying it. "That's not your job, Smith. You're a Constable Third Class. If you want to make Constable Second Class someday, I'd suggest you concentrate on doing the job you've been assigned. Do you understand me?"

"Yes, sir." She didn't add that it seemed unfair she was being reprimanded for doing her job *too* well. Everyone knew Peterson had applied for a job and promotion to Inspector in Kelowna. Everyone knew he'd not been offered the position and was not happy about it.

"Glad to hear it. Tonight I want you on foot. It might be a Monday, but college kids on spring break are pouring into town. I want a regular count of patrons in the bars and an eye on everything. Let the bouncers know we're out there. Let the drinkers and troublemakers know we're out there. Dave arrived on time for his shift, so he got the truck. I'll be around if you need me."

Smith smiled, hoping it looked natural and professional. Her teeth ached.

Peterson left the room. Molly Smith shrugged back into her jacket, pulled her gloves out of her pocket, and headed for the night life of Trafalgar.

The restaurants were busy, the bars less so. That would change in a couple of hours. Street lamps illuminated gently falling snow.

She pulled her collar up and walked down the street. Not too cold, fortunately, barely below freezing, so she wouldn't have to worry about staying warm.

In the doorway of Trafalgar Thai, Smith's favorite restaurant, a couple leaned together for a kiss.

Adam had arranged his shifts so he could go to Toronto for a week to visit his family and had left this morning. He'd wanted her to come with him. She made excuses about work, although she could have tried to juggle her schedule if she wanted to. She'd never been to Toronto, probably should go one day. The skiing was, apparently, dreadful.

It frightened her, thinking about going all the way across the country to meet Adam's family. That would mean there was something…permanent about their relationship. A commitment. The suggestion of the intention to possibly enter into a commitment. Different with her family. They were right here. Nothing more natural than for Molly's boyfriend to come for dinner now and again.

A few months ago, she'd suspected Adam was about to propose. But he'd drawn back, maybe sensing the wariness in her.

Why couldn't things stay the way they were? Everything was just fine, why did people always want more?

The kissing couple broke apart. Smith was surprised to see that they must be in their sixties. The man gave her a friendly smile, and the woman dipped her eyes shyly.

Of course, if things did stay the way they were, then Moonlight Legolas Smith would always be a constable third class.

The man took the woman's arm in his and they began to walk away.

Smith had only taken a few steps when she heard a sharp cry and a thud. She whirled around. The man lay on the ground, the woman's hands to her mouth.

"Are you okay, sir?" Smith hurried to his side. "Don't try to get up yet. Take a breath."

He groaned. All the color had drained from his face and his eyes were clenched shut. He tried to sit, but fell back with a cry. "My leg. Blast it all. My leg hurts like tarnation." The offending limb was definitely at a bad angle.

Smith activated her radio, called for an ambulance, and then crouched on the sidewalk beside the man.

His companion dropped to her knees on his other side. She placed her arm under his head, trying to keep it off the icy sidewalk.

"I help?"

Mr. Chan, the owner of Trafalgar Thai, stood in his doorway.

"A pillow would be good," Smith said.

A pile of red-and-gold cushions soon arrived and the injured man's companion lifted his head and slipped one underneath. "Oh, Robert," she said, "do you think it's broken?"

"Sure feels like it," he groaned through tight lips.

Smith upped her estimate of their ages by a decade.

They heard a siren coming down the hill. A small crowd gathered to do nothing much but stand and watch.

"We're on our honeymoon," the lady told Smith. "Robert wanted to go to the Caribbean for a beach holiday, but I insisted on a winter wonderland. I guess I was wrong."

"No nooky for you tonight," he said, sucking back pain.

Smith laughed. Mortified, she slapped her lips together. "Sorry."

"Not half as sorry as I am," the lady said, and Smith couldn't hold back the second laugh.

The paramedics arrived and Smith got out of the way to let them do their jobs.

Seventy years old if a day, both of them, and on their honeymoon.

Sweet.

Broken leg. Not so sweet.

She walked on. She didn't need to rush things with Adam. If she wasn't ready to talk about settling down, moving into his place, getting married, then she wasn't ready.

If she met a fun, good-looking guy who was attracted to her, who wanted to ski with her, what could be wrong with that? Nothing.

Nothing at all.

"Five-One." Her radio interrupted her thoughts.

"Five-One, go ahead."

"*Feuilles de Menthe* reports a drunk and disorderly patron refusing to pay."

"Got it." She set off at a light jog in the direction of the restaurant next door to her own apartment.

◇◇◇

Mark Hamilton did not appear to be at home. The phone rang; the answering machine picked up on the fourth ring.

Winters didn't leave a message. He didn't have another number to try.

Hamilton was unmarried. He had been born in Canada in 1967. He'd moved to Trafalgar last July. No warrant was currently out for his arrest, and he did not own a prohibited or restricted firearm. Legally, anyway.

Ray Lopez continued to dig. Winters would keep trying to locate Hamilton. He also wanted to go to Victoria to talk to this Elizabeth Moorehouse about her relationship with Gord

Lindsay. He leaned back in his chair and debated whether he should confront the man first, or hear what the woman had to say. Victoria was a quick trip. An hour's flight to Vancouver, a fifteen minute hop over the Salish Sea to the Island. Barely enough time to settle into his seat and open a book. He checked the weather forecast for the next couple of days.

Clouds and freezing rain alternating with snow.

The nearest airport was in the town of Castlegar. Which they called Cancel-gar because it was so badly situated, in a bowl of a valley surrounded by mountains, for winter flights. He called up the airport weather. The screen showed a row of yellow planes, meaning possible weather delay.

That might be a problem. Book a flight, go to the airport, waste possibly half a day sitting around and hoping the plane from Vancouver would get in and back out again. If it didn't, come home to try again the next day.

He could ask an officer from Victoria to visit the woman, but this wasn't something he wanted to delegate.

His phone rang.

"Winters."

Paul Keller, the Chief Constable. "I'd like an update on the Lindsay case, John. Do you have time to drop over and fill me in?"

"Sure."

"I've got a couple of beers in the fridge."

"Won't say no to that." Winters would check the flight prospects in the morning. Weather in these mountains could change as fast as a man could blink.

He called Eliza with an update on his arrival. "I've got to drop around and fill Paul in. He'll want to have a beer, chat for a while, but I'll try to get away as soon as I can."

"Poor man," Eliza said. "He's lonely. Perhaps we should invite him out to dinner one night."

"When this case wraps up, we'll do that. I might be going to Victoria tomorrow. Just a quick hop and back, with luck in one day, but the weather can be a problem."

He talked as he headed out the door. He'd take his own car, so he wouldn't have to return to the station after seeing Paul. "How was your day?"

"Uneventful. I've been worrying about Margo, though. She's been acting very strangely lately."

"In what way?"

"Just odd. Nothing important, I'll tell you about it later."

"Love you," he said, flicking the button on the key to unlock his car. It flashed its headlights in greeting.

"Bye," Eliza said softly.

Paul Keller's new condo looked exactly like what it was: the home of a middle-aged man left adrift by a sudden, unexpected divorce. Winters recognized bits and pieces of furniture from the house Keller had shared with his wife, Karen. A collection of photographs of their children, moving through time, decorated a table, but otherwise the living room was cold and sterile. No paintings on the walls, no small carvings on display, not even a carpet to add a splash of color to the gleaming hardwood floor. The room was painted real estate-friendly neutral. In the kitchen, other than a kettle, a toaster, and one mug turned upside down on a folded tea towel, the countertops were bare.

Keller greeted his head detective and went to the fridge to get a couple of beers before leading the way into his den.

That room, at least, was all Paul Keller's. His large wooden desk, the comfortable leather chairs, the rows of photographs on the wall marking the progress of his career. The Ikea bookshelves lined with volumes on policing, criminal psychology, politics, and history.

The scent of tobacco, hovering over everything. An ashtray sat on the desk, full of gray ash and ground-out cigarette butts.

Winters made himself comfortable in a well-used arm chair, the leather as soft and creamy as butter. Keller sat behind his desk and swirled the chair around so he faced into the room rather than out. Seated at his desk, he'd have a great view of the river and the hills on the opposite side. The headlights of cars shone in the distance, a thin line of light breaking the deep darkness of the winter woods.

"Looks like you're settling in well," Winters said.

"It's great. I can walk to work from here. I told the guys not to send a car for me anymore. I can use the exercise. There's a gym in the common area, a pool and a tennis court come summer. No driveway to shovel, no lawn to cut. Just great," he said, unable to hide the wistfulness in his voice. "I miss the fire, night like this."

Winters eyed the bare wall. The Chief's old house boasted an enormous open fireplace. "Can't have everything."

"No. Tell me what's happening with the Lindsay case. Did you get help from IHIT?"

"They sent me two warm bodies. I've got them helping Ray on the phones. They're going through Cathy Lindsay's cell phone, calling everyone in her address book and arranging an interview. We're trying to get in contact with the people she worked with. A good number of them are out of town, but in some cases we've got interviews set up for when they get back."

"Teachers," Keller said. "Not only a week in March, but all summer off and two weeks' vacation at Christmas."

"And a pretty tough job the rest of the time."

"No tougher than ours."

"Sometimes it seems as if they're almost the same."

Keller laughed and lifted his brown bottle. "I'll drink to that. Cheers."

"Cheers."

"I went around to Lucky Smith's for her birthday dinner the other night. Molly was there, Adam Tocek too. Molly sure hates it when her mom calls her Moonlight, but Lucky refuses to change. She considers it a personal insult that her kids don't like the names she and Andy chose. Samwise, for God's sake. Surprised the boy turned out to be half normal."

"I met a kid a while ago whose mother named him Beowulf."

Keller roared.

"She's young, but a good mother, I thought," Winters said. "Good parents can make up for a lousy name."

"Back to mothers. Cathy Lindsay?"

"By all accounts a nice, normal, middle-class Trafalgar woman. I've got a couple of lines to pursue." Winters filled his boss in on the school rumor about an affair between Cathy and a fellow teacher and the VicPD report of Gord Lindsay's suspected second life in Victoria. "But really, I can't see either of those leading to murder. Yes, the husband might have wanted to get rid of her if things were getting rough between them. But they aren't worth major money, not as far as we've been able to tell. So why not get a divorce? Nasty, unpleasant, but not unusual."

"As well I know."

"Right. There's nothing in Gord Lindsay's background that suggests he's got the wherewithal to get hold of the sort of weapon that was used to kill his wife, or how to use it with that degree of accuracy. The gun guys tell me it was an expert shot."

"Any chance they weren't aiming at Cathy?"

"If not, then what were they aiming at? Nothing's out there. This close to town, no one should be hunting. If they were aiming for the back window of one of the houses on the ridge, they were at a ridiculously bad angle and distance. As for the rumor of Cathy's affair, I'll follow that up when the guy in question answers his darn phone, but same question applies. If he wanted out of the affair, why kill her? Tell her to bugger off. You know as well as I do that domestics are nasty, vicious, sudden things. Pent up anger or overwhelming rage. Nothing like this. It was calculated, cold, planned. Parking his car in such a place that we'd lose it in a maze of tracks." Winters shook his head.

"A joy killing then?"

"I've considered that. Was Cathy a random target? The wrong place at the wrong time? In this town? I just can't see it. Maybe I don't want to see it, but my gut says no. For what that's worth. My gut isn't telling me anything at all about this one."

"They get any DNA off the cigarette butt found?"

"We're waiting for the results from the lab. A DNA sample's totally useless if there's nothing to compare it with." He finished his beer, set the bottle down on the table.

"Get you another?"

"Better not. I'm driving and I've got a long day ahead of me tomorrow."

"One other thing, while you're here. I had a call from the mayor last week. Someone's bought the Grizzly Resort site."

"Who?"

"Fellow by the name of Fernhaugh representing some sort of consortium. The bad news is they plan to go head and develop it."

Winters leaned back in his seat with a groan. That piece of mountain wilderness had been slated for development a few years ago. The deal had died, the partners withdrew and put the land up for sale. The Trafalgar City Police breathed a collective sigh of relief. Not that the TCP had any objection to development, but the project had been a flashpoint for environmentalists before the first shovel so much as hit the ground.

"I've a preliminary meeting with the mayor and this Fernhaugh on Wednesday. Not looking forward to it. We do not need that issue rearing its ugly head."

"You can say that again."

"I no doubt will."

"Have you spoken to Lucky about it?"

"Fernhaugh's been keeping a low profile. I don't think she's heard. Yet. I wouldn't want to be in the same room when she does."

Chapter Sixteen

By the time Molly Smith got to *Feuilles de Menthe*, the drunk had been dragged away by his embarrassed wife. He'd had some objection to the degree to which his steak had been cooked. The kitchen would have prepared him another, if he'd asked, the waiter told Smith. But he ate the whole thing without complaint, while consuming two bottles of an excellent Australian Shiraz, and then decided it wasn't good enough and he wasn't going to pay.

Smith asked for a description—middle-aged, average height, average weight, brown hair, black leather coat. The waiter shrugged. "Average guy."

"I'm afraid he's going to get behind the wheel," she said. "I don't suppose you saw which direction they went?"

"As it happens, I did. I wanted to make sure he didn't decide to come back. They turned left and crossed Monroe Street. You'll be pleased to hear I saw the wife take the keys out of her purse. And keep them in her hand."

"Good. Thanks. If he comes back…"

"I'll let you know."

She left, stomach rumbling. What with stopping in at the store for new gloves, and then waiting for Winters to arrive and hear Lucky's story, Smith hadn't eaten since lunch at the lodge. She was starving, and it didn't help standing on the street outside Trafalgar Thai while the scent of spices and aromatic herbs drifted out the door every time it opened. Or being here while waiters passed bearing plates piled with braised ribs or grilled salmon.

Anyplace she might be able to grab something quick that she could eat standing up—the bakery, the coffee shops—was closed at this time on a Monday night.

Wasn't there a snack bar at the rec center? Indeed, she thought with an inner smile, there was.

The nightlife district of Trafalgar was a small one. The rec center wasn't far from the east end of Front Street, next to the tourist info place. Peterson had warned her not to be spending her time investigating murders she wasn't assigned, or qualified, to investigate. He couldn't object to her getting something to eat, could he?

Better than her fainting on the street from hunger.

That sort of thing reduced the citizenry's confidence in the professionalism of their police service.

Happy with her logic, she set off down the street. She'd arrive about quarter to eight. In time to catch Mrs. Grady, her old teacher, before her game.

The parking lot of the rec center was almost full. Lights spilled from doors and windows. Little kids followed parents lugging enormous hockey bags; women with coats tossed over fashionable yoga pants headed for their cars, while women in shorts and carrying athletic shoes walked into the building.

The industrial-strength carpeting in the entrance was wet and dirty with rapidly-melting snow, the building filled with the acrid scent of generations of sweat-soaked shirts, damp socks, overly-stewed coffee, and stale popcorn. The floors reverberated with the tread of cleats and skate protectors. Children's laughter and parents' cheers bounced off the walls and the glass shield surrounding the ice rink. Smith knew her way around this place, and she headed for the gym. At the snack bar, pink hot dogs turned slowly on the grill and popcorn bounced in the machine. Business first and then a couple of those hot dogs. She hadn't had a proper hot dog, drenched in mustard and relish, in years.

In the gym, women were leaning against walls stretching, standing in small groups chatting, or kicking soccer balls back and forth. A few glanced over at the arriving policewoman, but most carried on with their warm-up.

Smith wondered if Cathy Lindsay had come here. That might be an avenue to explore. Although she couldn't imagine the woman had offended someone in aerobics class or Pilates so severely they'd take out a contract on her.

She spotted her quarry alone by the far wall, rhythmically doing squats. Smith made her way across the gym floor, highly overdressed in her winter jacket, uniform, equipment belt, and black boots among these sleek women wearing shorts, T-shirts, and running shoes.

"Hi, Mrs. Grady, how are things?"

"Moonlight, nice to see you. Is there a problem?"

"I remembered you play here on Monday, and I wanted to ask you some questions. It won't take long."

Mrs. Grady—Smith didn't even know her first name—glanced at the round white clock high on the wall. Five to eight. "What's this about?"

"Cathy Lindsay."

The teacher's face settled into dark lines. "Bad, bad business. I don't know what I can tell you."

"She taught at TDH I hear. Did you know her?"

"I knew her to see her. To say hi if I ran into her in the grocery store. I never had anything social to do with her, nothing outside of school."

"The first forty-eight hours are absolutely critical in a police investigation," Smith said.

"So they say on all the TV shows."

Smith tried not to grimace. "In this case, Mrs. Lindsay's place of employment is closed for another week. Sergeant Winters, the detective in charge, wants to speak to people who worked with her, but most of her colleagues are away or can't be reached. I remembered seeing you here the other day, and said I'd ask."

"I don't know how I can help you, Moonlight."

"It's come to our attention that rumors about Cathy Lindsay were circulating at the school."

Mrs. Grady's eyebrows pulled together and her face tightened. For a moment Molly Smith feared she was going to be chastised for doing a substandard job on her essay on the Brontë sisters. Gosh, that had been so awful. She minded Mrs. Grady's disapproval far more than she minded the D she got on that paper, or what her mother said when she saw it. Mrs. Grady's disappointment, as well as the smirk on Meredith Morgenstern's face when she was asked to come to the front of the class and read from her A+ paper on Wordsworth, rankled for a long time.

Smith pulled her head back to the present. She tried to look like a police officer interviewing a potential witness. It wasn't easy.

"Watch out," Mrs. Grady cried, leaping back. An out of control black and white soccer ball bounced off Smith's right leg.

"Sorry." A woman chased after the errant ball.

A whistle blew and the women fell into order. Mrs. Grady glanced at them.

"Cathy Lindsay?" Smith nudged.

"You're asking about a rumor?"

"Some students have said she was involved with another teacher."

"I don't know about *involved*." Mrs. Grady let out a sigh as she gave in. "Yes, Cathy is certainly at the center of the rumor mill lately. I guess I should say she was. Terrible, terrible business, what happened to her. She has…had…a, I scarcely know how to say it, a crush on one of the male teachers."

"A crush?"

"That seems to be the best word I can use. It was becoming embarrassing. She'd arrive at staff meetings late so she could pull up a chair beside him. She brought cookies and cupcakes she'd baked, saying she had a few extra and she knew a single man—emphasizing single—didn't get much home cooking. She asked him to give her a hand carrying things to her car or to class. The sort of thing she'd never needed help with before. In short, she mooned around like one of our grade-nine girls with a crush on the football team's quarterback."

"This man, how'd he react?"

"He was hideously embarrassed. We were all embarrassed. For the both of them. He leapt to his feet at one of the staff meetings when she came in late, offered her his chair, and ran to the other side of the room to stand against the wall. With his arms crossed so defensively he might as well have hung a no-trespassing sign around his neck.

"It's difficult sometimes for a male teacher, in such a female-heavy environment. And they have to be so careful about never being in a possibly compromising situation with the teenage girls. I'm sure he didn't need this complication. To be honest, Moonlight, I felt sorry for him. I was walking with him to our respective classrooms about a month or so ago when he said he'd forgotten something and whirled around and dashed off down a side corridor. Sure enough, who was heading our way but Cathy. She even started dressing better."

"Better how?"

"Better quality clothes, jewelry, high heels. Just nicer. Thank God, she didn't try to dress sexy."

"What's this man's name?"

"Moonlight, he didn't *do* anything. He didn't kill her because she was embarrassing him. If anything, I'd suspect she'd be more likely to kill him because he rejected her."

"Did he reject her? Tell her to piss off, I mean?"

"That I don't know."

"His name?"

"I don't want to get anyone in trouble, Moonlight. My game's started. We're short-handed as it is."

"I know his name, Mrs. Grady. I just want confirmation."

"You can call me Alice now."

Never.

Mrs. Grady surrendered with a reluctant sigh. "Mark Hamilton. He teaches math. And he's a very, very nice man."

"Thanks."

"I was pleased when you came back to Trafalgar, Moonlight. Pleased to see you became a police officer. We need young women like you, doing well in the traditional men's jobs."

Smith shifted her boots. They'd deposited a large wet puddle on the gym floor. "Thanks, Mrs. Grady."

The teacher ran onto the floor and sent a ball flying into the far wall with a well-placed kick.

It was ten after eight when Smith left the gym. The snack bar was dark, the glass window pulled across the counter, the hot dog cooker switched off, the popcorn machine silent, the coffee pot empty.

Smith groaned.

"I didn't do it!" A teenage boy shouted, raising his hands in the air. "It wasn't me. It was him. He did it all." His companion smacked him on the side of the head as they passed, laughing uproariously at their own joke.

Chapter Seventeen

Tuesday dawned dark and gloomy, threatening more snow or a nasty icy rain, the mountains hidden by thick banks of gray cloud. Not much chance of catching a flight out today.

John Winters wasn't too disappointed. He'd decided to talk to Gord Lindsay first. No point rushing off to Victoria, possibly wasting an entire day, without ensuring Elizabeth Moorehouse was at home. If he called to set up an interview he'd have to identify the police department he was with, and she'd be on the phone to Gord the minute Winters hung up.

He'd brought his laptop to the breakfast table and read the *Globe and Mail* online while munching toast and jam and sipping coffee. Eliza had her usual yogurt and berries with a sprinkling of granola as she checked stock market figures on her iPad. She kept a pad of paper at her elbow and alternately chewed the end of her pencil and her yogurt. She made a note, jotting down a string of numbers, chewed her pencil some more.

"Are you going into the gallery today?" he asked.

"Later. I have some work to do on our portfolio this morning. Oil's up again."

"Isn't it always?"

"No, John. Not always. You're thinking of gasoline."

Molly Smith had phoned him moments after he'd arrived home the previous evening to report what she'd learned about Cathy Lindsay and Mark Hamilton. He'd gone to his computer to jot down some notes and ideas, and Eliza had been curled up on the couch reading when he finished.

"You were going to tell me about something that happened at the store the other day," he said now. He tossed the last bit of toast into his mouth and shut the computer lid. "I got preoccupied and forgot to ask."

"Nothing important, really, but it was a bit worrying. A man came into the store, wanting to look at some sketches I have in. Judging by the look on Margo's face, you would have thought it was the Second Coming. She stared at the man so long and so hard, he pretty much fled in terror. When I asked her about it, she said he was her son."

"Her son?"

"Odd, eh? She's married, has a grown child and a grandchild."

"Perhaps she had a son who died."

"That would be sad, but why would she think he was in my gallery wanting to buy a picture?"

"Some people never can accept a sudden death. For years, they continue to think a mistake must have been made. Particularly if the body wasn't found or it wasn't in good enough condition for them to be able to see their loved one one last time. I was thinking about that yesterday. Gord Lindsay says he keeps expecting to see Cathy popping around every corner."

"That's understandable, isn't it? In his case. Her things would be everywhere, her scent in the air, a magazine where she'd left it, a corner turned down to mark her place. My grandmother lived with us for a few years when I was young. She broke her hip in a fall and for days after she'd been taken to the hospital, I kept hearing her footstep in the hallway or seeing her out of the corner of my eye. She went into a nursing home after that, where she lived for a good many more years, I'm happy to say. It was different with Margo. This was no glimpse of a shadow. She stared right at him. It was dreadfully awkward."

"Perhaps she needs some grief counseling."

"I scarcely know the woman. I can't suggest something as personal as that."

"If she didn't see a body, she might never have accepted the death. You could ask her."

"No, I'll leave it. She's my employee, not my friend. She doesn't need me interfering in her life. As long as she doesn't make a habit of chasing away interested shoppers."

He drained the last of his coffee and pushed back his chair. "I'm off."

"Meet for lunch?"

"Better not. It'll be another long, long day."

"The policeman's lot is not a happy one."

He gave her a kiss and went to work.

First stop: Gord Lindsay, philanderer.

Work never seemed like work. From the day Gord switched on his first computer, listened to the hum of the fan warming up, the whirl of the hard drive coming to life, saw letters and words appear on the screen, he'd loved computers. He was fortunate, he knew, that he was able to make a living, a good living, doing work he loved.

He'd been lucky to hitch up with a guy who had a solid head for business. Over the years, Gord had seen many people with good tech skills, the drive to work hard, the ambition to succeed, falter and lose their way, and eventually their dream, because although they were great at computers, they didn't know the first thing about how to run a business. How to make money. And, most importantly, keep it.

Computer people did not make good accountants or office managers.

Gord had recognized that he was lacking in that department almost as soon as he hung up his proverbial shingle. He'd invited a housemate from university, Ahmad Kashani, a business major, to partner in the company.

They'd never looked back.

Ahmad still lived in Victoria, had his fingers in other pies these days, but he kept his eye on the accounts and on the sales and marketing efforts, and he and Gord talked no less than once a week.

Yes, Gord had been lucky. In life, in business. In love.

Now he was getting over the shock of Cathy's death, he was beginning to consider that he might be lucky in this also. The marriage hadn't been going well no matter how much they both pretended, and he lay awake some nights worrying Cathy would ask for a divorce. For God's sake, she couldn't stop chattering on about some jerk at work. Mark had run a marathon. Mark spent the weekend hiking. Mark had done this and Mark had done that.

Mark, as far as Gord was concerned, was welcome to her.

But Mark was not welcome to a share of Gord's business. Or to his children.

Unlikely anything was going on between Cathy and this Mark creep. If she were playing games after school, she wouldn't talk so damn much about him.

Gord had checked her panties a couple of times, looking for traces of drying semen, after she'd come home following a night out with her friends and popped into the shower before bed. He'd pretended to kiss her as she came in the door while sniffing for the scent of sex or stray hairs on her shoulders.

Nothing.

She might have restricted her dalliances to times when Gord was in Victoria, but Gord didn't give Cathy credit for that much self-control. What Cathy wanted, she wanted now.

No, she wasn't screwing Mark-the-math-teacher. But if her eye was beginning to wander, who knows where it might have ended up.

If she ever found out about Elizabeth, and the house Gord kept in Victoria, Cathy'd be on the warpath.

This way, Cathy was out of his life. He kept not only all his money, but a life insurance payout would be coming in soon. And he had full custody of his kids. None of this joint-custody nonsense, seeing his daughter every second weekend. Custody of Jocelyn was what mattered. Bradley could hit the streets as far as Gord was concerned.

Elizabeth had heard the news about murder in Trafalgar. She'd phoned his cell, breathless, full of condolences. She knew he was married, knew where he lived. She knew, or thought she knew, that Cathy's family was very wealthy and she'd threatened to take her children to California, where her parents lived, if Gord ever left her.

That nothing in that story was true, didn't bother Gord. It kept Elizabeth docile. Kept her content to live in the house he helped pay for. Content to give him a much needed screw whenever he was in town.

Maybe it was all for the best.

He settled behind his desk with a travel mug of coffee his mom had made for him and a couple of his mother-in-law's muffins, fat with blueberries.

He'd come into work gratefully; he couldn't stand another minute in that house. Renee and Ann alternately wept and told each other they had to be strong and present a good front for "poor Gord and his poor motherless children." His father-in-law wandered around looking for loose screws or crooked picture frames and eyed Gord as if wondering if he'd murdered his daughter. Jocelyn was enjoying her grandparents' attention, but then she'd remember the reason for their visit, and burst into tears.

Bradley either slept or sulked, angry at the world.

The only good thing was all the cooking and baking that was going on.

Gord left the funeral arrangements to Renee and Ann. He trusted them, he said, tear in his eye, to do the best for Cathy.

The door flew open, and Justin, tech support, came in.

"Hey man, surprised to see you here. Sorry about your wife, eh? What do the cops think happened?"

Gord ignored the question. Work, all he wanted was to work. "Any calls yesterday?"

"Nothing important. Big Eddie's site went down, but I got it back up pretty fast."

"Morning." Adrienne, a web designer, sailed into the office. "Gord, I am so sorry. If there's anything I can do…"

"You can carry on as normal, Adrienne. We've promised Granger's Insurance to have their new web site fully operational by April first. I trust it's on track."

"Of course it's on track," she said, offended.

"Glad to hear it."

He pretended not to see the look she exchanged with Justin. Gord turned back to his computer screen. Words and images swam before his eyes.

Who the hell was he trying to kid?

Cathy. He'd loved her so much once. They'd had great times together. It didn't need to have all gone wrong. If he could have her back, if only he could have another chance, he'd do any-thing…anything to make her forget Mark-the-math-teacher. He'd gladly give up Elizabeth, if only his phone would ring, and Cathy would be on the line to remind him she and Jocelyn were going skiing. And did he know where Bradley spent last night because he wasn't in his bed.

He sensed a movement of air at his shoulder. He blinked through tears to see a box of tissues on his desk, Adrienne scur-rying back to her own corner.

Gord snatched a tissue and blew his nose.

Work. Time to get to work. What was he doing when he left on Friday afternoon, anyway?

Friday. Cathy had less than twenty-four hours to live. Did she know, did she have any inkling that her time on this earth was almost over? Any regrets for things not done and words never said?

He gave his head a shake. Right, he'd been working on a proposal for a web presence for a vacation condo development. It was going to be a big job and Gord wanted it.

The door opened once again. Instead of one of his employees, it was, Gord was not happy to see, the cops.

"I dropped by your house," Sergeant Winters said. "Your father-in-law told me you'd come into the office."

"Work needs to be done."

"I understand." Winters had come alone this time. Just as well. Gord didn't care for the steady, watchful eye of that young constable.

"What can I help you with? Has there been a development? Have you arrested someone?"

"Not at this time. I'd like a word in private. Is there some place we can talk?"

Gord glanced around the open-plan office. A 19th century warehouse, down by the river, converted into an office block. High ceilings with thick wooden cross beams, exposed red-brick walls, wide-planked, scarred floors, large windows. Justin and Adrienne were at their desks doing a poor job of pretending they weren't listening.

Gord got to his feet, feeling slow and heavy. "We can talk in the conference room."

The conference room of Lindsay Internet Consulting had a spectacular view across the park and over the river. When the clouds weren't so low they obscured anything further than the far side of the street. A long wooden table, gleaming with polish, and twelve accompanying chairs filled most of the space. A credenza held an empty coffee maker and stacks of mugs. No pictures hung on the walls, no flowers or plants on the surfaces. A place in which to conduct business. And only business.

"Tell me," Winters said, once he settled into the comfortable swivel chair. "About Elizabeth Moorehouse."

Gord simply shrugged. "You work fast."

Winters said nothing.

"I figured you'd find out about that. My marriage to Cathy is…was…a good one. Solid. But it happens that people, men anyway, over the years, start to need a bit of variety. You know what I mean? Spice up a middle-aged life."

Lindsay paused, no doubt waiting for Winters to say he understood. Between us guys, nudge nudge, wink wink. He did not. Silence stretched between them. The building was quiet. These old warehouse walls had been built strong and thick.

"Half of my business is in Victoria, where it began. My business partner lives in Victoria. I spend a lot of time there."

"What's your partner's name?"

"Ahmad Kashani. He's been with me since the beginning. He's not a full partner any more, but still supervises the accounts, the legal aspect of the business, that sort of thing." Gord hadn't even thought to contact Ahmad about Cathy's death. The man might not have heard. He rarely read anything other than the financial papers and international news.

"Tell me about Ms. Moorehouse. How long have you been seeing her?"

"Three years, give or take a few months. I go to Victoria regularly, as I said. I was getting tired of hotels, so suggested I help her out with the expenses on a house not far from the office."

"In exchange for?"

"You know full well in exchange for what. Sex of course. Elizabeth is what once might have been called my mistress. She owns a nice house in a respectable area. I pay a substantial portion of her bills. I sleep in her bed. I assume you got her name from that damned police report. I didn't want her to call the cops. I didn't want it on record that I'd been there, but when I was upstairs checking to see what else they'd taken, the bastards, she called 911."

"Did Cathy know about this arrangement?"

"She did not. Look, Sergeant Winters, you're barking up the wrong tree here. That I have a girlfriend in Victoria has nothing to do with Cathy's death. Instead of prying into my sex life, you'd be better spending your time checking into who was up there, on that path, that day."

"Rest assured, we're exploring all possible avenues, Mr. Lindsay."

Winters didn't think Gord Lindsay had killed his wife. He'd been in the house with his daughter when Cathy died. Sure, the girl couldn't account for all of her father's whereabouts, but he certainly didn't have time to get his shotgun, head off to the woods, wait for Cathy and her dog to come by, fire off a shot, pack up the weapon, walk down the hill to the church, collect his car, and drive back home.

He could have hired someone to do it. The killing had all the marks of an expensive hired hit.

But why? There seemed to be no big money in the family, on either side. Divorce and custody of children could get vicious—Winters had seen the fallout of that many times—but people tended to go into a divorce expecting it would all go well. Only when the lawyers got involved, the fees got expensive, and accusations and threats got flying, did the parties get angry enough to kill.

Winters studied the man sitting across the table from him. Gord Lindsay was overweight, balding and not trying to hide it. He chewed his fingernails when nervous (as he was now). His clothes were bought off the rack and didn't fit his expand-ing girth all that well. He had five employees in Trafalgar, four in Victoria. A moderately profitable business by all accounts, adequate to provide for a family in which the wife worked as a high school teacher. Not a company that generated the sort of excess funds that could pay for the hire of a professional killer. Unless money was coming in from somewhere else.

Did Lindsay have other business in Victoria, which was after all a major Pacific port, which the computer company might be a front for?

Had Cathy discovered something about that business? Had she found out about Elizabeth Moorehouse and threatened Gord if he didn't give the woman up?

Winters doubted it. He was pretty sure Gord Lindsay was exactly the middle-class family man, fooling around on his wife, which he appeared to be. But it was worth following up. Another reason for a quick trip to Victoria.

He glanced outside. The clouds might have lifted, just a tiny bit.

"I know you have to look into everything." Gord stood and walked to the window. He spoke to the glass. "Everyone and everything. I know that. But I didn't kill Cathy, Sergeant Winters. And I genuinely do not have the slightest idea why anyone would."

And that, Winters thought, was precisely the problem.

Chapter Eighteen

Eliza spent her morning on the computer, studying the business news, manipulating her portfolio. Sell a bit of this, buy some of that. Move money around. This was her happy place, the place where she'd sought refuge through the stifling, boring years she'd worked as a model.

That she made buckets of money from her investments was icing on the cake. And why she could afford to own two art galleries which were not simply failing to make a profit but bleeding money.

She ate a quick lunch of vegetable soup at her desk and then shut down the computer and got ready for work. She showered quickly, dried her hair and applied a light coat of makeup and a touch of pale-pink lipstick. She chose casual cream wool pants and a crisp white silk blouse accented with a scarlet scarf and earrings of dangling squares of red glass.

She studied herself in the mirror. Understated but fashionable. Well-heeled but not bragging about it.

She'd been modeling since she was sixteen years old, both on the catwalk and for magazines. She'd acted in TV commercials. She'd learned long ago how to play the part. How to pretend. Today she would play the businesswoman of excellent taste and independent means. The only role Eliza never played was cop's wife. She suspected some of the other wives didn't like her much. They thought she was stuck up and cold. She thought they were narrow-minded and provincial. She avoided police functions whenever she could.

The move to Trafalgar had been good for John. In the city, he'd been burning out, fast. Drinking heavily, hanging out in bars with cops after work. He was haunted, she knew, by some of his past cases. Some of the things he'd seen. Then the Blakely case, the worst of them all, a twelve-year-old girl, raped and murdered, by her own father as it turned out. The family prominent, rich; press attention relentless. She didn't know the details, but she knew John had almost made a mistake, almost arrested the wrong man. She heard him in the night, either pacing or wrestling with nightmares in his sleep.

So they'd moved to quiet, peaceful Trafalgar. He'd stopped drinking too much, didn't go out with the guys much, slept through the night, warm and safe beside her.

Eliza smiled at herself in the mirror and went to work.

She stood on the street and studied the window display of the Mountain in Winter Art Gallery. One of Alan Khan's sketches was gone, leaving a rather prominent gap in the display.

Next week it would all come down, and they'd set up for a fresh one-woman show. Which reminded her that she needed to check with the artist about the guest list for the opening reception.

"I see you sold a Khan in the window," she said to Margo as she took off her coat. "To Mr. Westfield?"

"No," Margo said with a small frown. "He hasn't been back. I wish he'd come in again. I saw him yesterday at Adventure Vacations, but he hurried away before I got a chance to speak to him. I was thinking…your husband's a police officer."

Eliza didn't care for that turn in the conversation. "We never discuss police matters." Not entirely true, but none of Margo's business. She hurried into the small washroom in the back to check her hair and face. Margo pounced when Eliza came out. "How do you go about finding someone's address or phone number?"

"The phone book? Canada411.com?"

"I tried those things. He's not listed."

"That would be because he doesn't want anyone to know where he lives, Margo."

"Maybe you could ask your husband."

"Certainly not. Even if I wanted to, it wouldn't be ethical for him to provide that information."

"Do you think he'll come in again?"

Eliza pretended not to understand. "John drops by sometimes to take me to lunch if he has time."

"I mean William Westfield. He's good-looking, isn't he? Although dreadfully thin. I wonder if he's married. I can't wait to meet his wife and children."

At that moment the door flew open and a smiling couple brought in a gust of cold air. Eliza gratefully retreated to her desk to work on the invitations for the opening.

Business was brisk throughout the afternoon, although a good many more browsers than buyers.

At five o'clock, Margo flipped the sign on the door to closed, and Eliza shut down the office computer.

"I was hoping he'd come in," Margo said.

"Who?" Eliza asked, fearing she knew the answer.

"William Westfield. He was interested in the Khan sketches. Perhaps he doesn't know we'll be taking them down next week. If you had his phone number, I could call and let him know."

Eliza Winters was not entirely an uncaring person, but she was a private one, and as she never shared confidences with anyone other than her husband (save the occasional weep on her agent and closest friend Barney's shoulder after a couple of martinis), she did not expect nor want people to confide in her.

She did not know what Margo's problem with William Westfield was. She did not want to find out.

"Oh, Eliza. I told Steve I'd seen Jackson. He said I was imagining things. I know I'm not. This time I'm sure."

This time?

Eliza fled for the closet. She fumbled to put on her coat. Couldn't find the sleeve. Margo held the back of the coat, so Eliza could get her arm in the right place.

When Eliza faced her, Margo's eyes were swimming with tears. "I know I'm right. I have to be right."

And Eliza found herself saying, "Tell me about your son."

Molly Smith rolled out of bed at noon. She'd worked until six, and was lying in bed, wide-awake, at six thirty. After night shift, she liked to read for a while, try to unwind before falling asleep. Knowing she had to get up to go skiing, today she hadn't. Instead she spent what passed for her night tossing and turning and punching her pillow, and it seemed as if she'd only fallen asleep as the alarm began to blast.

Grumbling, she made her way to the bathroom and then the closet.

She reminded herself that she didn't have to go. But, as usual, as she began to wake up she started looking forward to hitting the slopes. Even if only for a few hours.

She'd arranged to meet Tony at one. She glanced at the clock on the microwave as she headed out the door. Adam had called last night, as she was going to the Bishop and Nun to check out the crowd. He'd told her he missed her, muttered words of endearment, and asked what she was doing the next day.

"Skiing, of course."

He laughed. "Foolish question. Going with anyone?"

"No."

"I know you like getting out there on your own."

She'd made noncommittal sounds, said something was happening up ahead and she had to go. She didn't like the direction the conversation was taking. She wasn't being *unfaithful* to Adam. She was merely enjoying a few hours skiing with a man who was as good a skier as she. Nothing wrong with that.

So why hadn't she told Adam she was meeting Tony?

Simply, she assured herself, because Adam wouldn't understand. Men, even the best of them, could be possessive sometimes.

The clouds were low and thick, and it wasn't until she got almost to the top of the lift that figures emerged from the swirling snow and mist, and she could try to spot Tony. She was late.

She never came here in the middle of the day and had forgotten to allow enough time to park at the rear of the lot. So far back, she had to wait for the bus that made the rounds of the grounds, dropping up tired skiers and picking up new ones.

She expected him to have given up and gone off by himself, but Tony was waiting at the top of the mountain, his hands resting on his poles, not fidgeting, patiently watching skiers jumping off the lift chairs.

She knew the minute he spotted her. His goggles were pushed up onto his helmet, and she was close enough to see his eyes light up and his face break into a wide smile. She felt herself smiling in return, and lifted a hand in greeting. "Sorry I'm late. I forgot how far away I had to park at this time of day."

"Not a problem. I'm glad you came."

"It was nice of you to wait for me."

"That's why I'm here." He studied her face, and she did not look away. She felt color rising in her cheeks. "It's cold up here."

"Let's warm up. Ready?"

"Ready."

This lift sat at the conjunction of several blue runs and two black diamonds. Most people headed for the easier slopes. Smith followed Tony as he settled his goggles over his face and led the way to the lip of the mountain. She took a breath to feel the cold crisp air between her teeth and in her chest, settled her own goggles in place, and checked the path of the wind. She placed the tips of her skis in the direction she intended to go. A scattering of people were ahead of them, zipping in and out of the swirling mist, soon disappearing into the cloud cover. On a clear day, you could see a long way from up here: the line of mountains marching into the distance, toy cars moving along the strip of road twisting and turning through the dark forest, tiny figures mingling and separating, the lodge with smoke curling from the chimneys.

Without a word or checking to see if she was ready, Tony launched himself over the edge. She came hot on his heels, and they raced down the steep mountain. Visibility was almost nil with the cloud cover and falling snow. Only the crunch of snow beneath her skis, the whistle of the wind in her helmet, broke the silence. Tony found a section of fresh powder and he disappeared into it. She followed, moving blindly, trusting only to the feel of her skis and the reach of her poles, soaring on clouds, the cold air, full of the scent of pine trees and ice, fresh on her face.

She felt the ground level off and knew she was near the bottom. Lights from the lodge broke through the mist. She moved her feet into a hockey stop, driving the sides of her skis into the packed snow. Snow flew in a spray of white powder, and she punched her fist into the air with a cheer. She pushed her goggles up. Tony had reached the bottom no more than a second ahead of her. He watched her, grinning. Flakes of snow stuck to the stubble of his beard and his cheeks burned with cold and exhilaration.

"Good," he said, simply.

"Oh, yeah."

"Ready for another?"

"Let's try Blond Ambition next. Beat you to the lift."

She didn't beat him, but only because a girl, flailing wildly to control her feet and arms, slid into Smith's path.

They made several more runs. Smith was pumped, exhilarated. When she skied with Adam or Christa she slowed down, matching their pace. When she skied alone, she raced only against herself with no one to notice if she made a personal best or fell face first into a mound of snow.

This, racing with Tony, reminded her of when she'd competed. Pushing herself, testing the limits of her mind and body. She'd quit competition when she realized she was never going to be good enough to make the Olympics or even a national or provincial team. Maybe, she thought now, gasping to recover her breath, laughing at the snow on Tony's face, she shouldn't have been so quick to give it up.

"We should be able to get in one more run," Tony said.

She'd been having so much fun, she'd scarcely noticed the passage of time. A long line of cars, yellow headlights bouncing off falling snow, were pulling out of the parking lot and making their way in a single line down the mountain. Smith pulled her glove down and her sleeve up to glance at her watch. Almost five o'clock.

"Better not. I have to be going."

"You're not in a hurry, are you? Let's have a drink. We need something to warm us up, don't we? Something to eat? I didn't have lunch and I'm starving."

"Sorry. I'd like to, but I can't. I have to go."

"Why?"

She hesitated. She'd told him she worked for the city. She'd left it to him to assume she was a low-level clerk. Hard to say she had to go to work without him asking what sort of job started at six at night.

She headed for the bus pickup in front of the lodge. Lights were on in the building and along the deck. Warm, inviting. Inside, the fire would be blazing, the bar hopping, the kitchen serving for a while yet. Everyone talking about the conditions, about their runs, hoping for more snow tonight.

Tony was thinking the same thing. "You don't have time for one drink? What's the rush, Molly?"

She bent to snap her skis off. "I'd love to stay, but I'm due at my mom's for dinner. I have to get home and change first."

"Okay," he said, and she felt a twinge of guilt at the lie.

"Tomorrow?"

"No can do. Sorry." The bus approached. The line-up was long and everyone shuffled a few inches forward.

"I want to see you again, Molly. Soon. You name a time."

"Thursday. One o'clock?"

"Why don't I pick you up? No point in bringing two cars. Where do you live?"

The bus pulled to a halt. No one got off, and people climbed aboard, weighed down with skis and boots, backpacks, and overstimulated children.

"I'll meet you here. Lift at one."

"Can I have your phone number?"

But it was her turn to clamber onto the bus, and she left Tony with only a wave.

Chapter Nineteen

Her son. Her baby boy. Jackson.

Not a day had passed in the last forty-five years that Margo Franklin hadn't thought about Jackson. On her wedding day, she looked over the smiling congregation and imagined Jackson sitting in the front row, proud of his role as ring bearer. As she lay in the hospital bed cradling her newborn children in her arms, she wondered if Jackson had any adoptive brothers or sisters. When she went to the children's school to meet with their teachers or to soccer games to stand on the sidelines and cheer she hoped Jackson was getting a good education.

She rarely, if ever, talked about him. About her boy, stolen from her. Steve didn't want to hear it, and she'd soon come to realize that few people had any understanding. She'd been told more than once to "get over it."

She'd tried finding him using official channels. Everything had failed.

Jackson had disappeared from her life.

Until now. Now, he was back.

Margo enjoyed working at the art gallery. She'd trained as a typist and stenographer, started out at the bottom of the ladder in the typing pool at an insurance company. She'd taken a few years off to have the kids, but had been hired back when Ellen, her youngest, started school. She'd gradually climbed the ladder to personal assistant for a series of vice-presidents. She and Steve had retired with good pensions last year, when they both reached sixty. Looking to get out of the hustle and bustle of the city, they'd moved to Trafalgar a few months ago. Margo soon decided retirement wasn't all it was cracked up to be. Long boring days, particularly in the winter when she couldn't get into the garden; Steve underfoot all day.

This job was perfect. It was easy and the hours were relaxed. She enjoyed meeting the customers, and although she knew little about art she did think she had good taste and loved talking about it.

The job didn't pay well, and truth be told Margo spent all of her earnings (probably far more than she earned) on clothes and jewelry. She'd always thought she dressed well, but since working alongside Eliza Winters, Margo found her own long-suffering secretary and retired-housewife clothes drab and, dare she say it, dowdy.

Eliza was an easy boss; Margo got the impression she didn't take the art gallery all that seriously. She could be a mite aloof, even cold sometimes, but Margo was sure she'd break down Eliza's defenses soon enough. She'd been a famous supermodel once, no doubt she was used to not trusting people until she got to know them.

Today, for the first time Eliza suggested they do something outside a formal boss-to-employee relationship. Margo was delighted, and she leapt at the chance to talk about Jackson. "Let's go for a drink, why don't we? Do you have time? I'll call Steve, tell him I'm going to be late. He worries you know. After that horrible murder, I guess everyone's looking over their shoulder these days."

She made her call and they set off. The Hudson House Hotel was but a half a block downhill from the shop. Eliza led the way to the comfortable lounge. The bar was filling up with skiers, but the women found a two-person table tucked into a small alcove where they could speak in some degree of privacy.

The waitress arrived promptly and asked if they wanted menus. "No, thank you," Eliza said. "We won't be long. I'll have a Pinot Grigio, please. Margo?"

"Pinot Grigio? What's that? Is it nice?"

"It's a light white wine. Italian."

"I'll have that too." It sounded so sophisticated.

Young people were pouring in, laughing and slapping backs, shedding snow, pulling off gloves, cheeks ruddy with cold, faces exhilarated with the pure pleasure of being young and healthy.

Margo wondered if Jackson skied. He must, she'd seen him in Mid-Kootenay Adventure Vacations checking out the equipment on sale.

She hesitated, momentarily afraid to tell her story. Afraid Eliza would judge her. Judge her and condemn her. She saw Eliza glancing around the room, as if she were trying to find someone more interesting to talk to.

"I had a baby when I was sixteen," Margo blurted. She'd meant to start slowly, build up her story gradually, like stepping into lake water at the beginning of the summer. Instead, she found herself leaping straight off the dock.

"I named him Jackson. His father's name was Jack. I loved Jack, and he loved me, despite the age difference. But we couldn't be together. He was married you see, a good Catholic family man. Jack owned the drug store in our town, and I worked there part time."

Coasters and two glasses of wine appeared on the table. Margo picked up her glass. She remembered.

When she told Jack she was pregnant, he said no one must know. He swore her to secrecy.

Margo's family didn't have much money. Her dad worked at the sawmill and her mom stayed home. Margo was the oldest of six kids. She'd been so frightened, terrified to tell them she was pregnant.

With good reason.

Her mother found her throwing up in the toilet one morning. She looked at Margo as if she were a breeding cow, studying the enlarged breasts visible underneath the thin nightgown. "My worst fears have come to pass," she declared.

From then on, Margo wasn't permitted to sit at the dinner table with the family anymore. She had to take her meals in her room. Her dad said she disgusted him so much he couldn't keep his food down.

He told the other children she was a bad person, and they weren't to have anything to do with her. Margo's sister, Joanie, came to her room to show Margo her new doll. Their father snatched it up. Threw it into the stove, stuffed it into the flames with the poker. He said the doll was going to hell and Margo was going there too.

For many nights after Margo could hear her sister screaming in her sleep, having nightmares. But she couldn't go to Joanie's room. She couldn't comfort her. They wouldn't let her.

"Of course, I had to stop going to school as soon as my parents found out about the pregnancy," she said to Eliza. "Soon after that I left home. I remember that day, so well. Almost as well as I remember Jackson's birth. It was a Saturday, and Dad had taken all the kids into town to see a movie. A movie was a big treat in our family." By this time Margo had known not to even hope she'd be allowed to go with them. She wasn't good enough to get any favors. She was a disgrace to the family. She sat in her room, by herself, all day long. She was allowed out only to go to the bathroom and she was forbidden from speaking to her brothers and sisters. She shared a bed with Mary, the next sister down, and Dad told Mary not to talk to Margo. They gave Mary Margo's nicest clothes, not that she had much, said she didn't need them anymore. Mom brought in her meals on a tray. Burned potatoes and fatty bits of meat, what the others didn't want. She said the only reason they were feeding Margo at all was because the precious baby didn't deserve to starve because of Margo's evil.

Evil. Her own mother had believed she was evil.

Many years passed before Margo, with the love of Steve and their kids, began to finally understand that she was as valuable, and as flawed, as any other person on earth.

"They asked me who'd gotten me pregnant. My dad hit me, kicked me so hard my mom yelled at him to stop, when I wouldn't tell. I never did tell."

"A girl in my class went to stay with an aunt," Eliza said. She laid her hands on the table, twisting the stem of her wine glass between her long fingers, and focused her green eyes on Margo's face. "Everyone knew what that meant. When she came back she'd changed. She'd been a fun-loving girl before, now she was quiet, withdrawn. Sad. She never spoke of what had happened to her when she'd been away. We knew she'd had a baby, but we couldn't ask and she couldn't tell. We stayed away from her, even those who'd been her friends. It was as though she'd had the plague, and we were all in danger if we got too close."

"Yes," Margo said. "A disease so powerful it made parents hate their daughters. Turn from them and never want to see them again."

Lately two new words had begun to creep into Canadian consciousness. Honor killing. Murdering a daughter who'd been raped or gotten pregnant for the sake of the family's supposed honor.

Margo's parents hadn't killed her.

She sometimes wondered if that were only because their society hadn't given them permission to do so.

"Once everyone had gone to the movie, my mother told me to pack my things. I could take what would fit into one suitcase, nothing else. My uncle Pete came to get me. He drove me to the bus stop, leering at me the whole way. He wanted to know how it happened. He asked me if I'd liked it. What position I'd been in. He said my breasts were getting big, and he wanted a squeeze. A few years later, when I could think about that day clearly, I realized Pete, my mother's brother, had an erection the entire time we were in the car.

"My mother had given me money for bus fare to the city and a piece of paper with the name of a home for unwed mothers. She had not said good-bye. She had not come outside with me to wait for Uncle Pete."

Eliza dug in her purse for a tissue. She was crying now. They were both crying. The glasses of wine sat untouched on the table between them. The buzz of conversation from the bar had faded to white noise.

Margo never went back to her hometown and never saw her parents again. She didn't even attend their funerals. Once Joanie had grown up she sought, and found, Margo. Joanie was married now, to a nice man. They lived in Toronto, in a comfortable house with three cats, too much furniture, and a big garden. No kids though. Margo and Steve had spent a delightful Christmas with them the previous year.

"I stayed in a home for unwed mothers in the city," Margo said, and even after all these years, she shuddered.

It had been almost dark when the bus pulled in. Margo didn't know the way to this place where she was supposed to go. She didn't have a map, and her mother hadn't given her money for a cab. She had one cheap suitcase and a baby in her belly. She asked directions from the woman behind the ticket counter, who sneered as she eyed Margo up and down before telling her where to find the home.

It wasn't far. No doubt they put the home near the bus station on purpose, for all the disposable girls.

"It was during that walk," Margo said, "through the dark streets of the strange city, when I vowed I'd do anything for this baby. It would be him and me together against the world. Indivisible. Forever."

"Obviously, it didn't work out that way."

"No. That home." Margo took a breath. "If there's a hell on earth it was that place. I went back a few years ago. A sudden impulse. Steve was away on a fishing trip and I found myself buying a plane ticket. There and back in one day. I didn't want to spend the night. Before I knew what was happening, I'd rented a car and driven to the bus station. It's still there, seedier and more run down than I remember. I found where the home had been. It's gone now, replaced by a modern office building. I expected to find a bottomless black hole steaming sulfur where nothing green and living can grow."

"Do you keep in touch with any of the women you met there?"

Margo shook her head. "There's an online support group of girls who'd been there. I haven't joined. I can't face hearing their stories. I've heard talk about suing the organizations that ran those homes, but I don't care. If I could turn back the clock and have them be nice and kind, I would, but what's over is over. I don't need, or want, any money from them. Or their forced apologies."

"What happened to you there?"

Margo clung to Eliza's hand as if in a vice. Eliza did not try to pull away.

"They didn't beat us or starve us, but they made sure we knew we were disgusting, filthy creatures, not fit to live among decent churchgoing folk. We didn't even use our real names. They told me when I arrived my name would be Ruth. And that was that. We slept in a top floor dormitory, on narrow hard beds with little in the way of blankets. It was cold, so cold. I was there over a Prairie winter, and that might be what I remember the most. The cold. I'd left home at the end of summer, and hadn't thought to pack winter clothes. All they gave us to wear were loose maternity dresses, when our own clothes didn't fit any more. We worked hard, cooking, cleaning, laundry, mending. I never left the home. Not once was I allowed to go for a walk, to get a breath of fresh air. Some of the girls wanted to write home to their families, send letters. That wasn't allowed.

"They told me not one single thing about how the pregnancy would advance, what would happen when the baby would be ready to be born. I didn't even know how he would get out of me. We girls were forbidden to talk about it. We'd have privileges, whatever that meant, taken away if we were found to be engaged in conversation of an indecent nature. All we could do was exchange frightened whispers in the night."

Eliza let out a long breath. Her green eyes glittered like emeralds.

"One by one girls left, never to be seen again, and new ones arrived. Then it was my turn."

When she started labor Margo was put in a dark cold room by herself for several hours. When she was far enough along, they sent her to the hospital. Dropped off at the front door and the car sped away without so much as a good-bye or a good luck. Inside the hospital it was much the same. They, the unmarried girls, the wicked ones, weren't given pain relief or support. She was put in a bed and there she lay, by herself, laboring all through the night. Once in a while a nurse would pop in, spread Margo's legs, check the progress, listen to her heartbeat, and leave. Without saying a word of comfort or encouragement. The priest stopped by. The same nasty slimy creep who told them to beg forgiveness for their sins and wanted to hear every detail of the transgression at confession. One last chance to rail against the evilness of women and have a peek at her breasts.

Margo felt the ghost of a smile curling around the edges of her mouth.

Eliza noticed. "What is it?"

"Thinking of someone I met there. He did not come to a good end." She'd read the name of that priest in the paper about ten years ago. He died in jail, where he was doing time for the rape of a ten-year-old girl. The report said there were plenty of accusations against him, but the others had not made it to court. *Perhaps,* Margo thought, *there is some justice in the world after all.*

At last the ordeal ended and a baby boy was born to her. "They didn't give him to me to hold. They whipped him out of the delivery room before I realized it was over. I'd been told a decent churchgoing family would adopt him. I wanted him so much, I wanted to keep him with me, care for him. The world was a hard, harsh place. The only one who could be counted on to keep him safe was his mother. Me. But it was not to be."

What could she do against the church, the courts? Margo found out much later that legally she could have prevented the adoption. She didn't have to sign the papers. They'd told her at the home she'd be put in jail if she didn't sign.

She'd been too stupid, too bullied, to wonder why she'd have to sign him over if the law said she had to give him up.

"I saw my baby for the last time that night. I asked the woman who came to check on me if I could see him. She was very young, just a nursing student. She was kind. She told me to get out of bed. We'd pretend I was a married woman, and she'd take me to the nursery."

"Is everything okay?" the waitress asked.

Eliza and Margo jumped. Eliza picked up her untouched wine glass. "We're fine. Thank you."

"If you need anything," the woman said, glancing from one to the other, curiosity breaking through the aura of professional disinterest.

"The bill, please," Eliza said.

"So that's my story. I never went back to that miserable Prairie town. I never saw my parents again. The nurse who befriended me knew of a place that took in young women boarders, and I found a simple factory job. I worked hard. I was smart, and I was able to go to secretarial school at night. I was lucky. I've had a good life, Eliza. I could have ended up on the streets like so many sad abandoned women. Steve's a good man, and he's been a good husband. Our life hasn't been without its ups and downs, but my children turned out well and I'm blessed with a strong healthy grandchild. Before we married, I told Steve about Jackson, that I'd had a baby. I owed him the chance to leave me, to not be tricked into marriage with a bad woman." She felt herself smiling as she remembered. "He said he wasn't a virgin either. He'd lost his virginity in the rec room of a high school friend's house when the friend's mother said he was a big boy now, and she had something secret to show him. Oh, gosh. Don't ever tell him I told you that."

"I won't."

Margo sipped at her wine. "This is good."

"My dear, you saw that baby when he was one day old. And that was what, forty years ago?"

"Forty-five years. February 6th. Two a.m. I'll never forget him, Eliza."

"I don't think you should, but…"

"I've contacted groups that help children locate their birth parents. Nothing. Never a trace. Yet here he is. In Trafalgar. All my dreams have been answered."

Eliza did not smile as she placed her credit card on the table.

Chapter Twenty

John Winters spent most of the afternoon in his office, going over reports from the officers who'd been conducting interviews with Cathy Lindsay's friends and colleagues. A great deal of shock and distress. A big fat lot of nothing useful. No one had said anything about her apparent interest in the math teacher, Mark Hamilton. Winters had not told the officers about Hamilton. He didn't want to alert the man that the police were interested in gossip surrounding him. Not until Winters could have a chance to interview him.

He picked up the phone. "Ron, have you heard from the lab yet, anything on that cigarette butt?"

"John, I'm not going to keep it to myself, you know. When I hear, you'll hear. I can't give you what I don't have."

"Have you told them it's urgent?"

"Are you really asking me that?" Gavin said.

"I guess not. It's just that I have nothing. Absolutely nothing here. I need something to work with. Be nice if that butt is crawling with DNA."

"You know the story, John. The lab's behind, working as fast as they can. To them, every case is urgent. They'll get to it when they can. And when they do, you can be sure I'll let you know what's what."

"Thanks."

"Good luck," Gavin said, hanging up.

Winters tried Mark Hamilton's number again. He'd left a message, asking the man to call him, but people didn't always return calls from the police. The patrol cars had been told to drive past Hamilton's house regularly, checking for signs of habitation. Nothing yet.

"Still here?" Molly Smith's head popped around the corner. Her skin glowed with exercise and good health. Didn't have to be a detective to tell she'd spent her day on the ski hills. Personally, he didn't see the attraction. Plunging down the side of a mountain at the speed of a freight train and getting freezing cold to boot? No thanks.

"Still here."

"No developments, eh?"

"Early days yet. That's what I keep telling myself. When people go on vacation they should be required to leave contact information with their local police department. Just in case."

"Good luck with that."

"Did you want something?"

"No. Just saying hi. I'm about to head out."

"Hi. Have a good night. Hope it's Q." Police officers could be a superstitious bunch. In the way that actors never said the name of the "Scottish Play," cops never wished for a quiet shift. That would be sure to bring on the opposite.

He listened to the sound of Smith's boots heading down the hallway. The office was quiet, the day staff gone home. He took off his reading glasses and rubbed his eyes. The weather forecast clear skies tomorrow. He'd asked Barb to get him tickets to Victoria. The first flight out wasn't until eleven, and he wouldn't get to Victoria until early afternoon. The Victoria police had made an appointment with Elizabeth Moorehouse. By the time he made his way to her place, interviewed her, it'd be too late to get a flight home. Barb had reserved a room in a hotel in downtown Victoria, overlooking the harbor. A very good hotel. If he had to be away from home, he might as well stay someplace nice. He could afford to supplement the miserly daily rate the city paid.

He logged off from the computer and pushed his chair back with a sigh. He really, really did not like this case.

◇◇◇

Molly Smith made the rounds of the bars, saying hi to the bouncers, counting the numbers, sniffing the air, looking for trouble. Of which there didn't seem to be any tonight.

She leaned against the bar at the Bishop and Nun and sipped a glass of water. TVs scattered around the room played various sports channels, the sound turned off. Mike, the bartender, was regaling her with the exploits of his three-year-old nephew, the light of his life. He was a cute enough kid but one could only hear so much about nursery school, play dates, and a future in the NHL. They didn't usually run into much trouble at the Bishop. It was close to the center of town, meaning close to the police station, and catered for a middle-class clientele in search of a faux British pub. The accents were wood, the booths snug and private, and the papered red walls bore paintings of hunting scenes featuring unnaturally-elongated horses. A gas fireplace burned on one wall.

"I'll drop by again later," Smith said, finishing her water.

"See you, Molly."

She went through the back and emerged in the alley. Wires and cables stretched overhead, an urban jungle. She took a moment to shift her gunbelt, extended her arms to give them a good stretch. The muscles in her shoulders and thighs ached like the blazes. After intense skiing of the sort she'd had today she should have gone home and had a long bubbly soak in the bath with a glass of white wine resting on the side of the tub, and later met friends for drinks beside a fireplace burning real wood.

Instead, a quick leap into the shower, towel off, pass the dryer over her head for not long enough to get her hair thoroughly dry, pull on uniform and out the door. Alphonse's was closed and he hadn't even left her a treat of leftover baking on the landing as he often did. She hadn't had time to eat and the glass of water at the Bishop would hardly do for a meal. She was absolutely starving. Maybe she could get Dave Evans, who was in the car, to stop at the pizza place and pick her up something.

Yellow cat's eyes watched her from behind a pile of garbage bags laid out at the back of a convenience store. Until she could get that pizza, a chocolate bar would have to do. She heard a whoop of laughter followed by a crash and the tinkle of breaking glass. More laughter. She rounded the corner.

Three boys, underage almost certainly, were hiding in the shadows of the loading dock behind the hardware store. A garbage can was rolling down hill, picking up speed as it went. As Smith watched one of the boys swung a plastic bag against the wall. Glass broke. The other two took swigs from bottles of beer clenched in their fists. Brown glass glittered at their feet. They were laughing so hard at their own antics, they didn't notice her approach.

"I suggest you pour those out, guys,"

They jumped and she recognized them. Minor trouble makers. Fifteen, sixteen years old. Kids who lived with their parents in comfortable houses and went to school. Kids who'd grown tired of soccer league or church social groups, who hung around behind the bars because they weren't allowed in. It was early, not much after eight, so they hadn't, probably, been drinking for long. Not that their scrawny, still growing bodies had much capacity for alcohol in any event.

They turned and faced her, pushing the beer bottles behind their skinny backs, like ostriches stuffing their heads in the sand.

"Show me your hands, Kieran."

"I don't have anything, Smith. You can't make me."

"I can take you down to the station, if that's what you want. You're drinking in public and causing a disturbance. Think your parents want a call tonight?"

"Nah." He produced the bottle and held it out to his side. He flipped it over. Liquid foamed on the cold ground.

"You too," she said to the other boys. They exchanged glances, then the taller one shrugged and they poured out the beer.

"Thanks. I don't know you," she said to the tall one. "What's your name?"

"Who wants to know?"

"Keep up with the lip and I'll take you in. I asked your name."

"Rob. Rob Hardwin."

"Thanks, Rob. Pick up that broken glass. I see you have a bag. How handy. Put it in there."

"It's cold. Our hands'll freeze."

"Cry me a river."

Grumbling, they did as they were told, and then they tossed the bag of rubbish into the industrial garbage bin. They weren't bad kids, just restless with too much time on their hands, too much attitude, and surging testosterone. If they'd given her any backtalk, she'd have had no problem calling Dave Evans to come and pick them all up. March them down to the station, call their parents to fetch them.

Parents tended not to like having to do that.

Tonight, at least, she hoped she'd gotten to them before they could get themselves into any real trouble. "Okay. Kieran and Rob, you can go. Bradley, I want to talk to you."

Bradley Lindsay glanced around. His friends shrugged.

Smith jerked her head.

"Catch you later," Kieran said. Then he and Rob ran off, as if Smith would change her mind and arrest them after all.

"You can't keep me," Bradley said. "Not after letting them go. I wasn't doing nothing."

Molly Smith's degree was in Social Work. She'd been studying for her MSW but dropped out after the death of Graham. She no longer had any desire to go back to it, all she wanted now was to be as good a police officer as she could. But sometimes, she simply couldn't help herself.

"Don't you think your dad needs you at home, Bradley?"

The boy looked into her face, habitual sneer firmly in place. She returned the stare, saying nothing. His eyes were clear, pupils normal sized. He broke away. "My dad doesn't care what the fuck I do."

"I doubt that's true. But, even if you think it is, what about your grandparents? I'm sure they'd like you home."

He shrugged. "My grandmas are okay. Granddad's a bossy old fart."

"They're all hurting, you know."

He turned his head to the side and spat on the ground. "I got places to go, people to see. Couple of hot girls, older girls, meeting up with us later, get my drift? You can't make me stand here talking to you." He shrugged his thin shoulders in a display of braggadocio, stuck his thumbs into a loop on the waist of his over-large pants. "Unless you want to go someplace private like. And talk. Yeah, we can talk. How about your car? I've heard what goes on in cruisers. Late at night. No one around."

What a pathetic little jerk. She would have laughed if it hadn't been so sad. "You want to bug your dad, do you? How about I arrest you, take you in. Give him a call." This boy needed help. She didn't know if his dad would be able to give it. Bradley was in trouble before his mom died, minor stuff, teenage rebellion. Now, with all that rage against the world building up inside?

His eyes shifted to one side. "He won't care. Probably still at work. He's always at work."

"We'll get your grandmothers then. One them will come down to spring you, I'm sure." She pulled her handcuffs off her belt. Took a step forward.

He leapt back. His eyes dropped and all the aggression melted out of his body. "No. Okay, I'm sorry. I apologize, Constable Smith, if I insulted you."

"That's better. I'll let you off, but I want you to go home. If I see you out tonight, I will arrest you." She softened her voice. "Your grandparents would like to visit with you, don't you think?"

"Yeah. They're not doing so good. Grandma Renee in particular. My mom was her only child. She's having a hard time."

"Do you think she needs to be worrying about you?"

"Probably not."

"How about you, Bradley? You doing okay?"

His shoulders shook and for a moment she feared he was laughing at her concern. Then she realized he was struggling to hold back the tears.

"It's okay you know, to cry. She was your mother."

When he looked up again, his eyes were wet, a drop of moisture clinging to the long black lashes. "The last thing she said to me was not to go out. It was the first night of school holidays, and she wanted me to stay in. Watch a movie, play Settlers or something. Like we did when I was little." He sniffled and rubbed his glove under his nose. Smith dug in her pocket and found an unused tissue amongst all the detritus of a cop's uniform. She passed it to him. He twisted it in his fingers. "Who the hell wants to sit at home playing board games with their *parents* and a ten year old? I told her…I told her to stop being such a clingy nag. I told her to fuck off." The tears were running now, free and fast. Smith didn't touch him. She stood in front of him, quietly, saying nothing, letting him cry it out.

When Graham died, and later her dad, all she could think about for a long time was the things she *should* have said to them, before they left her forever. But she didn't know their time was coming to an end, and people didn't go around telling those they loved how much they valued them every time they walked out the door.

When was the last time she'd told her mother she loved her? Probably not since she was a kid, younger even than Bradley. But Lucky knew Molly loved her. It didn't have to be said.

"She wouldn't have minded, you know. That that was the last thing you said to her. She knew you loved her."

"But she didn't. She didn't," Bradley sobbed. "How could she have known? All the things I said to her, the names I called her. Now she's dead and I'll never see her again. Mom. My mom."

Smith's radio crackled. A car accident on the highway. Not her call, but she couldn't stand here counseling this kid all night.

"Have you had dinner, Bradley? I haven't and I'm starving. How about we grab something at Crazies? They're open until nine on Tuesdays."

He rubbed his eyes. Blew his nose. "Why?"

"Why? Because I'm hungry."

He hesitated.

"My treat."

She practically saw his tough kid armor settle back down around his shoulders. "Nah. Word got around I was with a cop, everyone would peg me for a snitch. Can I go now?"

"I'm not keeping you here. Why don't you drop into the youth center tomorrow? Someone there'll be happy to talk to you."

"I don't think so. That place's for wusses." He sneered and started to walk away. A decent kid trapped in a teenage boy's body. He hitched up his drooping jeans.

"Go home, Bradley," Smith called after him. "Your dad needs you. You're sorry you didn't say good-bye to your mom. You can make it up by being there for your dad."

He turned around. "My dad. What do I care? My dad's never been there for me. I doubt he much cares Mom's gone. See you around, Smith."

"Do it for your grandparents then. Or your sister. She's a nice girl. She doesn't have a mom any more. She needs someone who cares for her. What's her name again?"

"Jocelyn." His face softened. The sneer faded. He sniffled. "Her name's Jocelyn." He turned the corner and disappeared into the shadows.

Chapter Twenty-one

Wonder of wonders, Wednesday dawned bright and cheerful. As John Winters ate breakfast and lingered over coffee and the paper he was delighted to see the weak rays of the early spring sun poking out from between the mountains. Soon the snow would start to melt and before you knew it, crocuses and daffodils would be pushing their heads out of the ground.

"Victoria," Eliza said, glancing up from her iPad. "I haven't been to Victoria in ages. It's such a delightful city. Will you be taking afternoon tea at the Empress?"

"Think the city'll pay for it? I am going to interview a man's mistress. The setting would be appropriate."

"If they won't, they should." She nibbled on a slice of unbuttered whole-wheat toast.

His phone rang. Ray Lopez calling from the office. "Good morning, boss. I've got something that might make it an even better morning."

"Go ahead."

"Mark Hamilton. The math teacher? He served in the military for twelve years. 1994 until 2006."

"What'd he do there?"

"Infantry. A grunt. Entered as a private, left as a sergeant."

"Infantry means weapons."

"Firearms of many types. Training on how to use them. He did a couple of tours in Afghanistan. Left the military immediately after his last tour and went to UBC where he earned a four-year degree in mathematics. He then enrolled in the UBC teachers' program. Started working at Trafalgar District High in September of last year, his first teaching job."

"What's his police record like?"

"Before signing up he did a variety of odd jobs. Lumber camps, fishing boats, short-order cook. Seasonal unskilled stuff. He was in some trouble before he joined the army. Couple of arrests for punch-ups in bars, one drunk driving offense. He's been clean as a whistle since 1993."

"As far as the record shows."

"Precisely. You thinking what I'm thinking?"

"We know our guy had to be good with firearms, and this has moved Hamilton to the top of my list. Whether he had reason enough to want Cathy Lindsay dead, whether he was in the vicinity at the time, is another matter entirely. Ray, get his plate number and vehicle description. Send it out. RCMP and border guards. I want to talk to him, and I don't want to sit around any longer twiddling my thumbs waiting for him to come home."

"You got it."

"Get into his military records. Find out if he was in any trouble with the MPs. I want a peek at his medical records as well. Plenty of opportunity for trauma and psychological problems in Afghanistan. Look for a diagnosis or treatment of PTSD. Explosive temper, paranoia, that sort of thing."

"Will do. What time's your flight?"

"Eleven. I hate giving up a whole day, possibly two days, just to speak to this woman. Probably a waste of time, but it's necessary. She's not only close to Gord Lindsay, but she might have her own reasons for wanting his wife dead." Winters snapped his phone shut. Across the breakfast table Eliza's head was down as she read the screen of her iPad. The tip of her tongue was trapped between her teeth, and she drummed her pink fingernails against the table top.

"You heard nothing," he said.

"Really, John, after all these years you don't have to tell me." She lowered her reading glasses and fixed him with her amazing green eyes, sparkling with love. Or maybe only the reflection off the snow as the rising sun hit the untouched expanse of white and threw diamonds through the kitchen window.

Winters read reports all the way to Vancouver. He'd taken an aisle seat, not wanting to be distracted by the breathtaking view as the small plane flew low over the snow-covered mountains. He trotted through the terminal to catch the next leg of his trip. The even smaller plane had scarcely taken off before it began the descent into Victoria. This plane was so small everyone had a window seat, and he put his papers aside to admire the view. A sprinkling of verdant green islands were scattered across the blue sea like a giant child's handful of discarded marbles. No snow here, and when he got off the plane at the Victoria airport he shrugged off his winter jacket. It was a good fifteen degrees warmer than in Trafalgar.

"Sergeant Winters?" A woman approached him. Thirties, casually dressed in brown wool pants and matching jacket over a beige blouse. Her black hair was cropped very short, and although she could stand to lose a few pounds they carried well on her approaching six-foot frame.

"Yes?"

"Constable Louise Swanson. I'm your ride." She held out her hand, and he accepted the shake. Her grip was firm, her hand cool.

She led the way to her car. He didn't have luggage, just a backpack into which he'd stuffed a change of underwear and clean shirt along with his toiletry bag.

He told her it was nice to see some grass for a change.

"Got lots of snow where you're from?" she asked, in a tone that was almost wistful.

"Don't tell me," he said. "You're a skier."

"Every chance I get. That's the great thing about living in Victoria. I can take my kids up island in winter for skiing. In summer, we get out on the sail boat."

Pleasantries over, as soon as they were in the car, a nondescript blue van, pulling into traffic, Winters said, "Did you call Ms. Moorehouse yourself?"

"Yup."

"How'd she sound?"

"Not too concerned, I have to say. She said she wasn't surprised at my call. She'd heard about the killing in Trafalgar. The wife of my good friend, is how she put it."

"Tell me what you know about her."

"Not much to tell. She has no police record. She went to school in Smithers. Never attended university or college. Works at a local hardware store. Pretty dull life. On the surface."

"You never know what simmers beneath."

"And that," Swanson said, "is why you and I have jobs. Only one small item of interest. She was the victim of a serious knife attack a couple of years ago. Sounds like wrong time, wrong place sort of thing. The attacker was arrested on the spot, convicted, did some time. That happened before Moorehouse moved to her current address, and I could find nothing at all in that case to do with anyone name of Lindsay."

Elizabeth Moorehouse lived on a street of comfortable middle-class homes not far from the center of the city. Compact houses with huge trees on spacious lots indicated the age of the neighborhood. Swanson drove slowly, checking the house numbers. Spring was well underway here, and the neat gardens were lush with flowers and blossoms.

She pulled to a gentle stop in front of a small brick home, the front door and shutters painted a deep cheerful red. The street ended a few houses further down and Winters could see a flash of water. A canal or small river.

The police got out of the car and walked up the path. Winters knocked on the red door, and it opened almost immediately.

The woman was more attractive than he'd expected. Tall and slim with good skin and thick brown hair pulled back into a high ponytail. Her makeup was heavy but not untasteful. She wore jeans tucked into leather boots, a black T-shirt sprinkled with glitter, and a red leather jacket, nipped in at her small waist. A red silk scarf was wrapped tightly around her neck. At first glance she appeared to be in her early thirties. He looked closer, saw the fine lines at the edges of her eyes and around her mouth, the skin on her neck beginning to fold, and upped his estimate by a decade.

She smoked, a lot by the smell of it, and the tobacco struggled to compete with an expensive perfume, applied with a heavy hand.

"Right on time." Her husky voice was reminiscent of smoke-filled bars and whisky-soaked nights. "Come on in to my humble abode."

She turned and they followed. Swanson closed the door. A small dark hallway led into the living room. The furnishings were mass-produced from The Brick or Ikea. A vase of tall red roses, wilting slightly and browning around the edges, sat on the coffee table. Everything was neat and tidy. The room overlooked a large garden, shaded by old trees. A single lounge chair and a small table occupied the stamped-concrete patio.

"Have a seat." Moorehouse tossed herself onto a chair. A packet of cigarettes and an overflowing ash tray lay on the table beside her. She shook a cigarette out of the pack and lit it. Her hands contrasted with the rest of her. The nails were short and broken, the skin rough with a few nicks and cuts. She took a deep breath before saying, "I know you're here about Gord's wife. I read about it in the paper. Terrible thing." Her voice broke and she coughed.

Winters sat on the couch. As well as tobacco and perfume, the place smelled of an excess of air freshener. Overlaying the distinctive scent of pot. Not his concern; he wasn't here on a drug bust. Swanson's nose twitched.

"You're friends with Gord Lindsay?"

"Yes."

"Good friends?"

"Very good friends, if you catch my meaning." She dragged on her cigarette. The end glowed red.

"Gord lives here, with you, when he's in Victoria?"

"That's right. I'm sure you're too polite to ask, so I'll come out and say it. He sleeps with me. In my bed."

"How long have you known Mr. Lindsay?"

"Three years."

"This is a nice house. Do you own it?"

"If you've done your homework, you'll know I do. I bought it in 2002. Got a good deal, the price of homes in this neighborhood, big yards, close to the water, near downtown, have skyrocketed since. The house was pretty much a wreck, the yard a jungle. I worked hard, did most of the gardening and renovations myself." She looked around the living room, proud.

"Does Gord Lindsay contribute to the mortgage?" Winters asked.

"He chips in to help with my expenses. Why not? He lives here a quarter of his time. You're wondering how I can afford this place. Well I'll tell you. First of all, I work at the hardware store. That means I get tools and lumber and everything else I need at a hefty discount. It also means I make only slightly more than fuck all in salary. Fortunately, I have other sources to maintain my *lavish* lifestyle."

She unwrapped the scarf from around her neck. A scar, jagged, white, ugly, cut horizontally through the base of her throat.

Winters said nothing.

"I used to be a singer. A darn good one. A couple of moderately successful records but nothing made it big. I sang in jazz clubs and bars. I had a nice bit of a following. Did some backup vocals. Then, in May of 2002, I got in the way of a swinging knife in a fight in a bar. I got it right here." She abruptly lifted her hand and jerked it across her throat. "The doctors did a good enough job that I can talk fine, even sing a bit. But nowhere near good enough to get work anymore." She opened her mouth and sang. The note was clear and strong as it began to rise. Then it broke and crumbled as though into dust. Moorehouse coughed. "End of that career." She shrugged, as if she didn't much care, but pain shone in her eyes. She retied the scarf. "I got some insurance money, the guys in my backup band put on a fund-raiser for me. Together with what I'd managed to save over the years, I had enough to put a down payment on this house. My dad was a carpenter. I pretty much grew up sawing boards and hammering nails. So, now you know my life story. Sad, but not as sad as many."

"Gord Lindsay?"

"I knew Gord from the old days. He came into the bars where I was singing. Asked me to sign my CDs. That sort of low-level fan. After my accident," she made quotation marks in the air with her fingers, "I didn't see him until I ran into him three years ago in a coffee shop downtown. He recognized me. I didn't even know who he was until he reminded me. We talked, went out for dinner…You know the rest."

"It didn't bother you that he was married? Had a family in Trafalgar?"

She crushed her cigarette into the ashtray, twisting and grinding it down.

"Sergeant Winters, it didn't bother me one tiny bit. I was happy to share him. One week a month's about all I can stand of the guy."

"So why…?" Swanson spoke for the first time.

"Why does he stay here? Because I can't afford to keep this place on what I earn at the hardware store. Insurance and benefit money ran out long ago. I don't have much of an education, can't get a better job. I left high school at sixteen to become a singer. The taxes, the utilities, the upkeep are killing me. If I have to screw a fat man a couple of times a month to keep my house, I'll do it. I know what that makes me in your eyes, but in my eyes it makes me a survivor."

"You could rent out a room," Swanson said.

"Yeah, I could. But Gord pays more than any college student."

"Was his wife aware of this arrangement?" Winters asked.

"I doubt it. She didn't have the phone number. I overheard him on his cell to her a couple of times. He certainly didn't mention me, or the house."

"Did you ever meet her?"

"No."

Winters studied Elizabeth Moorehouse. She kept her face impassive; little emotion crossed it except when she talked about her home and the injury that ended her career. No reason for her to show emotion at the death of Cathy Lindsay. Not if she hadn't known the woman.

"Do you own a firearm, Ms. Moorehouse?"

"No, sir, I do not, but I can shoot. We lived near Smithers when I was growing up. In the bush. My dad had a rifle and he taught me to use it, but I haven't touched one since. I know why you're asking, but I had no reason to kill Gord's wife. I had reason not to—I don't want him making what we have permanent. And before you ask, I was here, at home all day Saturday."

"Was anyone with you?"

She shook her head. "All alone. I spent the day fixing up the basement. I'm putting in a second bathroom and guest room. Not that I ever get any guests. I lost contact with my family a long time ago. I don't go out much, except to work."

"Were you working at the store on Friday?"

"Took the day off. Business has been slow lately, they're cutting back our hours. I went to a party Thursday night with a bunch of my friends from the old days. I don't see them much anymore. It hurts, sometimes, when I remember what I've lost." She looked at Winters through dry eyes. "I could have made it big. Real big. International fame big. I was good enough. I just needed the break. Then...too late.

"So now I'll be looking for another sugar daddy. Want to apply for the job, Sergeant? It doesn't cost much, and the benefits aren't bad, if I say so myself."

"The party you mentioned. Can you give me the address please? And names of people who were there?"

"Checking up on me? Sure, no problem. They're mostly musicians, so you'd be better not to call too early."

"Did Gord Lindsay talk much about his wife? His marriage?"

"Oh, sure. She didn't understand him, and she'd let herself go over the years." Elizabeth snorted. "Like he was still some hot stud. He talked about his kids a lot. His daughter's perfect, the son a disappointing screw up."

"Did he ever lead you to think he was considering a divorce?"

"Nah. He spun me some line about how she had control of the money, and she'd make sure he never saw his kids again if he left her. A pile of rubbish. He was happy enough with our relationship as it stood, and so was I. No need to change anything."

Winters got to his feet. "Thank you for your time, Ms. Moorehouse." He passed over his card. "If you think of anything, anything at all, that might be important, give me a call."

She tossed the card onto the table. It landed in the ash tray. "Sure. Whatever." She did not get up to show them out.

"What do you think?" Swanson asked when they were settled in the car.

"I'd appreciate it if you can confirm she was at that party she mentioned. It's a long drive from here to Trafalgar. If she was in Victoria Thursday night, she would have had to have been on the road all day Friday. Then see if she caught a flight."

"Nice thing about living on an island," Swanson said. "If she took her car onto a ferry, they'll have a record of her license plate. I'll run that for you, too."

"Thanks."

"You think she might have been involved?"

"I'm not sure. She said she was happy enough with the situation with Gord, but I don't know if I buy that. She is not a happy woman."

"I'd say. Her unhappiness lies over that house as thick as the smell of pot. Understandable that she'd be bitter about losing her voice. I doubt she was on the verge of making it into the big time, but if she thinks she was…"

"What do you know about the attack on her?"

Constable Swanson pulled into the street and drove through light traffic into the city. "I looked it up before coming to get you. Pretty much what she said. Two guys got into a fight in a jazz club over a girl. One of them pulled a knife. Somehow, Elizabeth got in the way—she wasn't the girl in question—and she got cut. The guy with the knife spent three years in prison. He's out now, moved to Vancouver. Want me to drop you at your hotel?"

"Yeah. I've brought work to do."

She drove into the wide sweeping driveway of the Hotel Grand Pacific. The bell hop leapt to open Winters' door.

"Thanks for this. I don't know that I learned anything, but I got a feel for the woman. Keep your ears to the ground about her, will you?"

"Sure will. I'll call you later with the results of the check on the party and the ferry."

Across the street the wide, deep harbor sparkled in the sunlight. This time of year, it was quiet. Come summer the harbor area would be crowded with tourists, street artists, whale-watching zodiacs loaded with eager passengers, and tiny bright harbor tour craft zipping across the water. The gardens would be lush and the streets full. Now, it was after five, and dusk was deep. Tiny white lights lining the parliament buildings on one side of the square, the stately old Empress hotel on another, were switched on. Winters followed the bellhop into the lobby. He'd check in, work for a bit, and treat himself to a good seafood dinner.

John Winters dug a plump oyster out of its shell. The waitress brought a fresh glass of beer, rich amber in color with a thick foamy head. He gave her a smile of thanks.

The beer was good, the oysters even better. The gentle lighting of the restaurant shone on silver, crystal, and china. The place was almost empty, and he'd been seated at a booth for six. His laptop lay open in front of him. As he sipped his beer he read reports, one of which was interesting.

Molly Smith had come across Bradley Lindsay and his friends in an alley, drinking and causing a disturbance. She'd chased them off, but thought in light of the death of his mother, it was worth mentioning Bradley in a report. The boy had been hostile to her, offensive even, but she'd decided to take no further action. A wise decision, in Winters' opinion. Bradley's mother wasn't even in the ground yet. Gord Lindsay needed a break, even if his son didn't.

Winters thought about the boy. Could he have killed his mother?

If she'd been beaten in her home, struck on the head perhaps, even knifed in her kitchen, Winters would have considered it a possibility. But a shooting like that? Aside from the fact that, as far as they knew, the boy didn't have firearms training, it was a cold, calculated killing. Not the actions of an impulsive, angry-at-the-world teenage boy.

The weapon was no doubt lying at the bottom of the Upper Kootenay River or buried deep in the woods. On one hand Winters hoped it was —it couldn't be used again. But on the other hand they wouldn't find it in the back of some guy's closet or tossed into the trunk of a car.

No shortage of shotguns or rifles in the area. Lots of people who lived in the mountains, close to bears and wolves, kept long guns. Not so much in town though. Winters gave a sad thought to the now-crumbling long-gun registry. Once, he could have had officers pay a call on owners of 12-gauge shotguns. Ask if their weapon had been used recently or stolen. No longer.

The hovering waitress cleared the empty oyster platter. "Another beer?"

"Sure."

Elizabeth Moorehouse. She'd confessed quickly enough to familiarity with firearms. She'd seemed open, honest. Could have all been an act. Maybe she had been thinking it was time Gord Lindsay left his wife and married her, Elizabeth. Maybe she wasn't as content with their relationship as she seemed. Swanson had ascertained that Moorehouse's car hadn't left the Island recently. She had not rented a vehicle nor had she taken a flight.

Not using her own name at any rate.

He thought about the world she claimed to have left. Jazz clubs and bars featuring live music. People who slept all day, worked and partied all night. People who knew the sort of people who could set you up with false ID, loan you a car, no questions asked. Obtain an illegal firearm.

Had Moorehouse slipped into Trafalgar on Friday night? Had she been on the hillside the following morning? He made a note to check hotels for a woman arriving Friday. A single woman staying only one night would be remembered. Unlikely, if she had the wherewithal to cross the province secretly, she'd register in a hotel near her quarry, using her own name or not. But that was the sort of little slip-up that led to an arrest so many times. Gord Lindsay had told the police about Cathy's habit of a morning walk. Had he told his lover the same?

Had Lindsay known what Moorehouse planned to do? Had he put her up to it?

"Here you go, sir." The waitress loomed over him, bearing his plate, fragrant and steaming. He shoved his computer to one side. Lamb shanks in a rich tomato gravy, with a mound of fluffy mashed potatoes and glistening bok choy.

He dug in with enthusiasm.

After stopping to appreciate the first few bites, his mind went back to work. Moorehouse appeared to be as tough as the nails she used to renovate her house. Gord Lindsay, however, was not. If Lindsay had arranged for his lover, or anyone else, to kill Cathy, he had to be close to breaking.

The man would be an emotional wreck, either because of grief or guilt. Maybe both. John Winters would give Gord a gentle nudge. See if he fell.

His phone rang. A passing waiter threw him a dirty look. "Winters."

"Hi, Sarge. How's Victoria? The daffodils out yet?"

"Yes, and there's grass. Soggy, wet grass." He sipped at his beer.

It was Ingrid, the night dispatcher. "I got a call from Molly. She did a drive-by of a house at 762 Maybelle, like you requested. She reports fresh tire tracks in the driveway, and lights on that weren't on earlier. Do you want her to approach?"

"No. I don't want anyone doing anything. I'll handle it when I get back. Thanks, Ingrid."

"Having a nice dinner?" she asked. "I hear people in the background."

"A cheap pub," he said.

She hung up. Mark Hamilton lived at 762 Maybelle. Either the man was home or someone had dropped in who might know where to find him. Winters cursed under his breath. He'd like to go around right now, before Hamilton had a chance to settle in, maybe hear the news. That would have to wait until tomorrow. And, if Winters' flight into Castlegar was cancelled, as was always a possibility, he'd have to send Lopez around.

He checked his watch. Almost ten. His flight was at seven tomorrow, which would get him nicely into Castlegar at 9:30. He could be back in Trafalgar by 10:30.

"Would you like to see the dessert menu?" the waitress asked.

"Just the bill."

Chapter Twenty-two

The sky gods smiled on John Winters, and he was trotting across the parking lot at Castlegar airport heading for his car by ten the next morning. He had not asked the station to call Mark Hamilton's house to confirm the man was home, and if so instruct him to wait for John Winters' arrival. He wanted this visit to be as much of a surprise as he could make it. Almost certainly Hamilton would have heard the news about Cathy Lindsay, but if he hadn't, Winters wanted to be the one to tell him.

He'd left his Glock at the police station the previous day, not wanting to bother with the rigmarole of getting it onto the plane. He stopped by the office to pick up the weapon and check in.

One of the IHIT officers was in the GIS office, seated at a temporary desk, surrounded by paper coffee cups.

"Anything?" Winters asked.

"More of the same, Sarge. Nothing. Cathy Lindsay did not have an exciting life. Did you know she taught an adult class at the college on Monday nights?"

"Creative writing, I think Gord said."

"Yeah. I got the class register from the office, fortunately they have a secretary in for a couple of hours even though they're closed. I'm making those calls now. No one has much to say. My wife takes an Italian class at college. Same sort of night school thing. She's determined we're going to Italy on our next vacation. Night school's completely different than regular school. At night, for one thing, all adults for another. They don't socialize. Most of the class have families to get back to, jobs to go to the next morning. They don't get together to study or do homework. The teacher doesn't have an office and office hours."

"Which means?"

"Unlikely anyone in Cathy Lindsay's night school class would have reason to off her."

"Agreed. But we have to ask. Find out if she ever went out for coffee or a drink after class with any of the students or another teacher."

"I've asked. Mostly I get a shrug. Everyone picks up their books and heads off into the night the minute class ends. A couple of people said they sometimes saw her getting into her car. Alone. They couldn't be sure if she left by herself every week. I asked if Lindsay ever talked much about her home life, her habits."

"You mean habits like walking in the morning?"

"Right. Without saying so. Yes, a couple of them said. She told them she walks her dog in the woods behind her house every morning as soon as she gets up. The point, apparently, being that walking is supposedly good for the creative mind."

"Anyone in the class she seemed particularly close to?"

"Apparently not. One woman, a…" he checked his notes, "Elaine Federhalf said she didn't like Cathy and wouldn't be taking a class from her again. Federhalf told me she was taking this course because she's thinking of writing a book. Not to get an advanced degree."

"What does that mean?"

"Cathy was hard on the class. A tough marker and highly critical. She, the student, thought she should be getting an A for effort. Sour grapes, probably."

Winters sighed. "Keep at it."

Mark Hamilton lived on an old street at the foot of the mountain. Some of the houses had been gentrified to modern perfection, some cut into apartments and rented out, some allowed to slowly crumble back into the earth.

Hamilton's house was old but well maintained. The porch pillars had been replaced recently, the gutters and the front door looked new, and the paint was fresh. Winters parked in the street. The garage door, an old-fashioned wooden one, was closed, but the tracks of an SUV, clearly visible in the soft, melting snow, disappeared into it. The path from the garage to the front door had been shoveled.

A man, tall and handsome, thick with muscle, dressed in loose soccer shorts and a sleeveless T-shirt, opened the door on Winters' second ring. Sweat stained the shirt and ran down his face and neck. A blue towel was casually tossed around his neck.

"Help you?"

"Sergeant John Winters, TPD. Are you Mr. Mark Hamilton?"

"I am. What's this about?"

"May I come in?"

Hamilton stood back. "Is something wrong? My mom?"

"As far as I know, Mr. Hamilton, there's nothing to worry about. I have a couple of questions for you, that's all." The entrance hall was barely large enough for the two of them. It was crammed with an assortment of soccer shoes, hiking boots, winter boots, and running shoes, neatly lined in pairs on clean rubber mats. All the footwear was men's and appeared to be the same size.

"Yeah, sure. Come on through. I've been lifting weights." Hamilton wiped sweat off his brow. "I need a drink. You want something?"

"No, thank you."

Winters followed the man into the house. The small living room was a clutter of books, newspapers, stacks of paper, an open laptop. However, it was spotlessly clean and everything organized in some fashion. Winters studied the room while Hamilton went through to the kitchen. A tap turned on and water ran. Winters glanced at a pile of papers, spread out on the coffee table, spilling onto the floor. Exams.

Hamilton came back, sipping at a glass of water. "I've some marking to do before next week when school's back. I teach math at the high school."

"Which," Winters said, "is why I'm here."

"Really? One of the kids finally land himself in some serious trouble? Have a seat."

"I've been trying to get in touch with you for a couple of days. Where have you been?"

"Up north."

"Where up north?"

"A buddy of mine has a cabin outside Cooper Creek. I went there for a few days' vacation."

"Who was with you?"

Hamilton's eyebrows lifted. His hair was a mass of black curls coiling at the back of his neck. His eyes were a deep brown, and his cheekbones so sharp they might have been sculpted. His Adam's apple bulged as he swallowed.

"You'd better tell me what this is about before I answer any more of your questions."

Hamilton dropped into a chair. Winters remained standing. Hamilton appeared comfortable enough, as comfortable as anyone can be with an unexpected visit from the police. He didn't look like a man with anything to hide.

"You haven't heard the news since you got back?" Winters gestured to the newspapers on a corner table. The national and Vancouver papers were on top. No sign of the *Trafalgar Daily Gazette*.

"News? What news? You're talking in riddles, man. Spit it out."

"Do you know Cathy Lindsay?"

"What about her? I know her, yeah. She teaches English at my school. Did she have an accident or something?"

Winters studied the man. Hamilton's face was open, curious and a bit confused. Could be an act. Could be real.

"Cathy Lindsay was killed Saturday morning. Murdered."

A muscle twitched behind Hamilton's right eye. Otherwise he showed no expression. "Sorry to hear that. I can't help you. I left town after school Friday. Got home yesterday."

"How well did you know Mrs. Lindsay?"

"Not well at all. I saw her at staff meetings, in the halls. That's it. Don't know anything about her or her life other than bits and pieces of gossip I picked up."

"Much gossip about her?"

"No more than anyone else. I don't mean gossip as in spreading the muck. I mean as in what people do with their life outside of work. You can't suspect anyone at the school killed her? We're a pretty mundane bunch. The most trouble the kids get into is a bit of pot or a beer party now and again."

"I'll repeat my question of earlier. Who was with you this past week? Saturday morning in particular?"

"No one."

"No one? You went on vacation alone?"

"Yes I did, if it's any of your business. You can't possibly be asking me for my alibi." Hamilton got to his feet. The movement was swift, effortless. One minute he was sitting in a deep, badly sprung chair, the next he was on his feet, looming over Winters.

"Sit down please," Winters said. "We have to ask these questions."

"Are you questioning everyone at the school?"

"You don't have a family to spend your vacation time with? The school has your mother listed as your emergency contact. We called her. We got a nursing home, and the staff told us Mrs. Hamilton would be unable to help."

Hamilton dropped back to his seat. "I didn't have anyone else to put on that form. I guess I was hoping Mom would come around someday. She's gone downhill so damned fast. Doesn't know me; doesn't know where she is from one minute to the next."

"Did you visit her this past week?"

"No. She's sixty-four years old and as empty minded as a baby." He shook his head. "Her reward for a life of hard work, of never doing any harm to anyone. What a miserable world we live in." His face filled with anger. "I go to see her once a month or so. Have tea, check she's okay, talk to the staff. She doesn't know who I am."

"Your father still alive?"

"He died when I was a baby and my mother never remarried. Just me and Mom. I wasn't a good son when I was young. I try to make it up to her now, when it's too late to do any good.

"And before you ask, I'm divorced. It was an ugly divorce, bitter. On her part, more than mine. I don't keep in contact with my ex-wife and we didn't have any kids. I enjoy getting away from it all and went up to Cooper Creek. My buddy's place is in the woods, private, quiet. What I wanted." Hamilton shifted in his seat and rubbed at his face. The twitch was increasing.

"Did you see anyone on Saturday? Anyone see you?"

"I wanted to be alone. So I was alone."

"How about your friend who owns the cabin?"

"He lives in Vancouver. Leaves a key in a shed."

"They must have had a lot of snow up there. How'd you get in?"

"My friend has the private road ploughed regularly in case he gets the chance to get away for a couple of days."

"Did you see anyone Friday night? Or at any time on Saturday? Stop in at a store maybe? Buy gas?"

"I told you, I spent the time alone. I drove straight up after school got out on Friday. I'd filled up with gas and bought groceries the night before. I skied, I read. You can't seriously be thinking I had anything to do with Cathy's death. I barely knew the woman. You still haven't told me how it happened."

"School's back on Monday?"

"Yes." Hamilton pressed his fist into his cheek, hard. Trying to control the twitch.

"Were you having an affair with Cathy Lindsay?"

"What? Don't be ridiculous."

"I've heard you were close."

"Cathy might have wanted to be close. I did not." Hamilton got to his feet once again. He walked to the window, looked outside, walked back. "I'd like you to be going now, Sergeant. I have nothing more to say to you."

"You were in the army. Spent time in Afghanistan."

"I'm obviously a person of interest in this if you've been checking up on me. Yes, I did a couple of tours in Afghanistan.

I have no idea what that has to do with anything. I am what I am now. A small-town high school teacher. A divorced man who has no one to spend his holidays with."

"Thank you for your time, Mr. Hamilton," Winters said. "I have to ask you not to leave Trafalgar without letting me know."

"You can't possibly be serious."

"I am very serious. Is that a problem? Did you plan on going somewhere?"

"No. School starts Monday. I have to work."

"Glad to hear it." Winters headed for the door. He stopped, studied the array of footwear. Only one pair of winter boots of the type one would wear for a walk in the snow. Winters gestured toward them. "Mind if I borrow those boots?"

"What?"

"Just a formality. I'd like to check out your boots." Ron Gavin had taken prints of the tracks they'd found in the snow. Easy enough to compare them.

Hamilton's eyes narrowed. "Actually, Sergeant, I do mind. How am I supposed to get around?"

"You have plenty of other footwear. I'll return them tomorrow."

Hamilton shrugged. "Whatever. But I want them back. Tomorrow."

"Thank you."

"You haven't told me how Cathy died. Or why you think she was murdered."

"She was shot. From a distance. By someone who's a good marksman. Thank you for your time, Mr. Hamilton."

Chapter Twenty-three

Molly Smith collapsed face first into a heap of snow. Her left leg twisted and the ski detached itself from the boot. She sputtered and groaned and checked herself out for pain or anything not working as it should. She wiggled her toes, as much as she could in the solid ski boot. Everything seemed to be in order, and she flipped onto her back, spitting out snow.

Tony crouched beside her, his body at an awkward angle in his own skis. "You okay, Molly?"

"Just a tumble. Where's my ski got to?" She pushed her goggles up and wiped more snow off her mouth and chin.

"It's over there. Need a hand up?"

She held out her arm and he half lifted her to her feet. One pole was looped around her wrist, the other lay about five feet away. Her errant ski had come to a halt at the edge of the run, up against a tree.

She pulled off her glove and stuck her free hand into the neckline of her suit, scooping out snow.

People whizzed past, crouched low, moving fast, bodies tight.

Tony snatched her pole out of the path. "Better get out of the way." He took her arm and helped her to the side of the run. The wayward ski was unharmed, and she bent over and snapped it onto her boot. "Good to go."

"Do you need to rest a minute?"

"No, I'm fine." And she was fine. The landing had been soft, a straight forward face plant with no twisted limbs, encounters with snow-covered rocks, or trees suddenly appearing out of the cloud of mist and falling snow.

They'd been racing through powder, and she'd tried to overtake him. One wrong move, one moment of inattention as she gloated over her impending victory, and she was down. An *ignominious* lump.

"I've had about enough for today, anyway," he said. "Let's take it easy for a while."

They glided the rest of the way down and she enjoyed the slower pace, letting her muscles relax, letting her mind wander and appreciate the beauty of the woods and the day. The lifts would soon be shutting down for the night. She'd gotten off work at six this morning, napped until noon, met Tony at the hills at one. They'd pushed themselves hard, themselves and each other, one run after another, one race after another. In the valley temperatures were rising, the snow slowly melting into dirty, slushy puddles, but up on the mountain winter's firm grip still held.

The muscles in her thighs and arms ached and she knew she'd be in for it. She had tonight off, thank heavens, but had to be back at work tomorrow to put in an extra shift.

She needed some sleep.

"Care for a drink this time?" Tony asked.

"Sounds like a plan."

They left their equipment in the racks outside the building and waddled up the stairs to the lounge. One long room with the kitchen at the far end, the serving counters and cash registers, then rows of rough wooden tables and benches. Backpacks were slung across tables or hung on pegs, and the floor was wet and filthy with melting snow. The scent of frying food, bubbling grease, and curry spices mingled with the odor of socks and mittens steaming in the heat of the room. A small alcove tucked into a corner made up the bar, featuring a huge fireplace, cozy tables, and overstuffed couches.

At this hour, the lounge was emptying out as families headed home, and the bar was filling up with those eager to recount the highlights of their day.

"Whatca having?" Tony asked.

"Kokanee, please." She was driving, but one beer couldn't hurt. He pushed his way through the crowd at the counter, and she found a table for two close enough to the fireplace that they could admire it, not so close they'd roast.

She pulled off her helmet and ran her fingers through her hair. She was trying to grow it out, it was now at that horrible stage of being too short to make a bouncy ponytail but too long to look good ungroomed.

"Hey, Molly, Nice to see you."

She smiled up at a man standing beside her table, beer in hand. The mechanic from the garage which serviced the police cars. "Have a good day?" she asked.

"Great. The kids are with their grandparents. Not often we get a day on our own. This is my wife, Sandra. Sandra, Molly Smith, one of Trafalgar's finest." The woman, plump cheeks ruddy with cold and exercise, nodded in greeting. Smith struggled to remember the man's name.

He glanced around. "Adam here? He came by last week to talk about a truck and…"

Tony put two beers on the table and pulled out the spare chair. He looked at the mechanic, smiling, wondering if he was going to be introduced.

"Uh…No," Smith said. "This is Tony, my ski partner."

The men shook hands. "Sid Armstrong. Nice to meet you. See you around, Molly."

He turned back to his wife and their circle of friends.

Smith forced herself to smile as she picked up her beer. Tony dropped into the chair. "Cheers," he said. They clinked bottles.

Nothing wrong, she reminded herself, going skiing with Tony. Nothing at all. She and Adam weren't married, they weren't even engaged.

Adam had called her last night. She'd ducked into the doorway of a closed shop to take the call, and they'd talked for a long time. He'd talked, mostly, which wasn't like him. Nothing important, chatter about his parents and his sister and her family. Toronto had no snow, just a continuous cold, driving rain, making it difficult to entertain the kids. A man could only take so many movies suitable for the under-ten set. The kids were keen, he told her, to meet Norman. Maybe he'd invite them out in the summer. They were old enough to fly on their own. He could take them camping, do some hiking, kayaking. "Should be right up your alley," he said.

"Sounds like fun."

"Getting a lot of skiing in?"

"Not a lot. It's tough with working nights."

"You've got vacation coming, right?"

"Yeah, I do."

"Let's plan something. Something really nice. Spring skiing, maybe. How about Whistler? A top hotel, nice restaurants. Really spoil ourselves."

She hesitated.

"My treat. I'll even throw in a visit to a spa."

"Adam…"

"I miss you, Molly. I can't believe how much I miss you. And I've only been gone three days."

Her throat closed.

He tried to turn the sentiment into a joke. "'Course I started to miss Norman after two days."

"I never mind playing second string to Norman. Look, Adam, I gotta go. I'm supposed to be keeping the streets safe for the good citizens."

"And the not-so-good ones. I love you, Molly."

"Bye, Adam." She'd shut the phone carefully, slipped it into her pocket, and stepped into the sidewalk.

Terrifying a young couple who were sauntering down the street, arms wrapped around each other, paying no attention to anything or anyone until a dark-clothed, armed figure emerged from the gloom of a shop doorway.

"How about dinner tomorrow," Tony said, bringing Smith back to the here and now.

"Tomorrow?"

"Yeah, tomorrow. To celebrate good skiing." He lifted his bottle, his eyes fixed on her. "And new relationships."

She shifted in her seat and glanced to one side. The security guard was standing at the door, checking out the drinkers. He saw her and lifted a hand in greeting. She waved back, and Tony half turned.

"Just someone I know," she said quickly.

"You guys okay?" a waiter appeared at their table.

"I'll have another one of these. Molly?"

"No thanks."

"Where'd you learn to ski like that?" Tony said. "Did you ever race? Compete, I mean?"

"I grew up here, in Trafalgar. My mom says I could ski almost as soon as I could walk."

A fresh bottle appeared on the table. Tony chugged half of it in one long swallow. "I bet this was a nice place to live as a kid." He wiped his mouth on his sleeve.

Smith sipped her beer and told Tony about growing up in the mountains. Kayaking, hiking, skiing. She told him about her dad, Andy, encouraging her to be bold, to be unafraid. About her mom, telling her she could be all she wanted to be.

Tony listened, his head cocked to one side, his intense dark eyes focused on her face. She described growing up in the house at the edge of the bush, her first memories of coming to work with her mom, playing with ski equipment and hiking gear as other children played with toy trucks or Lego. Her dad teaching her and her brother to be guides, exploring the remote mountains and hidden valleys at his side.

The logs in the fireplace popped and flames leapt. All around them people laughed and chatted as they clutched bottles of beer or glasses of wine. Table tops were piled high with chicken wings, nachos, and discarded outerwear.

It felt strange to be talking about herself. She didn't meet many new people. In this small town almost everyone knew her. Many had known her since she'd been born. No one ever had to ask about her history or the history of her family.

At one point she laid her hand on the table. Tony put his on top of it. His index finger stroked her soft skin. She pulled away with a jerk, face burning. He reached for his bottle and took another drink.

She did not talk about Graham. Nor of Adam.

Or about her job.

"I'm sorry," she said. "I have rather gone on, haven't I?"

"I enjoyed listening to you. You sound as if you've had a great life."

"It hasn't all been good."

"Never is. Look, let's have dinner tomorrow. Most places'll be full on a Friday, but I'm sure we can get a reservation somewhere nice. You're the local, where would you suggest?"

"I can't. Sorry. I have to go to my mom's." The lie came easily to her lips this time.

"Again? You spend a lot of time with her."

"My dad died…recently. She likes having me around."

"Sorry to hear that. She can't cling to you, Molly. She has to let go sometime."

The waiter brought the group beside them their bill and exchanged a joke. By the time he turned, Tony had his arm in the air. "Get me another will you?"

"You're driving," Smith said.

"So?"

"Three beers in less than an hour? Not a good idea."

Something moved behind his eyes. Then it was gone as quickly as it had come, and she told herself it had been the shift in the light as people at the next table pushed chairs back and got to their feet.

The waiter slipped away. He knew Molly Smith. He knew she was a cop. If she said no beer, he wouldn't bring it.

"Whatever," Tony said with a shrug.

"Don't you have to work or something? Didn't you say you're a ski instructor?" No resort would let staff take vacation over one of the busiest weeks of the year.

"I quit Whistler a couple of weeks ago." He tilted his bottle to get the last drops of beer and began to turn looking for the waiter.

"Why?"

"Why? I didn't get on with the boss too well. Figured I'd look elsewhere. I have some money saved up, no rush to find something else. Decided to check out the Kootenays. I heard Red Mountain's hiring." He grinned at her. "But then I met this wicked skier and decided to hang around for a bit."

While he talked, his fingernails tore at the label on the bottle. She hid a grin. She made him nervous.

"This wicked skier has to be getting off home."

"It's not even six o'clock. Let's meet up in town, go for another drink."

She hesitated. She was bushed. She'd worked nights, and then slept fitfully for less than four hours over the past two days. Not to mention skiing full out all afternoon. She felt okay now, but knew that by the time she drove down the mountain, pulled up in the alley behind Alphonse's Bakery, and climbed the stairs, she'd be ready to drop. "I'm sorry. Not tonight."

His eyes narrowed. "I want to spend time with you, Molly. I want to get to know you better. I love skiing with you, but there's more to life than skiing."

She started to get to her feet. "I can do dinner on Saturday. How about…" She thought. Some place they didn't know her. Didn't know Adam. "*Feuilles de Menthe*," she blurted out. The restaurant in the block where she lived. Nothing wrong with having dinner with a friend. No need to sneak around as if she were going behind Adam's back.

Tony smiled, his brown eyes dancing in the firelight. "I know where that is. Seven o'clock?"

"Seven." She gathered her helmet and gloves.

"I don't have your phone…" he said, as she ran for the door.

Chapter Twenty-four

A man walked into the Mountain in Winter Art Gallery and gave Eliza a tight smile. He didn't seem interested in the art, more interested in peering around corners. He approached the counter where she sat with her book. "Hi." He wore a black winter coat with blue wool mittens. He did not take the mitts off.

"Good afternoon. Can I help you find something?"

"Don't take this the wrong way," he said, "but are you alone here?"

"How else must I take that question?" she said, placing her hand on the telephone. She *was* alone. People had been in and out all day, but right now the gallery was empty. Outside a couple stopped to study her window display, and then moved on.

"Your assistant. The older lady. She's not in today?"

"Margo has the day off. Why are you asking this?"

"Don't go anywhere," he replied.

He dashed out the door.

How odd. She took her hand off the phone and turned her attention back to her book.

The bell tinkled a moment later and all was explained. He was back, this time accompanied by the man Margo believed was her son. Eliza struggled to remember his name.

"Good afternoon. I came by the other day looking at the Khan sketches. Do you remember? I'm William Westfield."

She slid off her stool. "Of course, I remember. I'm pleased you came back. We have a few pieces left. They've proved to be very popular. I must apologize for my assistant's behavior. I don't know what came over her. She's a good saleswoman. Really."

"Don't apologize. I'm here now. Let me have a…have a…a look." He stammered, tongue struggling to form the words. She waited patiently until he was comfortable again. "Ah…uh… yes." He crossed the room to stand in front of the grouping of sketches. His friend left without saying goodbye.

Eliza returned to the counter, taking herself out of Westfield's way. Let him make up his mind, unpressured.

Eventually he turned to her. "The three across the bottom will make a nice grouping on the wall of my room."

"A good choice. Will you be taking them with you today?"

"They're small enough, no problem."

"I'll wrap them for you then." One at a time, she took the pictures off the wall and laid them on the table at the back of the gallery. She was reaching for the third when the door opened. She glanced up and smiled.

John.

"Be with you in a few minutes," she called.

"I can wait." He came over to join them. "Those are good."

"Amazing what a skilled hand can accomplish with no more than a couple of quick strokes," Westfield said. "You're Sergeant Winters. I've seen your picture in the paper." He held out his hand and the two men shook. "I didn't make the connection. You're Eliza Winters so this must be your husband?"

"Yes," she said, enveloping the art in sturdy brown paper.

"As long as I have you here," Westfield said to John, "I have to ask the question on everyone's mind. What's happening about the killing?

"Our investigation is progressing."

"I'm sure it is. Getting any help from IHIT?"

"Some."

"You can't talk about it, I understand. It's not just idle curiosity on my part. I knew her."

"You knew Cathy Lindsay?"

"Last term I took a course in creative writing at the college. She was the teacher."

"Did someone call you? Officers have been going through the class list."

Westfield shook his head. "Not yet, but I can usually be found at the bottom of any list. W." He laughed. "I'm sure you've found the same."

"What was your take on her?"

Eliza continued wrapping the art.

"I didn't know her socially, she was just the teacher."

"You must have had some impression of her."

"She seemed to enjoy teaching the class. She did say at one point she found it refreshing to teach people who wanted to be there. I assumed she meant as opposed to high school students. Who'd rather be just about anywhere else. I'm writing a novel. A gritty, hard-boiled mystery novel. Perhaps you could give me some tips, Sergeant Winters."

"I'd be happy to."

"My story's not very original, I'm afraid. Serial killer in a big American city. Hard-drinking, bitter, divorced cop. But I like it. It's my first attempt, see, and I figured I could use some help with the mechanical things. Dialogue, when to use description." His voice trailed off.

"Did Cathy Lindsay help with what you needed?"

"Oh, yes. She was very good at highlighting flaws."

Eliza had no interest in the conversation, but from where she stood, behind the counter, ringing up the sale price, she could hear the men's voices. She glanced up, startled at the bite William put in his last sentence.

John said, "Did she talk about her personal life at all? Mr. Westfield? Mr. Westfield?"

William seemed to be locked in place. His mouth was open, his jaw slack, his eyes did not blink. He looked as if, like Lot's wife, he'd been turned to a pillar of salt. His mouth moved, but no sound emerged. Seconds passed. Eliza reached for the phone.

Then he said, as if nothing unusual had happened, "She told us she taught English at the high school."

"Are you feeling all right?" John asked.

"Yes, thanks."

John and Eliza exchanged a silent question. Then he said, "If you're sure. Did Cathy seem to be close to anyone in the class? Any one in particular?"

"Not that I noticed."

"What about her life outside your class. Did she mention problems at home, with her friends, her work?"

"I can't really say."

"Can't or won't?"

"It's just an impression, you understand. I don't know anything."

"You can consider this a formal interview, Mr. Westfield. There's no one to hear us other than my wife, and she doesn't talk about police business." Eliza pulled her book out, flipped it open, and pretended to read. "If you know something, no matter how insignificant, you need to tell me."

"I was surprised to read in the paper that her husband owns a consulting business. I thought he taught at her school."

"Why?" The question was asked calmly, a routine inquiry. But Eliza knew her husband well enough that he might as well have lifted his ears and howled, a hound catching the scent of a fox.

She also heard the shrug in William's voice. "She talked about him sometimes. A math or science teacher. Can't remember his name offhand, but she would say things like so-and-so teaches his students that even in the sciences good writing's important. It's how we express ideas, create understanding and enhance knowledge. Or words to that effect."

"Did she get on well with the students in your class? Any problems you were aware of?"

"One incident, now that I'm remembering. Last day of class she handed out the final marks. This woman, Elaine, took offense at her result. She told Cathy she clearly didn't understand experimental literature."

"What did Cathy have to say about that?"

"She wasn't too concerned. It didn't come as a surprise to any of us that Cathy didn't like Elaine's writing. They'd clashed before."

"Thank you, Mr. Westfield. Here's my card. If you think of anything else, please let me know."

"Sure." William pulled out his wallet as he made his way to the counter. He tucked John's card in, and took his credit card out. Eliza rang up the charges. "Unlike many people," she said, "Alan Khan's spending the winter in B.C. and going to New Mexico for the summer. He should have some interesting desert sketches next year."

"Not for me, I'm afraid. Don't care for the desert. Bad memories." He picked up his parcel, said a cheerful goodbye and left.

When Eliza turned to face her husband, his look was dark and serious.

Chapter Twenty-five

Run. He had to run.

The streets were treacherous. Snow had fallen, melted under a steady pounding of car tires and pedestrian feet, frozen again, melted when the sun came out, and refroze when the temperature dipped in the afternoon.

Ice. Everywhere was ice.

First thing this morning, he'd gone to the grocery store to get in some supplies. On the way home, he'd seen a woman slip as he drove past. She'd stepped off the pavement to cross the road and hit the ground in a tumble of arms and legs, her mouth open in shock.

Mark pulled his car into a parking slot. He sat with his head down, breathing deeply, every nerve in his body quivering. Ashamed at not getting out to help her. Ashamed of being such a human wreck that the sight of a woman slipping on a patch of slushy ice made him think of explosions and gunfire. Men dropping in panic, screaming in pain and terror.

By the time he remembered that he was not in Afghanistan but in Trafalgar, British Columba, the woman had been helped to her feet by passers-by with better nerves than Mark Hamilton. She continued on her way without assistance, paying considerably more attention to the placement of her feet.

He needed to run, to escape the demons, to sweat them out. To pound the pavement, chew up miles and hours. If he ran hard enough he could escape time all together. Run so fast he would never have gone to Afghanistan.

But he couldn't run. Not today. He probably wouldn't get a block before slipping and falling. Some well-meaning passer-by would help him to his feet and tell him it wasn't a good idea to be out today. And pretend not to notice Mark Hamilton was crying.

Cathy Lindsay was dead. Murdered, the cop had said.

It had to have been the husband. Wasn't it usually?

So why was the cop checking out Mark? Peering into his background, opening his records? He'd done some things he wasn't exactly proud of. He'd been young and thoughtless. Full of himself, full of pride and arrogance and sheer stupidity.

He'd paid for it. Over and over and over. He was still paying for it.

He couldn't run, and it was too late to go skiing. The Alpine hills would be closed before he got there, and it would be too dark to head off cross-country.

He'd put in an hour on the treadmill. Not as good as breathing cold air and feeling the sharp wind on his face, but it would have to do.

He made his way downstairs. He'd created a fully equipped gym in his basement, with weights and benches, an expensive treadmill, a rowing machine.

He climbed onto the treadmill. Cranked up the speed, raised the incline, and ran.

He had tests to mark before Monday. Lessons to prepare for the new term. He'd get to that after the run. If he worked late into the night he might even be able to sleep.

As if that ever happened.

He'd burn out thoughts of the cop and what an investigation might reveal. Then he'd mark the tests. Most of the kids in his class didn't see the point of it all. They had computers, didn't they? Calculators. Machines to do their thinking for them.

Who, he tried to tell them, did they think created the machines in the first place?

They shrugged. Didn't care.

But a few students did care. They wanted to build computers, write video games, get jobs at Apple or Microsoft or a hot new start up. They wanted to be the next Bill Gates or Steve Jobs.

They wanted to understand.

Those kids kept Mark Hamilton alive. As long as he could teach math, he'd be okay.

He loved numbers, loved mathematics.

Nothing was unpredictable about math. In math, one plus one always equals two. It never comes out to three or to ten. It is what it is. It never equals a hollow-cheeked, dirty-faced child wearing a suicide vest, or a gunman hiding underneath a burka.

He adjusted the treadmill to an incline of seven degrees. The sweat was pouring freely now.

The cops were nosing around, asking questions. They'd taken his boots. The killer was an expert shot.

He couldn't go to jail.

He could run in prison. But he couldn't teach math.

Outside his basement, where the lights were never switched off, darkness settled across the valley.

Mark Hamilton ran on.

John Winters slapped his forehead.

He'd forgotten.

He'd promised Eliza he'd pick up a couple of croissants for breakfast tomorrow.

Ten to three. The bakery closed at three. He might be able to make it. If he was lucky, they'd have a few of the pastries left. Hopefully not just the chocolate ones. Eliza considered chocolate in a croissant to be a monstrosity on the scale of a Hummer in a residential driveway.

"I'll be back," Winters shouted over his shoulder to the dispatcher as he headed out the front door.

He jogged down Monroe Street, trying to stick to the bare patches of sidewalk, and turned into Front. His destination was in sight. He reached the bakery as Alphonse flipped the sign over.

"Please tell me you have some croissants left, or my life won't be worth living," Winters said as he stumbled through the door.

"I suppose you can make it worth my while." Molly Smith held up a paper bag. Winters glanced behind the serving counter. Three lonely loaves of bread on the shelf. The ovens were switched off, the staff gone home. The shop quiet and clean.

"Dare I ask what you have in there?" he asked Smith.

"Two fluffy, fresh-baked croissants. My supper. I'm on nights today. I *so* look forward to taking a break from the hard work of keeping our streets safe and tucking into some good French baking." Her blue eyes danced with amusement.

"Twenty bucks?"

Alphonse laughed as he hung his long white apron on a hook behind the counter.

"On the house." Smith handed Winters the smaller of her two bags. "I also got a baguette, so I won't starve."

"I'm in your debt."

"Night, Alphonse," Smith called as they left the bakery.

"My wife feels like having croissants for breakfast tomorrow. She doesn't often indulge so I said I'd pick them up. She said she didn't trust me, and she'd get them. I reminded her that my office is closer to the bakery than her store is, so I could manage. Imagine the egg on my face if I came home without them."

Molly laughed.

"As long as I'm out," he said, "I'm going to grab a coffee."

She fell into step beside him as they turned east, heading toward Big Eddie's. "Going back to the office?" she asked.

"I'm reading through the results of computer checks, interviews. Boring but necessary. Hoping something'll pop up and smack me on the nose. I'll do a couple more hours and then call it a day. You're working?"

"Volunteered to fill in for Scott so he could get an early start on the weekend with his kids. Six till six."

They turned into Elm and walked up the hill. "Can I buy you a coffee?" Winters said. "I owe you for the croissants. I hope they're not chocolate."

"Plain."

"If they were chocolate, Eliza'd know I'd left it until the last minute."

"A drink'd be good."

Big Eddie's was largely empty. One man waited while his sandwich was being prepared; a couple sat at a table near the door, heads close together, smiling, holding hands. Smith headed for a table in a far corner, and Winters placed their orders.

He sat on the bench beside her, both of them with backs to the wall.

"Can I ask," she said, "how the case is going?"

"Unofficially, it's going very badly. I've got next to nothing. I've been wanting to ask you about the son, Bradley. He was in trouble the other night and you were the officer responding. I hear he gets into trouble a lot. Tell me about him."

"Not much to tell. Typical kid. Spoiled, middle-class brat angry at the world for no reason whatsoever. No reason until his mom was murdered. He doesn't get on with his dad and is carrying a heavy load of guilt because he fought with his mom the night before she died. He seems fond of his little sister though, and his grandmothers. I hope he'll think about them before he acts out too much. I tried to plant a seed there."

He nodded and sipped his coffee. Jolene came out from the back and began stacking chairs onto tables.

"What'd you go to Victoria for?"

"Gord Lindsay has a girlfriend there."

"Interesting."

"Very."

"Did Cathy know about her?"

"I don't think so. If she did, she kept it pretty close to her chest. Gord says she didn't know, but men can be blind about that sort of thing. More importantly, of those of her girlfriends we've been able to contact, none of them said anything about it."

"You asked?"

"We asked in broad terms. Was there trouble in the marriage, was Cathy worried about anything."

"Maybe Gord's girlfriend didn't want to continue being just a girlfriend. Maybe she wants to be a wife?"

"I've considered that. I can't place the woman anywhere near Trafalgar. Doesn't mean she wasn't. But this doesn't seem like a woman's crime to me."

"Women can do lots of things that might surprise you."

"So my wife tells me." He gave her a smile. Molly Smith was smart and quick. Too impulsive still, but that would change with a few more years under her belt. She was a good cop. She might make a good detective someday. She had a feel for people. He'd never asked her what her plans were. Never asked if she were aiming for the top, or content to remain a beat cop in Trafalgar. Winters didn't know where she stood with Adam Tocek. These days marriage needn't interfere with a female officer's career ambitions, nor did becoming a mother. But staying here, in Trafalgar? That wouldn't lead to a stellar career.

She sipped her hot chocolate. "You don't have any suspects?"

Soft jazz played over the sound system. Jolene swept the floor.

"Your mom said rumors at the school say Cathy was involved with a teacher named Mark Hamilton."

"She wanted to be involved with him," Smith said. "That's different. Did you find out anything more about him?"

"Hamilton's a strange one. He'd been lifting weights when I arrived at his place. Built like the proverbial brick outhouse. Not my idea of what a math teacher should look like."

"People tell me I don't look like a police officer."

He grinned. "Appearances can be deceiving. We forget that at our peril. He's a good-looking guy, Hamilton. I wouldn't be surprised if a lot of the women at the school find him attractive. When I spoke to him, he claimed not to have heard about the killing."

"Did you believe him?"

"Not sure. He's hiding something. Might be anything. Some people are afraid of the police for no reason. Some people for a lot of good reasons we don't know about. He has a military background, which makes him a person of interest in this case.

He has no alibi. Says he was at a cabin in the mountains by himself. I managed to get him to lend me his winter boots. Ron gave the treads one look and said they weren't anywhere near a match, although the size was about right. Which only means if he was the killer he wasn't wearing those particular boots. And considering how efficiently our guy covered his tracks, I wouldn't expect to find evidence left lying around. He would have gotten rid of the boots along with the gun."

"No sign of the weapon?"

"No. The killer was fully in control of himself. Not the sort to throw the shotgun aside, or drop it in the nearest garbage can. Which is what makes this case so darned frustrating. What on earth was there about Cathy Lindsay, high school teacher, wife, mother, that had a man…a person…like that intent on killing her?"

"Maybe he mistook her for someone else."

"Entirely possible. My biggest fear is that there's someone out there with a bull's-eye painted on his back, and we can't do anything about it because we don't know who the hell it is."

"It's got the town spooked. People are, I don't know, quieter, looking at each other differently. Some people like to come over all dramatic about any situation, but many are genuinely concerned, wondering how something like that can happen here. Worried it will happen again. I don't like it."

"Neither do I, Molly." Even Shirley Lee, the most no-nonsense person Winters knew, was disturbed. He'd seen something in her face, something behind her eyes, which had concerned him. He knew very little about Doctor Lee. No reason he should, they weren't exactly friends. For a moment it had been as if she hadn't been there, in the morgue, beside him, but someplace else. Someplace she rarely went.

He almost shook his own head. Now who was getting dramatic? He finished his coffee. "Better get back at it. Keep yourself safe tonight, eh?"

She grinned. "Sure."

They took their empty mugs to the counter, calling good-bye to Eddie and Jolene. At the door, they stepped aside to allow a woman to maneuver a giant push chair into the shop. She was very young, with long straight hair the color of midnight, heavy black make-up outlining her eyes, black lipstick, an array of piercings, and a hoop through her nostrils. The child was bundled up in a snowsuit with nothing but his bright intelligent eyes peeping out from between swathes of scarf.

"Sergeant Winters, hi. How you doing?"

"I'm well. And you, uh…"

"Paula. Remember me? You came around to the women's center a couple of years ago asking about Ashley." She bent over and began unwrapping yards of scarf from the child's face.

"Paula. Of course I remember. I remember your son, too. Beowulf isn't it? He's growing fast."

"Sure is. Never stops moving. Beowulf, say hi to the nice man."

"Hi," the boy said, squirming to get out of the restraints.

"Beowulf?" Smith said, once they were outside. "She named her kid after a movie?"

"He was a Norse hero long before he was a movie character. Beowulf's saga is the first recorded story of a serial killer."

"She named her kid after a serial killer?"

"Beowulf's task was to hunt down the killer Grendel who was terrorizing the area. Grendel's sometimes referred to as the first serial killer."

He stopped walking.

"What's up?" Smith asked.

"Just an idea. I'm going to run some checks."

Chapter Twenty-six

Friday Gord Lindsay left the office in the middle of the afternoon. One of his best clients had cancelled a four o'clock meeting, no doubt thinking poor Gord wouldn't be able to concentrate on issues at hand. They were right, but he was angry at the cancellation nonetheless. He needed to work. He needed to forget the turn his life had taken, even if only for a short while, and bury his head in his computer.

No one would give him a moment's peace. He was thoroughly sick of the endless cups of coffee being brought to him by well-meaning female employees—all of whom normally refused to make coffee on feminist principals—with sad sympathetic eyes and offers of shoulders to cry on. The male employees kept slapping him on the back, suggesting they take a long lunch or break off work early and go out for a beer.

He headed home thinking he'd surprise Jocelyn, take her shopping maybe, try and have some fun together, but she'd gone to a friend's house and wouldn't be home until after supper. His mom and Renee were at the grocery store; however, Ralph there. Ralph had decided it was time to finish the basement. He'd also decided Gord was going to help.

Gord did not do handyman chores. If anything more elaborate than the change of a light bulb needed doing around the house he'd hire someone. Any other father-in-law would suggest they wash the car or tidy the garage to keep Gord busy. Ralph wanted to spend the weekend rebuilding the bloody house.

Gord slapped his head, said he'd forgotten an important appointment, and fled his house. He drove aimlessly through the streets, eventually finding himself at the city park, high above town.

The place was packed with families enjoying the end of the school holidays. The snow was icy and the ground bare in patches, but little kids didn't mind. They zoomed down the hill, laughing and screeching with terrified pleasure. Proud parents shouted encouragement, and dragged traditional wooden or modern metal toboggans to the top. A group of older boys were using flattened cardboard boxes.

Laughing kids, smiling parents, beaming grandparents. Everyone looked so happy.

Gord sat in his car and watched, ignoring the questioning glances of passing adults. When was the last time he'd gone tobogganing with Bradley? He couldn't remember. Had to have been many years ago. He bought an old-fashioned red sleigh and they'd come to this same hill. Bradley had been frightened at first, trying hard not to show it. Gord had sat at the back, his arms wrapped tightly around the boy's chest. Protecting his son. Keeping him safe. After a couple of runs, Bradley declared he wanted to go by himself.

And he had. While Gord stood at the top, waving, his heart in his mouth. He'd been proud to let the boy go.

He should have held on as long as he could.

He'd had a call from the principal of Jocelyn's school this morning. She wanted to invite a grief counselor into the school to work with Jocelyn and any of the girl's friends who might be having trouble dealing with the death of Jocelyn's mother.

Gord was okay with that. He told her so, and they talked about how her teacher would keep an eye on Jocelyn, be there in case the girl needed her. Cathy's funeral was scheduled for Monday, the first day back at school. A good number of Jocelyn's friends would want to attend. Gord told the principal his daughter would be in class Tuesday. They agreed that she needed to get back to routine as soon as possible. As if, Gord thought but did not say, Jocelyn's life would ever be the same again.

For the rest of her years, Jocelyn would miss her mother. There would be an empty place at her wedding; no one to give her kindly advice on the birth of her first child. No shoulder for her to cry on when life got too hard. No one to tell her to buck up, and suggest they chase away her worries by indulging in some retail therapy.

No one to tell her the facts of life.

Gord put his head in his hands and wept.

He wept for himself as much as he wept for his daughter. All that Cathy had done, all that she had been in their lives, would now fall on him.

He knew he wasn't up to it.

Renee was making noises about staying on after the funeral. To help out.

About the last thing Gord wanted was his in-laws hanging around. Renee could be as much of a bother as her husband. Gord couldn't put a glass down before she whisked it away to be washed. She dusted and cleaned, and two hours later she was back, dusting and cleaning again. She'd tidied up his home office when he was at work, and he couldn't find the rough notes he'd made on the proposal for the hospital job.

Worst of all, she made his bed every morning. It had given him a hell of a shock, the first time he'd walked into his room after an outing with Jocelyn. The bed neatly made, the top of the dresser tidied, his discarded socks and underwear in the laundry basket, all of Cathy's things put away. He told Renee never to do that again.

She said she was only trying to help, sniffing in that annoying way of hers.

The next day she made the bed and cleaned the room again.

Gord didn't bother to protest any more.

Cathy had been a slob. He'd thought it one of her best features, largely because he was no neat freak himself. Cathy did the laundry when she got down to her last clean outfit; she ran the dishwasher when it was full and washed the pots when it was time to use them again. She made their bed once a week when she changed the sheets. Why bother in the interim? It just got mussed again.

She expected Gord to pick up after himself, and if he didn't his things remained where they'd been tossed. The kids threw their sports bags and school supplies into their rooms and shut the door.

If they were having company, Cathy could turn into a version of her mother, cleaning up a storm. Gord would be handed the vacuum and a can of Pledge and told to have at it. The house usually managed to look presentable when guests arrived, the doors to the nonpublic areas of the house firmly closed.

Cathy had grown up in a house run like a military barracks awaiting inspection. Neatness was the order of the day, and Renee and Ralph considered any mess to be a personal affront.

She'd never gotten over her youthful rebellion.

Now, she never would.

Jocelyn was the neat one in the family. Funny how habits skip generations. Jocelyn made her bed before school, lining up her stuffed animals and dolls on the pillow to patiently await her return. She hung her clothes in the closet, most of the time, and knew where her school things were when she needed them. But she was just a kid and didn't take the neatness thing too far.

Gord feared Renee was rubbing her hands together in glee at the chance to turn her granddaughter into her version of herself.

As for Bradley…

He'd worry about Bradley later.

A family walked up to an SUV parked beside Gord's. Mom, Dad, two kids, a black Lab. The perfect family. They loaded toboggans into the trunk, and children and dog piled into the back. The father eyed Gord suspiciously. A man sitting there, alone in his car, observing a park where kids played? Then he seemed to recognize Gord. His face flushed and he looked aside, embarrassed.

Gord Lindsay watched the SUV drive away, and then he pulled his cell phone out of his pocket. He ran his fingers over it.

Elizabeth had called several times. She'd left a message telling him Sergeant Winters had visited her.

She left a second message demanding to know why he wasn't answering.

This morning, she'd called the house. Spoke to Renee, pretended to be a friend, concerned about Gord.

But Renee wasn't stupid, and she'd given Gord the message with an arch to her eyebrow and a question in her voice.

"Business contact," he said, hoping his guilt wasn't written all over his face.

He'd have to deal with Elizabeth sometime. Might as well get it over with. He flipped the lid, tapped buttons. Heard the ring.

"My god, Gord. I've been so worried. I've been calling and calling. Did you lose your phone? Didn't you get my messages?"

"I told you on Sunday not to call me. I've got a lot on my plate, you know. I got your messages, Elizabeth. As did my mother-in-law. Please don't phone the house again. How'd you get the number anyway?"

"Duh, it's in the phone book, Gord. I'll thank you not to take that tone of voice with me. I don't like having the police sitting in my living room, interrogating me, you know."

Elizabeth, unlike Cathy, was neat and tidy. One of the things he liked about visiting Elizabeth, aside from the obvious, was a calm, clean environment. He himself wasn't any neater than at the house in Trafalgar, but Elizabeth cleaned around him. She washed his clothes, cooked his meals, picked up his socks.

All very 1960s. Like an episode of *Mad Men* or something.

Would it be so bad living with Elizabeth permanently? She would never be a mother to Jocelyn, but she could be a wife to Gord.

Did he want a new wife?

What a goddamned stupid thing to be thinking. Cathy wasn't even in her grave and here Gord was making plans to fill her side of the bed.

He took a deep breath. "I'm sorry you had to go through that, Elizabeth. Really I am. I had no idea that cop would go all the way to Victoria."

"He had lots of questions. Questions about you. About you and me. Did you kill your wife, Gord?"

"What the hell? Are you crazy? You think I could do something like that?"

"I have no idea what you could do or not do," she said in that deep, damaged voice he found so incredibly sexy.

To his shame, he felt himself getting stiff.

He bit down on his thumb. Hard.

"The cops seem to think so," she said.

"It's routine. They always suspect the husband. I have an alibi, my daughter."

"When's the funeral?"

"Why are you asking?"

"I'm thinking of coming. Pay my respects."

"No, Elizabeth. I don't want you here."

"I'm not going to stand up in front of the church and tell everyone what I mean to you, if that's what you're afraid of. I guess I should say what I meant to you. This changes things. We need to talk."

"Give me some time. Everything's happened so fast."

"Monday."

"What?"

"The funeral's Monday. Three o'clock. I'm looking it up right now. I have property taxes due. If I don't pay, they'll start slapping on interest charges."

"You can't be asking me for money. Not now, not today."

"We have an arrangement, Gord. I bought a load of supplies for the basement renovations from the store and put it all on my credit card. I need to pay it off."

"Elizabeth…"

"I'll need a new dress for Monday. Something black and solemn. Shoes and a coat to match. Jewelry. I'm looking forward to meeting your kids, Gord. See you Monday."

A soft click, and he realized she'd hung up.

Teeth marks, deep, were pressed into the soft pad of his thumb, turning the skin deadly white.

Chapter Twenty-seven

"Did you and Francesca do something special before she left?" Smith asked.

"We had a private farewell," Dawn Solway said, unable to hide a grin.

Behind Solway's back Dave Evans rolled his eyes. Wisely he said nothing. One day he would. He'd say something so sexist or homophobic that Smith would have to lay a complaint.

That, she did not want to do. Those things never ended well. The entire office, civilians and officers, would come down on one side or another. Bad blood, recriminations, accusations. She wished Evans would transfer out of Trafalgar. She suspected he'd applied at some other police services. She suspected he'd been turned down.

Still, if Dave left they might get someone worse. Usually it was the older guys who caused trouble, the ones who fondly remembered the good old days when being a police officer was a man's job. And a real man, a manly man, at that.

Unfortunately some of the younger ones, like Dave, weren't all that much better.

Smith knew where she stood with Dave Evans. He'd have her back, as long as it wasn't too dangerous a place for him to be.

"What about you, Dave," Solway said sweetly. "Anything special for the weekend?"

He grunted. Evans was good-looking, tall and fit. He could do macho swagger along with the best of them, and some women liked that. He didn't have trouble attracting women and went through girlfriends at an alarming rate. At the moment he was girlfriendless. Station gossip said Sally, a waitress at the Hudson House Hotel, had thrown him over in favor of the new bartender. Dave Evans liked to be the one doing the throwing over.

Whatever had happened, Dave wasn't in the best of moods these days. Smith shuddered to think that might be because he wasn't getting any.

Friday evening. March Break. The last big weekend of skiing. They had a full complement of officers working tonight.

"When's Adam get back?" Solway asked.

They were reading the previous shift reports, waiting for Staff Sergeant Peterson to arrive and bark out tonight's assignments.

"Monday."

"Bet you're looking forward to seeing him," Solway said.

Smith glanced up. Solway's eyes were on the computer screen, her fingers moving the mouse to scroll through the text.

"I don't want to hear about it," Evans grumbled.

"Then don't listen," Solway said.

"I work here, you know. They pay me to sit on this chair."

"Is that all they pay you to do?"

"Enough of that," Peterson said from the doorway. "I want everyone bright and alert tonight. Most of the bars are expecting a capacity crowd. The Bishop has a popular band playing. The Potato Famine's advertising a wings and pitchers special, so they'll be busy."

"Ug," Solway said. "You wouldn't catch me eating anything cooked at the PF."

"Not everyone has your refined tastes," Evans said.

Solway ignored him. "I wonder if they reuse their grease."

"Is that allowed?" Smith asked.

"Pardon me, ladies and gentleman," Peterson said. "I'm talking here."

"Sorry, Sarge."

"The Mounties are running a Ride check on the highway, so they'll be close if you need backup. Brad's out in a truck already.

Dawn, you take a car. Molly and Dave, I want you on foot. I'll
be available if you need help. Any questions?"

They shook their heads.

"Then let's go to work."

The three constables shut down computers, shrugged into
outdoor jackets and gloves, and hit the streets.

Dinner and a movie. Like being back in high school.

Without, Lucky Smith thought, the insecurity and the acne.

She and Paul had eaten spicy noodles at Trafalgar Thai and
were now in line for tickets at Trafalgar's single movie theatre. It
showed one film, once a day during the week, twice on weekends.
If you wanted to catch a movie, and didn't want a long drive to
Nelson or Castlegar, you had to take what they offered. Tonight,
it was a sophisticated British comedy that had received generally
good reviews. Something they should both be able to enjoy.

Everyone in town was talking about little other than the
Lindsay killing. At the restaurant, Lucky and Paul had deliberately asked for a table in a back corner, near the bustle of the
busy kitchen, and Paul sat with his back to the room, unlike
police officers' preferred position. He'd muttered something
unfavourable about small-town gossip. Lucky hid a private grin—
nothing she liked better than engaging in small town gossip. Before
Moonlight had joined the police force, before Lucky herself had
become—friends?—with Paul Keller she would have been one
of the first to corral the Chief Constable and demand to know
how the investigation was proceeding and why hadn't they made
an arrest yet.

"Chief Keller, Lucky, good evening." They turned at the
sound of their names. A couple had joined the line. The man
smiled broadly, the woman nodded.

Darren Fernhaugh, the property developer.

Lucky scowled. "When you were in my store the other
day, you neglected to tell me you've bought the Grizzly Resort
property."

"I wasn't in the store to discuss business, Lucky. Just to do a bit of shopping. Still, I'm confident everyone will be more than happy with the plans we've come up with."

"The make-up of the city council's changed since Reg Montgomery's original plan for the resort, you know. You might not find them as development friendly."

"The land isn't in Trafalgar. I don't need the city's permission to develop it."

"True. But you will need the goodwill of the nearest town, which happens to be this one, if your so-called development proceeds and people start inquiring about buying."

"I don't expect that'll be a problem," Fernhaugh said with a smile. "We haven't even advertised yet and job applications are flooding in. Many with Trafalgar addresses, I might add."

Lucky ground her teeth. Jobs, always about jobs. Mr. Fernhaugh and his partners wouldn't give one fig about jobs if they could outsource the work to China or Bangladesh. But, as construction jobs first, and then waiting on tables and cleaning tasks couldn't be sent offshore, they'd loudly proclaim to anyone and everyone—politicians most of all—what a great service they were doing, bringing *jobs* to this remote community.

That jobs which now catered to people seeking a true wilderness experience would be redundant if the land was scattered with development projects, would be overlooked. Never mind the animals. They didn't need jobs. They just needed to be left alone.

Fernhaugh smirked. Then he turned to Paul. "I'm aware the resort area is outside your jurisdiction, Chief Keller. I'm working closely with the RCMP on security issues, but as we will have important facilities in Trafalgar, including our local sales office, I'd like to have regular meetings to discuss what we can do to help each other."

"I don't think that's appropriate," Lucky said. Paul gripped her arm. He gave it a squeeze. She snatched it away.

"Informal to begin with, perhaps," Fernhaugh said. He spoke to Paul, but he watched Lucky out of the corner of his eyes.

"I've joined the local branch of Rotary. I understand you're a member, Chief?"

"Yes."

"Good."

Lucky sputtered. Andy had been a Rotarian. He liked the group and considered it important for business contacts. After his death she considered joining. She never quite got around to it. Perhaps it was time.

"The line's moving, Lucky," a voice called. She glanced over her shoulder. No one stood between them and the ticket window. Paul Keller let out a grateful sigh and went to pay.

Lucky waited until they'd taken their seats before saying, "Odious prick."

"That's a bit harsh," Paul said.

"I don't like him. Or his awful resort. I thought that had been settled when Reg's partner pulled out of the project. What do you think he wants with you, anyway? Not special favors, I hope."

"You know full well I wouldn't give them even if he did. He's aware there's opposition to his plan. The tree huggers'll be descending on us from all sides. That means work for the police."

"Tree huggers!"

"Yes, the tree huggers. Never saw a tree they didn't think more important than giving a man a job and putting food on his table."

"Tree-huggers! How dare you use that term to refer to me? I've never hugged a tree in my life, but that doesn't mean I don't care about the environment. You know, the environment, the air we breathe, the water we drink. All that important stuff."

Paul glanced around. "Lucky, calm down."

"That's how they shut us up. Calm down. Don't create a scene. Be a good little woman. Really Paul, giving a man a job! What kind of job? A construction job that lasts a few months, a minimum-wage tourist job? These are the same sort of people who've destroyed manufacturing and industry in this county. Jobs that paid good wages, permanent jobs, jobs for…"

She snapped her mouth shut, aware that the lights had gone down, music had started up, and people were hissing at her to be quiet.

Paul put his hand on her arm. She pulled it away. All of the fun had gone out of her. She felt old and sad. She sometimes wondered if she were the only one in the world who still cared.

"I'm sorry if you're upset, Lucky," Paul whispered. "You know I care for you, but I'm the Chief Constable of Trafalgar and if anyone attempts to stop the resort development through illegal means, I will order my officers to prevent them, and if that fails, we will arrest them. Now, can we watch the movie before they throw us out?"

That Paul would uphold the law, she had no doubt. That was his job, and she wouldn't expect him to do anything else.

Tree huggers.

The way he'd said it had been an insult. Mocking. Pure and simple.

She couldn't expect, didn't expect, Paul to agree with all of her politics.

But she did expect some degree of respect for her heartfelt beliefs.

Even after twenty-eight years of marriage, a glimpse of Eliza could still take John Winters' breath away.

She wore a new dress tonight. Sleek and form fitting, falling to her knees. Silver fabric shot with green thread the color of her eyes. The neckline was scooped, accented by a necklace of a twist of thick silver and silver and emerald earrings. High-heeled sandals with thin straps showed off those gorgeous legs to their full advantage. She'd had to wear clunky, winter boots to get from the house to the car and then navigate the sidewalk into the restaurant. Still, the full effect, when she discarded boots and coat, gloves and scarf, was like a caterpillar emerging from its cocoon a radiant butterfly.

She took his arm and smiled at him. With her in those heels she was even taller than he.

They'd had long-standing plans to go out to dinner tonight. No special occasion, but Eliza believed in the importance of having an occasional date night. It was too easy, she maintained, for long-married couples to fall into a dinner-in-front-of-the-TV routine. Not that Eliza ever allowed them to eat dinner in front of the TV.

Tonight's date was going to be rushed. Instead of going home to pick her up and put on a suit and tie, he'd arranged to meet her at the restaurant. He wouldn't be drinking, and wouldn't be driving her home. But a man had to eat and he might as well enjoy a good dinner with his amazing wife. Before going back to the office and plowing his way through witness statements, looking for something—anything—to jump out at him as important.

Flavours restaurant looked great. Candlelight sparkled off starched white linen tablecloths, crystal, china, and silver place settings.

"I'm sorry, sir," the maitre-d' said, "we're running a bit behind, and your table will be a few minutes. Would you like a drink at the bar while you wait?"

"Sure," Winters said.

He ordered tonic with a slice of lemon, Eliza asked for a glass of white wine. She'd come in a taxi and would call one to take her home.

The bar was busy with groups and couples. Everyone laughing, some loud and forced, most natural, friendly and welcoming. He relaxed and settled in among the chatter of conversation, the clink of glasses.

Eliza lifted her glass. They toasted each other silently. Her eyes sparkled in the dim light, the reflection of her jewelry. She laid her hand on his arm and gave him a smile. He grinned back.

The crowd shifted and he spotted an attractive Asian woman at the other end of the bar. Something familiar about her. She looked up, caught his eye, smiled and waved. He recognized the shape of her strong, tiny hand first. Shirley Lee. He'd never before seen her out of a lab coat or with her hair unbound.

"Someone I should say hi to," he told Eliza. They carried their drinks over.

The pathologist wore loose, black trousers and a black blouse under a red jacket embroidered with gold. Her hair was pinned back by gold combs and fell in a waterfall almost to her waist. They introduced their partners. Shirley's husband was around her age, dressed in a good suit and silk tie. The couples chatted for a moment, and then Eliza asked Eugene Lee what he did for a living.

When their respective spouses were talking, Shirley leaned over and dropped her voice. "Have you made any progress on that shooting, John?"

He'd been thinking of Doctor Lee only this afternoon, remembering the effect Cathy's autopsy had on her. The only time he'd known the pathologist to show any interest in a case other than strict medical matters.

He lowered his voice to match hers. "Nothing concrete yet. A couple of people in mind."

"Time's passing. The longer it takes…"

"I know. Why are you so interested in this one, Shirley?" She was a blunt, plain-speaking woman. He saw no reason to beat about the bush no matter that they were in a fine restaurant, sipping drinks, rather than gowned and in the autopsy room.

She studied his face. Winters heard Mr. Lee ask Eliza for the address of her gallery in Kitsilano. Ever prepared, she slipped a business card out of her tiny silver bag.

"It happened to my mother," Doctor Lee said. Her voice drifted away, traveling through time and memory, back to the past. "My birth mother. It's almost the only memory I have of her. Cambodia. I was five years old. We lived in Phnom Penh. My father, a doctor, educated therefore an enemy of the people, had been taken away some months before. We were ethnic Chinese, and that was almost a crime in itself. I never found out what became of him. I have dim memories of a large comfortable house, with wide verandas, and gardens in which I would play. The memories are so faint, I am not sure if they are real or something I once read in a book and took to be mine.

So few of my memories are good ones. Along with everyone else, my mother and I were forced out of the city. I remember being hungry. I remember walking until my shoes were torn and then my feet. I remember wanting my favorite doll that I'd had to leave behind. I remember calling for my father, asking my mother why he'd left us."

Eliza and Eugene had stopped chatting. Eugene put his hand on his wife's shoulder. Eliza took a step closer to her own husband.

"Amongst all the noise and chaos, I heard a single shot. My mother fell into the road. Face first, the back of her dress turning red. Target practice probably, for a Khmer soldier. We were Chinese, our lives of no consequence. I remember nothing more until I was in a refugee camp. I suspect a Chinese family found me weeping beside my mother's body and took me with them." Shirley Lee's gaze was unfocused as she stared into her past. Eugene watched her with sad, loving eyes.

"No one was ever held responsible for shooting my mother. She died at the side of the road. I doubt anyone had time, or dared to expose themselves, to bury her. They left her for the dogs and the scavengers. I'd like to think…I hope…you can find the person who did the same thing to Cathy Lindsay."

"I will," John Winters said.

"You will try," she said, with a soft smile, "and although you may not succeed, I trust you do to the very best you can."

"Your table is ready, sir, madam." The Maitre-d' broke into their tight circle.

Doctor Shirley Lee physically pulled herself back to the present. Her shoulders stiffened, her head straightened, and the overwhelming emotion was wiped from her face. She had not cried, her eyes had not even been moist. John Winters wondered when she had last allowed herself to weep.

"Nice to meet you, Eliza. I hope you enjoy your dinner."

"Thank you."

John and Eliza watched them walk away, escorted across the room by a waiter. Eliza slipped her arm around her husband's waist and pulled him close.

Chapter Twenty-eight

As expected, the police had a busy night. To make matters worse, an icy rain began to fall.

Molly Smith was helping clear up an accident scene at Front and George when she got a text from Adam. A single word: "Love."

No injuries, fortunately, but the rusty old van was too damaged to move under its own power so the town's main intersection was blocked until a tow truck could arrive and haul it away.

She wrote back, "Love you," and pressed send as her radio called her to Trafalgar Thai where an overly-inebriated man was accusing a waiter of stealing his wallet. Before Smith arrived, the item was found under his chair.

At midnight she was in the Bishop and Nun leaning against the bar, sipping a glass of water. Her radio squawked, and she heard Ingrid asking Dave to go to the Potato Famine.

Then, "Five-One?"

"Five-One here."

"Four-Two on route to the Potato Famine. Asking for backup."

"Got it."

She left through the back door and cut through the alley, moving fast yet conscious of patches of ice on the surface. Wouldn't help anyone if she fell and broke a leg.

Dispatch said an ambulance was on route, as Smith rounded the corner and saw the pub up ahead. A cheap, rundown place,

The Potato Famine was frequented by those whose idea of a fun night out was as much about getting into a brawl as having a couple of drinks with friends. Signs advertising various brands of beer flashed on mounds of dirty snow piled on the sidewalk in front of the pub.

She entered the bar, her hand on her belt, her eyes on everything. The sour scent of unwashed clothes, sweat, spilled beer, overcooked grease, and far too much testosterone filled the gloomy room.

The band stood on the small raised platform that served as a stage, but they were not playing. People lined the walls, clutching glasses and beer bottles.

Smith pushed her way forward. In the center of the room a space had been cleared as if for dancing, but rather than happy couples, a man lay on the floor, shrieking in pain and anger. A knife protruded from the top of his thigh and his pants were drenched in blood. The bouncer knelt beside him, trying to hold him down, telling him to stay calm, bellowing for someone to call an ambulance. Dave Evans had a man pushed up against the bar, bent over so his face was flat on the surface, hands cuffed behind him, legs kicking, yelling something about, "let me at him." The second bouncer was helping Evans hold the man down.

"What do you need?" Smith called.

Evans didn't turn to look at her. "Take care of the guy on the floor. I'm okay until a car gets here."

There must have been two hundred people in the place, a drunken college crowd mostly, a few construction workers, celebrating the end of the work week. Every one of them stood watching, brown bottles clenched in hands, faces expressionless. This was not the sort of establishment where the police could expect citizens to step forward and offer help.

Smith went to the injured man, still bellowing in rage. She heard a fresh shout of anger, and spun around. A man pushed his way between two plump, heavily-made-up young women in short skirts and tight shirts with plunging necklines. He was short and square with a shaved head and a tattoo of a snake curling around his neck. His eyes were narrow and the muscles in his neck bulged. He held an empty beer bottle upside down by the neck. Letters were tattooed on his knuckles. His eyes were on Dave Evans, back turned, focus on the squirming prisoner. The tattooed man brought the bottle down on the surface of the bar, and it shattered in a spray of brown glass.

"Dave, watch out," Smith yelled. She was a good ten feet away.

Stupid, stupid, stupid. She'd followed Evans' instructions, rather than checking out the crowd first.

"Drop the bottle. Drop it, now." She pulled out her Glock. Women screamed. People rushed for the door. Chairs flew and tables crashed. Men shouted, some in fear, some in excitement.

The bouncer yelped and leapt back, taking himself out of the way. Evans whirled around, pushing the handcuffed man to the floor, reaching for his own weapon. His eyes meet hers.

"Police. Drop the bottle," Smith yelled, throwing all of her fear into her voice, trying to sound commanding, authoritative. Make him know she meant business. "Do it now." The man turned to face her. His eyes were clear, focused. Thank god he didn't look as if he was on something that would steal the fear from him. He knew she was there, knew she'd shoot if she had to. She fought to keep her voice steady. "Drop it."

He stared at her, not relaxing his grip. Dave hauled his prisoner upright and dragged him further down the bar. The bartender had a phone in his hand, and the first bouncer had left the injured man and stood at Smith's side.

The tattooed man held the bottle neck, the broken end pointing toward her, jagged glass glistening. He took a step forward. The bouncer retreated. Smith stood her ground, both hands firm on the gun.

She felt time slowing; she was aware of every breath she took, and every sound in the place. She held the Glock out in front of her, her hold on it solid but not gripping. "Put," she said, "it down."

"Pig bitch."

No one said a word. The band members were on the stage, holding their instruments. Watching. The only sounds were the man's deep breathing, the squeak of floorboards, and a woman weeping. Even the guy with a knife stuck in his leg had gone quiet.

Smith sucked in a breath. *Would she shoot?* Yes, she would. One more step would bring him in rushing range. She'd shoot all right.

A siren broke the silence. Blue-and-red lights washed the room. The tattooed man blinked.

"I said, put the bottle down. Now!"

The weapon clattered to the floor as Brad Noseworthy and Dawn Solway burst through the doors.

"Take three steps back," Smith said. "Up against the bar."

He did, his black eyes fixed on hers.

"Get down, get down, get down," Noseworthy screamed.

The man spat once on the floor. And then he dropped.

People were coming back into the room, everyone wanting to see what was going on now danger had passed.

Smith waited until Noseworthy had one knee in the tattooed man's back and his hands cuffed before holstering her weapon. Only then did she let out a long breath. She took two steps, grabbed the broken bottle off the floor, and straightened. She pulled a plastic bag out of her pocket and dropped the bottle neck in.

Noseworthy hauled the cuffed man to his feet. "Let's get these two the hell out of here," he said to Solway.

The watching drinkers parted to let them through.

Two paramedics arrived. They tended to the injured man, now swearing a blue streak. Smith stood where she was. Trying not to shake.

"Good job," the bouncer said to her.

"Thanks."

A guy broke out of the crowd of onlookers. He stood in front of Smith. "A cop. You're a goddamned cop." Tony. He was not smiling.

"Yup."

"You told me you're a clerk in an office." Tony was dressed in jeans and a short-sleeved T-shirt. His arms had always been hidden by his winter clothes; now she could see the tattoo of a string of barbed wire around his right bicep. A sword, decorated with runes, dripping red blood, covered his left arm, wrist to elbow.

"I said I worked for the city. Which I do."

His face was dark, his lips set in a tight line. "A lie of omission."

"I didn't intend it that way."

"Would you have shot that guy?"

"If I had to. A broken bottle's a formidable weapon. I'll do what I have to do to protect myself. To protect everyone in this place. Including you."

She studied his face, and didn't like what she saw. His eyes were narrow with anger, a vein pulsed in his forehead. His legs were spread, feet planted firmly on the floor. How on earth could she have thought this man attractive? "I have to go. It's a busy night, and I'm working. Whether you like it or not. About dinner tomorrow? Forget it."

"Damned cop." Tony walked away. He pulled a stool up to a table in front of the small stage, and shouted to a waitress, who was picking a chair off the floor, to bring him a beer. He yelled at the band to start playing.

Smith left.

Chapter Twenty-nine

The man with the knife in his leg, screaming threats now that the police had his attackers in custody, was taken away by ambulance. Brad Noseworthy accompanied them. The two fighters were stuffed into patrol cars and driven to the station to be processed into custody.

Smith got a ride with Dawn Solway. Evans drove Noseworthy's vehicle with the second prisoner.

"You okay, Molly?" Dawn asked, keeping her voice low as she switched the light bar off and the windshield wipers on. She'd only been inside a few minutes yet a light coat of ice covered the window.

"Yeah."

"If you're not, take some time, eh?"

"I'm good." Smith sucked in a breath and gave what she hoped was an encouraging smile.

"How about we drive outa town first," their prisoner suggested. "I can show you gorgeous *ladies* what a real man can do. You don't even have to take the cuffs off."

"Gag me with a spoon," Solway mumbled as she pulled the car into the street.

They processed the prisoners. These two would be spending a few days in jail until their hearing. Assault PO and assault with a deadly weapon.

The man Evans had grabbed, the one who'd knifed the guy, remained quiet. He grunted his name and address when asked, kept his head down and his eyes averted. The other one, who turned out to be his brother, swore a blue streak, alternately threatening to sue the police for everything they were worth and asking Smith and Solway to keep him company in his cell. He made Smith's skin crawl.

Finally the men were tucked up for the night, and Solway and Smith headed upstairs. The dispatch console was a circle of harsh white light in the dark and quiet of the offices.

"I need a drink," Solway said, "Molly?"

"Huh?"

"I asked if you want a pop? Are you sure you're okay? If we're charging that ugly guy with assault PO, that means you were in a fight, right? Do you want to talk about what happened?"

Smith glanced at Ingrid. The dispatcher had been around a long time, seen almost everything, probably had heard everything. "Just us girls here, Molly."

"I'm fine. Personal stuff on my mind. Really."

"If you say so." Solway went into the lunch room, and came back pulling the tab off a can of Coke.

Footsteps sounded in the hall, and Dave Evans joined them. "Coulda been a bad one."

"But it wasn't," Smith replied.

"I'm heading back out," Solway said. "You need a lift?"

"I'll walk." Smith said. "Check out the action in the back alleys."

The phone rang. The three young cops watched as Ingrid picked it up. "I'll send an officer around immediately," she said, before hanging up.

"The Youth Hostel. Woman was raped—allegedly—in a bedroom. Suspect has left the scene. Victim needs medical assistance."

"I'm on it." Solway downed the last of her drink and put the empty can onto the counter.

"I'll come with you," Evans said. "You'll need help taking statements."

They ran out of the building. Smith picked up the empty can and took it to the recycling bin in the lunch room. She turned the collar of her jacket up.

"Stay safe," Ingrid said.

Smith gave the dispatcher a wave and let herself out the secure door. The street entrance contained a small vestibule with a narrow bench, a corkboard displaying safety tips and wanted posters, a counter with a glass divider between the room and the main building, and a sliding partition the dispatcher could open to ask a caller their business.

Had she seriously been thinking of cheating on Adam, solid, reliable, adoring Adam, for a guy whose only virtue was that he was a good skier? She must have been out of her mind.

She pulled out her phone, flicked it open, and pressed buttons. She kept her face turned toward the street in case Ingrid had recently learned how to lip read.

Her call was answered before the second ring. "You okay? It's late."

"I'm okay. Wanted to hear your voice."

"You're hearing it," Adam said. It was a good voice, deep and strong. Authoritative when it needed to be, soft and warm when it spoke to her.

"I kinda forgot about the time difference. Sorry. I guess you're in bed."

"Not a problem. You can disturb me in bed anytime. Things busy there?"

"Yeah. We're hopping. Dawn's been called to a rape at the youth hostel. An alleged rape. How come if the victim had been stabbed in the chest, it wouldn't be called an alleged stabbing?"

He chuckled. "Been talking to your mom, have you?"

"I love you, Adam."

"Hey, Mol. I love you too. You know that. Did something happen tonight? You sound, I don't know, kinda sad."

"I guess I just realized for some reason that I really, truly do love you."

"Was that in doubt?"

"Perhaps the depth of it was."

"It's four o'clock in the morning where I am, and you're working. I want you sharp and focused out on the streets, not thinking about me. So I'm going to go now. Hell, maybe I do want you thinking about me. When I get back, I have something to ask you, Molly. Take care." She heard a soft click as he hung up.

She tucked her phone back into her pocket, and then turned and looked through the glass. Ingrid was smiling at her.

And Molly Smith realized she had a big, stupid smile on her own face.

Chapter Thirty

Mark Hamilton went skiing. In town it had rained overnight, but fresh powder had fallen on the mountains and conditions on the black diamonds were good. He skied hard and fast, muscles aching and face burning with the cold, until dusk began to settle and the lifts closed.

He'd received an e-mail last night, inviting him to an upcoming get-together in Vancouver, a rare invitation from his old buddies from the unit. He never went, so contact between them had largely dried up over the past five years. Some of the guys, he knew, were as fucked up as he was. They found strength in each other. As soldiers always had and always would. They might go to shrinks and mind-docs, where they'd talk about their feelings and pop pills, but no one else, they knew, could ever understand.

No one who hadn't been there. Done the things they'd done. Seen the things they'd seen.

Not that they'd ever talk about it. It was enough, to know your buddy was by your side when you needed him there.

Mark only knew this from talk he'd heard. He didn't exchange news or meet every now and again over a beer to complain about the civilian world or the incompetence of the department of veterans' affairs.

He wasn't good enough.

He'd failed in the worst way a soldier could.

He'd let a man, one of his men, die.

He didn't deserve their support, their friendship.

Their understanding.

It had been a good day on the slopes. He'd outraced his mind and exhausted his body. Back to work on Monday. It would be nice to see the kids again, even the sneering, surly grade nines and tens. Boys who thought they were so tough, but didn't have a clue.

Their innocence was a balm on his tormented soul.

The store was busy on Saturday, but James and Flower were both working and so Lucky Smith spent the day planning for the end-of-season sale.

Time to get rid of the skis and snowshoes and make room for hiking poles and kayak paddles.

She glanced round her small, crowded office. A picture of her and Andy hung on the wall. It had been taken the day the store opened. Andy had long blond hair and a droopy mustache; Lucky's flame-red hair had been ironed and parted in the middle of her head to fall in a smooth waterfall across her shoulders, and her skirt barely covered her pert little butt.

So young.

So many years, so many memories.

Unlikely she and Paul would have memories to share in their old age. Last night had not, to put it mildly, ended well. She'd been furious at his casual dismissal of environmentalists as tree huggers.

She was intelligent enough to realize that she probably would have let it go if she hadn't been on the phone to her friend Jane Reynolds only that afternoon. Jane who never, never gave up. Jane who spurred Lucky on when she sometimes felt like simply giving in.

Other people seemed to pass their lives without always finding something to be angry about.

Sometimes Lucky wished she could.

But that wasn't her way. She did like Paul, very much. She liked his company, she even respected him for the job he did.

A smile touched the edges of her mouth as she imagined her nineteen-year-old self, a sophomore at the University of Washington, heavily involved in student politics in the Vietnam era. On one of her first dates with Andy they'd gone to a SDS demonstration.

But that was long ago, and the past, as they said, was another country.

What to do about the past that was last night? Paul had obviously been hoping Lucky would stay over at his condo, but after their spat in the theater, and then a chilly walk, in more ways than one, back to his car, neither of them made the suggestion.

They drove out of town in silence. He pulled up to Lucky's house in the snowy woods. "Thank you for a lovely evening," she said.

"I'm sorry," he said, "if...that I upset you. I wouldn't like to think things such as that can come between us. Destroy our... friendship."

His hands were clenched on the steering wheel. She laid one of hers on his. "Our friendship is important to me," she said. "Good night Paul."

He didn't ask if he could come in. She didn't know what she'd have said if he had.

She got out of the car. He watched until she was inside and kitchen light came on and then he drove away.

She'd wanted to kick something. Instead, she opened the door again and let Sylvester out.

Chapter Thirty-one

The church parking lot was full half an hour before Cathy Lindsay's funeral service began, and cars began to spread out along the steep mountain roads, tucked between snowbanks. Two uniformed officers were in place directing traffic.

John Winters made sure he was one of the first to arrive. The day was clear but cold, so mourners would be unlikely to linger outside. He took his place near the front of the church, at the end of a pew where he could see everyone as they arrived. Ray Lopez stood at the back. The gleaming casket, all polished wood and brass, covered with a mass of flowers, had been brought in earlier and placed in front of the altar. Additional bouquets and wreathes filled the church, their scent sickeningly strong.

The church was late-seventies ugly on the outside, but inside it maintained an aura of dignity and grace. Plain pews, wood worn by decades of seated rumps and sweating hands, large tapestries, woven with biblical scenes, decorating either side of the choir loft. The unadorned altar, the plain wooden cross hanging above it, powerful in their simplicity. The stained glass windows were too modern for Winters' taste. Jesus' followers looked like a pack of Trafalgar neo-hippies rather than first century peasants, but the windows were pretty and allowed the low spring sun to pour through.

Winters recognized the mayor and numerous town dignitaries. His own boss, the Chief Constable, had come, as had Mark

Hamilton, the math teacher, and William Westfield, who'd been in Cathy's night-school class. Winters was surprised to see Margo, Eliza's assistant; he hadn't realized she knew the Lindsays. Perhaps she could be counted among the curious. Plenty of people would be here who only had a passing acquaintance with the deceased, if at all.

Today was Monday, the first day back at school after March Break. A substantial number of children were in attendance, classmates and friends of the daughter, Jocelyn, as well as Cathy's fellow teachers and her students. Some of Bradley's friends had turned up, for once neatly dressed and somber of appearance. Gord and Cathy's friends and colleagues had come, as well as most of the neighbors. The genuinely grieving and the mildly curious.

It was a spectacular case. A shocking, unsolved murder. Like those who called the police station with nothing of significance to report, some people would come to the funeral only because they wanted to be part of the drama.

John Winters studied the faces of everyone who entered. He didn't know what he was looking for, but he'd know it if he saw it. Guilt maybe? Gloating? Someone more interested in the reactions of the mourners than the service or tributes to the deceased?

The church was full to bursting. People crowded together in the pews, some had to take seats in the choir loft, everyone speaking in low respectful whispers. Laughing children were immediately hushed. An invisible organ played soft, sad music.

One of the last to enter the church was Elizabeth Moorehouse, beautiful in a severe black suit, black hat trimmed with fur, high-heeled leather boots. Women gave her curious glances and nudged their neighbors. Some of the men stared.

After the way she'd talked at her home in Victoria, Winters got the impression Moorehouse was happy to have Gord Lindsay moving out of her life. Either something had changed her mind or she'd been stringing the police a line all along.

Winters wasn't the only one surprised to see Moorehouse. She'd taken a seat at the entrance to a pew, making everyone else squeeze down. Gord couldn't fail to see her as he made his way toward the front surrounded by his family. Winters saw the man's face tighten and his jaw clench. Gord threw what could only be described as a furious glare at Moorehouse. She did not shy away, but stared at him until the family had passed.

VicPD had come back negative on Gord Lindsay. No hint of anything irregular in his business affairs. As far as they were concerned Lindsay Internet Consulting was precisely what it claimed to be, and nothing more. That the police hadn't found any skullduggery didn't mean everything was on the up and up, of course. Might just mean Lindsay was good at hiding it, but Winters doubted it. If Lindsay did have gang connections, Russian mob maybe or even the Yakuza, enemies so ruthless they'd killed his wife to make a point, the man would be cowering in terror, fearing they'd come after him or his children next.

Instead Lindsay simply looked sad. Sad and confused as to why this had happened to him and his family. He took his place at the front of the church and sat, back hunched, head bowed, his children on either side of him, his mother and Cathy's parents beside them. Jocelyn wore a plain blue blouse and skirt. Her long hair had had been washed and brushed to a high shine. Bradley sported a fresh haircut and had put on a clean white shirt, gray and blue tie, and dress pants.

Everyone sat down, the organ music drifted to a halt, and the minister stepped up to the lectern.

"Friends," she said, and the service began.

Winters slipped away. From this point on he'd prefer to be at the back.

While the mourners watched the service, Winters and Lopez watched the mourners. Some of the smaller children clung to their parents, a few of the older ones nudged each other and stifled giggles. Teenage boys yawned or kept their heads down, not in prayer or respect but because their thumbs were working their smart phones. Of the adults, women cried and men looked grim and solemn.

Gord Lindsay's right arm was around his daughter's shoulder. Bradley sat close, but not touching, his father. Cathy's parents clung to each other. They all, even the boy, openly wept.

People came forward to speak. Cathy's principal talked about the woman as teacher. A university friend told them about Cathy's youth. A local woman related a funny story about their book club.

Winters studied the crowd.

The only person acting at all out of the ordinary was Margo Franklin. She'd taken a seat two rows behind William Westfield, slightly to one side. Her eyes were fixed on him throughout the service, and she kept missing the cues to stand for a hymn and sit down again. Westfield continually glanced over his shoulder, although he did not smile at Margo or acknowledge her.

As Cathy's book club friend descended the stairs heading back to her seat, an agonized wail broke through the sound of rustling clothes and gentle weeping. People twisted in their seats to see behind them. In the second last row, mourners shifted their legs. Some half rose.

Mark Hamilton had been seated in the middle of the pew. He'd gotten to his feet and was fighting to get out. Sweat poured down his face, and the thick muscles of his neck bulged with strain. He knocked knees aside and didn't bother to excuse himself. He reached the aisle. He looked at Winters through eyes as round and white as those of a horse smelling fire.

Winters stepped forward. Hamilton brushed past him.

Winters followed the math teacher out of the church. "Are you all right, Mr. Hamilton?"

"I get." Hamilton gasped for air. "Claustrophobic. That's all. Too many people." He half ran, half fell down the steps.

"Catch your breath. It'll be over soon. They'll be serving tea in the…"

"I have to go. So many people. I can't breathe in there. I can't bear it."

Winters reached out one hand. He felt solid muscle beneath the man's coat. Hamilton shrugged him off as if the Sergeant were a pesky fly. "What can't you bear, Mr. Hamilton?"

"I have to go."

"You can't bear it that Cathy's dead? What exactly was your relationship with her, Mark?"

"I had no relationship with her."

Inside the church mourners began to stand, voices rose to sign a hymn. It would be over soon, people flooding outside into the cold sunlight.

Winters was aware of Ray Lopez standing behind him.

"You're reacting very strongly to her funeral, Mark, stronger than I'd expect from a colleague. Particularly an ex-military man. She liked you, you know. Students, teachers at the school have told me that." Winters lowered his voice. "Did you like her?"

"She was a nuisance. Always hanging around. *Oh, Mark. Please Mark. You're so nice, Mark.* Wanting help. Wanting *to* help. I told her to go away, to leave me the hell alone. But she wouldn't." The twitch started behind Hamilton's right eye. It grew stronger, pulling at the corner of his mouth, jerking his lip into a hideous half smile.

Winters' heart accelerated. *Keep the man talking.* He had to keep the man talking. In a few minutes people would be everywhere, chattering and crying.

"What did you do, Mark, when she wouldn't go away?" Once again Winters laid his hand on Hamilton's arm. The man was solid muscle. With his other hand Winters reached for the handcuffs on his belt. He felt as much as saw Lopez take a step forward.

"Do? What did I do? Nothing. I should have told her I don't like women. *Sorry, but I'm gay, don't you know.*"

"Is that true?"

"No. These days I'm nothing. Not gay, not straight. Nothing." The twitch began to slow. His mouth settled back into a straight line.

He jerked his arm out of Winters' grip and dashed down the rest of the stairs. He ran flat out, across the parking lot, down the hill, his coat streaming behind him.

"Want to have him intercepted?" Lopez asked.

"No. We know where he lives. I want a full check on Mark Hamilton from the army and as fast as possible. I'd say that man's suffering a full-on case of PTSD. I want to know if it began when he was in the army. Or when he killed Cathy Lindsay."

"Because she was a nuisance."

◇◇◇

Shouldn't be much longer. Molly Smith had been standing at this corner for two hours, directing traffic. She'd stepped in a slushy puddle, soaking her boots, and her feet were freezing. She stamped them to keep circulation going. Earlier, a steady stream of cars had gone up the hill; none had come back down yet.

The funeral was being held at the same church where Norman had gone in pursuit of the shooter. An inadequate parking lot, near the top of a steep hill. The overflow of cars blocked the neighboring streets. The roads were narrow enough in summertime, never mind with five-foot-high snow banks on either side, and people who were less than efficient at parallel parking but still wanted to get as close to the church as they could.

A man came down the hill, heading her way. His clothes, suit and tie, dress coat, indicated he'd been at the funeral, but he was running. Fast. As he approached, she could see wide anxious eyes, blinking rapidly, a face wet with tears mixed with sweat.

Had something happened in the church?

For a moment she thought of a shooting, a bombing, the roof collapsing under the weight of wet snow. No, there wouldn't be one lone man running away. She could still hear the distant sound of music. An organ playing and out-of-tune voices singing.

"Sir," she called. "What's wrong?"

He saw her. His frightened eyes took in her dark blue uniform, the blue hat with lighter blue band, the jacket with shoulder patches, the fully laden equipment belt. If anything, the terror in his face only increased.

"No," he said, a strangled cry. "No. I shouldn't have come."

He changed direction, and darted away from her, running hard. She stood in the middle of the road watching. He slipped on a patch of ice; his arms windmilled and he cried out, but he managed to keep his footing. Then he rounded a corner and disappeared.

Chapter Thirty-two

Now was her chance. Margo was almost giddy with excitement and possibilities.

Eliza had told Margo that William Westfield had been a student in Cathy Lindsay's night school class. In that case, he'd probably be going to her funeral. Margo didn't know Cathy, but that shouldn't matter. In a small town like this everyone either knew someone or knew someone who knew them. She'd go to the funeral to pay her respects. And if she ran into William, how nice. They could have a friendly chat over excessively-stewed tea and crustless tuna sandwiches at the reception after.

Margo had decided not to mention anything about the funeral to her husband until the last minute. She dressed in a subdued-gray suit suitable for the occasion and studied herself in the mirror. Perfectly respectable. Taking a deep breath, she went into the living room.

Steve was comfortably ensconced in his favorite leather chair deep in one of the political biographies he loved. He looked up as she came in, and a question crossed his face when he saw what she was wearing.

Margo told him she'd known Cathy from the art gallery. "She had a great interest in local artists. Liked to keep abreast of what we were showing."

"I thought you said you'd never met her." He lowered his book.

"I didn't know her name, but I recognized her picture in the paper. I'd like to go to the funeral and pay my respects."

He glanced at his watch. "You should have given me some notice. I scarcely have time to change."

"No! I mean, no, dear. I don't mind going alone."

"Margo, is there something you aren't telling me?"

She bent down, kissed him on the forehead. "I won't be long."

She was among the first to arrive at the church. She sat in her car, fidgeting with her necklace. Wouldn't do to go in too early.

Cars began arriving; a steady stream of people walked up the steps to the church. What if she didn't see him? So many people, bundled up in winter coats and hats. He might not even come.

She'd decided it would be better to approach Jackson—William—in public. She'd be more comfortable speaking to him, telling him the wonderful news, with people around. He'd be overjoyed, of course, to discover that she was his mother. His real mother. His birth mother.

Still, in case he wasn't initially as delighted as he should be, better to speak to him where he couldn't shut the door in her face.

Too bad he'd bought the Khan pictures when she wasn't working. The art gallery, with its soft music, good lighting, neutral walls, would have been the perfect place. Now that he had the three sketches, who knew when he might come again. Perhaps never.

She didn't know where he lived. He wasn't in the phone book, and he hadn't given an address to Eliza. Margo didn't know if he had a job, and the night-school creative-writing class might not be offered again now that the teacher was dead.

This was a bad idea. She should go home.

Then she spotted him.

He'd parked on the street and was coming up the neatly-shoveled church walk at a sedate pace, head down, shoulders hunched. He wore a fine wool coat and brown leather gloves.

So distinguished. So handsome.

Margo got out of her car. She hurried across the parking lot, taking care of her footing. She fell into step behind him. She'd wait until the service ended before approaching, anything else would be inappropriate.

The church was almost full when they entered. Soft organ music played, and people greeted each other in low voices. The flower-draped coffin was at the front, closed thank heavens.

William took a seat in the middle off to the left. Margo found a place two rows behind. A couple slid in beside her. They nodded polite greetings.

She studied the back of William's head. It was almost square, hair and skin stretched over solid bone. So much like Jack, his father.

She'd written to Jack when the boy had been born. Born and stolen from her. She asked his help in getting the baby back. He never replied. She'd believed at the time his wife must have intercepted her letters.

Years later, once she was married and a mother and knew something about the ways of the world, she finally understood that Jack Sorensen, small town drugstore owner, had been nothing but a lying cheat. A man prepared to seduce an innocent young girl from a cold, unloving family. No doubt Margo had only been latest in a long line.

She wondered if she'd been the only girl stupid enough, naïve enough, desperate enough, to fall for his oily charm.

No, she had no sentiment for Jack.

But she would not let her feelings about Jack reflect on his son. Her son.

She became aware that the people around her were getting to their feet. She scrambled to follow.

The family was coming down the aisle. So sad. The husband looking like he hadn't slept for a week. The little girl, neat and pretty, her nose and eyes red and swollen. A teenaged son and Cathy's parents or in-laws. The family reached the front of the church and everyone sat down.

Only the minister remained standing. She and John Winters. The police officer walked down the side aisle, heading for the back. His handsome face was set into serious lines, his eyes moving across the congregation. She gave him a smile of greeting, but he did not acknowledge her.

He had not come with Eliza so he must be working. Everyone said the police came to funerals, hoping the killer would be there and let something slip by their words or actions.

William shifted in his seat. He glanced behind him. He saw Margo, watching him. She threw him a smile.

He turned, focusing his attention on the minister, announcing a hymn. Once again people began to rise.

Later Margo couldn't remember anything about Cathy Lindsay's funeral. She popped up and down along with everyone else, mumbled a long-forgotten prayer, tried to look serious and somber. She'd been raised Catholic, hadn't been to church since the day her mother had locked her in her room in disgrace. The few funerals she'd been to over the years, including those for Steve's parents, had been held in the funeral home. This Protestant church seemed very plain to her. She rather liked it.

William Westfield kept glancing over his shoulder, checking to see if she was still there. She tried waving once, just a wiggle of her fingers. He glared at her, and she dropped her hand. Perhaps he was a religious man, and thought she wasn't being respectful.

She folded her hands in her lap and tried to pay attention.

At last the funeral service ended. Six men rose and approached the casket. They lifted it and carried it out of the church to the accompaniment of slow, solemn music, and much weeping. The family followed. After they'd passed, the rest of the mourners stood and made their way down the aisle.

Margo watched William. He was seated close to the side aisle and turned in that direction. She did also. She stood at the end of her pew, conscious of the people behind her trying to get past. She didn't care. She waited until William reached her and fell into step beside him.

"Lovely service," she said.

He grunted.

"Are you going to the reception? It's downstairs, in the church basement."

"Are you?"

"I might."

"Then I'm not."

They reached the narthex. A dimly-lit corner contained a table with a few items for sale, a book on the history of the church, a calendar, a donation box. Notices were pinned to a corkboard on the wall. Bridge group. Pot-luck supper.

People pushed past them, crowding the confined space. Margo found herself standing almost nose to nose with William.

"You know who I am, don't you?" she said.

"Lady, I haven't got a clue."

"Let yourself believe. I saw your face the day you came into the art gallery. I know you recognized me. Deep down, you knew it was me."

William glanced from side to side. They were hemmed in, pushed up against the wall. The area was narrow, creating a considerable bottleneck as everyone exited the church at the same time.

"I have absolutely no idea what you're talking about. And I don't particularly want to know."

"Your mother. For heaven's sake, son. I'm your mother."

His eyes opened in surprise. He sucked in a breath. Then he laughed. "Sorry to tell you this, lady, my mother's dead and buried. But last time I saw her, she didn't look one little bit like you."

"She's your adoptive mother." His eyes moved, and Margo knew she was right. "I'm your birth mother. I recognized you the moment I laid eyes on you. I knew. How could I not?"

He leaned forward. She breathed in the manly scent of him. His spicy aftershave, an underlying layer of sweat. For a moment she almost expected him to kiss her.

He spoke in a low, deep voice. "You're a lunatic, that's what you are. Stay away from me."

"Jackson…"

He pressed the tip of his index finger to her chest. It burned through her jacket, blouse, layers of skin and fat and bone. It touched her heart. "I said, stay the hell away from me." He pressed the finger deeper. "You're a nut case."

Then he was gone, mixing with the crowd, disappearing through the doors.

She laid her palm flat against the center of her chest, between her breasts. She felt her own heart beating. She could feel the power of their bond, the very essence of love. He was a man, pretending always to be strong and powerful. Like most men, unable to confess his yearning for her, his weakness, his need for her. For Mom.

He'd go home and think about what she said. Then he'd come looking for her. Ready to apologize, wanting to hear more.

Her entire body shuddered with excitement.

Chapter Thirty-three

"We've got a match."

"Go ahead."

"The lab found traces of DNA on that cigarette butt," Ron Gavin said. "I ran it and, ta da, a match."

"That is good news."

"Garfield Leonard O'Reilly. Done time for trafficking, living off the avails, break and enter. Now resident in Trafalgar, British Columbia."

"I know the character. A fixture of our fine town. Thanks, Ron."

Winters snapped his phone shut with a groan, not pleased at the news. Gar O, as he was known to everyone in town, spent his days walking from one end of Front Street to another. Gar had a long record, but he'd been reasonably clean since moving to Trafalgar about five years ago. Brain addled by drugs, right leg crippled by a knife wound he waited too long to have treated. Winters wouldn't have put him high on the list of suspects.

Still, you never knew what people were capable of.

He'd taken the call in the basement of the church following Cathy Lindsay's funeral. The tea had been drunk, the sandwiches and squares consumed, most of the mourners dispersed.

The interment was private. Gord Lindsay and his family had left long ago.

Time for John Winters to take his leave also.

He called Jim Denton at dispatch.

"I'd like to talk to Gar O. Have the patrol officers keep an eye out for him, and let me know when they have a sighting."

"Want him brought in?"

"No. He gets twitchy under pressure. I just want a chat."

"Will do."

His phone rang as he was pulling out of the church parking lot. Gar O had been sighted at the bus stop by the rec center. Winters arrived a couple of minutes later to find Dawn Solway chatting to the man, her posture comfortable and relaxed. Gar leaned back against the bench, good leg crossed over one knee.

As Winters walked up, Gar reached into his pocket and pulled out a packet of cigarettes.

"Hey, Gar."

"Sarge."

Winters studied the man. His stringy gray hair hung over his face and down his back almost to his belt, and his beard wasn't much shorter. He was around five foot four, and substantially overweight, looking like a hairy snowman with legs. He lit his cigarette and threw the match onto the sidewalk.

"What'd you do weekend before last, Gar?" Winters asked. "Stay in town?"

"Didn't kill no lady, if'n that's what you're askin'."

Gar might be short of brain power these days, but his survival instincts were as sharp as ever. He shrugged. "One day's same as the rest. I was in town, yeah. Don't travel much anymore. I might have had dinner at Maddy's place on Saturday, bunch of the guys were there. Or that might have been Sunday."

"Did you go for a walk?"

"Walked from my place to Maddy's. Streets were busy. Yeah, it was Saturday. Lots of cars with skis on the roof pulling in. School holidays startin'." He sucked on his cigarette. Blew smoke out of his nostrils.

"What about Saturday morning?"

"Sarge, you're askin' about a week ago. I don't know. Went to Eddie's for coffee probably, usually do." He broke into a smile, showing a mouthful of stained, broken, and missing teeth. "Hey, now I remember. I phoned my daughter. Asked what she and the kids were gonna do for the vacation."

"How's she doing?"

"Good. Real good. Got three kids now. Smart kids, good kids."

"Did you know a woman named Cathy Lindsay?"

"She the one killed, I hear."

"Did you ever meet Mrs. Lindsay?"

"Don't think so." Gar smoked. He was relaxed, his arm thrown out along the back of the bench, his legs crossed. He was dressed in white socks and running shoes, not boots. About six inches of bare leg was visible below his coat. Gar wore shorts all year long, never mind the weather. The hand holding his cigarette was still, not shaking. His clothes smelled of smoke, and not just cigarettes either. He'd clearly had a joint not long ago. Marijuana always made him agreeable and friendly.

He tossed the end of his cigarette to the sidewalk. Ground it out beneath his shoe, and then picked it up. He checked carefully that it was extinguished and, with a smile at Solway, he slid across the bench and dropped the butt into the sand-filled top section of the trash can.

He lumbered to his feet. "That be all, Sarge? I got places to go, people to see."

"Thanks Gar," Winters said. "Have a good day."

"Same to you, my man. And my lady." He walked away, with his awkward listing gate.

Winters peered into the trash. Cigarette butts stuck up out of the sand like trees in a forest after a fire had passed through.

"You think Gar had something to do with the Lindsay killing?" Solway said, her disbelief matching Winters'.

"No. I think someone's playing me for a fool." He hadn't dared hope a killer as organized as this one would accidently drop a cigarette brimming with DNA at the scene, but even the best of them made mistakes. Otherwise the cops wouldn't catch most of them.

The person who'd killed Cathy Lindsay had come into town, picked up a cigarette butt, perhaps from this very bin, tucked it into his pocket and carried it up the mountain to drop where he'd stood, aiming his sights at a woman out walking her dog. He'd left the 'evidence' as a gigantic screw-you gesture to the police.

Eliza's hand hovered over the phone, as her head spun with indecision.

Privacy, Eliza firmly believed, was a virtue. Everyone was entitled to privacy, unless they were committing an offence against another's person or possessions. Unless, in other words they were intruding on someone's privacy.

Otherwise, butt out.

She ran her fingers across the buttons of her phone as she glanced at the computer screen. Margo's home number was in her employee file as well as Margo's husband Steve's cell phone number in case of an emergency.

This was hardly an emergency. Margo had entrusted Eliza with her private information, trusted it would be used only if necessary.

Eliza made the call.

"Mr. Franklin," she said, desperate now that she'd made up her mind to get the words spoken as fast as possible. "I'm Eliza Winters, from the art gallery where Margo works."

"Hi. Nice to meet you at last, Eliza. On the phone at any rate. Can I help you with something? Are you trying to get hold of Margo? Isn't she off today?"

"Yes. I mean, yes, she's not working today. Which is why I'm calling, Mr. Franklin."

"Steve, please."

"Steve. This is difficult for me to say, but I feel that I must. I need to talk to you about Margo."

"Is there a problem?"

"Perhaps we could meet. Are you free this afternoon?"

"As it happens, I'm in town right now. I'm in the parking lot at the hardware store, about to go home. I could stop by the gallery."

"I'll be here."

He came through the door a few minutes later, a man in his sixties with a round belly, bulbous red nose, and a thick shock of pure-white hair.

He crossed the floor with quick, confident strides and stuck out his hand. She accepted it in her own. A bandage was wrapped around his forefinger, his palm was covered in scratches, and a healing cut bisected the pad of his thumb. He saw her notice and said with a self-depreciating grin, "Since I retired, I'm trying to do all the odd jobs around the house myself. It's a tough learning curve. Now, what's this about Margo?"

"She spoke to me in confidence," Eliza said, the words thick in her throat, "I won't reveal the contents of that conversation, although I understand you know."

"Go on."

"Something happened, here, in the store that worries me, and that is my business. We had a customer the other day, a gentleman aged around forty, forty-five. Margo seemed...unduly interested in him. She told me she believes him to be her son."

Steve grimaced. "Yeah, I figured it was something like that."

"The man wasn't happy at her attention. He left the gallery, and later sent someone ahead to ensure Margo wasn't here before he came in to buy what he wanted. I'm sorry, Steve, but as well as being concerned about Margo herself, I can't have her chasing customers away. I also understand she followed him into another store." Her voice trailed off. "I thought you should know, that's all."

"I appreciate it, Eliza. I do. I guessed this was happening. Again."

"Again?"

"Margo had a baby boy when she was very young, and he was taken away from her. That's never been a secret between us. I was okay with her trying to locate him through the usual channels. Nothing came of it. She was highly disappointed, but she seemed to accept that she wouldn't be able to find him. We had two kids of our own. A boy and a girl. Our eldest, our son Gerald, was killed in a car accident three years ago."

"Oh, dear."

"As well as Gerald, the accident killed his wife and their unborn child. As you can imagine that took an enormous emotional toll on Margo."

"It would on any mother. Or father."

"Once Gerald died, Margo began seeking her son, Jackson, again. This time she wasn't content to try to open adoption records. She started looking for him everywhere she went. We'd be walking down the street and she'd suddenly turn and chase after some random white man of about the right age."

"Did you get her any…help?"

"I tried, but she doesn't think she has a problem. It's created an enormous rift between Margo and Ellen, our daughter. Ellen thinks her mother's insulting Gerald's memory by wanting to replace him with, and I quote, "some best-forgotten bastard""

Eliza cringed.

"Precisely. Margo didn't care for that and they had quite the argument. Ellen also believes Margo's denigrating her, Ellen, because she's a girl and Margo wants to regain the preferred boy child. Which is absolutely not the case, but matters can get out of hand mighty fast when families start fighting. Things are said that can never be unsaid.

"We'd been planning for a long time to move to a small town when we retired. I hoped a change would help Margo get over this obsession. Obviously, I was wrong."

"You need to get her some professional help."

"I know, I know. Everything was going great when we came here. She stopped chasing strange men, stopped scouring the newspapers inspecting the face of everyone in every picture. I thought she was over it. Apparently not."

Eliza gave him what she hoped was an encouraging smile. "If there's anything I can do to help, please let me know. I do like Margo. Very much."

"Thanks."

The door chimes tinkled and two women came in. Well dressed, expensively groomed, laden with shopping bags. Steve nodded to them on his way out.

Chapter Thirty-four

"Give me some good news," John Winters said as he came through the office door, thoroughly discouraged after his chat with Gar O.

"Two things," Lopez said, swiveling his chair. "First, Mark Hamilton. I've got his army medical records."

"Thank heavens," Winters said, throwing himself into his chair, "for interservice co-operation."

"Nothing's amiss. He got a clean bill of health when discharged. He was never wounded, and there's no record of him receiving, or needing, psychiatric care. All negatives, from our POV."

"Negatives can be positive," Winters said. "You saw him at the funeral. The man looked like the devil and all the hounds of hell were after him. Total panic. What brought that on? I heard no loud noises, no unexpected screaming or shouting that might have prompted a flashback to a firefight."

"Can't hang a man for being upset at a funeral."

"Keep digging. The teachers say Cathy was irritating Hamilton. He tried to avoid her when he could. She appeared not to want to take no for an answer."

"So he gave her a no she had to accept?"

"Perhaps. I'd like to talk to one of his commanding officers. See if you can find someone for me."

"He's been out of the army a good few years. Gone to university, become a teacher, moved here."

"He didn't learn to shoot at teacher's college, and he didn't go into a full-blown panic attack because the church was full of well-behaved high school students."

"I see your point. In my spare time," Lopez grimaced, "I've been working on the ViCLAS report. I sent it on Friday after you thought about the serial killer connection, while, I might add, Madeleine tapped her toes and waited for me to finish before we went to her friend's for dinner." ViCLAS was the Canadian police interagency communication tool used for finding links between crimes in distant jurisdictions. Not easy to use, time consuming, but a lot better than the old days when they'd often not even know about a similar incident a few miles away if it had been committed in another province or state. "Someone must have had time to kill on the weekend, because I got a report back. They might have found something."

"Tell me about it."

"From 1986-1997 there was a series of sniper shootings in Arizona. A place a lot like Trafalgar from what I can tell. Small town in the wilderness, lots of tourists, full of arty types, and transients," Lopez wiggled his fingers in the air, "in search of their spirituality. Over the eleven years in question there were six sniper killings. All the victims were female, all of them white, all in the thirty to forty-five age group. Otherwise they had nothing in common, not religion, income group, marital status. Nothing. The victims were either hiking in the wilderness or walking in a sparely populated residential area when they were shot. The shooter always maintained a good distance from the victim, and he used a variety of weapons, various types of rifles or shotguns. Never a handgun."

"Indicating the perp disposed of the firearm after the killing."

"Right. Then in July of 1997, it ended. Not a single incident since."

"Grendel," Winters said.

"What?"

"Reminds me of a story. They have any suspects?"

"A few, but nothing concrete and nothing that would tie anyone to more than one of the victims, other than the fact that, like Trafalgar, a small town's a small town. No one was ever charged. Law enforcement came from all over to help out. And then it ended. The police pretty much assumed the perp had died or left town and that was the end of that. They were looking for a serial killer, but this case had none of the normal serial killer indicators. No trophies taken, no taunting the police, no cryptic notes to the press. Believe it or not, other than in police circles and the town itself, the case had a pretty low profile. Didn't get much national attention."

"The days before the Internet."

"Over the years, officers have questioned men arrested for similar shootings, but no one they came across had a connection to the Arizona business."

"That's interesting, but I doubt it has anything to do with our guy. Just another shooter."

"We can only hope. God help us if this was the first."

"First of what?" Barb Kowalski asked.

"Nothing," Lopez said quickly.

Barb stood in the doorway, carrying an ominous-looking envelope. She shook it and coins jingled. "I'm collecting. Marlene Hardcastle's retiring."

"Who the heck is Marlene Hardcastle?"

"The law clerk at the RCMP detachment. I have a card for you to sign, too."

Winters grumbled and pulled out his wallet.

Men chased each other around the ice. The puck skidded from one side of the rink to another. Sticks flew, bodies collided, the crowd roared their approval.

Gord Lindsay saw none of it. He sat in his favorite chair, an untouched bottle of beer and an empty bowl of chips on the table beside him. Renee had been through here a few minutes ago, dusting and tidying. She must have thought gremlins had snuck into the house while they were at the funeral—at Cathy's funeral—to mess up the TV room.

"Sure you don't want to come?" Ralph said. "Doesn't do you any good, sitting here brooding."

"I'm not brooding," Gord said. "I'm watching the game."

"Yeah. Right. Suit yourself."

Jocelyn dashed around her grandfather. She'd changed out of the skirt and blouse she'd worn to her mother's funeral and put on a well-worn pair of jeans and a long-sleeved T-shirt with sparkly lettering across the front. The sleeves were too short and the hem of the jeans rose above her thin ankle bones. She was growing fast; she'd need new clothes soon. Cathy would…No, Cathy was dead. Gord would have to be the one to take his daughter shopping.

"Please come, Daddy. Please."

"I'll be here when you get back, honeybunch. Off you go now, your grandmas are waiting."

"Please." She grabbed his arm, started to pull. "Please come."

He jerked his arm away. "Will you stop that goddamned whining. You're not five years old any more."

The girl's face crumpled and she burst into tears. Ralph muttered soft words, put his arm around her shoulders, and led her out of the room, throwing Gord a look that could sour milk.

"Everything all right?" Renee called.

The family was going out to dinner. Renee and Ann said they didn't have the energy to cook, not after the funeral. Gord simply couldn't face going with them. Squeezed into a booth at the Chinese buffet between his mom and Renee, both of them thinking they were keeping his spirits up by chattering away like a couple of birds who didn't see the tornado building on the horizon. Ralph shoveling in orange-tinged chicken and ribs coated in sauce the consistency of wallpaper paste.

Jocelyn's large sad eyes, watching her father, waiting for him to take all the pain away.

Bradley had been coaxed out of his room, away from the ever-present computer games, by his grandmothers and talked into accompanying them to dinner. Gord hated to think it took the death of his mother to turn the kid into a half-normal human being.

He flipped through the channels. Nothing worth watching. He continued flipping.

The doorbell rang.

He ignored it. Another well-meaning neighbor bearing a casserole or homemade cake. A stream of which were arriving at the house. Renee put it all in the freezer, provision against the day when they'd be gone and Gord would have to feed his children himself.

The bell again. Longer this time, as if someone were leaning against it.

It stopped.

His cell phone buzzed.

He glanced at the display. Oh god, Elizabeth. He hadn't been at all pleased to see her at the funeral. Dressed so no one could fail to notice or remember her.

He hesitated. He didn't want to talk to her. He didn't want her here, but she could be mighty persistent. Elizabeth could be counted on to stand her ground until she got her way. Once, he'd thought that an admirable trait.

"I can't talk now," he snapped into the phone. "My daughter's calling for me."

"No she isn't," Elizabeth replied. "She just left. The whole happy family, minus the grieving husband, piled into a van and drove down the hill."

"Where are you?"

The doorbell rang.

He scrambled out of his chair, bolted down the hallway, and threw open the door, Spot hot on his heels.

Elizabeth stood there, smiling, dressed as she'd been at the funeral.

"For god's sake, are you out of your mind? You can't come here."

"Why not?" She stepped forward. He didn't move. She took another step until they were almost bumping chests. Gord glanced around, down the street, at the neighbors.

He stepped back, and Elizabeth walked past him into the living room. Spot followed, sniffing at her ankles. Elizabeth scanned the room, ignoring the curious dog. "Nice house."

All neat and tidy. Nothing at all like the home Cathy had lived in. Gord shifted a china figurine so the arrangement was off center, just because he could.

"I don't want you here, Elizabeth. Please, this is Cathy's home. I live here with my children."

She plucked a picture off a side table. Gord and Cathy on their wedding day. Cathy: so beautiful, so happy.

"She was pretty," Elizabeth said in her deep, sexy voice.

"Yes, she was."

"Don't worry, Gord. I don't want to move in. I don't want to be a new mommy to your kids. Perish the thought." She shoved Spot away with the toe of her boot. "I certainly don't want to have to pick up after your dog. I don't want to cause you any trouble."

A great weight lifted off Gord's chest. "What do you want then? Why are you here, Elizabeth? Go home and I'll call you next week."

"What do I want? Thank you for asking. Twenty thousand dollars should do it. Then I'll never bother you again."

"What? Why the hell should I give you anything?"

She dropped into a wingback chair. Her coat fell open, exposing the long legs, sleek stockings, high-heeled boots. "Now that your wife's dead, you don't need to sneak around any more. You can live openly with another woman, once a suitable mourning period is over, of course."

"I don't want to discuss our future now. I…"

"See, Gord, it's like this. I don't want that woman to be me."

"What?"

"I don't want you, Gord, not now that you're single, but I have expenses. I have a house to maintain and a life to live. Twenty thou will see me okay for a while."

Gord stared at her. He'd been afraid Elizabeth had come here because she wanted their relationship to be more open. Permanent. Recognized. He'd been wondering how he was going to dump her.

She was not only dumping him but asking to be paid for it.

"I don't owe you anything."

"Consider it a farewell gift to an old friend."

"No. Even if I had that kind of money, which I don't, I'm not going to give it to you."

"You have life insurance, I'll bet. Cathy did, I mean. You'll be clearing a nice sum."

"That money, if I ever see it, is for our children. So I can pay for things Cathy did for them. What about that jewelry I bought you?" He almost groaned. When he'd first met Elizabeth he'd taken money out of the company accounts and splurged on some pretty—and pretty expensive—baubles trying to impress her. "You got insurance money from the theft of the jewelry, didn't you?"

"Yeah, I did. That's why I'm not asking for more. Twenty thousand by the end of the month, and you'll never hear from me again. You have my bank account details. If the money's not there, I'll be back. Your mother-in-law looks like a right battle-ax. Wonder how she'd take it when I come crying to her, saying you were about to ask Cathy for a divorce. And here, I'd paid all sorts of money on my house, to make a nice home for you and a second home for your dear sweet kids. Sniff sniff."

"She won't believe you."

"She will when she sees the photographic evidence."

"You filthy bitch. I didn't know you had it in you."

She threw back her head and laughed. "Yeah, Gord. I screwed you because you're *soooo* attractive. Such a hunk of a man. Get real. When I lost my voice, I lost any chance to make a decent living for myself. When I ran into you again, my money was running out, my bills and expenses climbing. It was you or the streets, a job see, like a housekeeper with benefits. I'm quitting, and I want severance pay." She got to her feet and put the wedding picture carefully back on the side table so Cathy faced Gord. He turned away.

"I'll see myself out," Elizabeth said.

Gord stood at the living room window, watching Elizabeth walk down the path. She'd parked her car, a rusty old banger, in the driveway. She opened the door, and then turned and gave him a cheerful wave.

Where the hell was he going to get twenty thousand dollars in little more than a week? Cathy's life was insured through her job benefits, but as he'd told Elizabeth, he needed that money to help him raise his kids by himself. To make up for Cathy's lost income. This house had a hefty mortgage—they'd taken out an extra loan to renovate the kitchen last year. He'd have a lot of additional expenses without Cathy home with Jocelyn over the school holidays. He wouldn't be able to spend time away in Victoria; he'd have to hire someone to manage that part of the business or give it up altogether.

Then again, he would no longer be helping to support Elizabeth in Victoria. Having two homes and two families wasn't cheap.

Perhaps Elizabeth would agree to getting the money in installments.

No, that wasn't a good idea. Then she'd have a hold over him until she got all she wanted.

He could simply not pay her. What would she do? He'd done nothing illegal. He'd never signed any papers promising her anything. She couldn't sue, had no grounds to take him to court.

She could talk to Ralph and Renee. To Gord's mother, Ann. Did Elizabeth really have pictures of them together? He'd never posed with her. But hell, every phone these days had a camera. All it would take would be a couple of shots taken while Gord slept. He never wore pajamas to bed in Elizabeth's house the way he did at home with Cathy.

How pathetic was that? As if sleeping naked made him some sort of stud. *A hunk of a man.* He slapped his ample stomach. Flesh jiggled and a hollow sound echoed.

Pathetic.

He could live with Ralph and Renee's disapproval—heck they'd never much liked him in the first place. But he couldn't bear to imagine what his mom would think if she found out about Elizabeth. If she saw, god help him, pictures of her son sleeping in another woman's bed. His tiny shriveled prick, his belly a match to the color and constancy of the Beluga whales at the aquarium.

He'd pay. He could get a loan, explain to the bank he needed to cover some expenses while waiting for the insurance money to come in.

Hell, twenty thousand wasn't all that much anyway. Not in the grand picture. That old house Elizabeth was so proud of positively drank money. She'd go through it fast enough.

And then what? Would she be back? Wanting more?

He'd worry about that when the time came.

He headed for the kitchen. His mom had made a casserole out of last night's leftovers and prepared a serving for his dinner. Ignoring the foil-covered dish, he reached into the cupboard and pulled out an oversized bag of chips.

Cathy never allowed junk food in the house.

Screw that. He was a grown man and he could have whatever he wanted whenever he wanted. He ripped open the bag, stuffed a handful of chips into his mouth.

They scratched at the inside of his cheeks, clung to the walls of his throat. Chemical spices burned his lips. He gagged on the salt. His stomach churned, his throat closed, and he choked. Gord Lindsay ran for the sink and spat out the mouthful of barely chewed food. He threw the bag onto the floor and brought his foot down on it hard, again and again. Broken chips flew everywhere.

Gord burst into tears. He sank to his knees and sobbed, surrounded by the dust of crushed salt and vinegar potato chips and the fading memory of love.

Chapter Thirty-five

It was a wonderful stroke of luck. Perhaps more than luck.

Margo had never doubted she was destined to find Jackson. Fate, that fickle creature, was itself giving her a hand.

She'd watched him leave the funeral. He climbed into a beige Corolla and drove away from the church. Margo was pleased to see that he stopped to allow people to cross the street and kept to the speed limit. She made a note of his license plate.

She worked in the gallery on Tuesday, the day following the funeral and her talk with Jackson. After closing, they took down the current display and began getting ready for the new one. It would be a one-woman show and the artist fussed and fussed all evening. Absolutely nothing was to her liking.

Even Eliza, as cool and composed as ever, could barely contain her impatience with the woman.

They finished about ten. The artist puffed and declared that *this* was not what she had expected, and departed with her head high followed by an entourage that consisted of a man with a scraggly beard, bad breath, and nicotine-stained fingers. Eliza locked up. The women left through the back door, heading for their cars.

"If she dares make one word of complaint at the reception on Thursday," Eliza said, "I will ban her from the gallery. I can't believe how difficult she turned out to be. She knew the size of my space. You'd think she'd been expecting the National Gallery."

"Nerves, I suspect," Margo said. "It is her first show."

Eliza sniffed. She could sniff in a way that indicated sophisticated disapproval. When Margo sniffed people handed her a tissue. "No excuse. If she thinks she's got something to be nervous about, she should try walking the catwalk in Milan in six inch heels a week after twisting her ankle. One can be a flighty amateur, oh so important and dramatic. Or one can be a professional and get on with the job at hand. I fear our Ms. Reingold has chosen the former and if so, this will be her first and last show. That boyfriend doesn't help. Sycophant more likely. I predict he'll slide up to me at the reception and inform me in a low voice that he makes art I absolutely *have* to see."

They reached their cars. "Thanks for staying late," Eliza said.

"I'm happy to."

"Is everything, um, okay, Margo?"

"Couldn't be better. I've spoken to Jackson. He's confused about what I told him, but that's natural. He'll want to be cautious. He's going to look into opening his adoption papers. I'm so excited."

"He's adopted?"

"He was very close to his adoptive parents and didn't want to hurt them by seeking his birth mother. But now that I've approached him, he's keen on the idea."

Eliza chewed her lip. "Have you told Steve about this?"

"I'm saving it to be a surprise. Don't worry, Eliza. It's all going to turn out perfectly well. Good night."

"Good night."

Eliza got into her car. Margo watched the rear lights drive down the alley and disappear as they turned into the street.

She called home. Told Steve they'd run into a problem and it would be closer to midnight before she finished. He told her to take care, and she said she would.

She then drove slowly through the streets of Trafalgar, up and down, back and forth. Looking for a beige Corolla, checking license plates. March Break was over and family groups had left, but lots of tourists were still in town, getting in the last bit of skiing before the snow melted and the season ended for another year. Vehicles were parked outside restaurants or returning to hotels. Margo had trouble identifying the color of cars in the dark, and she wasn't all that familiar with vehicle designs. She checked the main street, the parking lots beside the better hotels, before deciding she'd have better luck on the residential streets. No doubt Jackson would be at home this time of night, maybe he'd park his car outside, not in a garage.

Once she found his car, she'd know where he lived and she could call on him in the morning. He'd been abrupt at the church, but as she told Eliza that was only to be expected. He was a man after all, and although an indescribable something would be telling him Margo was his mother, he'd have doubts. Men liked to be presented with facts. They didn't trust their intuition the way women did.

Once she had a chance to tell him the details of his birth, and he could compare that to what he knew, then he'd realize she was on to something important.

She drove slowly up Cottonwood Street, foot hovering over the brake pedal, her head moving back and forth as she scanned the sides of the road and driveways.

Jackson might not live in town. If he had a place in the mountains it would be hard to locate him, but he had to come into town for shopping and such. All she had to do was keep searching.

A sharp blast broke through Margo's happy thoughts. She started and then peeked at her rearview mirror. Red-and-blue flashing lights.

Oh, dear, the police must be after a speeder.

She dutifully put on her turn indicator and pulled slightly off to the side of the road to let them pass.

To Margo's extreme surprise, the police car came to a stop behind her. The door opened and a uniformed figure approached. Margo rolled down her window.

A woman. She stood beside Margo's door, slightly toward the back. She shone a flashlight around the back seat, then into the front.

"Can I see your license, insurance, and registration, please," she said in a calm and efficient voice.

"Of course." Margo fumbled first in her purse and then in the glove compartment. So many papers, she had trouble locating the insurance. She found it at last and handed everything over. "Is there a problem, Officer?" Margo peered up at the face. Young, fair, and pretty. The policewoman did not smile.

"Wait one moment, please."

Margo watched in her mirror as the policewoman returned to her car, and then she looked around. Snow fell lightly, flakes caught in the beams of her headlights. This was a street of neat houses; most of the lights were off. The flickering blue glow of a TV shone in a couple of windows. A man walking a dog passed by on the other side of the street, giving Margo a long look. Cars slowed as they approached, curious drivers glancing at her.

She felt her face burning. How embarrassing. She hoped no one she knew would recognize her, stopped at the side of the street like a common criminal.

What on earth was taking that woman so long?

Margo fidgeted in her seat.

Finally the door to the police car opened. The officer stood at Margo's window, but didn't pass the papers back. "Thank you, Mrs. Franklin. Can I ask what you're doing?"

"Doing?" Margo's voice broke. "I mean, what am I doing? Why I'm going home. I worked late tonight."

"Do you not know where you live?"

"Of course I know where I live. What sort of question is that?"

"We received a call from the Hudson House Hotel saying a car was going through the parking lot, checking out the vehicles. I've followed you for several minutes. You're driving very slowly, apparently aimlessly up and down the streets. Why?"

Margo swallowed. Oh dear. She'd never so much as had a speeding ticket in all her life. She didn't know what she'd say to Steve if she were arrested. "I'm looking for someone."

"Looking? On the streets? At night? Don't you think that's a bit odd, Mrs. Franklin?"

"My friend's in town, but I don't know where she's staying. So I'm trying to find her car."

"Why don't you phone this friend and ask?"

"I've lost his...I mean her...number."

"Mrs. Franklin, you can't possibly drive around all night checking out every car. Suppose your friend has parked in a garage?"

Margo said nothing.

"I'm advising you to go home. If your friend wants to contact you, he will. If I find you behaving like this again, I have grounds to detain you. You look very much like you're checking out unlocked cars."

"I most certainly am not."

"Glad to hear it. Is there some reason you cannot go home? Is it unsafe for you there?"

"I can go home."

"Good. Would you like me to escort you? Or call someone to come and collect you?

"No."

The policewoman passed Margo's papers through the window. "Good night," she said.

Margo tucked her license into her wallet and her registration and insurance into the glove compartment. She switched on the engine. Easing back onto the road, she was highly conscious of the policewoman behind her.

The flashing lights of the police car switched off, and the vehicle did a U turn, heading back to town.

Margo let out a long puff of air. How dreadfully embarrassing. But not nearly as embarrassing as if Steve had been called to come down to the police station and bail her out.

She'd go home, as she'd promised. Try again tomorrow. It would be easier to see the make of the cars and their license plates in daylight anyway.

She pulled to a stop at the corner of Ninth Street, intending to turn right and head home. A beige Corolla drove through the intersection.

Margo turned left and followed.

Chapter Thirty-six

"I'm impressed, Ms. Jenaring. Highly impressed. That's a solid piece of work."

Michelle Jenaring, age seventeen, beamed around her mouthful of braces. She lifted her fist into the air and pumped it. The class applauded.

Mark Hamilton laughed. He had high hopes for Michelle, one of the brightest of his students. She planned to major in math at university, and he was proud to think he'd played a role in helping the shy girl find her true calling in life.

He glanced at the clock on the wall. One minute until the end of the school day.

It had been a good one. The grade nines had slumbered through their class, as usual, the grade tens had complained about the amount of homework, also as usual, but the grade twelves had been interested and engaged. He enjoyed having the advanced pre-calculus class last period, ending his day on a high note. These kids were taking this course because they wanted to be here. Most of them were headed for university to major in the sciences.

The bell rang, and students scrambled to gather up books and bags.

"Mr. Hamilton to the office. Mr. Hamilton," announced the PA system.

He grumbled under his breath. What was it now? Had he placed a comma in an incorrect place on some kid's report card, or neglected to tick a box on his employment record? At least it wouldn't be that ridiculous Cathy Lindsay wanting his 'help'. He immediately chastised himself for the thought. Sure the woman had been a nuisance, but she didn't deserve to die because it made Mark Hamilton's life a fraction easier.

He'd made a damned fool of himself at the funeral on Monday. One minute he'd been in the church, squeezed into a pew between an elderly woman with a heavy hand on the cologne bottle and a fat kid with sharp elbows who sent text messages the entire time. Next minute, he'd been at a ramp ceremony in Afghanistan, watching as they loaded the coffin of Corporal Fred Worthing onto an airplane for the long journey home. Fred, good old Fred, father of five, who never met a kid he didn't want to play soccer with. Who died because Mark Hamilton didn't have the guts to save him.

He'd watched them carry the flag-draped coffin across the tarmac. Soldiers saluted, music played, and civilian women wept.

Sergeant Mark Hamilton had also wept. He stood at attention, ramrod straight, his arm in a stiff salute as tears streamed down his face. Everyone thought he was crying for Fred, but he wasn't. He cried for himself. He cried for the wreck of a man he'd become.

As they said the meaningless words over Cathy Lindsay, Mark cried for himself once again while the ever-present demons laughed and danced the jig on the grave of his pride.

Perhaps the demons had had enough fun for a while. Since he'd fled the church, he'd been feeling okay. Better than he had in a while. He'd even slept last night; his sleep not disturbed by nightmares he could not remember come morning.

The grade twelve pre-calculus students always made him feel good. He saw his own love of mathematics reflected in the best of them. As long as there were students who loved math and wanted to learn, he knew he could cope.

He made his way to the office through the throng of laughing, chatting teenagers, hoping he could wrap this up and get to basketball practice on time.

◇◇◇

John Winters arrived at Trafalgar District High as school was letting out. He wanted an official presence, so he'd brought Molly Smith and a patrol car.

Teenagers poured out of the school, everyone of them eyeing the police vehicle prominently parked in the no-parking area by the front doors. A couple of droopy-panted boys made an abrupt change of direction and bolted back into the school. No doubt to find another exit.

He wished he could ask them to turn out their pockets.

Instead, Winters and Smith climbed the steps and went into the building.

"Did you go to this school?" he asked her.

"Yeah. It sure is weird wearing this uniform here. Look at those girls. They make me feel about a hundred years old."

The girls in question, all long swinging hair and thin hips, burst into giggles when they saw Smith looking at them.

The two women working in the office stopped whatever they were doing to watch the police enter. One rose and came to the counter, a greeting on her mouth, concern in her eyes.

Winters showed his identification, although the presence of a uniformed constable was probably ID enough. "I'm looking for a teacher here. Mark Hamilton. Was he in class today?"

"I believe so."

"He should be on his way to the gym," the second woman called. "Basketball practice today, and Mr. Hamilton's the coach."

"I'd like to speak to him. Can you page him to come to the office, please."

"Certainly." The woman exchanged a glance with her colleague as she headed for the public address system. "Mr. Hamilton to the office. Mr. Hamilton."

Mark Hamilton soon arrived, shock on his face when he saw who waited for him. Kids drifted to a stop in the hallway. They lingered outside, exchanging questions, peering through the glass walls.

"Sergeant Winters," Hamilton said. "What can I do for you?"

"I have a few questions regarding the death of Cathy Lindsay."

Hamilton's right eye twitched. "Okay."

"We can't talk here. I'd like you to come to the station."

"I'm not finished for the day. How about if I come down after work?"

"Now, Mr. Hamilton."

A drop of moisture appeared at Hamilton's hair line. His eye twitched again, and he grasped his hands together so tightly the skin turned white. Winters could have phoned Hamilton, asked him to drop into the station. He could have come alone, in a plain vehicle, to pick the man up. But he'd chosen a patrol car with a uniform escort because Mark Hamilton was clearly a man under pressure. Add a bit more pressure, tighten the screws.

Stand back and observe the fallout.

Hamilton's eyes darted around the room: the policewoman, standing behind and slightly to one side of Winters, the watching staff, the growing pack of kids outside the office.

"I have questions for you regarding your relationship with Mrs. Lindsay," Winters said.

"I had no relationship with her." Hamilton looked at the watching women. "You know that, right? I had no interest in Cathy."

"That's right. Why Mark was never anything but polite no matter how much she swanned over him. Isn't that so, Betty?"

Betty, no longer smiling, muttered words of agreement.

This was not, Winters realized, a supportive audience. Clearly Mark Hamilton was popular here. He glanced at the windows, murmurs building in the hall as word spread and students gathered. He cursed himself. Coming here had been a mistake. A serious one.

He hadn't wanted to pull Hamilton out of class, so he waited until school was finishing for the day. It had been a long time since John Winters had been in a high school. He'd forgotten this was precisely the time when the halls would be most crowded and the kids wouldn't be hurrying to their next class.

"Let's go," Winters said.

"Are you arresting me?" A vein began to beat in Hamilton's neck. Sweat poured off him, although the room wasn't overly warm.

"No, Mr. Hamilton, I am not arresting you. I have questions and I thought it would be better if we talked where we could have some privacy. Not here."

"You can use Ms. Herchman's office. She had to go to a meeting and won't be back today," the helpful receptionist said.

"Mark." Winters tried to sound both forceful and friendly at the same time. "Let's go."

"What about basketball?"

"I'll go down to the gym, tell the boys practice is cancelled for today," Betty said.

Molly Smith stepped forward. She placed her hand on Hamilton's arm. He flinched.

Betty gasped.

"That won't be necessary, Constable," Winters said. "Mr. Hamilton is not, as I said, under arrest." If he were under arrest Molly would be handcuffing him. Winters hated to think of the reaction to that. "Shall we go?"

Hamilton's eye was twitching so badly it might have been doing a dance. He clenched his fists, took a deep conscious breath, and let it out slowly. He was a big guy, powerfully built. He might be more than a match for a middle-aged man and a woman.

Winters decided to drop it. Hamilton showed signs of being unstable, which was why Winters had thought bringing him down to the station would be a good idea. Clearly it wasn't. He was about to tell Hamilton to go to his practice and come to the station after, when the man uncurled his fists and said, "Not a problem. You have to find out what happened to Cathy. We all want that, don't we?"

The staff mumbled agreement.

"Janet, the boys can have their practice without me. Tell Randy he's in charge." Hamilton gave Winters a smile as warm as that of a grinning corpse laid out for Doctor Lee's inspection.

Winters nodded to Smith, telling her to leave first. As she opened the door a wave of sound rolled over them. A hundred or more students must have been in the hallway. They stood watching, some muttering, no one smiling. Kids blocked the path to the doors. Two boys stood at the front of the pack, arms crossed over chests.

Smith stepped forward. Her back was straight, every muscle in her body tense. She did not, Winters was pleased to see, have her hand resting on her pepper spray or, god forbid, her Glock.

The boys didn't move.

Winters was aware of how quiet it had become. The murmurs had stopped; no one spoke. In the office, Janet held a phone in her hand.

"You kids have nothing to do?" Hamilton said, his voice surprisingly strong, pitched to carry. "Martin Robotham, if the results of your last test are any indication, you should be home studying."

Some of the kids laughed. A tall gangly boy with a buzz cut and a few stray whiskers on his chin turned to the onlookers and lifted his arms in triumph.

The tension broke, and the crowd shifted. Winters could see the doors ahead. They walked on. Behind them, the path closed as the kids followed.

Smith held the back door of the car open for Hamilton, but she did not put her hand on the top of his head or shove him in.

Winters got into the passenger seat. He turned and faced the man in the back. "Thank you, Mark."

"I didn't kill Cathy Lindsay, you know."

"Glad to hear it."

Chapter Thirty-seven

Margo spent the day in a state of fevered excitement. Eliza had not come in, and Margo was in charge of the gallery. She was busy, lots of people wanting to see the new show, preparations to be made for the formal reception tomorrow evening. Eliza would be pleased to see red stickers on two of the paintings, and the show wasn't even officially open. Renata Reingold's art was too abstract to suit Margo's taste, but she didn't have to like the work to sell it.

She'd followed the beige Corolla last night, through the twisting streets hacked into the side of the mountain, close enough that her headlights lit up the license plate. It was him. Jackson! They hadn't gone far before the Corolla slowed to turn into a driveway. The garage door opened automatically, the car drove in, and the door shut behind it. Margo pulled up across the street, hoping the driver would have to come out of the garage to get into the house. But he didn't. In a few moments lights began switching on inside.

She sat in her car, palms wet, heart beating, debating whether or not to approach the house. Eventually, she decided against it. It was late, probably not the best time to talk to a man with life-changing news. Besides Steve might have stayed up, waiting for her.

Now she knew where Jackson lived, Margo could return at a more-suitable time.

The curtains were pulled back and she could see him moving about. He walked up to the window, lifted his arms to draw the drapes. Then he stopped, peering out into the night. Margo's heart leapt into her throat. He sensed her. Knew she was close. That bond they shared, reaching out to him. A car drove by, throwing light around her. Jackson didn't acknowledge her, and the curtains were pulled sharply closed.

She put the car into gear and drove home almost bursting with happiness.

She'd barely slept. Lying in bed, watching the celling, beside a gently snoring Steve, Margo had made her plans. When the gallery closed at five, she'd go home, have dinner with Steve, tell him she had to hurry back to work to finish preparing for the reception. She didn't like to lie to Steve, but he didn't understand how she felt about Jackson, and so she'd sometimes not told him the whole truth. She didn't want to upset him.

Steve couldn't understand. Ellen, her daughter, refused to understand. How could they? They'd never had a child stolen from them. Two children. Gerald killed in a car accident, her grandchild along with him. Gerald would not be coming back, the precious grandchild would never have a chance at life, but everything would be good now that Margo had found Jackson. Her baby boy. They'd taken him away, but he remained in her heart. Never forgotten.

"It's good, but I'm not comfortable with the use of so much yellow. Is there something a bit less colorful perhaps?"

"What?" Margo snapped out of her dreams. The customer was addressing her. "Colors. Renata is known for her bold use of primary colors." She'd read that in the brochure. "There is one small watercolor on paper that might be more to your taste." She led the way across the room.

Margo would go to Jackson's house tonight.

He'd be thrilled.

Molly Smith dropped Sergeant Winters and Mark Hamilton, the high school teacher, at the station and took the car back out on patrol.

Wasn't that a potential nightmare? For a while there she'd feared they were about to have a riot on their hands. If they'd taken a resisting Hamilton out in handcuffs, they probably would have. She got cold shivers simply thinking about it. A riot in a school. She'd didn't know if she'd have the fortitude to defend herself, if it came down to it.

Thank god she hadn't had to find out.

Was it possible Hamilton had killed Cathy Lindsay? He didn't seem the type. Seemed like a nice enough guy, and the kids obviously liked him. Of course, that had nothing to do with anything. Didn't everyone say, when they found out their neighbor was a serial killer or mass murder, that he seemed like a normal guy who kept to himself?

She could see why Winters was interested in Hamilton. She recognized him as the man who'd fled Cathy Lindsay's funeral, running down the hill as if the hounds of hell were in pursuit.

Today, in the school office, she'd sensed something in the man. Fear, violence, she hadn't been sure what. It was there, under the surface, yet close enough to the top it threatened to overwhelm him. He'd broken out in a sweat as soon as he'd seen the police, every muscle in his body tensing. And that tick in his eye, what was that about?

It might mean nothing. Lots of people didn't like to be interviewed by the cops, no matter how innocent they might be.

"Five-one."

She grabbed the radio. "Five-one. Go ahead."

"If you're free, you're wanted back at the office for a ride."

"On my way."

The ride, as she guessed, was Mark Hamilton. He was sitting on the hard, narrow bench in the vestibule when she got there, shoulders hunched, hands clenched between his knees.

"Mr. Hamilton, I'll take you back to the school. Mr. Hamilton?"

He looked up. His right eye twitched in an unbalanced rhythm. His face was deathly pale beneath his winter tan and his brow dripped with sweat.

"Are you okay, sir?"

"I…I need to go for a run. Take me home, please."

"It's kind of icy for running. The temperature's been dropping all day and the melting snow's refreezing. Treacherous stuff."

"I have a treadmill in my basement."

"That's good." She hesitated. "Don't you want to go back to the school and get your car first?"

"There will be people…questions. I need to run now."

"Okay, home it is." She hesitated before holding out her hand. He took it, and she pulled him to his feet. Hamilton was shaking like a leaf in a strong wind, his hand slick with sweat. He clung to her. Embarrassed, she jerked free. She glanced into the office. Winters stood by the console, watching, his face drawn. He gave her a small nod.

She took Hamilton to her car and helped him into the passenger seat. Approaching six o'clock, thick threatening clouds had brought an early night.

They said nothing as she drove through the streets, the only sound the hum of the engine and the soft ping of ice pellets clattering against the car windows as a cold rain fell. She pulled into Hamilton's driveway and he leapt out of the car with a sudden burst of energy.

"Sorry about that, Officer," he said, giving her a smile so strained it was more of a grimace. The tick in his eye had stopped and his color was recovering. "I don't care much for enclosed spaces."

"Good night, sir."

"Good night. Thanks for the lift, eh?"

She waited beside her vehicle until he was inside.

Strange guy.

Over the next couple of hours, as she drove up and down the streets, watching for trouble or someone needing assistance, Molly Smith thought about a lot of things. About Cathy Lindsay, gunned down. She probably wondered, if she noticed it at all, why someone had punched her in the back. And then she was dead. Before she hit the ground, they said. Her poor husband, her poor kids. Winters seemed to think Hamilton might have been the shooter. Smith doubted it: the way his hands shook he'd have trouble hitting a barn door unless the barrel of the gun was touching it. Who then?

They probably never would find out. Smith herself figured it for a fun killing. The perp long gone, heading for another town, another person out for a walk on a nice day.

God help us all.

The sign was turned to closed at Mid-Kootenay Adventure Vacations. Her parents had had a pretty good marriage. They'd been together since their university days, and Andy had learned to let Lucky have her way. Which usually wasn't a problem as they agreed on most things. Lucky's relationship with Paul Keller was going to be a darn sight more tumultuous. Smith wondered if the Chief had any idea what he was getting into. He probably did. He'd known Lucky for a long time, and often from the other side of the barricades. Things with the new resort would be heating up come summer when construction crews moved in. When they started chopping down trees and damming the river.

Molly Smith did not want to ever again see her mom at a riot.

She found her thoughts drifting to Adam. She hadn't seen him since he got back on Monday. He'd been busy with a convenience store hold up some distance away, and then a grow-op raid. He'd suggested they go out for dinner tomorrow night, someplace *special*, said he'd get someone to cover for him so he could relax and enjoy the evening. Special. She wondered if he was going to pop the question. Would he have a ring in a small blue box, would he get down on one knee, would a bottle of expensive Champagne be waiting in the wings? Or would he just be Adam and say something like, "Wanna move into my place? Save on rent."

She decided that whatever he said, her answer would be yes.

She'd risked hurting Adam, or worse, by flirting with Tony. She'd had a narrow, and lucky, escape. Never again.

If she'd come to realize one thing with this Cathy Lindsay business, it was that life comes with no guarantees. No point in waiting for the right moment, waiting for opportunities to present themselves, or the circumstances to be exactly to your liking. Wait long enough and the right time might well never come. She glanced at the clock. Almost eight. She'd swing by the convenience store and get herself a drink and a bag of almonds. Another quiet night in Trafalgar. As she reminded herself not to say the Q word, the radio snapped to life.

"All units, all units. Report of an active shooter at 87 Lakeview Drive. Injuries."

Smith slapped the console, bringing up lights and sirens. She took the corner into Pine Street on two wheels while startled pedestrians watched her go. The car fishtailed on the road, but the tires gripped, and she raced up the mountain.

Chapter Thirty-eight

John Winters did not think Mark Hamilton had killed Cathy Lindsay. Unless he was a heck of an exceptional actor.

Winters had felt about as bad as he could while doing his job. Hamilton was a basket case, no doubt about it. He'd twitched and sweated all through the interview but managed to remain lucid. Cathy Lindsay had bothered him, yes. She clearly liked him and wanted him to pay attention to her. He didn't have any feelings for her and never encouraged her.

He had never arranged to meet her outside of school hours. He had never been to her house, didn't even know where she lived, and she had never been to his.

"Do you own a long gun?" Winters had asked.

"No, sir, I do not."

"Not even for hunting? There would have been opportunities for hunting at the cabin you went to last week."

Hamilton shuddered. "I don't hunt. I don't eat meat. I can't stand the sight of blood. Not after the things I've seen. The very idea makes my skin crawl."

"What sort of things."

"In Afghanistan."

Mr. Hamilton, have you sought treatment for PTSD?"

"I can handle it." Hamilton lifted his head and fixed his eyes on Winters. "When I'm left alone."

"Cathy Lindsay didn't leave you alone."

"Cathy Lindsay was a minor annoyance. If she'd come to my house uninvited, invaded my privacy, I might have struck out at her. But she didn't. And so I didn't hurt her."

"There's no disgrace, you know, in needing help to deal with trauma. The police get counseling these days. After a shooting or a killing or any highly stressful incident we're sent to a psychologist. Have to keep going until the doctor says we're back to normal. Whatever normal means. It's the same in the army, isn't it?"

"No disgrace, no, not usually. For me, though, no forgiveness."

"Why?"

"Because I'm a filthy coward. Because I hid under a truck afraid to move while a man lay in the dust and died." Hamilton began to cry, soundlessly. Tears dripped down his face. His voice was so low, Winters had to lean forward to hear. "An IED, a street on the outskirts of Kabul. Our truck hit it. Flames, smoke, people screaming, guns firing. Corporal Fred Worthing got the worst of it. He was under my command, and I failed him. I groveled in the dust, covering my head, crying like a baby. Fred had been thrown into the street, out in the open. Blood everywhere, most of his legs nothing but red mist. He screamed and screamed. Calling my name, screaming for help, but I couldn't move. I heard a shot and the screaming stopped. Then more of our guys arrived and the crowd scattered. I stood up, pretended I'd been under fire myself. Fred lay in the road, not moving. A single shot in the forehead. Killed where he lay by some cowardly piece of shit, unable to defend himself."

"You can't keep blaming yourself," Winters said, knowing how feeble his words must sound. "If you'd gone to your buddy's aid, they would have shot you too."

Hamilton's eyes were streaks of red. "I only wish they had."

The guy was a mess. Winters knew he was largely to blame, at this moment at least.

Still, a murder investigation was a murder investigation. He had a job to do, never mind how many innocents got hurt in the process.

Hamilton had been pretty much his only suspect. Back to square one. Almost two weeks had passed since the shooting. The trail was getting cold fast. Time to head home, and hope something new came to light tomorrow. He told Hamilton he was free to go.

John Winters watched Molly Smith lead Mark Hamilton to her car, his head down, his steps fumbling. He slipped on a patch of ice and her arm shot out to catch him. He recoiled as if she'd struck him.

Winters had begun to turn when out of the corner of his eye he saw another man hurrying toward the station, head down, collar pulled up against the icy rain.

Perhaps John Winters wouldn't be going home quite yet.

He opened the door. "Mr. Lindsay, what brings you here?"

"Elizabeth. Elizabeth Moorehouse. You know her, right?"

Winters nodded. "We've met."

"She killed my wife. She murdered Cathy."

"That's a serious accusation, Mr. Lindsay. Are you sure?"

"As sure as I can be. Elizabeth's gone back to Victoria. That is, she told me she was going home. You'll send someone around to arrest her, won't you?"

"Why don't we talk this over first?"

Winters escorted the man to an interview room. The nice one with a painting on the wall, comfortable furniture, good lighting, plastic flowers in a plastic vase. Rather than to the suspects' interview room, stark and bare, intended to be intimidating, which was the room where he'd brought Hamilton. Probably another mistake. "If you'll wait here a moment, I want to ask my colleague to join us."

Winters went to his office. He still had the services of one IHIT guy, still working the phones. Ray Lopez had been taken off the Lindsay case. Crime didn't stop just because they had a murder to investigate.

"Ray, Gord Lindsay's here. He's accusing his girlfriend, Elizabeth Moorehouse, of the murder of his wife."

Lopez swiveled in his chair. "Wonder what brought that on?"

"You think he's got a point?" IHIT said.

"Check with VicPD on Moorehouse's whereabouts, will you. Tell them I might need them to pick her up. Ray, I want you in on this."

"You got it."

Gord Lindsay was perched on the edge of his chair when Winters and Lopez came in. His eyes darted between the men. Winters introduced them.

"Can I get you something, Gord? A coffee? Water?"

"No. Thanks. I want to get this over with."

The police took seats and waited for Lindsay to begin.

"This isn't easy for me. I spent most of last night tossing and turning, thinking about it. Didn't get a darned bit of work done today. I don't know what else I can do. Elizabeth came to my home on Monday, after the funeral."

"I saw her in church."

"She's played me for a right jackass all along. I guess that's why it's taken me this long to come and talk to you. I feel like a stupid teenage boy. I thought she, well I thought she cared for me. Turns out all she wanted was my money."

Winters kept his face impassive. How many times had he heard that before?

"We had a nice thing going. I had…company when I was in Victoria, she had a man around the house some of the time. When Cathy died, I was afraid Elizabeth would want to move in with me. Get married." He laughed, the sound bitter, self-mocking. "Hardly. What she wants is money, and never to see me again."

"How much money?" Lopez asked.

"Twenty thou."

Not, Winters thought, a heck of a lot. "Be that as it may, I don't see how that leads to murder."

"She's a crack shot, raised in the wilderness in northern B.C. Her dad hunted for food and taught Elizabeth to hunt alongside him."

"Does she own a firearm?" Winters asked.

"Not that I've seen. Doesn't mean she couldn't go out and get one, does it?"

"Have you ever been shooting with her? To a range, hunting?"

"No."

"Then how do you know she's a crack shot?"

"She told me so."

"Let's go back a few steps. About this money. Did you tell her you'd pay?"

Gord Lindsay told them about the blackmail threat. He talked about his in-laws, always disapproving of him, about his mother, who pretty much put him on a pedestal. His shame, his regrets.

He talked about Cathy, about what a great woman she was and how much he loved her. Winters let the man talk. He'd never entirely written Lindsay off as the killer of his wife. His alibi was only his young daughter, easy enough to put ideas in her mind of where her dad had been and when. He was sad now, remembering all the good times they'd had, the love they'd shared.

Regret?

Had Gord Lindsay set Elizabeth Moorehouse—the crack shot—up to kill Cathy?

Was her blackmail attempt over more than illicit sex? Was Gord threatening to back out of their deal?

No. Not if Gord was here, at the police station, telling them about it, pointing the police in the direction of his lover. The man wasn't that devious, or that clever. Or that stupid.

A soft knock and the door opened a crack. Ingrid's head popped in. "Sergeant Winters, can I speak to you for a moment?"

"Excuse me." He got to his feet, followed Ingrid into the hallway, and closed the door. He could hear sirens as vehicles pulled out of the parking lot behind the station. A uniformed officer ran past, pulling on his jacket.

"What's going on?"

"We have a report of an active shooter. A woman shot on the street. No sign of the perp."

A small-town cop's worst nightmare. For a brief moment Winters thought of Elizabeth Moorehouse. Had the woman stayed in town, not gone home as she'd told Gord Lindsay?

He dismissed that idea as quickly as it had come. He'd pursue Lindsay's accusation of Moorehouse for Cathy's murder, but for the life of him Winters couldn't think of any reason she'd start shooting up the streets.

Mark Hamilton. Winters groaned. He'd let the man, broken, depressed, highly trained, go.

"Get rid of Mr. Lindsay, will you, Ingrid." Winters threw the door open. "Ray, you're with me. Now."

Recriminations would have to wait.

Chapter Thirty-nine

Molly Smith reached the scene in minutes. People had gathered in nervous clusters in the middle of the road. They turned to wave at her, and a woman shouted, in a voice high with panic, "Over here, over here." Smith could see more people kneeling around an object on the sidewalk. Others were coming out of houses, standing on porches, or hurrying toward the excitement. Rain, mixed with snow and ice, continued to fall, but the onlookers paid no attention to their physical comfort.

She pulled her car to a stop in the middle of the road, heart beating rapidly. She hesitated for a fraction of a moment. Ingrid had said an active shooter. Somewhere, out there, in the night, was a person with a gun. It was not unheard of for a cop hater to create a scene, to deliberately draw the police out into the open.

Then—bang.

A child ran past her vehicle, heading for the group on the sidewalk. A boy, running flat out, his unbuttoned jacket billowing behind him. Smith slapped a control on her console, killing the piercing noise of the siren, and then she leapt out of the car. "You. Go home, get out of here, now."

The boy whirled around, eyes wide. He did as she'd ordered.

Sirens, lots of them, heading her way. Her radio squawked with commands, and she shouted into it to tell them she was at the scene.

The streetlights cast puddles of yellow light into the rain and through naked branches. Some house lights were on, some shrouded in darkness. More houses loomed over them as the hill rose sharply up. The shooter could be absolutely anywhere.

"Did anyone see what happened?" she yelled, pushing her way into the crowd. "Did anyone see who did this?"

"I heard a noise," a woman said. "A bang. Very loud. She was only a few yards in front of me. I saw her fall. I thought she'd tripped. Then I saw the blood." She began to wail, "Oh my god. Oh, my god."

"Anyone else see anything?"

Heads shook. Arms reached out to comfort the sobbing woman.

"I heard the shot. I didn't know what it was, but then the screaming started, so I came over," a man said. "I was going to do what I could to help, but the doctor arrived."

"Get off the street," Smith told them. "Go home. An officer will be around to talk to you shortly."

A woman lay on her back on the pavement, face white, coat soaked with blood. Two people squatted beside her. A woman with her hands pressed against the wound, blood up to her wrists. A man next to her, coat off, bare chested, ripping up what looked to be his own shirt. "I'm a doctor," the woman said. "Got to stop the bleeding."

"Ambulance is coming."

Smith turned back to the onlookers. "All of you people, get away from here. Go home." She considered telling them the shooter might still be out there. Not worth the panic, she decided. People began to break away from the pack. Some left, some stepped back a few feet.

To her infinite relief, she saw Staff Sergeant Peterson pull up. Not her responsibility any more.

More vehicles were arriving, screeching to a stop in the street. City police, Mounties, an ambulance. Headlights broke the night, and sirens and men's voices broke the quiet of the neighborhood.

"Smith, you're with Evans," Peterson shouted. "Check out these houses. Backyards, alleyways, sheds. You," he directed a

Mountie, stuffing uniform shirt into jeans as he approached, "get these people off the street."

Smith glanced behind her as she moved to do as she'd been ordered. The eyes of the woman on the ground were closed, her face drained of color. Blood continued to pump through the fingers of the Good Samaritan, and that meant she was still alive. A man stood over the group, holding an umbrella up in a feeble attempt to provide some protection to the wounded woman and her helpers against the freezing rain.

Evans gave Smith a nod and they slipped away from the throng, drawing their weapons. Evans held a flashlight. Guns clutched in hands trying not to shake, watching their footing on the thin crust of ice coating the snow, the two officers made their way into the backyard of the closest house. A motion detector light switched on. Ignoring the rain dripping down collars, soaking through pant legs, they crouched in the cover of the building, leapfrogging each other, one moving forward, staying low, the other maintaining guard, using hand signals to communicate.

She pushed all conscious thought to the back of her mind. If the shooter were here, hiding, watching, she'd deal with him. That was all she needed to know. Back in Police College when they did use-of-force training, the immediate rapid deployment instructor had been a woman by the name of Sergeant Angelina Sullivan. Tough as they came, Sullivan ripped the head off anyone who dared call her Angie. Smith had been surprised to come across Sergeant Sullivan at the mall one evening. Leading a tussle-headed toddler by the hand, pushing a stroller, laughing up at a tall handsome man carrying shopping bags, she looked like a real human being. Smith thought of Sullivan now. Tried to remember everything she'd learned from the woman.

It was all a blur.

She remembered making a mistake, bursting into a room that supposedly contained the shooter, seeing movement to one side, turning toward it, yelling at it, "Get down, get down, get down." It was a dummy, set up to represent a hostage, while the trainer playing the shooter came up behind her and said, "bang."

The class laughed as Smith's face burned with embarrassment. Get it wrong now, and she'd be a lot more than embarrassed.

Smith whipped around the building, gun up, moving from side to side. *Dig your corner, dig your corner,* Sullivan bellowed at her. All was still. Thank heavens for snow. Unless the shooter could fly, he wasn't here. The lawn was an unmarked, pristine carpet.

They cleared the yard, moved on to the next house. A garden shed stood in a dark corner against the back fence. The snow here was heavily trampled. Kids probably, out playing. Tracks in and out of the shed. Evans jerked his head toward it.

Smith went first. She stacked right; Evans positioned himself on the left. He gave her a sharp nod. She swallowed and tightened her grip on her Glock. She reached for the door knob. She twisted it, threw the door open and crashed in, gun up in a two-handed grip. Evans followed, swinging the flashlight from side to side, checking out the corners.

Nothing here but rusty garden implements and a jumble of sleds and snow shovels.

They moved from house to house, garden to garden, tension twisting their guts. Dogs barked and the curious peered out kitchen windows. Her radio told her Mounties were sweeping the other side of the street. Every officer who lived within a hundred kilometers was being called in.

Peterson ordered Evans and Smith to return to the scene. Start a door to door, ensure the shooter wasn't holding some innocent family hostage.

Crime scene tape had been strung up, strong lights arranged to illuminate the area. The cold rain seemed to be lessening. The injured woman had been taken away. A patch of black blood soaked into the ice where she'd lain. Ron Gavin knelt on the sidewalk. The street was full of marked and unmarked police vehicles, red-and-blue lights flashing. Smith recognized Adam's truck. He'd have Norman out, trying to get a scent. Unlikely they'd find anything, so many people had been milling about.

A couple of men from the *Trafalgar Daily Gazette*, cameras and notebooks ready, stood behind the tape. Other reporters held microphones in front of witnesses. No TV cameras yet, but they'd be here soon.

Smith and Evans took the house closest to where the woman had fallen. A man and boy stood in the window watching them approach.

"Hey," Smith stopped so abruptly Evans almost crashed into her. "Give me a sec."

She ran back to the road.

Winters huddled in a circle with Paul Keller and Ray Lopez. Keller said, "Worst possible situation. A random shooter."

"Have you ID'd the victim?" Smith said.

"We found a purse beside her," Winters said. "Alison's going through it."

"Alison," Smith called, "is the name Franklin?"

"Got it in one."

"I thought I recognized her. I stopped her yesterday. Last night."

"What? Where? Why?"

"She was driving through town. Up and down the streets, going slow, checking out cars, driveways. I thought she was looking for unlocked vehicles so I pulled her over. Ran her license and plates. An older woman, nicely dressed, nervous, car neat and tidy. Hardly the type to go in for a bout of smash and grab."

"Did she tell you what she was doing?"

"Said she was looking for a friend whose phone number she'd lost. She got her pronouns muddled, said the friend was a she and then said he, back to a she. I figured she'd been having an affair with some guy, he dumped her, and she was trying to find him. I told her to go home or I'd bring her in. It was so weird her name stuck in my mind. As I remember, her address is near here."

"A witness said she lives in that house on the corner. He didn't know her name, though. I knocked, but no one answered. Place's quiet. What happened after that?"

"Nothing. I told her to go home and then I left. Didn't see her again."

"I can't believe that's a coincidence," Ray Lopez said.

"No."

Townshend held up the wallet, open to the driver's license. "Margo Franklin. Sixty-one years old."

"What the hell?" Winters said.

"You know her?" Keller asked.

"I might." Winters pulled out his phone. "Molly, wait right there. Hi, yeah, no time to talk. Margo who works for you. What's her last name? Thanks. It'll be a late one." He put his phone away.

"You're onto something," Smith said, reading the gleam in his eye.

"Margo Franklin works for my wife at the gallery. Perfectly pleasant lady, the times I met her. Recently retired, new to town. She's been stalking a man."

"What?" Keller sounded as surprised as Smith was. One never thought of middle-class, elderly ladies as potential stalkers. Molly remembered her own mom yelling at the police from behind the barricades, and decided that middle-class women were capable of just about anything.

"She claims he's her long lost son," Winters continued. "Eliza told me Margo's obsessed with this man. I saw her at Cathy Lindsay's funeral, paying more attention to this guy than to the service. He bolted out of the church soon as it was over. I wonder if Margo approached him. Eliza had a talk with Margo's husband, and he told her that she, Margo, has been somewhat unstable since the death of her son a few years ago."

"So," Smith said, "she's unstable. That doesn't help us. She didn't shoot herself."

"No. She didn't. But she was making a nuisance of herself." He chewed his lip. Ron Gavin shouted, "Move that light closer." Alison Townshend went to give him a hand.

"Someone else said something of interest to me earlier today. *If she'd invaded my privacy, I might have struck out at her.*"

"What's this guy's name?" Lopez asked.

"William Westfield. Sound familiar?"

"Don't think so."

"Seems a stretch," Keller said.

"Maybe not. He knew Cathy from night school class. When we interviewed the people in that class, one of the students said she'd told them she went for a walk every morning in the woods behind her house. Easy enough to find out where she lived, hang around a couple of days to see what time she walked. And then wait for her."

"You think this is the same shooter?"

"Ron's got the slug. Went in her side and out again. Same type of weapon, far as he can tell.

"I'm going to pay a call on William Westfield. This is only a hunch, so I don't want to drag a lot of people away. We need to check these houses in case the shooter's still here, start asking questions, interviewing witnesses. Ray, our friends from the press are here, and we can be sure the big city boys will be descending ASAP. Toss them a bone, will you, and then see if you can locate Margo's husband. Eliza might have a number for him."

He looked at the officers. Everyone watched him. His eyes settled on Molly Smith. She saw a flash of indecision, and then he said, "Smith, you're with me."

Chapter Forty

They took a patrol car.

Smith punched William Westfield into the computer, brought up his address. Picton Street, high above town.

"Any word from the hospital?" she said.

"No. I'm not entirely sure this Westfield's our man. I'm acting on the assumption that he is. We're going in hot and heavy. Guns and noise. You will follow my lead in everything. Let's hope he's home. Not somewhere on the hillside, watching our people, another shell in his weapon. Keep the siren on until we get to his street. Then turn it and all lights off. Glide up to the house. Park as close as you can get. Block other cars if you have to. Then move."

Winters glanced at the young woman beside him. He'd decided on the spur of the moment she was the one he wanted with him, if Westfield was indeed the guy they were after. Winters didn't know most of the Mounties well enough; he wasn't sure of Dave Evans. Evans was a hot head, and hot heads could turn cold fast when the pressure was on. The rest of the TCP uniforms were checking the houses. Winters didn't want to take the time to pull them off. Ray Lopez would have been a good option, but Winters needed a uniform. If he was going to charge into a man's house, gun drawn, he didn't want any possibility of anyone not understanding they were the police.

He should have a freaking platoon at his back, but the situation at the scene was too fluid. He couldn't pull any more officers away. They had to act on the assumption that the shooter was still in the vicinity.

When Winters arrived at the shooting, he'd taken the time to observe the watching crowd. Curious faces, some crying, some shocked, many pressing forward eager to get a better look.

Was he there?

Had he hung around in order to observe the results of his handiwork?

Was he inside a house, hiding behind the curtains, gun to a baby's head? *Not a word.*

Winters searched faces for one more interested in the reaction of the crowd than the body or the cops. He hadn't seen anything other than shock, fear, horror, curiosity.

Whoever this guy was, he was a cool one.

Winters remembered the case in Arizona back in the '90s. Six women shot and killed. No clues, no evidence. No suspects. Another cool one.

What had Westfield said that one time Winters met him? Something about the desert landscape and bad memories.

His gut churned.

Westfield was the one. Guaranteed.

The streets of Trafalgar were eerily empty, no teenagers hurrying home after sports or music practice, no one walking dogs or taking a stroll after dinner, not even cars moving through the rain-slicked streets.

"Kinda reminds me," Smith said, reading his mind. "Of one of those post-apocalyptic movies. Everyone's gone. Only their stuff remains."

"Obviously, the news has spread. Which is good, we want people off the streets. Goddamn it, Molly." His temper boiled up out of nowhere. This was a good town, a great town. A fabulous place to live and to visit. It did not deserve to cower in the shadow of a killer, all the life drained out of it, neighbors watching neighbors, peering over their shoulder every minute of every day. Children hustled from car to door, patios and parks abandoned. He punched the dashboard. "If we don't catch this guy, now, tonight, this is going to be a ghost town."

Smith switched the light bar off. Then the vehicle's headlights. She turned the corner and they glided down Picton Street, shrouded in darkness. The rain had stopped, leaving roads and sidewalks greasy with wet ice.

Lights were on in the house they were interested in. Garage door closed, curtains drawn.

Smith and Winters slipped out of the car. No interior light came on to illuminate them. He gave her a nod and pulled out his weapon. She did the same.

Winters gestured to the front door. The path hadn't been shoveled all winter, and snow lay icy and deep. They ducked low and passed in front of the windows at a crouch. Smith took a breath and then shot across the doorway. She pressed her back against the wall. Her breathing was calm, her eyes intent. She held her Glock in two hands, barrel pointing to the sky. Her hands did not shake.

The door didn't look anything special. He'd kick it in, step back, let her go first.

Hopefully catch a guy watching TV in his pajamas.

Might as well see if it was unlocked before going to all the trouble of trying to break it down.

He nodded to Smith. She reached out, turned the handle.

The door swung silently on oiled hinges.

Smith was inside. She took the left, Winters went right. They were in a hallway, steep, narrow stairs leading up. Stairs were never good. A single pair of heavy men's boots were neatly placed on a drying mat, wet with melting snow. Smith sucked in a breath at the same time Winters saw it.

A shotgun in the corner, propped up against the wall. She threw a question at him, and he nodded. She crossed the small room, moving fast, keeping low, and snatched the shotgun in her left hand, keeping her Glock in her right. She broke it open. A casing, bright red, fell out. She emptied the last shell into her hand.

"Sergeant Winters," a voice came from inside the house. "That was quick."

Chapter Forty-one

Molly Smith dropped the shotgun shell into her pocket as a calm voice beckoned to them from inside the house.

Winters pointed to himself, meaning he'd go first. He pointed right: he'd take that side. She nodded. She was encumbered by the shotgun. Couldn't hold her Glock in both hands, couldn't leave the shotgun behind in case a second person was in the house.

"Move," Winters shouted. He cleared the doorway. She followed, yelling, "Moving." Went left, dug her corner, kept her back to the wall, swept the room.

They were in a living room, tastefully decorated in shades of beige with green accents. A handsome wooden bookshelf, full of neatly displayed hardcovers, filled one wall, a large flat-screen TV was mounted on another, good art was prominently displayed throughout the room. A comfortable cream leather sofa decorated with sage pillows faced the TV. On the far side of the room a man sat in a wingback armchair with his right leg crossed casually over his left. He held empty hands in the air, palms out. He smiled at them, a smile without a trace of humor or welcome.

"Sergeant Winters, come on in. You've brought a young lady, how nice."

The man was severely emaciated, cheeks sunken, eyes dark caves in a white face, the knuckles on his hands as prominent and lumpy as burls on trees. He did not move. "As you can see," he said. "I am unarmed."

"Don't move," Winters shouted.

"No need to yell. I can hear you."

"Smith, cuff him. Put the shotgun in the corner where I can see it."

She lowered it to the ground, slipped her own weapon into her holster, pulled cuffs off her belt. The man gave her his creepy smile and held his hands out in front of him, wrists together.

"No," she said. "Stand up and turn around."

He didn't move. She reached out, grabbed his arm and pulled him upright. He was as light as a child. She flipped him around, pulled his arms back, twisted his hands so palms were facing out, and snapped the cuffs shut.

She patted him down as Winters said, "William Westfield. I am arresting you for the murder of Catherine Lindsay and the attempted murder of Margo Franklin."

"Won't do you much good. I'll never go to trial. I doubt I'll spend a day in jail."

"You're rather sure of yourself." Winters' words had a bite to them the like of which Smith rarely heard. She dared a quick glance. His face was set into a tight grimace and his eyes were dark.

"Sure as I can be. I'm not feeling well. You have to call my doctor."

Winters jerked his head toward the door.

Smith pulled on her prisoner's arm. "Let's go, buddy."

He took a step, then another. When they reached Winters, the man stopped. "The perfect crime. Police officers will be talking about me for a long time to come."

"Not so perfect. As you're on your way to jail."

Westfield shrugged. He had almost no muscle tone in his arm. "Only because I decided to take out the second bitch. She thought she was my mother. Reason enough to off her right there. I congratulate you. You found me faster than I expected. When I decided to eliminate Margo, I knew I was exposing myself to discovery. But, as I said, it no longer matters."

"Get him out of here," Winters spat.

"You will be calling my doctor," Westfield said. "And he will order you to release me."

They hustled Westfield out of the house. Winters snatched up the shotgun. He pulled off his jacket and wrapped the weapon in it.

"You may not remember me, Miss Smith," Westfield said, as they crossed the yard. "I saw you at your mother's store recently. A nice woman, your mother. I'm sorry I won't be able to drop in any more." She did remember. That was scarcely two weeks ago, and Westfield looked like he'd aged about twenty years as well as being on a hunger strike.

He seemed to be taking this all quite easily. Smith glanced at Winters. He shrugged. Was Westfield going to claim mental instability in his defense?

Smith put her hand on the top of his head and shoved him into the back of the car.

Winters took the front passenger seat, resting the shotgun across his lap. He pulled out his phone, flipped it open. "I'm bringing him in. I've got what's almost certainly the shotgun we're after. Ask Gavin or Townshend to meet me at the station immediately. I want an ID on this gun fast. If we can link it to the shooting, we can call our excess people off the search." He snapped the phone shut.

"I can assure you, that is the weapon used tonight. It'll match with Cathy Lindsay."

Curiosity was eating Smith alive. Winters sat placidly in his seat, watching the dark streets pass.

"Are you going to ask why I killed her?" Westfield said.

"In due course."

They arrived at the police station. The garage doors rolled up, and Smith drove in. She and Winters got out of the car. Only when the bay was secure did she open the back door of the vehicle. She reached in and took Westfield's arm. He started to slide toward her, but fell back with a sharp cry. Eyes closed tight, he groaned. Sweat broke out on his forehead, and his entire face crunched up in pain. His skin was a sickly gray.

"Don't give me that act," she said. "I barely touched you. Come on."

"A minute, please," he whispered through clenched teeth. "Give me a moment."

She glanced at Winters who'd come to stand beside her, still holding the shotgun. He said, "Mr. Westfield, are you in need of medical assistance?"

Westfield said nothing. He simply breathed, slow and deep. Time passed. Smith waited for orders. She didn't want to have to wrestle the guy out of the car.

"I told you I was," he said at last. His voice wasn't confident now, not mocking, not trying to be friendly. The words were clipped, the breathing behind them labored. "My doctor's card is in my shirt pocket. The pain's passed. I can move now."

He slid out of the car. "Thank you for your kindness."

She wanted to knee the playacting bastard in the nuts.

Winters reached into Westfield's pocket with his free hand and pulled out a business card. "Constable Smith, process Mr. Westfield. I'll make the call and hand this weapon to forensics."

She led Westfield into the cell block.

"I need to sit down," he said.

He did look pretty awful, she had to admit. Hard to act up a sheen of sweat out of nowhere. She nodded at a chair. He dropped into it.

"You can take the cuffs off now. I'm in no condition to resist."

"I don't think so." She logged onto the computer. "Full name? Address? DOB?" He'd spend the night here, in the city jails, be brought before a judge in the morning. Winters would want to interview him, but if Westfield asked for a lawyer, he or she wouldn't arrive until tomorrow at the earliest. She glanced at Westfield. His color was better, not exactly healthy looking but no longer deathly pale. His light-blue eyes were on her, fixed, unblinking.

Weird.

Winters came back. He did not look happy.

"Doctor Singh is on his way."

"I told you he would be."

"He wants to take you now, tonight."

"He's been after me for a couple of weeks to move, but I had one last job to do. Now, I'm ready."

"What the hell?" Smith said, forgetting herself. "Are you nuts? You're not going anywhere but cell number two."

"Want to talk to me first?" Winters said, ignoring Smith.

"Happy to. As I said, I intend to go down in the annals of criminal justice. No need to call a lawyer for me. I'll never make it to court."

"Constable Smith, take the prisoner upstairs. Interview room one. I'll be along shortly."

She took Westfield's skinny arm once more and pulled him to his feet. Upstairs to the interview room. The walls were industrial beige, the table steel, bolted to the floor, the chairs uncushioned and uncomfortable. A camera was secured to a high corner. The black eye watched them enter.

"Take a seat," Smith said.

He did so. She did not offer her guest anything to drink. She stood with her back against the wall, feet planted, and watched William Westfield. She studied his face, searching for evil. For some sign. For something she'd recognize if she saw it again.

Nothing. His eyes were fixed on her. Her skin crawled, but she knew that was only because she knew what he'd done. If she met him on the street she wouldn't have thought him anything out of the ordinary. Hell, she had seen him in her mother's store, didn't give him a second glance.

The door opened. John Winters, followed by Ray Lopez and a man Smith had seen at the hospital, short, darkskinned, not smiling.

"Evening Doctor," Westfield said. "Sorry to drag you out at this time of night."

"I simply cannot credit what Sergeant Winters is telling me. Is this true?"

"Yes."

"Unbelievable. William has been my patient for three months, and I had absolutely no idea."

"I'm allowing Doctor Singh to sit in on this interview," Winters said.

Smith's head spun. He was what? Winters did not look at all happy. Ray Lopez's face was a picture of displeasure. She wouldn't exactly expect them to gloat in the presence of the killer, but she'd have expected them to look a little bit pleased with themselves.

"Constable Smith," Winters said, "Uncuff the prisoner. Stay in the room for the interview."

Smith walked behind Westfield. He stood so she could take off the handcuffs. He rubbed his wrists and sat back down. The men took seats. Lopez had brought an extra chair. Smith remained standing.

Lopez switched on the recording equipment, and Winters began the interview by stating the time, the place, those present.

"I've had a call from the hospital," Winters said. "Margo Franklin came out of surgery well. She's in critical condition, but is expected to recover. The slug missed all vital organs."

"A stab of pain came on me at the moment I pressed the trigger. I couldn't help but flinch, which jerked the shotgun. Once she was down, a tree blocked my sight. By the time I got into position to fire again, people were in the way."

Doctor Singh moaned.

"Why?" Winters asked.

"Because she was an interfering bitch. She thought she was my mother. She wanted to be my mother. She was following me everywhere, even to my house, and that was the last straw. I want to pass my final days in peace, not haunted by some creepy old woman."

"Cathy Lindsay?"

"She didn't like my writing. She gave me a D on my short story, said it was hackneyed and repetitive. It wasn't."

"What was your story about?" Winters asked.

The edges of Westfield's mouth turned up. "A killer, far too clever for the dumb cops who're looking for him. Obviously I wasn't thinking of you, Sergeant."

"You killed her because she gave you a D?" Lopez couldn't keep the disbelief out of his voice.

"I killed her because she dared to judge me. I wanted to wait for Easter, hoping for a nickname. The Easter Bunny Killer has a nice ring, don't you think? But I knew I was running out of time."

"If not Mrs. Lindsay…"

"Then it would have been someone else. The perfect crime, Sergeant Winters. No motive, no evidence. The cigarette butt was a clever touch, wouldn't you agree? I picked it up out of an ash tray by the bus stop."

Winters said nothing. Westfield continued, "No motive, no evidence, no linkage to any other crime. Most importantly, no bragging and no loud-mouthed accomplice. I've had that weapon for a long time. I stole it, of course. No paper trail."

"A game. You took a woman's life for fun."

"Not entirely. I told you, she judged me. She mocked me. She said my story was excessively violent. Misogynist. But yes, I will confess, I did it because I could. Because I'm capable of the perfect crime, and I wanted everyone to know it. I'm aware that the truly perfect crime would go undetected. No one would even know a crime had been committed. What fun would there be in that?"

"Tell me about Arizona."

Westfield smiled. "You are clever, Sergeant, to make that link. I killed a few women in Arizona when I lived there."

Doctor Singh buried his head in his hands.

"Then nothing for fifteen years? Or were you doing your killing someplace else?" John Winters studied William Westfield. The man was smiling slightly, pleased with himself as he calmly described the destruction of a life, of many lives if you considered Cathy Lindsay's husband and children. His eyes were an attractive and unusual shade of pale blue, but they glowed with such malicious pleasure that they brought to Winters' mind a line from the saga of Beowulf, as the hero encounters the killer, Grendel: *two dots of fire against a veil of blackness.*

"No more killing." Westfield explained. "I retired, so to speak. My mother died, and I went to Florida to settle up her affairs. When I got back, somehow I didn't feel like killing any more. I'm sure you want to know all about my mother, but I don't want to talk about her. She wasn't my mother anyway. I was adopted. My real mother, whoever she might be, was, my adoptive father never failed to remind me, a slut and a dirty whore who couldn't keep her legs shut and threw me away like a discarded tissue." Westfield's mouth was open, ready to continue with his story, his self-justification, his self-pity, but no words came out. His jaw moved; he stared across the room without blinking, directly at Molly Smith.

Her blood ran ice cold.

Winters began to rise.

"Give him a minute," Doctor Singh said. "His brain is, in lay terms, not firing properly. The pathways are becoming blocked as the tumor grows and his brain is searching for another route to form the words."

"My adoptive father moved around a lot," Westfield continued, as if there had been no interruption. "He had trouble keeping a job. He constantly fought with his co-workers or ran into trouble for smacking his wife. He knocked me around too, when the mood came on him. She could have stopped it. She could have stood up to him. But she didn't. He died in a bar brawl in Flagstaff. Fellow followed him into the parking lot and shot him in the back. No tears from me. She wept buckets, of course. Such a good man, she told everyone at the funeral. Not that many people bothered to show up."

Smith's fists were clenched. She tried to wiggle some blood back into her fingers without anyone noticing. Brutal father, passive mother. Why did that always turn out to be the woman's fault?

Why did other women have to die for it?

Westfield let out a gasp of pure pain. He lifted his hands to his head. He rocked his body back and forth and moaned.

Doctor Singh leapt to his feet. "I'm afraid this interview cannot continue."

"Very well," Winters said. "I have all I need for now. About all I can stomach too."

Smith stepped forward, ready to take Westfield back downstairs. Lock him up for the night. The cells in the police station were not intended to be comfortable. A steel bed, no mattress, no blankets. A toilet in the corner, a camera overhead.

"My situation has gotten a lot worse in the past two weeks." Westfield lowered his hands and eyed them through narrowed eyes and spoke through teeth clenched against pain, his face slick with sweat. "I wouldn't be able to maintain a stakeout or make that walk through the woods any longer. With Margo, I had to sit in my car until she came out of her house."

"What happens now?" Doctor Singh said.

"Mr. Westfield will be taken to the hospital," Winters said, biting off the words. "As you pointed out, we can't care for him here."

Molly Smith almost swallowed her tongue.

"No, not the hospital," Westfield said, his voice stronger as the pain passed. "I've a room waiting for me at the hospice, right, Doctor? You'll send someone around for my things? I don't think we locked the door behind us. I'd like a few pieces of art. The new sketches in particular."

"You're going to the hospital," Winters said. "I won't disrupt the patients—the deserving patients—at the hospice by putting you there. You'll have a guard on you, round the clock. And be secured to your bed at all times."

"You can't do that," Westfield protested. "I'm dying. I deserve to be at the hospice."

"You deserve," Winters said, his composure breaking, "to be in hell."

Westfield turned to his doctor, "Tell them," he shouted. "Tell them what we arranged."

"I can give you the care you need at the hospital as well as anyplace else," Singh said, his voice dripping with disgust. "And that only because my oath requires me to do so."

"Detective Lopez," Winters said, "Escort Doctor Singh and his patient to the Trafalgar hospital. Westfield is to be restrained at all times. Tell Staff Sergeant Peterson to arrange a twenty-four hour guard on him. Constable Smith, cuff him."

Chapter Forty-two

"You going to tell us what the hell's going on, Sarge?"

Smith and Winters, along with a good number of officers, stood at the windows watching as William Westfield, his doctor, Ray Lopez, and Dave Evans got into a patrol car and drove down the dark, abandoned street.

Winters grimaced. "Can't blame you for being mad, Ingrid." He turned to face the group. "All of you. It's a damned crying shame. Doctor Singh told me William Westfield has stage four glioblastoma. Meaning a brain tumour that's eating him alive. He has, at the most, a couple of weeks to live. The tumor was detected three months ago and he refused treatment, claiming he'd rather die than drag on for at best another year. The doctor's been trying to get him into the hospice. Westfield said he had a few matters to take care of first. I guess we know what that means." Winters looked as if he wanted to spit on the floor.

"It means he gets off scot-free," Ingrid muttered.

"Saves us the cost of a trial," Ron Gavin said. "Saves us having to sit in court and listen while some expensive lawyer explains to the judge that his client's misunderstood."

"Sick bastard," Adam Tocek said. "In more ways than one." He stood beside Molly Smith, his hand resting lightly on her shoulder, the closest they'd allow themselves to get while in uniform.

Her face was pale, her mouth tight, and her eyes blazed with so much anger they reminded Winters of her mother. "He killed Cathy Lindsay for nothing at all."

"Pretty much. He's right. We never would have caught him if he hadn't gone after Margo. Whoever cleaned up his house after he died might have turned in the shotgun. Might not. He would have been remembered, by the police anyway, for a killing that remained unsolved.

"Be that as it may, we still have jobs to do. The Chief's at the mayor's office now, preparing a statement. Ron?"

"I pulled in a few favors, got someone out of bed to run tests on that shotgun. To my eye, it's the one that killed Mrs. Lindsay. We'll get confirmation pretty soon. Alison's still at the scene. Just because the guy confessed doesn't mean we can pack up."

"Thanks for coming in everyone. If Ron doesn't need you, and you're not on duty, I guess you can go home now."

They began to move away, muttering and shaking heads.

Adam Tocek gave Molly Smith's shoulder a squeeze and said, "Talk to you tomorrow."

Winters should have been elated. He should have been ready to go out and celebrate.

Instead he was just sad. What a goddamned waste. Cathy Lindsay, her husband, her kids. Everyone caught up in this because of some smarmy bastard who wanted to be remembered as a killer smarter than a bunch of small town cops.

Right now he wanted nothing but to go home, but first he'd pay a call on Gord Lindsay. The guy deserved to know they'd caught his wife's killer. He'd drop in on Mark Hamilton tomorrow and apologize.

Winters turned to Molly Smith. "You did good today. I'll mention it to Al."

"Thanks. Why don't I feel good?"

"It's not up to us to feel good, I'm sorry to say. We did our jobs. We caught the bastard before he could do any more damage."

"Does it matter? He's going to be dead in a couple of weeks anyway, you said."

"Look at it this way. Suppose some other woman offended him tonight or tomorrow. Took his parking space, cut him off with her grocery cart. Didn't bring his meds fast enough in the hospice. And he decided he had one more score to settle."

Smith's radio crackled. "Five-one?"

"Go ahead."

"Sergeant Peterson is asking if you're going to hang around the office for the rest of your shift, or intend to get back out there."

"Message understood."

Winters gave her a small grin. "I suspect you'll be spending the rest of the night answering questions."

"That's not a bad thing."

"No, it isn't."

Chapter Forty-three

Mark Hamilton studied the object in his hand. Cold metal gleamed in the flickering glow of the gas fireplace.

The lights in the house were turned off, leaving only blue and yellow firelight to see by.

All he needed.

The radio blasted out heavy metal, cranked up loud. There'd been another shooting in Trafalgar, and earlier the reporter had called in from the scene, breathless, excited. In the background, sirens, people panicking.

Would the cops be here soon? Knocking down his door, breaking in, guns drawn, boots pounding on the floorboards?

He hadn't killed anyone, didn't even know the person they were saying had been shot this time. But what did that matter? Once again he had no alibi, no friend to say they'd been tossing back a beer together after work or watching a game on TV.

He'd come home from the police station a few hours ago, dropped off by the pleasant young woman. In the old days, he would have flirted with her, asked if she wanted to go out for a drink. Now, he muttered thanks as he got out of the car, and then he headed straight downstairs to run for an hour, lift weights for half an hour.

It hadn't helped. All he could think about was going to prison.

Prison and Corporal Fred Worthing, dying in the dust so far from home.

Mark stroked the gun. Smith and Wesson J Frame. Small. Big enough to do the job.

He hadn't lied to the police. Sergeant Winters had asked if he possessed a long gun, a rifle or shotgun. He hadn't asked if Mark had an unlicensed, restricted weapon like a handgun. Which was a crime in itself.

He'd bought this revolver when he returned from Afghanistan. Ready to do himself in when it all got too bad.

Then, to his considerable surprise, he'd been accepted at university as a mature student. His mom had been so proud. The revolver had been tucked away in the back of the closet, mostly forgotten. But nothing could be forgotten forever. Over the months and years following the incident, he'd often dreamed that Fred was standing silently in the swirling dust, beckoning, telling him to be a man. To do it. To eat his gun.

To join him in hell.

Mark Hamilton owned one bullet. He didn't need any more.

He lifted the gun. He opened his mouth. He tasted it, tasted the bitter, cold, harsh metal against his lips. His mom would never know he'd stopped coming to visit. He had enough to keep her in the home as long as she lived. He bit down on the barrel, closed his teeth onto it. He swallowed, fighting against his throat, which had closed against the intrusion. His finger twitched, sought the trigger.

"This just in!" The radio exclaimed, cutting Guns and Roses off in midnote. "Trafalgar City Police have made an arrest in the killing of popular teacher Cathy Lindsay. They report that the same person was allegedly responsible for this evening's coldblooded attack on Mrs. Margo Franklin. Chief Constable Paul Keller has this to say."

The Police Chief said something about an arrest, about good policing, about the two shootings being linked. Then over to the mayor to chatter about a safe community and a good place to live and raise a family.

Mark didn't want anyone from the school to find him in his living room with his brains spattered across the back of the chair, so he'd stuck a note on the front door, warning them to call the cops and not come in.

"Now," the radio guy said, "back to the scene of this evening's shooting. Lorraine Quinn reporting live."

"Thanks, Warren. I'm with Michelle Jenaring, a student at Trafalgar District High who heard the shots from her house and was one of the first to arrive. Michelle, what's your reaction to the news?"

At first all Mark could hear was crying. Then the girl gulped and said, "I'm so glad. So glad it's over and they've caught him. Now our lives can go on. I'm so looking forward to going to school tomorrow and hugging everyone. I was going to go into computers but after seeing how that doctor saved the woman's life, I've decided to switch to medicine."

The reporter thanked her and went to talk to more people.

Michelle Jenaring was in Mark Hamilton's precalculus class. She wanted to get a degree in math. Her family didn't have a great deal of money, and her older twin brothers were already in university. Michelle was on track for several good scholarships and Mark planned to write recommendations for her.

Thursdays he had the grade twelves right after lunch.

Would they have found him by then? Would a somber principal come to the class and tell them, tell Michelle, that their teacher had decided life was not worth living?

That hopes and dreams and ambitions were an illusion. They'd all be better off dead.

What would happen to Michelle if she didn't go to university? What would happen to that brain which loved nothing more than solving a math problem?

He pulled the revolver out of his mouth. He took his finger off the trigger.

He spun the chamber and took out the single bullet. He got up from his chair and went into the kitchen. He studied the bullet for a long time, twisted it in his fingers, examined it. So small. So inert.

He dropped it into the sink where it landed with a clatter of metal on metal.

Mark Hamilton turned on the tap. He gave the bullet a nudge with his finger and pushed it into the drain.

It disappeared.

Tomorrow, he'd take the revolver around to the police station. Hand it in.

Maybe he'd see the pretty blond policewoman again. He'd smile at her and hope she'd smile back.

Then he'd go to school and teach math.

Chapter Forty-four

Eliza Winters peeked out from behind a huge bouquet of peach roses, her smile radiant. "We're absolutely delighted to see you looking so well, aren't we, John?"

Margo Franklin lay in her hospital bed, hooked up to beeping machines. Truth be told, John Winters thought, she didn't look well at all.

She looked like a woman who'd been shot and had almost bled to death in the street.

Her husband, Steve, stood beside her, beaming.

Eliza put the flowers on the windowsill, joining other bouquets, cards, even a teddy bear with a red ribbon around its neck. "We've been told we can't stay, but we did want to pop in and say hi. I've cancelled tonight's reception. Ms. Reingold wasn't too impressed, but I hardly wanted to put on a celebration. I'll reschedule for when you're back on your feet."

"We'll look forward to that," Steve said. "Won't we, dear?"

"You got him?" Margo croaked. "The one who did this to me?" Her daughter, Ellen, lifted a glass of water to her lips.

"We did," Winters said.

"Why?"

"Mistaken identity," Steve said quickly. "Isn't that right? He mistook Margo for someone else."

Winters didn't reply. He didn't need to. Margo's eyes had drifted shut and she slept.

"I'll walk you out," Steve said.

"Thanks for coming," Ellen said.

Steve had phoned that morning, to let Eliza know Margo was out of danger. She'd lost a lot of blood, but blood can be replaced. The shell had entered her side and exited without hitting any vital organs. The doctor was confident she'd suffer no lasting effects.

"Is he her son? The boy she called Jackson?" Steve asked once they were in the hallway.

Winters studied the man's face. "It's possible. I don't know if she needs to hear it though."

Steve nodded. "What a nightmare. All these years, searching for the guy, and then he shoots her."

"I'll tell you what I know. You can decide what to say."

"Suppose she asks for a DNA test?"

"He'd have to agree to that. We have his DNA on record now, but it can't be used for a private matter without his consent, even after death, simply because Margo asks for it.

"Eliza told me the date and place Margo said her baby was born. It seems to be the same as records show for Westfield. He was adopted immediately after his birth. There's a shade of resemblance, particularly in the eyes, between the two of them, but I might see that only because I was looking for it. What you want to tell her is up to you, Steve, although I can't imagine it will do Margo any good to believe her son tried to kill her."

"The doctors here said they'd recommend a good therapist. Margo needs to get over this obsession. God, it almost killed her. Regardless of who Westfield might, or might not, be she has to realize she can't go around telling strange men they're her son." Steve laughed without humor. "What a choice. If I tell Margo her son tried to kill her, she'll know she found him and can stop seeing him everywhere she turns. On the other hand, what will that do to her head?"

"You'll do the right thing." Eliza placed her hand lightly on his arm. "I know you will."

"Ellen was on a plane the minute I called. It'll do them both good to spend some time together. Thanks for coming. And, John, thanks for everything."

Chapter Forty-five

Gord Lindsay flipped pancakes. Bacon sizzled in the cast iron frying pan. Maple syrup and butter were on the table.

The kids were in their rooms, supposedly getting ready for school. He didn't plan on fixing a substantial cooked breakfast every morning, but today he'd make the effort. Renee and Ralph had left yesterday morning, and Gord had put his mom on the afternoon plane. He hadn't been sorry to see them go. He needed to have his house back, spend some time with Jocelyn, just the two of them. Spend some time with Bradley too, if the boy'd let him.

He heard the news on the radio last night, a shooting in Trafalgar. He'd almost flown across the room to turn it off, not wanting Jocelyn to hear. Not wanting to hear any more himself. Another shooting. Gord couldn't imagine another family going through the pain he and his children were.

If the killer was the same person, then it couldn't possibly be Elizabeth. He'd called her at the house in Victoria, and she'd answered. He heard a man's voice in the background.

Gord muttered something about putting the money together and hung up.

He'd pay Elizabeth her twenty thousand. And hope to hell he never heard from her again.

Sergeant Winters had stopped by. It was late, Jocelyn asleep, Bradley watching TV, Gord sucking on a beer, mindlessly munching potato chips, and wondering how he was going to live the rest of his life without Cathy. When Gord opened the door to see the man standing there, for a moment he thought Winters had heard he was going to pay Elizabeth the blackmail money and had come to warn him against it.

Instead Winters said, "Have you heard the news?"

"Yeah. Another shooting. God, man, what's happening here?"

"I knew you'd want to hear it from me. We got him, and he's confessed to killing Cathy."

Gord's legs buckled. Winters grabbed his arm. "Steady there."

"Who? Why?"

"A stupid, stupid thing. He was a student in Cathy's night school class and took exception to the mark she gave him."

"What?"

"He killed my mom over a grade!" Bradley stood in the hallway, dressed in jeans, sloppy but not too oversized, and a Vancouver Canucks T-shirt. His feet were bare and his hair tousled.

"Your dad needs to sit down," Winters said.

Gord was aware of his son's arm around his shoulders, a strong hand under his elbow. They went into the living room and Gord dropped into a chair. "You're sure?"

"Yes."

"He's not going to get off, is he? Not on some stupid technicality."

Winters rubbed his chin. "The biggest technicality of them all."

And he told Gord and Bradley that Cathy Lindsay's killer would be dead before this time next month.

In a way Gord was glad the bastard would never come to trial. He, Gord, wouldn't have to face him, day after day. See his ugly mug in the paper, listen to everyone in town talking about the case.

Spend the next forty years fearing the guy would get out on parole and come back to Trafalgar.

Gord lifted bacon out of the frying pan and placed it on paper towels to soak up the grease. "Breakfast," he called, tossing pancakes onto plates.

"Yeah, pancakes." Jocelyn bounced into the kitchen, hair trailing behind her, Spot at her heels. Yesterday, she'd clung to her grandmothers and begged them not to leave. Ann and Renee wept, but Ralph had said, in his gruff voice, that they all had lives to lead and he'd be at the other end of a phone anytime Jocelyn needed him.

This morning the girl's eyes were clear as she pulled a stool up to the breakfast bar. The dog's nose twitched at the scent of bacon.

"Go and get your brother," Gord said.

"I'm here," Bradley said. "That smells great, Dad."

"Maybe we can go skiing on Saturday," Gord said to Jocelyn. "Would you like that honeybunch?"

"Yeah. Can I ask Leslie to come with us?"

"If you'd like to."

Bradley grabbed a slice of bacon off the tray. He broke it in half, tossed one half into his mouth, the other to the dog. "My old equipment should be good for another run. I'll have a look after school, Dad."

"That'd be good, son," Gord replied.

Chapter Forty-six

Lucky Smith delayed going into the store this morning. She lingered at the breakfast table while coffee cooled at her elbow, reading the online newspapers. Another shooting in Trafalgar. It scarcely bore thinking about. Lucky lived here, alone, out in the woods. She owned twenty acres of mostly trees and rocks; the nearest neighbor wasn't within shouting distance. It had never occurred to her to be the least bit worried, either when the kids were young and Andy might be away, or since he'd died. She didn't lock the doors most of the time. Her friends knew they could pop in and out whenever they wanted. She'd often arrive home to find a magazine with an article marked or a gift of vegetables from someone's garden on the table.

Once Moonlight became a police officer she began nagging her mother to lock the doors and take more care. She even suggested motion detector lights and a security system. Lucky put that down to police paranoia, and said she'd think about it.

Last night, she'd put her book to one side and gotten up from her comfortable chair by the fireplace in the living room after she received a phone call telling her about the shooting in town.

She locked the doors and instructed Sylvester to be on guard. Sylvester yawned.

Moonlight phoned later, a quick call from the police station, to let her know they'd caught the guy, and were sure he was the one who'd killed Cathy Lindsay.

Lucky breathed a sigh of relief but did not unlock the doors.

This morning's news reported that William Westfield, resident of Trafalgar, had been arrested and charged with both shootings. Lucky thought she might have met Westfield at one time. Didn't he come into the store now and again? She wasn't really sure.

The story was vague about what happened last night. Westfield was apparently under guard at the hospital. Strange, if he'd been shot during the arrest you'd think it would have been mentioned.

Lucky tried not to think too much of what her daughter's job involved. She hoped Moonlight had been well out of it last night.

The sound of tires on gravel had Lucky shutting her computer and getting to her feet. Paul Keller's SUV was pulling up in front of the house. He stayed in his seat for a moment before climbing out of the car and walking up the path between piles of dirty, melting snow thick with ice crystals. Sylvester provided an enthusiastic escort.

Lucky opened the door. She'd not locked it after letting the dog out earlier. "Paul, good morning. What brings you here? Is everything all right? I've been reading the news. Thank goodness you've arrested him. Come in. Come in. Would you like a coffee? Breakfast?"

He stood in the doorway. "I'm not going to stay, Lucky. You have to get to the store, and I'll have a pile of paperwork to do this morning. I've been up most of the night, thinking about this business. It's a terrible case, but I'll leave you to read about it in the papers and hear the gossip on the streets. Can't help make me think sometimes we don't know how short a time we have left."

"Paul."

He lifted his hand. He hadn't taken off his gloves. "Hear me out. Do you care for me, Lucky, even just a little bit?"

"I do. More than a little bit. But we're so different. Your job. My activities. Someday perhaps…"

"Someday might never come, Lucky. Life's too unpredictable. I want to be with you. I'm not asking for us to move in together. I have a feeling that would be too sudden for the both of us. I want to spend time in each other's company. I want to see you, to talk to you. To love you, Lucky."

She looked at him. He didn't make a move toward her. He stood there, dripping snow on her floor, holding his hat in his hands, a middle-aged, overweight man who smoked far too much and exercised too little. Sylvester sniffed at his boots.

Lucky Smith felt a great joy rise up into her chest. She laughed, and held out her arms.

Chapter Forty-seven

That had been the anticlimax to beat them all.

They'd had dinner at Flavours, the best, most expensive restaurant in Trafalgar, the previous night, the day following the Franklin shooting. Adam had worn a suit, strikingly handsome in a crisp white shirt and perfectly knotted blue tie. She'd worn a sexy dress with a plunging neckline and a swirling skirt, and sky-high heels. She'd ordered a green salad, followed by the salmon. He'd had sweet potato soup and a steak, rare. They talked about work, about how the town was still in shock over the revelations about William Westfield, about Adam's family back east and Molly's family here in Trafalgar. They talked about the possibility of a summer vacation to Europe, where neither of them had been.

The waiter cleared their plates and asked if they wanted dessert. Adam chose his favorite, pecan pie, but Molly demurred. "Coffee, please."

When her coffee arrived, it was just a cup of coffee. Adam dug into his pie with gusto.

She'd been expecting a bottle of Champagne, carried high by a grinning waiter. Maybe a little blue box on her saucer.

She'd thought he was going to propose.

He hadn't.

After dinner they walked through the quiet streets to her apartment, where Norman waited. Adam took the dog for a quick walk while Molly put on her sexiest nightgown.

Adam came back. They went to bed. They made love—and it was good—and then they slept.

She awoke when he got up, still dark outside. He had to go to the town of Nelson for a meeting this morning.

He kissed her. He left.

She lay in bed looking up at the celling, feeling a total fool.

She didn't have to wait for Adam to pop the question. She was a modern woman, she was her mother's daughter, she could propose to Adam herself.

Somehow that didn't seem right, though.

She thought about Graham. His proposal had been not the least bit formal. They were in university, didn't have any money. He'd propped himself up on one elbow in bed and said, "Why don't we get married when you finish your degree?"

She'd said yes.

She glanced at the clock. Six-thirty, the welcome start of a four day break from work. She planned to spend the day running errands, doing laundry, cleaning the apartment, meeting Christa for lunch at George's.

Adam was off tomorrow and they were going to Blue Sky for the day.

She hoped they didn't run into Tony.

She rolled out of bed and padded to the bathroom, and then into the kitchen to put the kettle on. She lifted the lid off the tea container.

A piece of paper lay there. A small blue box beneath.

She opened the note, hands trembling slightly. Adam's writing. "I intended to do this in person, but got so nervous I've lost my voice. Marry me, Molly. I love you so much." She lifted the lid off the box. A square-cut diamond mounted on a golden circle flashed in the harsh kitchen lights. She took the ring out and slipped it on her finger. A perfect fit.

Her heart grew in her chest. She threw back her head and laughed and then she reached for her phone.

She typed a quick text message. Ten-Four.

Molly Smith pressed send.

To receive a free catalog of Poisoned Pen Press titles, please contact us in one of the following ways:

Phone: 1-800-421-3976
Facsimile: 1-480-949-1707
Email: info@poisonedpenpress.com
Website: www.poisonedpenpress.com

Poisoned Pen Press
6962 E. First Ave. Ste 103
Scottsdale, AZ 85251